The Keeper

Alastair Gunn is an experienced magazine journalist. *The Advent Killer* was his first novel in a series featuring DCI Antonia Hawkins, followed by *My Bloody Valentine*. *The Keeper* is Alastair's next DCI Antonia Hawkins thriller. Alastair lives in Hertfordshire with his fiancée, Anna, where he is working on his fourth novel.

The Keeper

ALASTAIR GUNN

PENGUIN BOOKS

PENGUIN BOOKS

UK | USA | Canada | Ireland | Australia
India | New Zealand | South Africa

Penguin Books is part of the Penguin Random House group of companies
whose addresses can be found at global.penguinrandomhouse.com.

First published 2016
001

Copyright © Alastair Gunn, 2016

The moral right of the author has been asserted

Set in 12.5/14.75 pt Garamond MT Std
Typeset by Jouve (UK), Milton Keynes
Printed in Great Britain by Clays Ltd, St Ives plc

A CIP catalogue record for this book is available from the British Library

ISBN: 978-1-405-93301-8

www.greenpenguin.co.uk

Penguin Random House is committed to a
sustainable future for our business, our readers
and our planet. This book is made from Forest
Stewardship Council® certified paper.

For Anna

Prologue

He hit the tree hard.

It knocked him off course, scrabbling for grip in the dark as his feet slid on the wet ground. But he stayed up, making it to the next trunk, pulling himself in tight. Fighting for breath; trying not to cough.

The night stretched away in every direction, crooked black shapes bleeding into one another. Shadow on shadow.

He felt sick.

He fought it down. His lungs were burning. He needed time to rest and think. But there was none.

He tried to control his breathing; to calm his banging head. He was shaking. The freezing air tore at his lungs, and he could taste blood on his teeth. His body hurt, the stab of damaged ribs, the arcing wound on his left shoulder leaking sticky wetness down his arm, the screaming pain from his shin. It felt like he'd been running for hours, ducking left and right through dense scrub, wanting to scream for help; knowing it would do more harm than good.

Get a fucking grip.

He wiped his eyes and stared into the gloom, sharp for any movement among the splinters of moonlight filtering down from above. Around him the sinister woods creaked, his attention flicking from one tiny sound to the next; an animal up in the canopy, the slurred rustle of wind in the trees. But still nothing to see except craggy shapes clawing at the night.

How far had he come? It felt like miles, but he might have been going in circles for all he knew.

His head shot round as the cracking noise came from his right; the sound of someone stepping on dry leaves. Someone else moving out there in the darkness.

Not far away.

His breath caught in his throat.

Keep still . . . stay down.

Another crack. Nearer this time.

Panic took over.

Then he was running again, into the blackness.

Where are you going?

He didn't know.

He pushed harder, skidding across the greasy forest floor, looking for a way out.

And there they were.

Headlights, rounding a bend through the trees ahead, a way off, but worth the risk.

'Help!' he shouted. 'Over here.'

But his voice was weak. The car didn't stop.

'Hey!' Louder. 'Stop. Please!'

The headlights moved away.

Then he heard someone else running, somewhere behind him in the dark. Another person's feet pounding the ground in time with his own, someone else's breath coming in bursts.

Close.

Pete drove himself harder.

Don't look round; just get to the road.

Then his ankle folded.

He crashed sideways, crying out. There was a white flash, then a ringing sound. He blinked hard. *Get up!* He tried to right himself, but his muscles had turned to mush, and he slumped back down.

For a second nothing happened as he stared into the darkness, blinking, confused. Had it all been a dream? Was he in bed, sleeping off a night on the sauce?

He tried to twist, felt agony erupt in his shin.

It's real.

And suddenly there were hands on his throat, strong thumbs clamping his windpipe, choking him.

No!

Pete grabbed the wrists. Clasp and rotate, *break the hold*. But the grip on his neck tightened, and his vision filled with swirling patterns of red and black.

He forced his eyes open; saw his hands pawing at the arms stretching away. Felt the buzzing panic as his head began to go light.

He was six years old, standing on Brighton Pier, calling for his father to come and put money in one of the rides.

But as the whiteness seeped in, his assailant formed out of the confusion. An alien face, all angles and glassy green eyes. It came closer, its breathing rapid and rough. As if it enjoyed his pain.

What if this is the end?

Then the pain was gone, and the question gently dissolved.

I

There was a painting on the wall of Brian Sturridge's office, its colours quiet greys and blues, its brass-leaf frame ragged and cracked. It depicted one child teaching another to read from a large, hard-backed tome. It was valueless; the artist unknown.

But, aside from his Mont Blanc fountain pen – a gift from his late father – the picture was the only object that had accompanied Sturridge throughout his thirty-year service, surviving two office relocations and three refurbishments, purely because it epitomised the founding principle of his work: *to help or be helped, each party must collude in mutual pursuit of that aim.*

And yet, although he would never capitalise on the lucrative potential of his vocation, and move beyond the stuffy confines of counselling within the Metropolitan Police Service, Sturridge found high-ranking officers testing his patience on an increasingly regular basis.

For example, the woman in front of him now.

According to her record, DCI Antonia Hawkins was accomplished, respected, and destined for greater professional heights. She was attractive, with a slim, athletic figure, incredible eyes and dark shoulder-length hair that framed an effortlessly graceful jawline. Attractive enough that, had he not already been down that road and lived to regret it, he might have been tempted. Plus she was young enough – now in her mid-thirties – to change the course of her life if she wished.

So why, when she referred herself for these sessions six months ago, had DCI Hawkins clearly done so with little or no intention of dealing with her considerable and deep-rooted personal issues?

The most likely possibilities were that she agreed to these sessions as a way to avoid something worse, or that she recognised the need for them, without then being able to follow through. Either way, he was growing tired of the lip service she consistently paid his best efforts to help.

Every one of their subsequent weekly meetings had descended into cerebral tennis, with Sturridge attempting to coax her into debate, and Hawkins deftly skirting all the unpalatable subjects they most needed to discuss.

There were two main issues: habitual discomfort with human interaction, and the near-fatal knife attack that had almost killed her ten months ago. Historic difficulties with family and friends, the encompassing need to achieve, volatile personal relationships therefore destined to fail. Sturridge had ascertained all this during their first session. His problem, as often became the case, was getting the client to accept such inconvenient truths.

And the last few moments of silence suggested she wasn't going to respond to his last question.

He asked it again. 'How do you feel now . . . about the attack?'

Her gaze lingered on the painting for a second, having followed his there, before she turned slowly back to meet his eye.

Another pause, then, 'It's nice. Do you still paint?'

Her usual tactics: pleasantries aired only when the alternative was less comfortable, insight revealed purely to distract.

He sighed. 'Not since college. It was my final piece.'

'A pivotal moment?'

Sturridge nodded. 'Something like that. Did the same thing happen to you?'

'No.' Her attention drifted away. 'It was only ever going to be law enforcement. If I was good at anything else, I'd probably be doing it by now.'

'Is that why you're here?'

Her expression gathered. 'Maybe.'

'Did the attack change the way you feel about your work?'

Hawkins studied the space between them before replying, her head tilting to the side. 'I thought about leaving. Briefly, after it happened.'

Progress. 'Why?'

She thought for a moment. 'Because it had become personal . . . more than just a job.'

'So why didn't you? Leave.'

Hawkins shook her head, as if waking up from a daydream, and whatever spell had inspired her brief mood for revelation was gone.

She shrugged. 'Never say never.'

2

Hawkins realised she was sucking her teeth as she slowed the car and turned off the main road. She stopped herself, quietly cursing Brian Sturridge and his pious bloody counselling sessions. Surely you were supposed to leave that sort of thing feeling less wound up than when you arrived. So why, after every stupid obligatory visit, did she come away feeling exhausted, as if she'd just been subjected to interrogation?

Probably because it was getting harder each time to skirt the steadily burgeoning elephant.

Eventually she'd have to talk about the attack.

But talking about it wasn't something she'd been able to do in almost a year since it happened, not with family or friends, not even with Mike, and certainly not with a bored Met counsellor who spent more time thinking about her hemline than her mental health.

Part of her said there was nothing to be gained by baring her soul, anyway, having survived eleven near-fatal knife wounds inflicted by a psychopathic serial killer with a personal grudge. She hadn't needed time away, once physical barriers had been overcome.

She had simply put her head down and got on with it, returning to lead a major case within weeks; the successful solution of which had earned her permanent promotion to DCI.

OK, so she had the odd nightmare.

Who didn't?

Hers might have been recurring, and based on real events, but they had been less frequent recently, and opening up those memories might make things worse instead of better.

What she needed was to forget.

Over the summer, Hawkins had undergone laser surgery to remove the last traces of physical scarring. The treatment had worked so well that even *she* could no longer tell where the marks had been. But the mental abrasions were taking longer to erase. Her boyfriend Mike had borne the brunt of their effects, but the really rough patches were behind them now, and fortunately he was still around.

DI Mike Maguire, an African American New Yorker, was Hawkins' closest ally on the force. Over the course of three or four investigations when they'd worked together, a few years ago, intuitive bonds had turned into emotional, then physical ties, before either of them had realised it was happening.

But the news hadn't gone down well with Hawkins' then fiancé.

Annoyingly, Mike had done the 'decent' thing, taking a secondment in Manchester for six months, giving the couple a chance to sort things out, but Paul hadn't been able to forgive. He'd moved out a few months later, leaving Hawkins to buy him out of their mutual home; the two-bed semi in Ealing she still occupied.

Mike's return last winter had led to the relationship being resumed. But she'd been attacked before things had a chance to develop, and one way or another they'd been dealing with the fallout ever since.

For a time afterwards, Hawkins had struggled with intimacy, but Mike's patience and empathy had allowed trust to be rebuilt, and now their relationship was stable, if as fiery as ever. They'd been living together for almost a year.

Work, however, wanted something more formal.

Mental wellbeing was the Met's latest byword. The commissioner had signed off a new initiative called *Time to Change*, a network of services designed to assist officers who experienced traumatic events in the course of duty. For a few months after the attack, Hawkins had been dealing with the upshot from their last major case, and her body healing from the assault. But, as soon as the furore died down, and she was declared physically fit, she'd been summoned by the Mental Health Team for assessment.

Hawkins had 'not received' the first letter sent home, and ignored the next, but they were nothing if not determined. An MHT officer had appeared in her office two weeks later to arrange their first meeting.

She had politely informed him that no help was required; everything was fixed. She could cope.

Thanks anyway.

But that had simply pushed them into official channels.

DCS Vaughn called her the following day, drawing her attention to the small print in her job description. Basically, she was obliged to attend.

The terms and conditions of her permanent promotion to DCI stated that routine psychological assessments would be conducted biannually, and as required should she be involved in a potentially distressing incident. If she didn't go, she was in breach of contract, and could be removed from duty henceforth.

She had arrived at the first session defiant, expecting to go through a few motions, tick the relevant boxes; get signed off by appointment number three. Now, six months later, it looked like there was only one way to end her unhappy relationship with the counsellor.

One of these days, she'd have to open up.

Hawkins pushed the thought away as she approached the biggest house on the estate, pausing to let two unfamiliar but expensive-looking Audis pull off the drive. Their presence, along with lingering daylight, emphasised a recent but welcome trend. In the last few weeks, a lighter than usual workload meant that for the first time in years, Hawkins had been able to do shifts vaguely resembling her contracted hours. This, combined with weekly counselling sessions at five in Brent Park, which sat conveniently between work in Hendon and her Ealing home, meant she'd be closing the front door behind her by half six. And for someone who normally rolled in with takeaway food somewhere between eight and ten p.m., that almost qualified as a day off.

Hawkins steered her Alfa Giulietta, a recent purchase

inspired by Mike's love of Italian cars, around the final curve on to her sweeping cul-de-sac. Increasingly she'd been missing the convenience and freedom of having her own transport, but had also wanted something with charisma, so she'd persuaded Maguire to take her around the local forecourts. He'd driven her straight to the Alfa Romeo dealer, and within the hour her search had been over: a top-spec deep blue metallic model with climate control and satnav. She'd written the deposit cheque sitting in the soft leather driver's seat, silently admitting to herself that, for a Yank, Mike actually had taste. She'd fallen for the looks straight away, and even if the reviews said it was nowhere near the best in its class, compared to the maltreated buckets you normally got from the Met's selection of pool cars, it was a sodding limousine.

It was a shame that recently she'd been a lot more in tune with the car than with the man who'd advised her to buy it. But tonight was going to be different, if her plan worked.

Hawkins glanced at the passenger footwell, where two bottles of wine were being propped up by the ingredients for an authentic Italian carbonara, and a small but sinful New York cheesecake. Romantic dinner for two, a few glasses of Chablis, and amour might just be on the cards.

Her optimism climbed as the parking area beside the house came into view. Mike's Range Rover wasn't there, which meant she could have preparations for the meal well underway by the time he got back from the gym. But the mood stalled when she slowed to turn in, and caught sight of the empty car parked outside on the street.

Siobhan's tasteless white Nissan Qashqai only ever turned up here for one of two equally sporadic reasons: an obligatory invitation to a family event from their mother, or by complete surprise. Today its appearance was unexpected.

Which meant Siobhan wanted something.

3

Hawkins spun. 'You fucking *what*?'

'Shhhh!' Siobhan hissed, closing the kitchen door and turning back to glare at her younger sister. 'The kids will hear you.'

'Sorry,' Hawkins lowered her voice, as a loud thump from the living room emphasised the fact that the hurricane tag-team were now completely unsupervised. They both waited a beat, in case the bang was to precede tears, but a moment later the ruckus resumed.

Hawkins turned back. 'Say that again.'

Siobhan hated being spoken to that way, but the fact she was here for a favour meant no rebuke followed the frown. 'I can't go to Mum's.'

Hawkins bit her tongue. She always called it *Mum's*, as if their father didn't exist. 'Why not?'

Siobhan looked out of the window for a moment, huffed before answering. 'Because I haven't told them.'

'Well,' Hawkins eyed the phone handset on the bench between them, 'there's an easy way to fix that, isn't there?'

'You wouldn't!' Siobhan blazed.

Hawkins let her hang, feigning consideration. 'How come *you* moved out, anyway? Surely if you've got the kids, he should be tapping up *his* siblings.'

'I needed to get out. I just can't be there at the moment.'

Hawkins rubbed her neck as she heard the cat flap go, and Admiral Kirk, her overweight rescue cat, waddled in. He took one look at Siobhan and turned on the spot, disappearing back into the garden.

'Anyway,' Hawkins continued, 'there isn't room. Five people into one bathroom doesn't go.'

Siobhan's brow fell.

'You remember Mike,' Hawkins prodded. 'Tall black guy, talks with an American accent. Came to Dad's birthday.'

Nothing.

'Tell me you remember Dad.'

'Oh shut up,' Siobhan snapped. 'I know who Mike is; I just didn't know he was . . . *here*.'

'He's been *here* for almost a year.' She snorted. 'Isn't it funny how much more interested you become in people's lives when you want to gatecrash them?'

There was a lull in hostilities, which as usual Hawkins spent wondering how sisters almost similar enough in appearance to be twins could so effectively rub each other up the wrong way.

At last she asked, 'What happened, anyway?'

Siobhan slumped, waving the details away. 'It's over. Things haven't been right for ages. He's just so . . .'

'Boring?' Hawkins felt her eyebrows rise. 'I did tell you.'

'No.' Her sister looked suddenly wounded.

'Obsessed with work, then. I told you that, too.'

'It's not his work. He's just so . . .' It took her a moment to find the appropriate word, ' . . . average.'

Hawkins frowned. 'I thought that's what you liked about him.'

Siobhan fake-laughed. 'It's what *Mum* liked about him. I didn't get much of a say.'

'So buy him a sodding sports car.'

'Enough!' Siobhan's shoulders hunched, hands tensing. 'It's done, OK? I can't go to Mum's; I can't go home. And no one else has room for the three of us.'

'*I* don't have room.'

'Don't make me beg.'

'Rent something nearby; I'll help with the kids.'

'There's no money. We spent it all on the house.'

'You have a job.'

'Not any more. Malcolm got promoted, so I left. I promise it won't be for long.'

Hawkins almost stamped a heel. 'No.'

'*Please*, Antonia.' And there they were: the piteous eyes Hawkins hadn't seen since Siobhan, at eight years old, was so desperate for a pony that she'd temporarily mortgaged her frosty exterior. Mum had been so taken aback that Dad's Christmas bonus for that year went on *Toby*, a pretty piebald colt, who'd endured two winters of neglect before being stolen, and practically two more before a re-frozen Siobhan realised he'd gone.

Hawkins crossed her arms and exhaled. 'So run this by me again. I get to put you all up for free; endure this chaos day and night and, as a bonus, I get to lie to Mum and Dad about the whole thing?'

'We'll be no trouble. The kids can sleep in with me.'

'You're damn right they can.'

Siobhan gave a timid half-nod. 'Just till I arrange something more permanent.'

Hawkins shook her head. 'Two weeks, no longer.'

4

The flames were dying.

He got up and walked to the hearth, shivering despite its residual heat, to nudge at the ashes, drop a fresh offcut on to the fire. The embers danced as they tasted new fuel, and slowly the wood blackened as it succumbed.

He glanced at the window, catching his crooked reflection in the blackness outside, drawing himself up, proud and assertive like Ash.

He drew the curtains and drifted back to the armchair, slumping in the seat, head dropping into his hands. Their last exchange replayed itself in his mind. Again he picked at each word, searched every sentence for what he might have said; what he'd done to drive his mentor away.

Still no answer came.

This was torture.

Ash had been mad with him in the past, of course. But he'd rarely been *ignored*.

And never this long.

Over the last few hours he had returned to the memorial in the woods several times. But on each occasion he'd been met by the same silence.

That was the only place he felt close to Ash any

more. It was all they had left; the tiny stack of pebbles and stones he'd made to honour his friend. Was it too small? He'd worried about that at the time. But he'd also been wary of making the pile too obvious, in case strangers passed close to the house. It was their business, nobody else's.

Perhaps he had visited less often over the last week or so, but he'd still been every day. Yet nothing seemed to make any difference. No amount of pleading produced any response.

The longer his friend stayed away, the more powerful the anger seemed to become. And he knew of only one way to mute this awful torment . . .

He stood; taking his coat from the hook by the door, checking the pocket for keys.

His only option was to keep going.

Get out there.

Find the next.

5

'No way, Toni,' Maguire asserted, 'not your sister, not here.'

'Shhhh!' Hawkins hissed, shutting the kitchen door. 'The kids will hear you.'

'You drive each other *insane*. And she still hasn't apologised for what happened at your dad's birthday.'

Actually, Siobhan was unlikely to hear their conversation from the bathroom, where she was bathing Rosie and Kyle, but Hawkins didn't want the situation getting any further out of hand. Sod's Law had plenty to answer for already today.

Not only had Siobhan's unannounced arrival ruined her plans for a romantic evening, but a pulled muscle had brought Mike home early from the gym. Otherwise she'd have had their less-intimate-than-intended dinner ready, the kids in bed, and Siobhan hidden away upstairs, so she could break the news in a calm and controlled way.

As it turned out, Maguire had walked in to find a hallway full of suitcases, Hawkins hastily clearing up leftover takeaway, and Siobhan trying to coax two screaming children off the furniture. Immediately the challenge had become peeling the kids off their adopted uncle, and getting them all out of the way so that Hawkins could begin applying damage limitation.

She took his hand. 'Look, I know Siobhan gets . . . *opinionated* when there's wine around.'

'*Opinionated?*' Mike chimed. 'She said you were obsessive compulsive.'

'She has some odd views. But it's mostly diversionary tactics, to take the focus off how unhappy she is.'

'What?'

'She lashes out when she's sad. She doesn't mean it.'

Mike's eyes narrowed, but he was coming round.

Hawkins capitalised. 'It minimises disruption for the kids.'

'Can't we take Malcolm? I like Malcolm.'

'It's a chance to bury the hatchet.'

'Whatever.' He sighed. 'Don't say I didn't warn you.'

'It's too late anyway, I already said yes.'

He sighed once more. 'How long?'

'Two weeks.' She watched his eyes widen again. 'At most.'

'It's gonna be tight, you know. It was bad enough when your dad was here.'

'Only because you're incapable of tidiness.'

That earned another glare.

She countered, 'Besides, there's nowhere else, so we'll just have to get on with it, OK?'

Maguire was about to respond when Hawkins' mobile buzzed. She retrieved it from her bag, accepting when she looked at the screen that Sod's Law wasn't done with them yet.

White Post Wood
Havering
Body found

6

Rachel pulled her jacket tight around her shoulders, shifting from one leg to the other, rubbing her calves together. She yanked the zip up to her chin, trying to ignore the ad board on the lamp post next to her as it flapped noisily in the wind.

'Fuck offff,' she growled at the weather, wishing she'd worn stockings under her micro skirt. Earlier on it had been a decent day, but since the sun had gone down it had turned fucking freezing. No wonder she was the only girl out tonight.

And to cap it all, business was shit.

She looked over at the bright lights of the KFC drive-through, at the cars creeping round from hatch to hatch, fighting the urge to jack it in for the night, thinking about what her best mate, Usha, always said.

Never eat before making your first sale.

If she gave in now, next thing she'd be home in front of the telly, arguing with her little brother; answering a million questions from Mum about where she'd been and why she never ate at home any more.

Sometimes it was torture working right opposite a fast food place; she spent the whole fucking time hungry. But this was the best pitch in Leyton, and most of her trade came from drivers who pulled in for dinner and watched her standing around on the corner while they ate.

Rachel turned back to the road, thinking about the college course she could almost afford: the one that would get her a job in beauty or fashion; one that didn't involve haggling with hairy old men about the price if they didn't wear a condom. If she worked hard and got promoted, she'd be able to rent somewhere of her own, a room, maybe a flat.

Being trapped at Mum's with Trevor made her sick. All she could think about were the nights a few years ago when Niall was at Dad's, and Mum still worked at the pub. The nights Trevor would insist on them watching TV together, sliding closer and closer, pulling her on to his lap.

One time she had tried to shop the arsehole, but he denied it, and Mum had believed him because she'd made a few things up in the past, shoplifted here and there.

At least he'd stopped.

So Mum and Trevor could go fuck themselves. The thought of getting out was the only thing that kept her going these days.

It would mean leaving Niall behind, which was hard, but he'd be OK. Trevor wasn't into boys; she knew that much for sure. And anyway, once she had a place and he was old enough, Niall could move in with her.

She lit a cigarette, cupping her hand round the flame, eyeing the few cars parked up outside KFC. The crappy Ford was empty, and she'd get nothing from the people carrier where a guy was trying to silence two screaming children, or the smartly dressed woman in the Audi, glaring at her over the steering wheel between bites.

Rachel took another drag and walked towards the bridge. Trade might not be as steady there, but punters were more likely to stop because it was dark under the arches.

She reached the junction and started to cross. But a horn blared as she stepped off the pavement. She stumbled backwards, landing on her bum as a car swerved past and roared away.

Rachel sat for a moment, breathing hard, making sure she hadn't broken a heel before struggling back to her feet. Her half-finished cigarette lay on the ground but she ignored it, and was brushing the gravel off her hands when another car pulled off the main road and stopped, its passenger window sliding down.

A quiet voice came from inside, difficult to hear over the noise of passing traffic. 'I s . . . saw what happened. Are you OK?'

'Yeah.' Rachel rubbed her backside. She took a step forwards and bent down to look inside, but all she saw was the dark shape of a man in the driver's seat. 'It was probably my fault anyway.'

'No . . . he d . . . didn't signal.'

'Whatever.' Rachel straightened, expecting him to drive away, but there was a pause, then . . .

'Can I . . . g . . . give you a lift somewhere?'

A punter after all.

'Sure.' She leaned on the sill, already back in work mode. 'Where did you have in mind?'

'I . . . I don't know.' The guy edged backwards in his seat, which was always a positive sign. Often the bolshie blokes just wanted to humiliate you, but the nervy ones stared at you like confused puppies for all of the two minutes it took them to finish. This guy looked harmless. It would be an easy fifty; quarter of an hour tops.

'I'm Ruby,' she said, trying to relax him. 'What's your name?'

He scratched at his chin, obviously a first-timer. 'R . . . Rupert. I can d . . . drive you . . . wherever you want.'

'Great.' Rachel opened the door and slid into the seat as the interior light came on, letting her skirt ride up, checking things out while he was distracted. His clothes weren't expensive, like the car, but everything looked clean; another good omen. There was no cash on show, nothing except a hip flask in the cup holder, but then the richer ones never waved it about. More often it was the flash bastards with sports cars who were broke.

She closed the door. 'We'll have to head for Walthamstow if you fancy a hotel. They know all the girls around here.'

The interior light faded, but she could see his eyes darting this way and that. He was breathing hard, looking in his mirror at the traffic on the main road, probably checking for cops.

'Which . . .' he stammered, 'which . . . way is it?'

'Well that depends on what you can afford.' She placed a hand on his thigh. 'And what you want.'

He tensed, blinking hard, looking at her hand on his leg. 'I d . . . don't . . . understand.'

'Hey,' she soothed, 'I'll be gentle.'

'N . . . no. This isn't . . . right. Not right at all.'

Rachel frowned. Did he really not get what was going on?

'Sorry, mister.' She withdrew. 'I don't really need a lift.'

'Oh.' He breathed. 'Oh dear.'

'Sorry,' Rachel repeated, opening the door and stumbling out. She closed it and stood back as the car pulled away.

Watched its tail lights disappear along Dunton Road.

7

The Range Rover's headlights rocked and jolted as Mike turned off the service road, bouncing over the speed bumps at the entrance to the car park, pulling up beside the SOCO truck and a few other vehicles parked neatly on the far side. Two uniformed officers stood beside a police-liveried Astra at the back, its sidelights and roof-mounted LEDs casting eerie beams out into the black air.

Maguire killed the engine. 'What a way to spend your night.'

Hawkins grabbed the empty Burger King bags as they climbed out, taking a small detour to deposit them in a bin before following Mike across the shingle surface, stray leaves crunching beneath her wellington boots. She caught up as they met two uniformed officers at the wood's' edge.

'Hi.' She showed her warrant card. 'Do all these vehicles belong to our people?'

'Yes, Chief Inspector,' the taller constable replied with a West Country tinge. 'Car park was empty before we got here with the SOCO team.'

'Good.' She peered at the forest. 'So where's the party?'

'Over there, ma'am, straight through the trees.'

Hawkins followed the line of his outstretched arm, eyes straining to penetrate the blue glare from the cars. Then she saw what he was pointing at: floodlights ahead of them through the woods, the lamps' intensity tempered by the cluster of shapes stabbing at the darkness between. 'Who's in charge?'

'Tanya Goddard.'

Hawkins nodded. Goddard was deputy forensic pathologist at the Home Office, which meant her boss, Gerald Pritchard, was either on holiday or otherwise engaged. The man rarely missed a murder scene, so it was likely to be the former, although Hawkins wasn't going to complain. Pritchard's wandering eye often distracted her from properly assessing a crime scene, making Tanya a welcome substitute.

'Has the landowner been informed?' she asked.

'Yes, ma'am. He's the farmer, lives on site, whacking great place just north of here. He already knew about the discovery, from the people who found the corpse, but the SOCO team called ahead and cleared it on their way over. He knows you'll want to speak with him, but he'll stay out of our way till he's needed.'

'Fine.' She turned back. 'How do we get to the scene?'

'As the crow flies, I'm afraid, but you can't use the pathway; orders from the forensic team. They need to sweep the access routes for traces, but they'll do that when it gets light.' He held out a torch.

She took it. 'Is there a proper cordon on the way?'

'Absolutely. All be sorted in the next half-hour.'

'Good.' She looked at Mike. 'Shall we?'

'Right behind you, Chief.'

Hawkins thanked the uniforms, flicked on the torch, and led off. They passed through a break in the railway sleepers acting as the car park's perimeter, and headed into the trees, keeping clear of the path.

Mike stayed close behind, fending off the hanging branches that Hawkins' more modest height allowed her to duck. Thanks to recent rain, progress across the slippery, uneven ground was slow, giving Hawkins time to get her bearings.

According to the navigation software they'd used, this was White Post Wood, a medium-sized copse on the edge of Belhus Woods Country Park, near South Ockendon. The relative countryside they'd negotiated in the final part of their seventy-minute drive from Ealing seemed distinctly un-Londonesque, yet even here there was a faint background hum from the M25, less than two miles to the east, while they were a similar distance north of the Thames.

Qualified Met turf.

The fact that most murder investigations took place in more urban environments meant Hawkins' career rarely brought her to such places, although its rural attributes made an interesting, if challenging, change. She edged her way down a small drop strewn with exposed tree roots, trusting her weight to the sturdiest-looking branch within reach, telling Mike to watch his step.

She righted herself at the bottom, checking ahead.

They were nearing the edge of the trees, beyond which four free-standing spotlights formed a circle five yards in diameter, pointing down into a central zone. In their glare, stark against the surrounding blackness, several figures in white overalls were working away at ground level with tools and evidence bags. Among them another anti-contamination suit moved from point to point, camera flash sparking in the wider dark.

According to several texted updates on their journey there, the scene itself was still relatively fresh, having first been exposed ninety minutes ago. Purely by chance, the SOCO team had been fifteen minutes away on a burglary and arson job in Rainham when the call had come in. They'd downed tools and driven straight over, using the hour before Hawkins' arrival to begin excavating the gruesome discovery.

The last message Hawkins received from the team said that the body had been found by two civilians – buried beneath the surface of this field. A lack of decomposition on the hand that had initially been exposed indicated it hadn't long been there.

As well as liberating the corpse from its makeshift grave, they were now in a race against time to establish the victim's identity. The faster that happened, the sooner they could move on to determining motive, which should lead straight to a shortlist of likely suspects.

Or so theory went.

Muted conversations became audible as they emerged from the trees, and Hawkins shielded her eyes against the dazzling spotlights, trying to make an assessment of their environs.

Above them, a three-quarter moon hung in the cloudless sky, casting a soft grey light across land that fell gently away from the medium-sized field they had just entered. Woods framed one side of a plot whose remaining edges were bordered by sturdy-looking fences, beyond which further clumps of trees broke up other sectioned off areas of land. A few dimly lit windows in the distance probably belonged to the farmhouse that the uniformed officer had mentioned, and chill winds swept across the open ground between, lending an unexpectedly icy blast that suggested winter wasn't far off. The air was noticeably cleaner than just a few miles to the west, and every breath felt like it had been sharpened to test her lungs' resilience.

'Chief Inspector.' Tanya Goddard arrived beside them, removing a pair of soiled nitrile gloves, to greet Hawkins and then Maguire with a controlled handshake each. Goddard was a stocky woman in her late forties, whose conversation rarely strayed beyond her forensic profession, and never left the area altogether. Hawkins hadn't worked with her much, but a spotless reputation and a reported lack of kids, partners or friends backed up the implication she lived for her work.

'No Gerry tonight?' Hawkins asked.

'Sadly not,' Tanya said without expression. 'He's been off since yesterday afternoon.'

'Nothing serious, I hope.'

'His wife died on Thursday. A brain aneurysm nobody saw coming. She was forty-eight.'

'Oh.' Hawkins fished for the right words.

But Goddard had already moved on. 'Grab some overalls and I'll show you what we've got.' She waited while they collected white suits and overshoes from the supplies officer, a humourless man called Chad, whose demeanour as he handed them over was so woeful that he might as well have been asked to hand out the family silver.

'Follow me,' Goddard instructed once they'd suited up. 'Stay in the marked areas.' She wheeled round and stalked away with the detectives in tow, all three treading carefully inside the narrow taped access route.

Hawkins switched to breathing through her mouth as the familiar tang of recent death filled the air; turning to study the small crater slowly forming in the centre of the spotlit area, where forensic officers were painstakingly excavating their grisly find. The two men positioned nearest the cavity were working away with small trowels, picking at the edges as if carving a sculpture into the earth. Each trowel load was deposited carefully into white trays held by secondary officers, who sifted the contents before placing them into one of two large plastic barrels further out.

The hole itself was two feet in diameter; and almost the same in depth. Slowly emerging from its base, Hawkins could see an adult male head and shoulders, greying skin patched with soil, the rest of the body still buried in the surrounding dirt. The corpse lay on its right side, arms folded neatly across the chest, right hand resting on top of the naked left shoulder.

Goddard stopped them a few feet from the hole. 'Here he is: *Homo-Depositus*, IC1 male, mid-twenties, found two hours ago by a couple of civvies doing some metal detecting. They're at the farmhouse with the owner.' She waved down the hill before turning back to the grave. 'You're lucky he's still recognisable, actually, having been buried instead of just dumped. Everyone loves a free dinner,' she nodded at the treeline, 'especially the local wildlife.'

Mike peered at the body. 'We got a name?'

'Not yet,' the pathologist said. 'Obviously we're still to see below shoulder height, but assuming the killer has any sense, they'll have removed all clothing to minimise traces of DNA. If we find a wallet or other personal effects down there, it'll be a bonus.'

'Absolutely,' Hawkins agreed. 'You said metal detectors found him, but I can't see any piercings or rings. What did they pick up?'

Goddard sighed. 'We're not sure yet, but there's a hefty scar on the left shoulder, so he may have some surgical steel in there. I'll be able to say for certain following autopsy.'

'How about cause of death?'

'Again, it's difficult to say, but if I had to guess I'd go with strangulation. The pattern of bruising on the neck is consistent.'

Mike said, 'Lone attacker?'

'Not necessarily,' Goddard told him. 'One finisher-off,

perhaps, but I can't say yet how many people were involved in getting him to that point.'

'How long has he been down there?' Hawkins asked.

'Well,' Goddard's head rocked from side to side, 'there are residual signs of rigor mortis. So given the lack of blistering and skin decay . . . I'd say between eighteen and thirty-six hours, and that he was buried shortly after death.' She saw Hawkins' mouth open and answered the question before it arrived. 'Definitely dead before he went in, that's clear from the lack of tracheal ingress. If he was buried alive, he'd have inhaled dirt, as a reflex if nothing else.'

Hawkins nodded. 'OK. What about digging the grave?'

'Tricky to say.' The deputy pathologist cocked her head. 'For a lone male of average strength and size, working flat out in dry conditions with soil of this type . . . a couple of hours at least.'

'Which suggests premeditation.' Maguire picked up Hawkins' train of thought. 'Our perp ain't gonna risk digging out here for two hours straight with the body propped against the nearest tree, in case he's interrupted.'

'What if he had assistance?' Hawkins challenged.

Goddard thought for a moment. 'A second person would speed things up, obviously, but any more than two working simultaneously on a hole this size would be tripping over each other.'

Maguire carried on. 'So whether it's one guy or more, the smart bucks say they dig the hole up front, which

35

means they can sell any old jazz about archaeology or environmental research if anyone starts asking questions, and go dig someplace else. They probably made the grave a while back, boarded it up, covered it with mud and leaves. Unless someone treads right on it, which ain't likely out here, no one finds it, which means they could have back-up holes all over.'

Hawkins accepted his logic, looking around, speaking more to herself than anyone. 'It's actually a good location. A short walk from the car park on a quiet road, but hidden from that side by the forest, plus it's near enough this edge of the trees to be obscured, while still getting some natural light from the moon, so our digger wouldn't have needed a torch. And any potential passers-by would be visible in advance across the open fields, or given away by their headlights upon arrival. Either way, whether he's digging the hole or dumping the corpse, the killer gets sufficient warning and a selection of escape routes, so he can scarper if he's disturbed.'

'Right,' Maguire said. 'Only risk is if he's seen but not approached, and someone's waiting for him to come back.'

Hawkins made a mental note to check if the farmer or his people had seen anything, and ask how often ramblers crossed this land. It was likely the killer would have worked under cover of darkness, of course, but there was still a chance he could have been seen, and that the observer hadn't found it weird enough to report at the time. And in all fairness, who *would* raise an eyebrow to somebody digging a hole on a farm? Probably just the farmer or one of his staff.

She turned back to Goddard. 'So where *was* he killed?'

'Interestingly there's evidence to suggest right here,' the pathologist glanced down at the grave, 'or somewhere similar, at least. The victim has minor gouging and scratches on his hands and forearms but nowhere else, indicating that he was still clothed during the chase. We've also got more serious bruising to the shoulders and upper arms, all consistent with moving at speed through dense foliage like this in the dark, navigating more by touch than sight.'

Hawkins interrupted. 'So let's say the killer plans the whole thing and digs this hole in advance. That way the body won't be exposed for long, plus he can get to know the area and its exit routes well enough to have a good chance of escape if he's seen dumping it. Somehow he gets his victim to woodland, either here or somewhere like it, and attacks. The victim breaks free and runs, but he's chased through the trees and strangled before being moved here and buried in the prefabricated grave.'

'It's plausible,' Goddard said. 'We'll wait for daylight before we go poking around the woods for evidence of a chase, or any previous bouts of violence, but if it did happen here and the victim had trouble negotiating the trees, chances are his killer did, too. We'll sweep for footprints in softer mud, and traces of torn clothing on the trees, plus any signs of the body being dragged to this location, although it's always possible he was carried. If we're really lucky, we might even get some blood. We'll look at the access routes for tyre and footwear imprints, as well, although most of the surrounding roads are tarmacked.'

Hawkins nodded. 'How soon can you get him in for autopsy?'

'Freeing the body undamaged is the slow part.' Goddard checked her watch. 'But if I call in a few favours, we should have him back to the lab pretty soon, so if all goes smoothly I'll have some answers for you before breakfast.'

Hawkins thanked her and asked to be informed when the autopsy was due to begin. Goddard agreed and went to check on her team.

'OK.' Hawkins turned to Mike. 'So we've got a lone male who appears to have been murdered in this vicinity, following a chase through the forest. Given the lack of vehicles in the car park when our team arrived, the most likely premise is that victim and killer drove here together, with the murderer taking that vehicle away with him afterwards. The less probable alternative is that the chase started on foot not far from here.' She waved at the landscape. 'Get whoever's on duty to start mapping out the area. Mark any buildings, residential or otherwise, and we'll go door to door in the morning. Hopefully there won't be many in surroundings like these. Restrict the search to a two-mile radius at this stage; this terrain is rough, so the chase probably won't have been long. We can always widen it later.'

Maguire nodded. 'How 'bout the press?'

'Issue an appeal for witnesses; anyone who might have seen the grave being dug, or anything of the chase itself. Also, assuming there's no ID buried down there, and unless someone's registered him missing, we need to get this guy cleaned up and photographed. Run his prints, too – I want to know who he is.

'More importantly,' she turned back towards the car, 'let's get our chat with the metal detectors and the farmer done quickly. We need to be up even earlier than normal tomorrow.'

She saw Mike's questioning glance, and added, 'I'm glad you've already forgotten, but we've got a fight on our hands for the bathroom.'

8

'It's about time,' the farmer mumbled at the sight of Hawkins' warrant card, swinging the heavy wooden door aside. 'S'pose you better come through. They're in the kitchen.'

He turned without acknowledging Mike, and lumbered off down the poorly lit corridor towards the back of the farmhouse.

Maguire closed the door behind them. 'I like him already.'

Hawkins shushed him and followed their host, picking up vestiges of stewed coffee above the musty aromas of dog and damp carpet.

They shuffled until fresh light cracked ahead as another door opened, the farmer's broad silhouette giving way to a room Dickens would have been proud to capture. Hawkins arrived on a threadbare grey mat over terracotta tiles, where she stopped to take in the space.

The beamed ceiling hung low, enhancing the sense of claustrophobia created by more dim lighting and disparate heavy furniture, antique sideboards jammed against Great War appliances, everything chipped or rusting through its paint. Beneath the grime, surfaces overflowed with old jars, faded ornaments, blackened pans.

A weathered Labrador raised its head from a basket in the far corner, gave the visitors a rheumy look, and slumped again.

And at a battered table in the far corner, surrounded by the carefully propped equipment to blame for their collective presence, two fifty-something men in wing-back chairs, ignoring cups of murky brown liquid, looking expectantly her way.

'Gentlemen.' She moved towards them, hand extended. 'You must be the metal detectors.'

'Detector*ists*.' The less wiry of the pair straightened, completing the shake. 'That's a detector.' He nodded at the glorified golf club next to his chair. 'We're detector*ists*.'

'My mistake.' Hawkins turned to his thinner companion, who introduced himself as Jim.

'Ignore Grego.' He waved at his friend. 'He thinks the whole world gets its kicks from traipsing round muddy fields, digging up rusty old shit, pardon my French.'

'Don't worry about it.' She smiled. 'Can you tell us a bit more about what you found?'

'Mostly just rifle casings.' Grego dug in his pocket. 'But the old girl never lets me down altogether.' He cast affectionate eyes at his detector, holding a small piece of metal out to Hawkins. She stared at it as he added, 'That's a Goose Helmet Silver Unit. Twelve hundred years old. Properly rare.'

Jim shot eyes at his mate. 'She means the body, you tit.'

'Oh.' Grego withdrew his offering. 'Right.'

The thinner man continued: 'Sorry about him. He's

got a nose for finding valuable crap, but don't expect much besides. What do you want to know?'

'This area,' Hawkins said. 'Have you ... detected here before?'

Jim shook his head. 'First time. We don't normally have to come so far from home, but now they've started dumping that *green waste* from landfill everywhere. It's full of tin foil and hypodermic needles, which ain't exactly the best stuff to be growing vegetables in, is it? Anyway, it buggers our game; all we get is interference.'

She nodded. 'Tell me about the grave: how did you come to find it?'

'Ground was covered with leaves,' Jim shrugged, 'which ain't odd that close to the trees, but out of nowhere Grego picks up a non-ferrous reading of eighty-five. That's pretty high, so we have a closer look, except instead of the massive stash we're hoping for, we find some geezer's hand. And when we clear the rest of the leaves, the outline of the grave becomes obvious. That's when we called you lot.'

'Good. How solidly packed was the soil when you started to dig – tight enough to have needed more than one person's weight to pack it down?'

The detectorists looked at each other before Jim answered. 'Wouldn't have thought so. Ground was pretty loose, as it goes.'

'Last question. How much time did you spend today in or around wooded areas?'

'None, really.' Grego this time. 'We were out in open fields till we got up here.'

Hawkins turned to the farmer. 'What about the last few weeks – have you noticed anyone hanging around your farm, especially near the trees?'

Their host, now leaning against the kitchen side, shook his sizeable head. 'You're the first intrusion I've had for months. And I already checked with most of the lads. No one's seen anything odd.'

'OK.' She raised eyebrows at Mike, who indicated that he had nothing to add, before turning back to the detectorists. 'We're almost done, though you'll need to wait here a bit longer, till the forensic team can take contact details and swabs of your DNA.'

Jim responded first to his friend's panicked expression. 'So they can count us out, moron.'

'Exactly.' Hawkins pointed at their feet. 'They'll also want samples of the mud on your boots, and imprints of the tread.'

She thanked the farmer for his time and hospitality, and was almost at the front door with Maguire when Grego caught up with them.

'S'cuse me, love,' he said, prompting them both to turn. 'But do you know what was down there, I mean, what the detector picked up?'

'Not yet,' she told him truthfully. 'And I have no idea who has first refusal in these situations, but if there's anything of value down there, I promise you'll be the first to know.'

9

Hawkins woke to a faceful of green fluff.

Her head snapped back and she coughed, instinctively knocking it away. She mumbled something, still not fully conscious. But the words arrested in her throat, as her eyes flicked open.

Rosie stood beside the bed in a blue net dress, with Hawkins' feather duster in her swiftly withdrawn hand. They stared at each other for a good three seconds before Rosie began shouting.

'*Mummy. Auntie Antonia said fu*—'

'No, no.' Hawkins shot upright, reaching for her niece. She missed, but thankfully the speed of her movement startled Rosie into silence.

'Let's not bother Mummy with *that*,' she soothed, forcing a smile past the headache already parallel-parking itself between her temples. But Rosie continued edging towards the door as Hawkins fished for something else to hold the attention of her sister's eldest.

'What are you doing with my duster?' was all she managed.

'Dusting, silly.' Rosie rolled her eyes. 'Mummy says your house is a disgrace.'

'Oh, does she?'

Ungrateful cow.

Rosie returned to her dusting, obviously having catalogued Auntie Antonia's outburst among all the other indiscretions she liked to regurgitate whenever their most judgemental family members were present.

Hawkins checked the far side of the bed, disappointed to find only dishevelled bedclothes. Mike, as the best thing since a Disney DVD on repeat, would undoubtedly have handled this better. But until he returned from the bathroom, Hawkins realised she was flying solo.

For some reason, she and kids had just never gelled. Anyone under the age of twenty-four remained a complete mystery, and Hawkins had finally capitulated when her failed attempts to bond with baby Rosie were followed eighteen months later by depressingly similar results with her brother, Kyle. Admittedly, the fact she and Siobhan were proverbial chalk and cheese wouldn't have helped, but she couldn't lay blame for the whole situation there. Maybe children sensed fear.

She eased herself into a sitting position on the edge of the mattress, as Rosie finished sprucing her bedside cabinet and skipped towards the far side of the room, singing some tuneless number and waving the duster, releasing a small cloud of airborne dirt on every upswing.

'That's a pretty dress,' Hawkins announced, moving to intercept.

'It was,' Rosie began as she was grabbed by the armpits and hoisted at arm's-length on to the landing, 'until my stinky brother tore a hole in it.'

'How awful.' Hawkins picked her way across the toy-strewn carpet towards the stairs, wondering how to distract her niece while she got ready for work. Siobhan still took every opportunity to show off the tiny scars on Rosie's forearm, from when she'd watched Auntie Antonia applying mascara, and tried to recreate the effect on Admiral Kirk.

'Shouldn't you be getting ready for school?'

Rosie sighed. 'Yes. Mummy said you'd help me.'

'*Siobhan?*' Hawkins yelled, dumping her niece on the top step when she realised she'd been dangling her over the drop.

'*What?*' The shouted reply came from behind the bathroom door.

She spun, now hoping that Mike rather than Kyle was responsible for the clanking sounds coming from downstairs in the kitchen. 'What are you doing?'

'*Having a bloody bath, if that's all right with you.*'

It had already started. 'I need to get ready for work.'

'*I only just got in.*'

She managed to count to four before the answer burst free. 'You're unemployed, Siobhan. You've got all day once I've gone. Get out.'

A short pause. '*So you give a huge shit about the fact my marriage is over, then?*'

'More than you do about swearing within earshot of your four-year-old.' Hawkins turned, flinching when she found an empty space where Rosie had been.

'Five minutes,' she warned. 'Then I'm breaking this door down.'

East Ham Public Mortuary was a squat brick building set back from the High Street, sufficiently depressing in appearance to justify most visitors' decisions to wait until death or unavoidable work commitment before turning up. A few skeletal trees failed to soften the mid-Victorian exterior, and the narrow tiled corridors echoed mercilessly as Hawkins and Maguire were shown to the dissection room.

Which stank.

The smell of disinfected dry meat grew as they pushed through into the main chamber, where Tanya Goddard and a second, younger woman stood behind a robust, height-adjustable slab. Both were dressed in pale green overalls with hoods and visor masks, and in front of them on the steel surface lay a naked male cadaver, clearly in peak physical form.

Hawkins recognised the same greyish blue face she'd seen emerging from the bottom of a hole the previous night. What hadn't been obvious then was that the body remained in one piece. The young man had been cleaned up, but it had done him no favours; a lack of mud only serving to highlight the horrific cuts inflicted during autopsy, patches of exposed flesh where skin had been systematically lifted to inspect subcutaneous damage, as well as the vestiges of whatever violent happenings had led to his death. He was a pallid patchwork of welts and scars, deep purple stains across lower sections denoting where now redundant blood had pooled.

'Tanya,' Hawkins instated a smile and crossed the room, trying not to gag, 'thanks for fitting us in so fast.' Barely twelve hours had passed since the body was found, and it was highly unusual for any post-mortem to happen so quickly afterwards. Evidently the mortuary was benefitting from the same quiet patch as the Met.

She stopped opposite the pathologist and her colleague, wondering how anyone with an olfactory bulb spent more than five minutes in this place, let alone a career.

'Good timing,' Goddard mumbled, stuffing the last few handfuls of human offal into an unsympathetically large cavity in the man's midriff. 'We're pretty much done.' She straightened and looked at her assistant. 'Give us a minute, would you, Sam? I'll shout when we're ready to close up.'

Sam nodded and shed her slimy gloves into a bin, before disappearing through a door at the back of the room.

Hawkins fought the urge to follow, addressing Goddard instead. 'So, what can you tell us about this guy?'

'A profusion, actually.' The pathologist's lips curled up at the edges, as if she was pleased with her odd turn of phrase. 'Would you like the injuries in physical or chronological order?'

Hawkins thought for a second. 'Can you give us a timeline?'

'Sure.' Goddard looked down at her subject. 'He's a bit of a mess, but the narrative's clear enough. We begin with a heavy physical assault. Everything from broken teeth to widespread contusions and two cracked ribs either side, all consistent with being beaten in a non-specific manner, by which I mean that the injuries are spread across the body, as if our assailant went at whichever part of his target was nearest. That suggests an impassioned attack, rather than a considered one. Having said that, none of these injuries were concentrated on vulnerable areas, and none are life-threatening.'

Mike frowned. 'So whoever did it wasn't out to kill?'

'Not at that stage,' Goddard clarified. 'More interestingly, though, there's a complete absence of retaliatory damage to the victim's extremities.'

'You mean he didn't fight back?' Hawkins said. 'So what . . . he was unwilling or unable to?'

'Or he thought he deserved it,' Mike added.

'I don't think that's it,' Goddard told him, carefully lifting the corpse's right arm to reveal scuff marks on the elbow. 'There's evidence he was trying to defend himself; even gouging to fingertips and nails, as if he attempted to drag himself away, but there's no corresponding damage to knuckles, knees or shins, which I'd certainly expect to see from a two-way fight.'

'Drunk or drugged, then,' Hawkins said.

The pathologist nodded. 'There are strong traces of alcohol and Benzodiazepines in his blood. Both are used recreationally these days, of course; so probably just a heavy night on the tiles. But yes, he was inebriated at the time of the attack.'

Maguire leaned closer. 'What about weapons?'

'No need.' Goddard turned the man's head, revealing a badly swollen jaw. 'Worst injury is a fractured mandible, while capillary damage elsewhere suggests an attack consistent with fists and footwear. If, as it appears, the victim was heavily intoxicated, our assailant wouldn't have required artillery.'

'When did the attack happen?' Hawkins asked.

Goddard's mouth twisted. 'Well . . . as we know, he'd been dead for a day or so before we dug him up, but histological examination of the bruising from the initial assault shows these injuries had begun to heal, so he lived for around twenty-four hours afterwards. I'd estimate he was first attacked three days ago.'

'Monday, then.' Hawkins looked at Mike. 'Which means whoever did this should still be carrying physical repercussions.' She turned back. 'What happened next?'

Their host eased her glasses up her nose with the back of a hand. 'There appears to have been a gap of about another day, during which I can find no evidence of further physical assault.'

'Maybe he got free; hid in the woods,' Mike suggested.

'Perhaps,' Goddard looked at him, 'but this is where it gets slightly weird. At some point in this hiatus he received . . . medical attention.'

Maguire blinked. 'You think it's weird he went to hospital after taking a beating?'

'That's just it; he didn't go to hospital.' Goddard leaned over and retrieved a few plastic bags from the bench behind her, holding them up to show their grubby contents. Each packet contained a mangled, bloodstained patch. 'These dressings were covering some of his worst cuts from the first attack, but they aren't of medical grade, not even close. They're just cheap domestic plasters, badly applied to wounds that hadn't been cleaned. Frankly, he'd have received better treatment at the Somme.'

'Maybe he put them on himself,' Maguire offered. 'Short-term.'

Hawkins realised what the pathologist was getting at. 'But where did he get them?' Mike didn't answer, so she went on. 'If he'd made it home or to a shop, he'd have cleaned himself up. Even tissues or antiseptic wipes would have helped if he didn't have access to water. Or are we suggesting he had plasters with him? If you're expecting a fight you take a weapon or a mate, not a first aid kit.'

'Actually there's more,' the pathologist interjected. 'Stomach contents say he didn't eat during this break, either, not since before the first attack, in fact.'

Mike didn't hesitate. 'Yeah, but his jaw's all busted up, right? So he ain't exactly craving Big Macs.'

Hawkins still wasn't convinced. 'Go back to the timeline. There was more violence?'

'Yes,' Goddard said. 'I've dissected a few of the most

damaged areas from both incidents, and following the twenty-four-hour pause we have what looks like a chase through the woods, judging by the dirt ingress and contusion profile of the more recent damage, which is consistent with recurring incidental collision. Put simply: running into trees in the dark. And finally we have the tracheal bruising that confirms death by manual asphyxiation, as I thought.'

Hawkins spoke slowly. 'He's beaten up, left alone for a day, and then strangled. So how do we account for the gap?'

'Easy,' Mike said. 'Someone tries to off him but he gets away. He spends twenty-four hours thinking he's in the clear, but then the killer catches up and finishes the job.'

'Maybe,' she accepted. 'But I think there's a better explanation.'

Expectant gazes turned her way.

'What if he was being held for ransom?'

She waited for her suggestion to sink in, watching Maguire turn the possibility over before he replied. 'So . . . the first attack is to tame the guy and get him locked away, and they patch him up so he don't expire before time. The twenty-four-hour gap is used to contact his family, demand the dough and wait for them to pay. Maybe they find the cash; maybe they don't, but then either he escapes or they give him a head start. Killer hunts him down, and *adios*. Kinda makes sense.'

'I'm glad we agree.' Hawkins turned back to Goddard. 'Thanks, Tanya. Keep us up to date with DNA stuff, if you can, and I'll send someone down later to take some pictures and set up an e-fit. We need a name for this guy to have a decent chance of finding whoever did this.'

She turned away, her brain already filling with strategies to trace the dead man's roots, but the pathologist called her back.

'Perhaps I should have said.' A smirk ghosted across Goddard's features. 'But I already know who he is.'

11

'Peter Barnes,' Hawkins announced, attaching the last photograph to a freshly cleared investigation board, then turning back to her team. 'A plasterer from Tottenham, twenty-four years old at the time of his death: three days ago, after a hard night's partying, judging by the drink and drugs in his system. Body was discovered last night, and autopsy happened earlier this morning, confirming strangulation as cause. Constriction blemishes on the neck are consistent with an average adult male hand span.'

She explained what they suspected so far of Barnes' final days: how he'd been beaten and badly patched up, apparently chased through the woods and then killed, and how two metal-detecting enthusiasts had mistaken his submerged remains for bounty.

She paused, allowing time for Amala Yasir to finish taking notes in her hard-backed A4 pad. The petite DS was a prolific note-taker, and during their four years working together, Hawkins had genuinely come to suspect that, somewhere, almost every detail of the twenty-nine-year-old sergeant's life would be documented in one way or another; all ordered and categorised for later analysis. Not that she was complaining, of course; Amala was diligent and efficient, never late for anything, and she turned up every day with her jet-black hair so immaculate and her clothes so well pressed that Hawkins sometimes wondered where she found time for sleep. If she could only batter some independence into the young DS, Amala might be the perfect officer.

Unfortunately, the same could not be said of her counterpart, the second detective sergeant currently assigned to their team. Aaron Sharpe defied Hawkins' theory that nobody 'fell' into a Met police career. As usual, the flaky remains of his breakfast Danish adorned the front of his ill-chosen shirt, and she'd be surprised if he did anything fast enough to dislodge them before the end of his shift. She had worked with Aaron on and off since the forty-something DS was seconded on to her team last December. And if she hadn't been preoccupied at the time, leading the biggest serial murder investigation the UK had seen in a decade, she might have been able to offload him before he'd become entrenched. Now his knackered brogues were firmly under her table, though at least his presence meant no other teams had come to Hawkins, cap in hand for Amala, in case their request for support ended up being filled by Sharpe instead.

The worst thing was that, even given the opportunity, she couldn't afford to let him go. Recent cuts meant resources were stretched more tightly than ever, making the extended team she'd managed to keep until earlier that year look positively indulgent. Hawkins' enforced absence in January had left Mike temporarily in charge which, combined with two high-profile serial killer cases in quick succession, had been enough to secure the services of two additional DIs.

Frank Todd might not have been Hawkins' biggest fan, and his acidic Geordie wit not always appropriate or welcome, but he was competent and experienced, and she'd definitely felt his absence since his move to the hate crimes unit four months ago.

The back of Steve Tanner, of course, she'd been less sorry to see. The self-assured and Chief Superintendent-endorsed prodigy had been drafted in during their last big case, supposedly to bolster their ranks and learn the Chief Inspector ropes from Hawkins. She'd recognised his annexing intentions straight off, even though others had been fooled, but Tanner's insidious ways had come close to undermining her at a difficult time. He'd been reassigned following a battle of wills that Hawkins had only just won, but he was still a pair of hands that hadn't been replaced, leaving her to scrounge constables and favours from elsewhere when workloads began to challenge everyone's commitment to the job. Which meant that, for the moment, any sergeant, even Sharpe, was better than none.

As if to emphasise the point, the lanky DS eased back in his chair for a stretch so theatrical he could have been going for a part in the West End. He finished and looked up, catching sight of Hawkins' palpable irritation, and quickly dropped his arms, his left elbow catching Amala's shoulder on the way down, knocking her pen to the floor and earning him a scolding glare as she bent to retrieve it. Amala said nothing, but the plastic wheels on her chair groaned as she increased the gap between herself and Aaron.

Hawkins waited for them to settle, glancing at the third and last member of her present squad. Normally Mike would be grinning by now, but this time he simply raised an eyebrow, reminding Hawkins of the struggle they'd endured that morning to exit the house on time. Despite the fact that it was now eight forty, ninety minutes since he'd stepped barefoot on a Lego brick, she could still feel the irritation radiating off him. But all eyes were on her again, so she put the pending tiff on hold and resumed her morning brief.

'Here's how Barnes' body was found,' she pointed at the first image, 'in this shallow grave on a country park not far from South Ockendon. It was deposited shortly after death, and had been stripped of possessions and clothes. I think it's safe to assume our late subject would have been dressed beforehand, so unless there was something sordid going on, our perpetrator's obviously aware that clothing tells a much more detailed story about a corpse than bare skin does. Finally, the hole was deep enough for the killer to be called unlucky that it was found so fast, maybe at all. Both elements suggest a premeditated attack, and that our murderer is intelligent and well prepared.'

'How did we make a positive ID so fast, Chief,' Amala asked quietly, 'if there were no clues with the body?'

Hawkins raised a hand to one of the other pictures,

which showed a dull metal plate in a tray, and the series of digits lasered on to its smooth grey surface. 'Luckily for us, Mr Barnes was into motocross, which led to a disagreement with gravity in 2012. He lost, of course, ending up with a broken wrist, a snapped clavicle, and a left shoulder blade held together by this surgical steel implant. Apparently this sort of thing sets off metal detectors like a retirement fund, so it's no surprise they dug him up. But here's the good bit; thanks to the good old Medical Devices Regulations Directive 2002, all surgically fitted devices must be CE approved and registered, so a quick records check revealed everything we need.

'Sadly,' she added, 'that's about all we have. Last night, after visiting the scene, Mike and I spoke to the farmer who owns the land. Neither he nor his workers noticed anything unusual recently, no unfamiliar vehicles; no one digging holes. There's also a shortage of DNA under the victim's fingernails, suggesting that he was too physically weak and disorientated to fight his assailant's grip. Unsurprisingly the area isn't awash with CCTV, although the relatively rural location should make outsiders the subject of local gossip, so maybe we'll get lucky there.'

She turned to the map Yasir had stayed late the previous night to produce, pointing at the crudely drawn cross and spade in the centre. 'Here's where the body was found, just beyond the treeline at the edge of this small wood. Amala has also marked all known properties and outbuildings in a two-mile radius. We'll focus the local investigation on this area for now, mainly because the victim was already injured when the chase began, so he wouldn't have been capable of covering much terrain. The other possibility is that one or both parties arrived by road, making this secluded car park a point of interest, too. The whole place was cordoned off late last night, and the forensics guys have been out since dawn, searching the woods for traces that might give us clues as to the direction the chase took, or the identities of those involved. You'll hear if they find anything, of course. Any questions?'

'Ma'am.' Amala's hand crept up. 'You said there was a day's gap between the first attack and the murder. If he was being held, could they have been trying to get information out of him?'

Sharpe piggybacked, 'Or coerce him into doing something for them?'

Hawkins nodded. 'Both are possibilities, but the post-mortem showed a clear lack of physical abuse between the two main bouts of violence, during which rudimentary first aid was applied, none of which fits a torture scenario. Our best guess at this stage is that we could be looking at a hostage situation. The victim may have been taken in order to extort money from his loved ones. I know twenty-four hours isn't long to wait for capitulation, but it's feasible he escaped, and was killed in the ensuing chase.'

She waited for more comments, but everyone seemed content, so she moved on. 'We need to put together a history for Barnes. How and where he spent his free time, friends, enemies; definitely anyone with an interest, financial or otherwise, in his death. Mike and I will visit his family and friends this morning, and try piecing together his movements over preceding days. We'll tread carefully, though. If any of them were asked for money, nothing was reported, so in that case there's a question mark over why. Otherwise it'll be a shock, because somehow the press have missed this one; we haven't even had reporters at the scene, although that luxury won't last. We're organising a TV appeal for news programmes in the surrounding boroughs, which can be aired once the family has been informed.

'Aaron, I want you on door to door, moving outwards from the burial site. Drag a couple of uniforms over to help, and find out whether any of the locals saw anything. We're after details of cars or people in the vicinity on or around Tuesday night, and any unfamiliar activity in recent weeks. It's likely the killer prepared this hole and possibly other back-ups elsewhere in advance, so anything that ties in with that would be good.'

She turned to Yasir. 'Amala, you're on background duty. Start with social media, phone records, text messages and bank accounts. Was Barnes on social services' radar, or known to any crisis associations? If he was killed because of something he was mixed up in, then maybe there's a clue among that lot.'

She finished up and sent the two sergeants on their way. Amala spent a moment at her desk and then disappeared, leaving Sharpe faffing at his desk.

Hawkins picked up the folder compiled by the night shift. It contained all the information amassed on the Barnes family so far, including Tottenham addresses for the mother he'd lived with and the father who'd made a token bid for custody ten years ago when the marital relationship dissolved. Three older brothers were listed, along with aunts and uncles, plus a few grandparents here and there.

But there was no question in Hawkins' mind, as she and Maguire left the incident suite, about where they were heading first. According to the four County Court judgements and one bankruptcy against her name, Peter Barnes' mother was heavily in debt.

Increasingly, unscrupulous loan sharks were using threats against debtors' relatives to exert leverage, and if Mrs Barnes had fallen into such difficulties, it wasn't too much of a leap to imagine her family becoming targets.

Especially, perhaps, her youngest son.

12

Hawkins banged heavily on the polished metal door of the Boilerhouse, and turned to watch the traffic drifting back and forth along a surprisingly sunlit Ferry Lane. The thick velvet rope strung across the entrance between two shiny poles, and the heavy metal gate blocking the entrance to the rear car park reinforced her suspicion that she'd be lucky to find anyone here, mid-morning on a weekday, but it had been worth a try. According to the large billboards dotted about nearby, the club was purpose-built, two minutes' walk from Tottenham Hale station, to serve its clientele seven days a week; trendy commuters who dressed well enough for work that they could come straight here on their way home. Allegedly week nights were *Firmly in the Chillout Zone*, while weekends were reserved for those who wanted to *Party like it's 1999*.

Hawkins couldn't remember the last time she'd wanted to visit any such place, although 1999 probably wasn't a bad guess. But then thirty-something detective chief inspectors probably weren't their target audience.

Behind her there was still no sign of anyone coming to the door, so she began descending the steps towards the car.

Hawkins' Giulietta was the only vehicle in the

sweeping U-shaped drive, obviously designed for long-wheelbase limousines to pull off the main road and deposit champagne-fuelled hen parties to maximum exposure. She slid into the driver's seat, digging in her bag for the list of Peter Barnes' disparate friends and family which she and Maguire were slowly working their way through.

So far that morning, Barnes' recent history had remained resolutely clouded. The local radio appeal for potential witnesses had yielded nothing yet, although Hawkins had greater hopes for the TV coverage they were due to get later in the day.

Instead they'd found themselves restricted to family, none of whom seemed to know much about how or where the victim spent his time, and neither had they been able to locate Nick Barnes, the eldest brother, whose record contained enough mid-level violence to make him worth questioning.

So they'd focused on lower hanging fruit. Mike had spoken to the father, who'd seen precisely none of his children for the best part of six months, but still made all the appropriately stricken noises when informed of his youngest son's death, and the two middle siblings, who'd been more interested in finding out on whom they should take revenge than what had happened to their younger brother. Once the Jeremy Kyle-esque overblown reactions were done, however, it transpired that none of them could say whether Peter had enemies, or where he'd been working in the weeks before his death. Maguire was now on his way to see a painter and decorator who, according to Barnes' father, he had shared work with in the past.

While it hadn't been any more cultured, Hawkins' day had at least provided some sort of progress. Peter's mother lived at the rough end of nearby Broad Lane. Dina Barnes was a recovering drug addict whose recent switch on to methadone tallied with a subsequent reduction in the frequency with which she was arrested for soliciting and petty crime. The dilapidated state of her council property gave an indication as to why her son had so regularly chosen to be elsewhere, but she swore she'd cleared her debts to high-interest loan companies, and that she'd never borrowed money from an illegitimate source.

She was also the one relative who seemed to know something useful about her son's exploits.

Apparently Peter's long-time best mate had managed the Boilerhouse since it opened three months ago. Dina didn't have a home address for the friend, but the club was quickly becoming one of Tottenham's most popular venues, and Peter often spent his evenings there. Which made it their best opportunity to map some of his recent affairs.

For now, though, there was no one here, which gave Hawkins two options: either begin chasing Companies House for details of whoever owned the place, and ask them to drag their bar manager down, or go and interview some of Peter's aunts and uncles, and come back when the club was open for business.

She was reaching for her keys when her phone rang.

A withheld number at this time of day could only be the Chief Superintendent.

She answered, mentally preparing the brief progress update Vaughn would expect. 'Hawkins.'

'Detective.' An unusual edge to his tone.

'Sir.' She hesitated. 'How are you?'

'Concerned, actually.'

Definitely something wrong.

Hawkins filled the silence. 'It's still early days, but we already have a name for the vict—'

'Not about the case, Antonia. I'm sure you're handling that with typical proficiency.' A beat. 'Are you alone?'

'Yes.'

'Good. Because I'm calling about *you*.'

'Sir?'

'Your welfare, to be precise.'

Sturridge.

She feigned confusion. 'Has something been said?'

'Not exactly. I'm reading your therapist's notes, since you volunteered for post-traumatic event counselling. No show, late, no show, cancellation. Even the sessions you *do* bother to attend show no significant progress.' Hawkins heard computer keys clicking. 'He cites *suppressed mid-stage neurosis, with a median risk of PTSD if not addressed.*'

She tried to counter. 'You know the demands of the job, sir. Investigations would suffer if I attended regardless. It's not easy, but I'm working through it.'

'Really? Then I must have the wrong notes, because Sturridge records *this* patient as *obstructive* and *wilfully introverted.*'

'Oh.' Her defence stalled.

Vaughn ploughed on. 'This needs addressing, Antonia. You went through a highly traumatic, life-changing event. But it's been almost a year now, and I can't afford to have a senior officer's judgement called into question because we didn't follow procedure. We have to put ourselves beyond reproach.'

'Understood. Leave it with me.'

'I want to see change.'

'Absolutely.' She drew breath, eager to get away.

'Antonia?'

'Yes.'

'I mean now. Call Sturridge back and put something in the diary this week. Get this sorted.'

Bollocks. 'Of course.'

She rang off, and sat staring out of the windscreen at the traffic jostling past on the main road, thinking about how much things had changed. Five years ago, no one at the top of the force's food chain would have shown the slightest professional concern about how well their workforce slept. But now mental health was a political hug toy, Vaughn's job was becoming more about duty of care to his officers than any commitment to actual law enforcement. These days you ended up in front of a shrink for crying at romantic comedy, so near-death experiences and their potential fallout were everyone's business.

Which meant, despite her best efforts to date, and regardless of how long she kept them up, he wasn't going to let the subject drop.

Hawkins sighed, and was looking through her contacts for Sturridge's number when her attention was dragged above the dashboard, as a large truck with a Carlsberg advert on the side turned off the main road and pulled up at the entrance to the club's rear car park. The horn sounded, and a moment later the powered shutter began to open inwards. As soon as the way was clear, the truck eased through, and the gate started closing again.

But Hawkins was already inside.

She followed the truck along the walled service road, which opened out at the back into a reasonably sized parking area, empty aside from two vehicles. A battered old Fiesta sat next to a sporty-looking Nissan coupé. The Nissan probably belonged to whoever was in charge; the Fiesta to whoever was cleaning the place today.

The truck stopped in the near corner, parking across the back of the building. Two men were climbing down from the cab, both fortyish; both in overalls. They saw her straight away.

'All right, darlin'?' the taller one called in a heavy Scottish accent. 'How'd you get in here?'

Hawkins wandered over. 'I followed you.'

'That's a relief. Thought you'd spent the night in one of them cars. Seen that happen here a few times, right, Gary?' He nudged his shorter colleague, who grinned. 'What're y'after?'

She produced her warrant card. 'Whoever let you in.'

'Oh.' He pulled a face. 'No serious, I hope.'

Hawkins shook her head. 'Nothing that'll put you guys out of a job.'

'Aye.' He seemed to relax. 'Well, the owner's nay here just now; only his bar manager, like.'

'He'll do.' She looked over at the building. 'Is there a bell I can ring?'

'Nah, but we're about to open the cellar there to unload. Inside door's probably no locked, so you can just wander through to the bar.'

'Perfect.' Hawkins waited in the sunshine while they opened the cellar and waved her through. She walked in, feeling the chilled air bite as she passed out of the daylight into an air-conditioned storage area. Stacks of multi-coloured plastic crates lined one grey brick wall, opposite rows of large metal casks. Hawkins headed straight for the exit at the back of the room, hearing the clank of barrels start up as she closed the door behind her.

A short corridor led through to the main room of the Boilerhouse, an open rectangular space with huge metal pipework running up the walls and across the ceiling, above a dance floor and DJ stage. Dark, seated booths lined the perimeter, interspersed with tall circular tables, and dull white lights that picked out antique-look brickwork in between. Dance music swirled quietly in the air.

But the place was deserted.

Hawkins moved out of the shadows, noting a bar to her right, with softly lit alcoves in the back wall housing optics and promotional displays. To her left, a closed door was marked 'staff only'.

She tried the handle. Finding it unlocked, she walked through into another corridor with three doors set in the left-hand wall. Hawkins had just started moving along the line when the far one opened, and a well-built guy in a close-fitting white shirt and dark trousers stepped out.

'All right there?' he said warily, moving towards her.

'Sorry to intrude,' she offered. 'I tried knocking, but nobody came. Your delivery guys let me in.'

The man nodded, still cautious, glancing back along the corridor. 'Yeah, saw you on the cameras. We're closed.'

He arrived in front of her, and she watched him scan her up and down, noting the subtle change in his demeanour from vigilance to charm. 'Not to worry, though. What can I do for you?'

'Jamie Lister?'

'Yeah.' The frown returned. 'Who are you?'

Before Hawkins could answer, the door he had come through opened again, and a slender blonde girl emerged, wearing a tight black dress and platform heels. A suspicious look ghosted across her face as she strode towards them, clearing as she asked them politely to let her pass.

'Staff meeting,' Lister said quickly when she'd gone, his cheeks flushing. 'Anyway. Where were we?'

'DCI Antonia Hawkins.' She held up her ID. 'Is there somewhere we can sit down?'

'Sure you don't want one?' Jamie Lister eased into the booth opposite Hawkins, holding what looked like three fingers of neat Scotch. 'Bar's always open for a pretty detective.'

'Bit early for me.' She kept her eyes off the large bottle of Jack Daniel's behind the bar, where the blonde girl was now stocking up the fridges, teetering back and forth from the store on her heels, bringing in half a crate at a time.

Faux leather groaned as Lister eased back in his seat, sipped his drink. 'What's this about, anyway?'

'A friend of yours. How well do you know Peter Barnes?'

'Barnsey? We're mates.'

'When did you last have contact?'

'Probably the last time he was in here.' The look of suspicion grew. 'Why?'

'Call it professional curiosity. When was that?'

'Can't say I remember.' Lister placed his drink on the table between them, suddenly defensive.

Hawkins nodded at one of the cameras dotted around the room. 'That's OK. I'm sure a check of your CCTV records will clear up any confusion.'

'Are we being accused of something here?'

'No, but now I'm curious as to why you'd think that.'

Lister chewed his lower lip, sniffed hard. 'Look, there's no illegal shit going on, all right? I run my club properly. No fighting; no drugs, I won't have it.'

'Would Peter?'

'Listen, darling, normally when ladies come in asking after Pete, it's because they're either smitten or about to be. I don't reckon you're either, so you'd better tell me what you think he's mixed up in before I say anything else.'

'Fair enough. Peter Barnes was murdered on Tuesday night.'

'Murdered?' Lister's face fell, but Hawkins had seen

70

the flicker of panic in his eyes. His gaze drifted out towards the middle distance and stayed there for a moment before coming back. 'You sure?'

'I'm afraid so. He was identified from the surgical steel plate in his left shoulder.'

'Fuck,' he whispered, his eyes closing for a few seconds. 'What happened?'

'We aren't sure yet; that's why we need your help. Did Pete have enemies?'

'No.'

'Had he fallen out with someone; become involved in something he regretted?'

A small shake of the head. 'Not that I heard about.'

'Was he in debt?'

'How the fuck should I know?' Lister's composure broke, and he shoved himself up off the seat.

Hawkins leaned across and grabbed his arm. 'We aren't done.'

Lister stopped and looked back at her, before slowly sitting down. He stared at the table top between them, breathing hard. 'Sorry. It's just a bit of a shock.'

'I understand. But maybe you didn't know him as well as you think.'

He eyed her. 'What?'

'You may discourage them here, Jamie, but Peter had large quantities of euphoric drugs in his system the night he was killed.'

'No fucking way!' Lister flared. 'He didn't *touch* that shit.'

'Look, I know you're upset, but the only way you can

71

help Pete now is by being honest with me. Surely you owe him that much.' She waited, watching the club manager wrestle with his conscience.

'It's probably nothing,' he said at last, taking the hint from her silence that she wanted to hear it regardless. 'Barnsey liked a bit of skirt, that's no secret, especially if it wasn't . . . available.'

Hawkins leaned forwards. *'Available?'*

'Single,' Lister explained. 'Too easy otherwise. Pete only went for girls with rocks.' He raised his ring finger. 'So they weren't in a position to get heavy.'

'Go on.'

'Normally it's just a one-time thing. He'll bang them in the bogs, send them home with a smile, and there's no hassle because they have more to lose than he does. But recently there was this girl, Lauren. Pete tried to play it cool, of course, but I could see he liked her. She's a regular, in here a few times a month. They were becoming a bit of an item.'

'Which didn't sit well with her husband.'

Lister rubbed the back of his neck. 'Word is he's a bit of a psycho; ex-boxer or something. She warned Pete; said the geezer would go ballistic if he found out, but Barnsey wasn't fussed; said he could handle himself.'

'Were Pete and Lauren here last time you saw them both?'

He nodded gently. 'They left together.'

'When was that?'

Lister looked up at her, his mouth twisting. 'Monday night.'

13

Hawkins locked the Giulietta and wandered round towards the driver's door of the Range Rover parked alongside, trying to keep her tall leather boots out of the large potholes full of mucky water.

She had just finished a brief phone conversation with Brian Sturridge's secretary, and was trying not to think about the appointment now booked for the morning. Instinct said discussing her trepidation with Mike would help, but common sense argued that highlighting such anxiety after months of telling him the sessions were a soon-to-be-forgotten formality might simply put him on wet-nurse alert, too. And she could do without lectures from both sides. She'd raise it later.

Maybe.

To her right, Eastern European accents shouted back and forth, drifting across from the fenced-off concrete area where several cars were being jet-washed. Cool mists arrived a few seconds after each burst of pressurised water, dusting Hawkins' skin as she reached the driver's door, where Mike was waiting.

'Hey.' He smiled. 'Got your voicemail. What's going on?'

'Peter Barnes' lover,' Hawkins explained, 'or the latest in a long line, at any rate, helps to run this cab firm.'

She pointed at the scruffy Portakabin on stilts at the rear of the parking area. 'Her name's Lauren, and she was a regular at the club managed by Barnes' best mate. They were both there on the night he was first attacked, and they left together, so she may be the last person to have seen him alive.'

'That's cool,' Mike agreed. 'But you know I trust you to talk to members of the public on your own these days. Why drag me all the way out here to Tottenham?' He pronounced *ham* like a separate word.

She gave him an admonishing look. 'There's a husband, a big tattooed one with a fuse you'd need forensics to find, who might not be thrilled that his beloved has been putting it about. He owns the business, so he might be here.'

'Got it.' Maguire nodded slowly. 'I'm here to protect that beautiful bone structure of yours.'

'No, you're here to protect Lauren, and to help me wrestle Rambo if he kicks off.'

'Whatever you say, boss. So theory's that he already knew she was hooking up with this other guy.' He shrugged. 'Gives him motive, I guess.'

'Exactly. So if he ends up being a suspect we might have to take him in, which is the other reason I brought you along. I hope you had Weetabix this morning.'

'Four.' Mike grinned. 'So if you're lucky, I might have energy left to protect your bone structure, too.'

They headed for the Portakabin, as Hawkins made a quick assessment of the place. The sign above the windows, a blue background with *Swiftcabs* written across it in large yellow letters, was strapped on with bungee cords, and the address it displayed didn't match this location. Jamie Lister had sent them straight here, however, which meant they'd been displaced for a while, suggesting the business was in trouble, probably having had to give up former premises. Another reason to watch the husband's temper, should he be about.

As they neared the entrance, a short middle-aged guy came out, trudged down the wooden steps and got into a dark Skoda saloon with the Swiftcab logo on the side. He started the engine and drove away, leaving the area in front of the cabin empty, which at least minimised the number of people they were likely to meet inside. Hawkins climbed the stairs and walked in ahead of Maguire.

The door opened straight into the seventies, a room around ten feet by six, with wood-effect walls and brown metal filing cabinets. An exhausted health and safety poster hung beside the entrance, and a large map of Greater London dominated the rear wall. Opposite, under the windows, a cheap laminate desk held a stack of radio equipment, a telephone, and a red anglepoise lamp that must have pre-dated all three of the room's occupants. From the uncomfortable-looking chair in front of it, a young woman looked up.

'Can I help you?'

'Lauren Coleman?' Hawkins approached the desk.

A frown cut the woman's brow as her gaze flicked to the window and back. 'Who are you?'

Hawkins introduced herself and Maguire, producing

ID and watching their host as she studied the warrant card. Her question had been almost rhetorical, because the woman fitted Lister's description perfectly: five seven, mid-twenties, blonde, with a small tattoo on her left forearm; certainly not the kind of girl normally found behind a desk in a dirty Portakabin. Unless an overbearing husband was trying to hide her away.

'Yeah, I'm Lauren Coleman,' the woman said, still cagey. 'So what are you, private investigators?'

'Met Police,' Hawkins told her, 'and for now we just need some help. We understand you know Peter Barnes.'

A small shake of the head, another glance towards the window. 'Who?'

'Come on, Lauren,' she pushed, 'we know you're a regular at the Boilerhouse, just like Peter. The manager there told us you're close.'

'Look, I . . . I never met anyone called Peter Barnes.' Coleman raised an arm, inviting them to leave. 'I'm working. You have to go.' As if on cue her radio bleeped, and a garbled message came through.

Hawkins gambled. 'OK, Mrs Coleman, let's make a deal. You feel free to keep lying to me, and I'll be gentle when I tell your husband about your affair with Mr Barnes. Does that work better for you?'

She felt Maguire bristle, but held the position, watching her opponent shrink.

Lauren sighed and looked out of the window, clearly about to concede, when something outside made her tense. She shot to her feet. 'Shit.'

Hawkins took a step forwards and followed her gaze. Out in the car park, a large black pickup had turned off the main road and was heading towards them.

'It's my husband.' Lauren ran a hand through her hair. 'He'll go ballistic.' She moved towards them, hands clasped as a car door slammed outside. 'Listen, I was sleeping with Pete, OK? I'll meet you later, tell you everything, just not here. Please . . . pretend you're after a cab. He'll kill me otherwise.'

Hawkins shook her head, about to explain it wasn't that simple, when the door beside them opened and Mr Coleman walked in, almost having to turn sideways to get his bulk through the narrow opening. He was older than his wife, perhaps late forties, with a shaved head and a honed physique for his age. But Hawkins was more interested in his hands, the knuckles pitted and scabbed.

Recent damage.

Coleman stopped just inside, head tilted, unable to move past the two visitors in the restricted space without acknowledging them. Hawkins looked at Lauren, whose pleading expression would have given her away, had her husband not been staring coldly at her and Maguire.

'What's going on?' Coleman asked in a heavy North London burr, addressing his wife without looking at her.

She stayed silent, clearly playing for time.

Coleman's eyes narrowed, moving slowly from Hawkins to Maguire and lingering for a moment before he turned to his wife. 'I said, what's going on?'

'What are you on about?' Lauren tried to make light of it, but her obvious unease told Coleman everything he needed to know.

He turned back to Hawkins. 'Smells like a fucking pigsty in here.'

'Calm down, Mr Coleman.' Hawkins kept her tone neutral and held up her warrant card. 'Your wife is helping us with an investigation, but she isn't implicated in any way at this stage.'

His expression darkened. 'What investigation?'

'The murder of a local man.'

A flicker of confusion entered Coleman's expression, but it was replaced immediately by renewed aggression. 'What the fuck's that got to do with her?'

'Your wife knew the deceased.'

Coleman breathed heavily at Hawkins for a few seconds, before turning slowly back to Lauren. 'You better start talking, woman.'

'I . . . I didn't know him,' she fumbled. 'I was just telling them.'

There was silence for a good fifteen seconds as Coleman stared her down. Hawkins watched the tears build in Lauren's eyes, a clear mixture of fear at her husband's rage, and shock at the news of her lover's death. Hawkins had intended to break it more gently, but she'd also wanted to gauge Lauren's reaction to being told. Except thinking time was over.

'You cheating slut!' Coleman shouted, barging past them towards his wife.

Hawkins tried to grab his arm, but he shoved her away. She stumbled backwards into the flimsy wall, watching Lauren cower as he bore down.

Before he could reach her Maguire lunged, interlocking an arm with Coleman's trailing elbow, grabbing his other bicep and yanking the shorter man back, trying to lock off the hold. Coleman reacted, his head snapping backwards, making heavy contact with Maguire's chin. Mike gave a stifled grunt and let go.

Coleman regained his balance and went for his wife again. She tried to run, knocking over her chair as he swung, glancing her jaw with a vicious hook that sent her sprawling into the desk, sending piles of radio equipment crashing to the floor.

He was lining up for another shot when Hawkins clattered into him from behind, surprised to find her weight having almost no impact. He spun, but this time she was wise to his tactics, expecting the elbow he tried to smash into her face. She swayed, evading the attack, sliding her hip under his and using momentum to throw her adversary. Coleman went down hard, landing head first on the stained carpet tiles. Hawkins followed, driving a knee into his spine, wrenching his arm back in a wrist lock. Coleman thrashed, trying to free himself, but Hawkins leaned on the joint, making him yelp.

'All right,' he yelled, relaxing at last. 'Ease off.'

But she didn't, shifting her weight forwards instead, letting her knee slide into the crease between his neck and the base of his skull. Bones ground as she felt the sinews in his arm approach breaking point; ligaments beginning to tear.

'Toni.'

Hawkins blinked as a hand touched her back, bringing the room into focus.

Then Maguire was beside her with blood on his teeth, easing her aside, pulling Coleman's wrists together behind his back, applying cuffs.

Hawkins wrenched herself away and stood, trembling, letting him fully take over.

It took a moment to find her voice.

'Mitchell Coleman.' She watched their captive being pulled to his feet. 'I'm arresting you for assault, against my officer and your wife.' She read him his rights as he stared spitefully at the wall, before Maguire marched him outside and off towards the cars.

Hawkins righted Lauren's chair and helped her on to the seat, noting the angry red mark on her jaw that would soon become a hefty bruise. It must have been singing, but she didn't seem to notice.

'Pete's . . . dead?' Lauren breathed, looking up at her.

Hawkins nodded.

The woman's gaze dropped away, breaths coming in short, traumatised shudders. ' . . . How?'

'Come with us to the station,' Hawkins said. 'I'll explain everything there.'

She waited while Lauren organised someone to take over and locked up, then helped her down the steps. They headed slowly for the Alfa, with Lauren still unsteady on her feet, and Hawkins trying not to count any chickens.

But she found herself suppressing a triumphant glow as she helped the young woman into the passenger seat of her car.

Because it looked very much at the moment as if they had their man.

14

'How long can these wankers keep me here?' Mitch Coleman demanded, before his brief's backside had even hit the chair.

'Once you've been charged, you should be free to go.' The solicitor responded calmly, obviously used to such treatment.

Both men turned to face Hawkins and Maguire with almost choreographed precision, clearly practised in addressing unwanted police attention. Although with a temper like Coleman's involved, that was no surprise.

The solicitor had introduced himself outside as Morris Paul. Hawkins didn't recognise him, which meant he was probably an expensive remnant of Coleman's semi-professional boxing days, now here to help out a mate, rather than for any major financial reward.

'My client fully admits giving your colleague a playful tap,' Paul continued, eyeing Maguire's split lip, 'and that he lost his temper, briefly, with his wife. But the marriage is in crisis, and Mr Coleman wishes to express regret. He's seeking help to address his personal issues, and will attend court, should it become necessary to resolve the matter. But for now he should be released.' Beside him Coleman smouldered, clearly not having voiced any such sentiments, but savvy enough to understand his predicament, and the resulting need to appear contrite.

Hawkins was about to answer when her mobile buzzed. She fished it out of her pocket, saw Yasir's number on the display and put it away. Amala could wait ten minutes.

She sat back from the table, making them wait, taking in the walls of the interview room at Tottenham station, a monotonous grey expanse broken only by the red panic strip. 'We'll get to charges, gentlemen, but first there's something else we need to discuss.'

Paul stood. 'If you aren't going to caution my client, he's under no obligation to stay.'

'Go if you want.' Hawkins watched Coleman stand, too. 'But we'll just arrest him again, as soon as he leaves the building. Surely it looks better on your client's record not to have been detained twice in one day.'

Everyone looked at the solicitor, who thought for a moment before asking, 'What other issue?'

Hawkins motioned for them to sit.

'Stitch-up time, is it?' Coleman sneered, as both retook their seats.

Hawkins held his gaze. 'Your solicitor says your marriage is under duress. Why is that?'

'That's none of your fucking business.'

'Did you know about your wife's affair?'

'No.' Coleman snorted. 'Not till you fuckers crawled out from under your shitty rock.'

'Charming.' Hawkins suppressed a smile, aware that the intensifying spite behind his insults meant Coleman hadn't enjoyed being put on his arse by a woman half his size. She crossed her arms. 'But you must have suspected something, at least, to catch on so fast.'

The carpet burn on their suspect's cheek twitched. 'Why would I?'

'Well, Lauren's a regular at the local night club. A wife half your age enjoying all those nights out? You must have questioned her motivation.'

Coleman looked away. 'Don't talk to me about that whore.'

'That's going to be tricky, I'm afraid,' Hawkins told him, 'because we're investigating the murder of a man with whom your wife was romantically involved. You say you weren't aware, but I don't believe that, which promotes you and your volcanic temper right to the top of our suspect list. So I thought you might care to contribute something at this point, to convince us you're not responsible for Peter Barnes' death.'

Coleman stared at her, sucking his teeth.

She pressed on. 'Keeping the attention of an attractive younger woman can't be easy, unless you inject a little drama here and there.' She paused, watching him stew. 'We saw how scared of you she is, so you could have stopped her going to that club if you really wanted to. But maybe you both like a bit of adrenalin, is that it? Show your commitment by forgiving her infidelity, and your virility by battering the guys she screws. Except maybe you went a bit further than battering this one.'

Paul leaned in, trying to break her eye contact with Coleman. 'You're harassing my client.'

'We're just establishing a few things.' She produced several photographs of Peter Barnes' blanched cadaver from the folder on the table and spread them out in front of him. 'This is what became of your wife's lover, Mr Coleman, but you already knew that, didn't you?'

No response.

Hawkins went on. 'We just spent an hour with Lauren. She's been telling us about Monday night, when she and Mr Barnes were at the Boilerhouse, the last time he was seen alive. They left together. Barnes put her in a cab outside the club, and then began walking towards his flat on Jarrow Road, twenty minutes away. Shortly after that he was violently assaulted, and twenty-four hours later he was dead, strangled and dumped in a shallow grave.' She watched Coleman's face as she spoke, but his expression didn't change.

She thought of his wife, currently sitting in another interview room along the hall, obviously a lot more upset by her lover's death than her husband's arrest. But the combined shock, on top of being attacked by her cuckolded partner, had reduced Lauren to a sobbing, monosyllabic wreck. It would be tricky to get anything useful out of her for a while yet.

'So where were you on Monday night?' she asked, half hoping he'd say at home, because Lauren had already told them the house was empty when she'd arrived.

Coleman considered his answer. 'The gym.'

'At that time of night, are you sure?'

'I know the owner. We had a drink after hours.'

'How long were you there, exactly?'

He thought about it. 'I was doing homework at the cab office till just before ten, got to him about quarter past, left around midnight.'

Perfectly covering the period in which Peter Barnes was attacked.

'And he'll back you up on that, will he?'

He shrugged. 'Course.'

'Which gym?'

'Kings, on the High Road. His name's Kenny, he wears size nine Adidas, and he's got a nice goatee beard with little grey hairs in it. You want directions?'

She ignored the gibe. 'And after your drink, you went straight home?'

'Yeah. I'd only had a couple so I drove. Was in bed by half twelve.'

'OK. I'm sure your wife will confirm that for us.'

He shook his head. 'Don't count on it. She was snoring like a squaddie when I got in, so she won't know.'

Hawkins made a mental note to check times with Lauren and changed tack, nodding at his damaged knuckles. 'What happened there?'

He glanced at his hands. 'Bag work. Should have wrapped up.'

Hawkins' mobile buzzed again, but she let it go to answerphone, keen to keep momentum while she had Coleman talking. 'We'll check all that with your wife and your friend at the gym, but let's assume for now that your alibi's a complete fabrication. I think it's much more likely that you knew Lauren was seeing Peter Barnes, so you went to the Boilerhouse that night to teach him a lesson. You saw him put your wife in the cab and walk away, so you followed and attacked him. But I'm still working on what happened in the twenty-four hours after that. I can't decide whether he escaped, and it took you that long to track him down again, or if you had him locked away somewhere, letting him think about his mistakes before you got rid of him for good. What made you decide to do it? Did he taunt you about sleeping with Lauren, or threaten to press charges about the assault?'

He shook his head. 'Bullshit.'

'Maybe.' She leaned forwards, placing her elbows on the table. 'But Lauren says you weren't at the house when she got back that night, and that she didn't see you again until the next day.'

Coleman's gaze drifted up towards the ceiling, and he took a deep breath before letting out a protracted sigh. 'I never touched him.'

Hawkins was about to retaliate when she heard Mike's mobile vibrate. He took it out and glanced at the screen before showing her Amala's name on the caller ID.

'Take it outside,' she instructed, turning to Coleman. 'It's one of our detectives. Maybe she found you a witness.'

They waited while Maguire extracted himself from the tight interview room and stepped out into the corridor.

'You stated before,' she said to Coleman when the door had closed, glancing at the recording equipment to reinforce the fact he was being taped, 'that you were unaware of your wife's infidelity. Is that correct?'

His eyes narrowed. 'That's right.'

'So why does your record show that you've been arrested on three previous occasions for assaulting her, and in each case you cited marital infidelity as reasonable provocation?'

He sniffed. 'They were different geezers.'

'Right.' Hawkins nodded slowly. 'Let's recap. You've got opportunity and motive, not to mention damage on your knuckles consistent with the attack suffered by Peter Barnes. You've attacked your wife in the past, for infidelity, and then you assault her and my officer without provocation. And you expect us to believe you had nothing to do with this man's murder?'

Coleman leaned forwards and stared straight at her, his tone full of stifled aggression. 'I told you. I . . . never . . . touched him.'

'Fine . . .' Hawkins was about to end the session, send Coleman to the cells while they investigated further, when she was interrupted by a knock at the door. She turned to see Maguire leaning in.

'Got a minute?' he asked, with a look that said: *you need to hear this.*

Hawkins paused the session and joined him in the corridor, carefully closing the door so that Coleman and Paul wouldn't hear. 'What is it?'

'Amala.' Mike held up his phone. 'She's back at the burial site.'

'Go on,' Hawkins said, hoping for a minor break-through that might help confirm or deny Coleman's involvement, maybe a local witness who saw the killer's vehicle, some DNA retrieved from the scene they could use.

'The search team called her.' Maguire hesitated.

'Spit it out, then,' she urged, starting to worry.

He sighed. 'Sorry, boss. They found another body.'

15

'Ma'am. Over here.'

Hawkins turned towards the remote voice, peering through the trees, and picked out Yasir's diminutive form, leaning out from a group of SOCOs away to their right.

She relaxed a bit. She was never fond of excursions into near pitch-black labyrinths, darkness having descended on their forty-minute drive from Tottenham to Havering. The autumn nights were closing in.

They'd already spent ten minutes fighting the undergrowth, after arriving at the same car park as the previous evening, and heading out into the small forest on foot to find the new burial site. But the freshly discovered scene was situated deeper inside White Post Wood than the original one, and had been trickier to find.

'Come on,' she told Maguire, veering off on to a less even path, using her torch to light their way.

'We're supposed to be damn city cops,' Mike grumbled from behind, crunching through bracken with uncharacteristic inelegance.

Hawkins sped up. She'd been teased too many times about her choice to carry wellingtons permanently in the boot of her car not to enjoy this. *Don't forget your knee-highs*, he'd say, *rubber-lover command might call a snap demonstration outside Downing Street this afternoon.*

She allowed herself a smile at hearing him stumble and crash along in her wake. The going was hard enough in her wellies, never mind the gripless brogues Mike hadn't had time to go home and change.

'Chop, chop,' she teased without looking back. 'Lateness displeases rubber-lover command.'

As they walked, Hawkins tried to piece together recent events. Yasir's phone call to Mike at Tottenham station had revealed that her and Sharpe's day of doorknocking had produced nothing of interest. Of the twenty or so locals they'd canvassed, none reported seeing anything beyond the regular trickle of vehicles carrying walkers and associated mutts to and from the woods. Depressing news, but Amala had followed up in typical arse-about-face style with a bombshell that changed the trajectory of the whole sodding case.

Another body, buried within two hundred yards of the first, was too much of a coincidence to be anything but the work of whoever had killed Peter Barnes. And whether Mitch Coleman was to blame or not, a second death also meant premeditation on the killer's part, on one if not both occasions, turning what had initially looked like frenzied retribution into something far more sinister.

Could multiple murders indicate some kind of campaign?

They stopped at the edge of the small clearing, no more than a bald patch in the forest, fifteen feet across at its widest. A jagged pool of cobalt sky hung above them in the empty space. Nearer the ground, frame-mounted spotlights cast shadows out on to the surrounding trees, magnified black fingers that stretched and jerked against the wider canopy whenever the wind reared. A dozen white overalls were clustered here and there, reducing the spectrum of associated parties to a family of uniform drones, distinguished only by height, bulk, and patches of face distorted by anti-contamination masks.

Yasir finished her conversation and wandered across to join them, sturdy walking boots poking out from the tops of her overshoes.

'Sorry to disturb your evening, ma'am.' She handed over two Tyvek romper suits and associated paraphernalia.

'We weren't exactly asleep in front of the TV.' Hawkins fought with the wrapper, looking at the far side of the clearing, where another gang of SOCOs with dirty knees huddled above the new crater. 'What happened?'

Amala turned towards the scene. 'One of the search teams was out here earlier tonight, looking for evidence from the Peter Barnes chase. They were about to call it a night when they found a partial boot-print in the soft ground over there. They were taking photos when one of them noticed the soil nearby had recently been dug over and packed down.'

Hawkins nodded, watching Maguire's brogues slowly sinking under him. 'When was that?'

Amala rolled back her sleeve, checked the time. 'Two

hours ago, just before it got dark. Sevenish? They spent some time taking samples before digging down, but I rang you as soon as it was confirmed. They found the feet first, but they've just uncovered the head.'

'Do we have a name?'

'No.' Yasir began wringing her hands; another habit that Hawkins was still trying to knock out of her. 'This corpse appears to be naked, like the last one. They're still digging, but no personal effects so far.'

She hid her frustration. 'OK. What *do* we have?'

Amala wrung harder. 'The victim's male, Caucasian, mid- to late-twenties, with long hair and a beard. It's too early to say for sure if he's been physically assaulted, but strangulation looks like cause of death again. Tanya says he was buried around a week ago.'

'Right.' Hawkins zipped up her overall and began filling Yasir in about their arrest of Mitch Coleman earlier in the day, and why he was now a murder suspect. Add the fact that their newly discovered victim fitted the same profile as Peter Barnes, and it was starting to look like the couple's marriage had been tested before.

She looked at Mike. 'Call Hendon and get someone to look at missing persons reports in the North London area. Focus on eighteen- to thirty-year-old men who disappeared in the last few months. Mitch Coleman walks in eighteen hours unless we can tie him to either of these deaths, and I'd rather not have to chase him around the Mediterranean for another chat.'

'Got it.' Mike found his phone and moved aside, scrolling through his phonebook.

Hawkins turned back to Yasir. 'Go home and get some rest. I need you back here at first light to organise things when the search starts again.' She finished fitting her overshoes and straightened. 'Because we aren't just searching for traces any more. Now we're looking for graves.'

16

'Wait.' Hawkins stopped in the darkness, halfway up the garden path.

Mike, ahead of her, turned. 'What?'

'Is it too late to get a hotel room for the night?'

'Probably. Why?'

'I don't know if I can face another morning like today.'

'Oh.' He came closer. 'Look, I know the kids are full on, but it's late; they'll be asleep, right? What say we go inside, hit the sack, and tomorrow I'll run interference; keep the little guys out from under your feet?'

Hawkins sighed. 'It isn't the kids; it's *her*. We drive each other up the wall. Always have.'

She stared past his shoulder at the house: usually an oasis of calm and tranquillity, no matter how disordered her day. But that oasis had been occupied, stripping her of the retreat whose importance she hadn't appreciated till now.

To make matters worse, a glow from behind the lounge curtains suggested Siobhan was still up, probably halfway through a bottle of Hawkins' best red, watching some vacuous satellite rubbish about people who have surgery in order to look like their pets.

'Look,' Mike said, 'I know things are tough for you right now, but—'

She cut in, '*Tough* for me,' eyeing the half of his face not hidden in shadow. 'Do you think I'm being unreasonable?'

'Now hold on. That's not what I meant.'

'So what *did* you mean?'

He fished. 'Just, you've dealt with a lotta shit this last year. Two massive cases, stepping up at work, the attack, now counselling . . .'

'Oh I see. It's *understandable* that I've been such a bitch.'

He shook his head. '*What?* Look, Toni, I'm not trying to pick a fight here. I'm on your side. Please tell me you get that.'

'I . . .' Hawkins felt her fury stall. She sagged, bringing a hand to her forehead. 'Maybe I am a bit stressy and reactive. Sorry.'

'Hey,' Mike enveloped her, 'you're amazing. There ain't many who could deal with it all like you do.'

'*Am* I dealing with it? Sometimes I wonder. Sleeping in a bloody madhouse doesn't help.'

'Come on. She's your sister, and she needs you right now. What's more important than that?'

Hawkins thought for a second before groaning. 'OK, maybe you've got a minor point. And I don't mind you being right sometimes, but let's not go mad.'

He laughed. 'Atta girl. Let's get inside. You head straight on up, I'll go fetch the rum.' He dropped his voice. 'If we're quiet, I guarantee I can take your mind off your sister.'

'Oh really?' Hawkins relaxed into him, feeling his

warmth. 'That sounds like a distraction worth investigating.'

They wandered up to the house entwined, pausing to kiss on the step. Then she unlocked the door and opened it.

On to bedlam.

The racket hit them as soon as the door seal broke; a brash cartoon voice singing to loud reggae music, and somewhere in the background, Rosie laughing.

'What the . . . ?' Hawkins stepped into the hall, as Admiral Kirk came flying out of the front room, almost colliding with the far wall as he fought to turn his impressive bulk at speed. Behind him came Kyle, also at full pelt.

'Oi!' Hawkins stepped between them as the cat turned the corner and shot upstairs. 'What's going on?'

Kyle stopped and stared up at her, apparently no longer interested in the cat, yet his pudgy expression conveyed neither apology nor embarrassment; more simple distaste. They held each other's gaze for a moment before Kyle turned and drifted back into the noisy front room.

Hawkins looked at Mike, who had stepped in behind her. 'Did you *see* that?'

'Unbelievable.' He shook his head, looking up at the cat, now glaring at them from the top of the stairs. 'I'd have bet anything that fat moggy couldn't run.'

'Funny.' She turned and strode into the lounge, rounding the corner to see Kyle slumped on the carpet, inches from the blaring television. And beyond him,

Rosie, bouncing up and down hard on the settee, the angle of its cushions already suggesting irreparable damage beneath.

'Down!' Hawkins shouted, chalking up a minor victory as her niece froze. 'Now!'

Rosie slid to the floor, head bowed. Hawkins snatched the remote control from her, muting the TV. 'Where's your mother?'

'Antonia!'

Hawkins spun at the husky tone from her kitchen doorway. *'Aunt Susanna?'*

'Hello, darling.' Sue swept in for a hug, brandishing a perilously full glass of wine. 'We were just getting a drink; didn't hear you come in. How the devil are you?'

'We?' Hawkins queried as they embraced, watching Aunt Lucia follow her sister out of the kitchen, also toting red. 'Where's Siobhan?'

'It's date night, isn't it?' Lucia explained as both women greeted Maguire, having to negotiate the kids, who had surrounded him the moment her attention was drawn.

Hawkins' head already hurt. 'But . . . she only left Malcolm five minutes ago. Who with?'

Susanna sneaked over, making sure the kids were still preoccupied with Mike. 'Some bloke her friend Sophie set her up with.'

Lucia followed. 'She's just testing the waters. We thought you knew?'

'Why would I?' Hawkins shrugged theatrically. 'I just run the bloody hostel.'

Sue looked at her sister. 'That explains why we got no effing notice for tonight; I told you Antonia would've booked us months ago. Still, no harm done. Grab our coats, Luce.'

'Hold on.' Hawkins blocked the doorway. 'Where do you think you're going?

'Up town, obviously.' Sue spread her arms, displaying the glad rags Hawkins hadn't noticed. 'I didn't spend all afternoon waxing my pits to sit around here with you lot.'

Hawkins shook her head in disbelief, gesticulating at Rosie and Kyle. 'What about these two?'

Sue pulled a face. 'I imagine it's well past their bedtime.'

'I know that,' she snarled. 'I meant who's going to *put* them there?'

Her aunts exchanged another glance before Lucia replied. 'Siobhan told us you'd take care of all that. Didn't she . . .'

'Discuss it with me first?' Hawkins fumed. 'Of course not. For crying out loud, I might have said no.'

Susanna's frown lifted slightly. 'Do you want us to stay?'

'No, we'll be fine.' She stomped to the bannister, snatching their coats.

'Are you sure?' Lucia took the jacket being thrust at her.

'Absolutely,' Hawkins told her. 'I wouldn't want either of you implicated in Siobhan's ghastly murder.'

She rushed everyone through ritual goodbyes,

tutting at her aunts' excessive cooing over the kids, finally closing the door and turning to see the two youngsters jostling for space behind Mike.

'Right.' She pointed. 'Upstairs now, both of you. Pyjamas on. We'll be up in a minute to do teeth.'

She stood, sentry-like in the hallway, as the kids silently gathered favourite toys from the living room floor and drifted upstairs. She watched the bedroom door close before turning her glare on Mike.

He flinched. 'Wowsers. You ever lose your passion for childcare, Sandhurst's always on the lookout for good drill sergeants.'

'I'm glad you find this amusing,' Hawkins shoved past him, heading for the kitchen to see if Sue and Lucia had left her any wine, 'because you're doing bed-time stories.'

'Happy to.' Mike followed her. 'How hard can it be?'

17

The wailing began in the small hours.

It started low; a barely audible moan creeping in through the walls, dismissible at first as the wind playing tricks. But it rose, slowly gaining volume and pitch, until it became the unmistakeable cry of a child.

Hawkins reached out, flipped the alarm clock on to its face and wrapped her head in the pillow, cursing her naivety. For some insane reason she had expected respite, given the full ninety minutes of tantrums and arguments she and Mike had negotiated just to get both kids tucked up and going to sleep. The fact they were sharing a room – Kyle in the double bed next to where his mum should have been; Rosie on the blow-up mattress on the floor – hadn't helped. Her one consolation had been the thought they might be sufficiently exhausted from it all to sleep through till morning.

Fat chance.

OK, so the residual stress of coercing the intractable duo into bed had already demolished any chance of meaningful sleep, but at least the mid-night peace and quiet had allowed her to think about the case.

She uncovered an ear, to check if the noise had stopped.

And there it was. Louder again.

She moaned and rolled on to her back, jogging Maguire with a shoulder. He mumbled something and turned over, but his breathing settled again. Hence her elbow to the ribs.

'Huh?' He lurched, inhaling hard. Then, groggily, 'What's going on?'

'One of the kids is crying.'

'Oh.' A few seconds of silence. 'Where's your sister?'

'Exactly.' Hawkins rubbed her forehead. 'Did you hear her come in?'

'No.' He yawned. 'What time is it?'

'After three.' They groaned in tandem as a second wail joined the first. 'What if she still isn't back?'

'You think she'd do that?'

Hawkins snorted. 'They're still crying, aren't they? Even if she *is* here, she's clearly too sozzled to care.'

Mike exhaled protractedly. 'Want me to go?'

'Would you? I've hardly slept.'

'Sure,' he mumbled. 'Just gimme a minute . . .'

Hawkins rolled back, trying to ignore her bladder's growing insistence that she needed the loo. She decided to wait till Mike got up. The flush would give her away, of course, but by then Maguire would already have engaged the enemy, allowing her to sneak back to bed and leave him to it.

The kids liked him better anyway.

She lay still, waiting for him to get up, trying to relax, cursing when the twin cries grew louder again . . .

Just as Mike started to snore.

18

The muffled voice reached them from the far side of the heavily panelled door. 'Come.'

Hawkins held her breath and followed the secretary inside, wondering why someone with quite so deliberate an air of informality should encourage such eighteenth-century practices as having his clients escorted in.

'Miss Hawkins,' the older woman announced, waiting for her employer's nod before she wheeled and departed, re-securing the door on her way out.

'Antonia.' The counsellor looked up from his documents. 'Please take a seat.' He motioned generally at the room. She chose an upright chair in front of his desk, reading his expression somewhere between smugness and curiosity.

Sturridge waited for her to settle. 'So what brings you here, Detective? Between appointments.'

Hawkins sucked at her teeth, summoning the reluctantly composed phrase. 'I, uh, don't feel that we've been making progress.'

His head tilted. 'What do you mean by *progress*?' He was enjoying this.

But she had to dance.

She cleared her throat. 'Until now I may have ... subconsciously been reluctant to talk about the attack.'

'Hmm.' Sturridge sat back in his chair, blinked. 'So what do you see as the solution?'

Hawkins glanced at the ceiling, inhaled before looking back, let the breath out. 'We should discuss what happened. Its . . . effects.'

He thought for a moment. 'OK. Where do you think we should start?'

'Probably with . . . him.'

'Your attacker.'

'Yes.' She paused. 'I assume you've read the file, that I don't need to explain how we came to know each other.'

A nod. 'My focus is on how it affects you today, if at all. How does thinking about him now make you feel?'

Hawkins sighed internally. At least she wouldn't be forced to lie about their history. As far as everyone but Mike knew, she was attacked because she'd been leading the investigation.

Nothing more.

Sturridge remained silent, but Hawkins realised she hadn't spoken for a while. The question still hung.

'I rarely think about him,' she said truthfully. 'He's gone . . . If anything I pity him now.'

'So do you have *any* lasting psychological trauma?'

Their eyes met, as Hawkins flirted with the idea of saying no. It was tempting: the crack of an opportunity to get her *counselled* badge, take a lolly and get out; put this torture behind her. But Sturridge wasn't stupid.

It wouldn't wash.

She let the silence stretch, dignifying the fragment she was about to offer.

'I have nightmares.'

Not even a flicker. 'Go on.'

'Not often. Maybe . . . once a month. But always the same.'

'What about?'

Hawkins felt herself shudder. 'About the knife. How it felt going in, over and over. Not being able to move. The helplessness.'

'I see. Do you talk to anyone about these dreams?'

She shook her head.

'Why not?'

'Because discussing them gives them significance.' She paused. 'Because I was hoping they'd stop.'

Sturridge seemed to think for a moment before he asked, 'How does it affect you during the day?'

'At work?'

'Yes.'

Heat crept up Hawkins' neck. 'I don't let it.'

'I see.' Sturridge looked down, made a note. 'What is it that you suppress?'

Mentally Hawkins kicked herself. She hadn't intended to acknowledge any impact on her career.

'If anything I'm less trusting.' She rallied. 'Although that could be down to eleven years of dealing with criminals and murderers.' She smiled, shielding the truth: that anxiety haunted her.

The fear that an inability to trust had become entrenched.

Every so often, meeting someone new would trigger memories: a reminder that the more you trusted others, the more vulnerable you were.

But Sturridge's calm grey stare didn't waver. 'Does this lack of faith ever lead to frustration?'

She swallowed, aware that she was now too far down the road to turn back. 'Perhaps.'

'And does that frustration ever lead to anger?'

'Sometimes. A little. Maybe.'

'How about aggression?'

And there it was, the word Hawkins had been willing him not to use. She frowned, portraying someone genuinely confused by the notion, as a single moment played itself out in her head. The moment she had driven her knee into Mitch Coleman's back.

Far harder than the technique demanded.

'Antonia?' Sturridge asked as her silence stretched. 'Have you ever felt the urge to lash out?'

'Absolutely not.'

Another awkward pause.

'You seem very sure.'

'I've been doing this work a long time.' She felt panic rise, heard the conversation between the counsellor and Vaughn. *She's unstable . . . a risk.*

Not in control.

That familiar alarm repeating itself.

If you open up, they'll remove you from duty.

The reason she was here: all they really wanted to know.

Could they trust her not to do something stupid?

The room went hot.

Her attacker's face flashed through her mind. She resisted turning in her seat. To make sure he wasn't there.

Then she was standing.

Sturridge looked up. 'Are you OK?'

Hawkins heard the words leave her mouth, the opportunity for self-control gone. 'I know what's going on here.'

The counsellor shook his head.

'I'm being lined up,' she stormed. 'Coaxed into indicting myself. That's how these things work, isn't it?'

'Miss Hawkins,' Sturridge began, 'please—'

'No.' She cut him off, already opening his office door. 'I won't sit here and talk my way into redundancy. If you want me out, you'll have to do it without my help.'

She began pulling the door closed behind her, turning to add, 'Session over,' just as it slammed.

19

The light ebbed into existence.

It was just a crack at first, growing a little more each time, before collapsing on itself. Raymond let himself doze a moment and tried again, at last managing to edge the darkness upwards and away.

The ceiling swam above him, its blurred greyness twisting. He blinked hard, stretching his jaw, willing the haze of sleep to clear.

He lay still, panting, waiting for things to stop spinning, trying to think. But his thoughts were clouded by the slow whump of a headache; the muted but powerful kind that told you your hangover, when it arrived, would be horrific.

Ray groaned and turned his head towards the brightness, his left hand drifting automatically out towards his glasses. But his arm fell through space where the bedside cabinet should have been, its unsupported weight pulling him on to his side.

What the . . . ?

He blinked hard, trying to pull the world into focus, feeling the scorch of a sore throat as he coughed.

He tried to concentrate, force more information from his surroundings. But they refused, fighting his attempts to pick out details in the mixed-up blur of a room. *Was he in hospital?* No. The colours bleeding into one another around him were rustic yellows and browns, not stark clinical tones, and there was a mustiness in the air, a mixture of dampness and dust. *So where the hell was he?*

A flash of memory. The woods, leaves crunching under his boots, light filtering through the trees.

Then it became a cascade. The empty forest, his attempt to cross the riverbed, his fall. The man in the car. How he needed to get home for Maura.

Jesus: Maura.

Suddenly he was fighting his way off the bed, hazy shapes whirling around him, as he attempted to straighten fragile, watery legs. The headache was really kicking in now. He slumped, breathing hard, hands clamped either side of his head.

What the fuck was going on?

Wherever he was, it wasn't hospital, and it wasn't home. He had no recollection of arriving here, and for however long he'd been here, his wife had been alone.

He reached for his mobile. But when his hand found only the fabric of his jumper, Ray realised the fuzzy shape hanging on the back of the blurred chair a few feet away must be his coat. He stumbled forwards and dug breathlessly in various pockets. He found his glasses and paused to fumble them on to his face, blinking as the room shot into focus, marred only by the spidery crack in the right lens. But he ignored his surroundings and returned to checking his coat, going back to feel each pocket several times to make sure, although it soon became clear.

The phone wasn't there.

Ray scanned the room for it, able to see detail for the first time. He knelt and checked the floor, lifting the bedspread, pulling the chair aside to make sure it hadn't fallen out of his coat.

Nothing.

His headache throbbed as he stood, taking in more of the room. He was in what looked like a traditional farmhouse, with thick wooden floorboards, bare brick walls on two sides; rustic plaster opposite. The ceiling was low and the window small, making the room dingy and dark, despite what seemed like a bright day outside. Above his head, the eaves creaked in time with the wind.

It wasn't a big space, either, no more than eight feet by ten, but the bed and chair were the only large pieces of furniture, so it didn't feel cramped. It looked like a normal home.

The guy in the car; this must have something to do with him. Was there a memory swimming in the back of his head about them having turned the wrong way? He couldn't think.

Ray hobbled towards the door, determined to find the owner, explain that he needed to get home for Maura. But as he gripped the ball-shaped handle and twisted, the door refused to move. He twisted it the other way and tried again, but the thing wouldn't budge.

Panic flared as he glanced round at the window, and

again as he noticed the tight metal bars running across it, outside the streaked and mucky glass. Then his gaze settled on the small wooden chest in the corner.

It couldn't be . . . could it?

Ray stepped forwards to inspect the dark wooden box, finding a lid and lifting it, confirming his worst fears.

A commode.

He spun, limping back to the door and grabbing the handle again, wrenching it left and right. He braced his shoulder against the wood, tried to jerk it in its frame, in case it was just a tight fit. But after a moment's exertion he let go, finally accepting the truth.

It was locked.

'Hey!' He banged the heel of his hand against the wood. 'Open this door!' He stepped back, breathing hard, listening for signs of movement.

None came.

Then he saw a small hole in its surface, just above his eyeline. It was roughly rectangular with jagged edges, as if chiselled through the surface in a rush. Ray stood on tiptoes and pressed his face to the door, peering through the small letterbox into the next room.

He couldn't see much through the gap, but it was obviously a kitchen, blackened pans hanging against the wall in the far corner, next to a rustic display cabinet crammed with various patterned bowls and plates. Three other sturdy-looking doors were set in the walls. Sunlight streamed through a large, latticed window above the sink.

But the room was deserted.

'Please!' Ray shouted. 'Let me out of here. My wife's unwell. She needs me.'

He stayed on his toes for as long as his bad ankle allowed, praying for someone to enter the room; come rushing to the door, apologising for their mistake. But no one did.

Ray dropped on to his heels as his senses went light, exhaustion overwhelming him. He limped back to the bed and sat, resting his face in his hands, blocking out the light, trying to calm his pounding head.

How had things gone so wrong? He'd left home in complete control, able to protect his wife, convinced he'd be back before she woke. But somehow, through a series of calamities, he'd wound up with cracked glasses and no phone, locked inside a house he'd never seen. He had no idea where he was or how he was going to get home. And every minute that passed made it more likely that Maura would hurt herself.

But everything in him froze as somebody spoke in a delicate, muted voice away to his right.

'Hello, Raymond.'

20

'Sorry.' Lauren Coleman placed the photograph on the stone and glass coffee table in front of her and looked up, blinking rapidly, the way people often did when they were about to lie. Her tone was heavy and distant. 'I don't know him.'

'Are you sure?' Hawkins asked.

Lauren pushed the picture away with trembling fingers. 'I don't think so. It's hard to say with all the . . .' She waved at her chin, simulating the matted beard that obscured the dead man's lower face.

'Please.' Hawkins pushed it back, making a mental note to ask the coroner to remove the beard and take further photographs once autopsy was complete. 'This is important.'

Lauren chewed her bottom lip, eyes pleading briefly with Hawkins to let this unsolicited interrogation end, before she picked up the picture and looked at it again. She was clearly traumatised, still bearing the red eyes and vacant stare of shock, though it was hard to say if that was down to news of her lover's murder, her husband's temporary incarceration, or just because she didn't enjoy being shown pictures of the dead.

But as she observed the woman's breathing quicken as she stared at the newly discovered victim's face,

Hawkins would have sworn that Lauren Coleman was hiding something.

She maintained her silence, letting any feelings of guilt that might be affecting Lauren play out. She'd cracked easily the last time they'd pressed her for information, back at the cab office, so the longer she held out now, the less likely it was that Lauren had been physically involved with this other man. But then Mitch Coleman didn't need much of an excuse to start swinging, especially for perceived competition. Perhaps this time he got the wrong guy.

Yet there was no question about the same killer being responsible for both murders. Just like Peter Barnes', the new corpse had been stripped of clothing and personal effects, and buried a short distance away, mere days in advance. The victim had also been starved prior to death, bore similar scratches and injuries, and even had Benzodiazepines in his system. The final point increased the chances that the drugs, rather than being taken recreationally by the victims, were administered by the killer, perhaps to subdue his prisoners during captivity, or in advance of the chase.

But the latest post-mortem had thrown up differences, too.

The new victim hadn't been assaulted until right before death. His wounds had been fresh when he died, indicating that, unlike Barnes, he hadn't been taken by force. He did, however, have bruising to his knuckles and arms, indicating that he had tried to defend himself.

But none of that helped them with an ID.

If they couldn't identify the dead man from DNA, medical records, or someone already involved who recognised his face, Hawkins would have to decide how much information to release to the media, in order to balance potential leads with the downside of probably alerting the killer. Although the possibility of a breakthrough here remained.

Lauren was still staring at the photo, so Hawkins assessed the Colemans' compact and congested front room.

Light streamed in through the French windows facing the garden. The modest seventies two-bed terrace confirmed Hawkins' suspicions about their business having underperformed. The room would have struggled to accommodate any more than just the two of them, thanks to being crammed with oversized furniture obviously purchased for a larger property, including the ornate wooden clock on the mantelpiece, which said they had just over four hours to charge Mitch Coleman with assault or murder. Otherwise he was back on the street.

Hawkins had made the short journey from Hendon to Haringey alone, hoping that Lauren would feel more comfortable at home. And that if the circle of infidelity and lethal retribution *were* some kind of sick ritual between the couple, perhaps she could be lulled by another lone female into letting something slip.

So far, zero.

In the meantime, Hawkins had spread her team across the capital. Mike had returned to Tottenham station, poised to confront their suspect, should anything of interest be gleaned here. Mitch Coleman would currently be looking at the same picture his wife was being shown, although Hawkins fully expected him to deny recognising the dead man. Such a statement could prove crucial later on, of course, assuming they could prove it a lie. It all came down to leverage; cranking up the pressure in small increments till something gave.

Amala was back at White Post Wood, helping to organise the burgeoning collection of search teams. A second body had compelled Chief Superintendent Vaughn to escalate the matter, greasing the wheels further up to release additional resources. With the greater numbers now on site, they were on track to have the small forest searched by nightfall, so they would at least be able to say for definite if there were any further graves. Of course forensics' operation would expand accordingly, although nobody was keen to specify boundaries at this stage. Unfortunately, there were still no rules to govern where murdering psychopaths could bury their victims, and White Post Wood was one small thicket among dozens inside the M25 alone.

Their greatest chance of success remained in identifying the new victim and linking him somehow to the Colemans or Peter Barnes. Aaron Sharpe was already leading efforts to establish who cadaver number two had been, and how he might have ended up two feet below the Havering soil. At the moment Aaron was working his way round Barnes' family and friends, finding out if any of them recognised the second man.

It was such a simple thing, but without a name, lives couldn't be cross-referenced; potentially common locations or interests explored; corresponding enemies assessed.

Or ex-lovers questioned.

Hawkins' attention returned to Lauren Coleman, who was now staring out at the garden, where a low wall separated a raised rear section from the small patio, apparently unaware that she still had company.

'What aren't you telling me, Lauren?'

Hawkins' question surprised them both. She hadn't planned to confront the issue so bluntly so soon.

Lauren turned, looking even more nervous. 'What do you mean?'

'Look, I'm not saying you had an affair with this man, but you may still be the common factor here. Could Peter or your husband have known him? I understand it might feel like you're making things worse for Mitch, but two people are dead, and if he's involved, we'll find out eventually. If you know who he is, Lauren, you need to tell me.'

'I already said I don't know him.'

'Fine.' Hawkins tried to think through the fug of exhaustion. It had taken her forty minutes to settle both kids during the night, just having returned to slump beside Mike when Siobhan had rolled in, tripping over furniture, waking them all again. She'd been face down in bed when Hawkins returned for round two.

Everyone else had been fast asleep when she and

Maguire left a few hours later. Siobhan wouldn't enjoy looking after two tired children with a hangover, but Hawkins' only regret about that was that she couldn't be there to watch.

She focused on Lauren. 'What about East London? Did their jobs ever take Peter or Mitch out that way?'

'Where exactly?'

'The Havering area. A place called White Post Wood.'

Lauren's frown deepened. 'Maybe. Pete worked all over London, and I suppose Mitch could have taken fares out that way.'

'But neither of them had any regular reason to be over there.'

'No, why?'

'It's just part of the investigation.' Hawkins reined in her frustration. 'Let's go back to the last time you saw Pete. You caught a cab home. What time did you get back?'

'I don't know. Just before twelve, I think.'

'Was Mitch here?'

Lauren paused; shook her head.

'OK. When did he come in?'

'I don't know. I'd had a few too many at the club, so I fell asleep straight away. When I woke up the next morning, he was in bed beside me.'

Hawkins saw her eyes waver. 'Come on, Lauren, there's more to this story, isn't there?'

She waited, watching the younger woman's gaze drop towards the coffee table, coming to rest on the dead man's face. Lauren was clearly holding back, obviously afraid of making things worse. Whether that fear was *for* her husband or *of* him it was impossible to say, but as she drew breath and looked up at Hawkins, it seemed as though the truth was about to be told.

Just as Hawkins' mobile rang.

She sighed, watching Lauren's defences rise again. She thought about leaving the call to answer machine, but the moment had already gone.

'I'd better take this.' She stood and moved out into the hallway, seeing Amala's number on the display as she answered.

'What do you have?'

There was a pause, which meant the news wasn't good.

'They've found a third body, ma'am, and I'm afraid it doesn't fit with your theory about Mitch Coleman knocking off his wife's lovers.'

Hawkins glanced back into the lounge, where Lauren was now standing near the window, arms crossed, staring at the horizon. 'Why not?'

Another hesitation. 'Because this one's a teenage girl.'

21

Ash stood up, dropping his cigarette and stamping it out. 'I'm going inside.'

'No.' Rupert grabbed his jumper; pulled him back down into the long grass behind the dead log. 'I don't want to.'

For a second Ash seemed angry, the way he did sometimes when Rupert tried to stop him pulling the legs off insects, but then a grin spread across his face. 'Come on, pal, it'll be a laugh.'

Rupert hesitated. 'But there are . . . ghosts.'

'Don't be soft.'

'Mummy says people died in there.'

Ash shook his head. 'She only says that to stop you coming here. You'll believe any old crap if she lays it on thick enough. Anyway, so what if they did? People die all the time; it doesn't mean the place is haunted.'

Rupert looked up at the house towering over them, at its peeling grey paint and saggy roof, at the yawning black holes where windows used to be, the raggedly painted sign that said DAN-GER, KEEP OUT. The building looked like it was in pain, its gutters angled downwards like an evil glare; its front door hanging open in a silent scream.

As if it was possessed.

The clearing was surrounded by tall trees and bushes, greenery stretching from the grass right up to the pale blue sky. But all the trees near the house were dead, with flaking bark and no leaves;

the ground lifeless and grey. Dead vines snaked their way up the outer walls.

Ash was staring at him. 'It'll be fine. Let's go.'

'I don't want to.'

Ash frowned. 'Well I don't care what you want. I'm going in.' He stood again and stomped off towards the abandoned house.

Rupert watched him go, not knowing what to do. He'd never stop his friend now. Ash was six months older than him, already thirteen, and not afraid of a thing. The teachers at school said Ash was wasting his intelligence; Mummy said he was smart but wayward. Except that wasn't the problem.

The problem was that Rupert didn't want to stay out here alone.

It was a bright summer morning; he'd been sweating on the walk over, but suddenly he was cold. The sky had clouded over and the blackened trees seemed to move, jagged branches reaching over him like claws.

He shivered and glanced round at the fields they'd crossed to get here, wondering if he should leave. But what if something happened to Ash?

How would he explain that?

He turned back, guts twisting when he saw that Ash had reached the house. His friend stopped at the entrance and looked around at him. Rupert couldn't make out his expression, but something dragged him to his feet.

They stayed like that for a few seconds before Ash disappeared inside. But Rupert was already moving, hurriedly crossing the crunchy grass towards the house, his heart beating harder the closer he got.

He wished now that he'd gone to school. Ash said his parents had arranged for them to have the day off again, and Rupert had been glad at first. He hated school, with its boards full of confusing numbers and words, its crowded corridors and its noisy breaks, when the other kids played in large groups, full of sayings and jokes he didn't understand.

But Ash was different. He didn't need jokes or noise. Ash had time for Rupert when everyone else ignored him; listened when no one else would. They were best friends; only friends. Friends no matter what.

He sped up as he passed halfway, wanting to call out for Ash to hold on; afraid that one of the trees might grab him if he did.

Rupert reached the house, pausing at the entrance. The hallway was impossibly dark. He swallowed hard, glancing towards home one final time. But the sky seemed even darker now, and a sharp breeze swept across the fields, urging him on.

He turned back, placed one foot on the step.

'Ash?' he called in a loud whisper, his voice echoing off the dirty walls.

No reply.

He took a deep breath, tried to stop himself shaking.

And went inside.

22

Hello, Raymond.

Ray turned slowly towards the voice, needing a moment to find his own. ' . . . Hello?'

Silence.

Had he imagined it?

'Hello?' He stood, wincing, and edged round to face the door, from where the voice must have come. The light wasn't good enough for him to see out through the jagged hole in the wood, but his senses flared as he picked up the slightest of movements in the darkness beyond.

'Are you OK?' the voice asked quietly.

'No, I'm not.' Ray started forwards, stopping himself mid-stride. 'I have to get home to my wife. She needs me.' He waited, watching the hole. 'She's ill.'

No response.

He took another step, feeling the tremor in his voice. 'Why is the door locked?'

More silence.

'Please,' he pressed. 'Why am I here?'

Another pause. 'You f . . . fell asleep in the car.'

Ray's gaze drifted away. *Had* he? He remembered feeling drowsy, watching the hedgerows scrolling by, drifting off . . . Maybe he'd been concussed from his fall in the woods, and the guy hadn't known where to take him. But none of that explained the bars on the window. Or the locked door.

He struggled to remember the driver's name. '. . . Rupert?'

The voice took even longer this time, but at last it answered simply, surprising him. 'Yes.'

Suddenly more came back to him. The car, Rupert introducing himself but not shaking hands, the drink.

The drink.

'Did you . . .' he began, the panic starting to rise more violently within him now. 'Did you *drug* me?'

He waited again, thinking about how quickly he'd started feeling drowsy after taking a few sips from the guy's flask.

What the hell had he been given?

'Please, let me out of here. My wife . . . Maura, she has Alzheimer's. There's no one else at home, and if I'm not there and she gets hungry, she might try to cook. Anything could happen.' Ray heard his voice shaking as he stumbled to the door. He grabbed the handle and wrenched it round, trying to force his way out. But the lock held.

He slumped, exhausted again. His heart hammered against his ribs, his head felt ready to explode.

'You can't keep me here,' he managed weakly, half to himself.

This time there was no response. The only sound was of footsteps on the other side of the door.

The sound of his captor walking away.

23

Rupert took another step into the hall, felt the air turn cold as he moved out of the sun.

'Ash?'

He stood still, afraid of moving further inside. The house smelled old and dirty. The paper was peeling off its walls, and chunks of ceiling hung down here and there. The floorboards were broken in places, their jagged ends sticking upwards like traps. It seemed darker than it should have, too, as if even daylight was afraid to come inside, and a gust of wind blew in, stirring a ragged net curtain hanging over the window by the stairs. Like a ghost it flared, appearing to wave; warning him to run.

He almost turned and fled, but something held him fast. Ash was here somewhere. He couldn't leave without his friend.

Again he called out, but no reply came. There was no sound, no sign of anyone else here at all, even though he'd seen Ash walk in just a moment ago.

Rupert swallowed, felt a tingle grow in his fingertips as he moved forwards, the floor creaking under him. He reached the bottom of the stairs, breathing hard, trying to decide where to check first, when a small bang made him jump.

He looked up. The noise had come from upstairs; there was no doubt about that. But why wasn't Ash answering?

Shaking, Rupert started to climb, carefully testing each step before transferring his weight. He listened out for more noises as he went, but it was hard to hear with his heart thumping so loud. He stuck to the middle of each stair, afraid of dirtying his clothes. If Mummy knew he'd been here, she'd be cross.

He reached the landing, another dingy corridor that turned back on itself, with three doors leading off to different rooms. The rickety house creaked around him. Huge cobwebs hung from the corners, some kind of plant snaked its way up the wall.

Rupert shivered, edging to the first doorway and peering in. Empty. And so was the second: nothing but a few bits of old rubbish scattered here and there, a broken rocking chair crumpled in one corner. And still no sign of Ash.

He moved on, afraid to find another empty space; of having to make his way home alone, explain to his mother that the house had taken his friend. But as he reached the door and pushed, he saw the room wasn't empty at all, and for a moment Rupert forgot his fear.

Unlike the others, stripped of their contents years ago, this bedroom looked almost undisturbed. It was a young child's, and if it hadn't been for the layers of dust coating everything, he might not have been surprised to see her sitting there, playing happily. To one side, a tiny pink bed still wore its duvet set, faded pictures of rabbits spread across its stained and crumpled surface. Toys littered the floor, cuddly animals and dolls abandoned as if their owner had been called away mid-game. Against the right-hand wall, a once-white wardrobe and chest of drawers, and beside him next to the door, a large blanket chest.

Curious, Rupert stepped inside, momentarily forgetting his fear, wondering why the room had been left this way. He stood in front of the blanket chest, reached for the intricate metal key sticking out of the hole just below the lid, hearing the lock release, and eased the lid upwards, resting it back against the wall.

The box was empty, maybe having been home to all the toys scattered across the floor. But when he reached out to close the lid, a crashing sound made him spin, as Ash burst out of the wardrobe with a yell.

Rupert cried out as Ash bowled into him, felt his legs go as he fell backwards. He hit the wall and slumped into the box, screaming again as Ash appeared above him, shoving his arms and legs into the blanket chest and slamming the lid.

Everything went black.

Rupert heard the lock turn, and Ash laughing loudly outside. Panic shot through him as he tried to kick his way out. But there wasn't enough room to move.

'Ash,' he shouted. 'Let me out.'

But Ash just laughed, louder and louder.

Rupert's heart felt like it was going to explode. 'Please. I don't like this.'

The lid didn't open.

Rupert sagged, exhausted, his breaths coming ragged and fast, tears starting to stream down his face.

'Please,' he managed weakly between panting sobs.

It smelled inside the box, of wood and dust and rot.

For a moment there was no reply, but then Ash's voice reached him in the blackness, the words turning his fear to dread.

'See ya, cry baby.'

'No,' Rupert whimpered. 'Don't leave me, Ash. Please.'

Then he heard footsteps fading away.

For a few seconds Rupert lay still, listening for the sound of his friend coming back, before panic took him again.

He started to scream.

24

Ray leaned closer, focusing through the crack in the lens of his glasses, and sagged.

The window frame had no exposed screw heads or joints; no obvious weaknesses for him to exploit. He'd already inspected the levers, looking for hinges with pins that might be worked loose. But there was nothing. It wasn't even worth smashing one of the small panes, because he'd never be able to fit through the gaps, and the bars themselves were some kind of metal, too strong to be bent without tools.

He straightened and stepped back, his head going light.

He could feel thirst and dehydration eating away at him, draining his resilience; breaking him down. Rupert, if that was really his name, hadn't returned since their first exchange through the door, even though Ray had returned to the hole regularly, hoping to catch a glimpse of his captor, and plead again for release. But there had been no sign of the younger man, and Ray was starting to worry that he had simply been left here to starve.

Even his early attempts to break out of the room, before hunger really kicked in, had been feeble; the sturdy lock on the thick wooden door repelling prolonged onslaught with ease. And the more force Ray exerted, the harder his head throbbed.

He'd been fighting fatigue for at least an hour, aware that his body had used its downtime to process whatever he'd been tricked into taking, rather than charging its reserves. There was also no way to know what kind of drugs he'd been given, so only time would reveal any side effects he was yet to experience. He had started feeling dangerously faint.

But he couldn't afford to sleep.

The shadows now cast on the far wall had slunk there from the other side of the room, their slow but unimpeded progress goading him, marking the passage of time. At least several hours since he'd come round.

Which meant Maura had been alone for more than twenty-four hours, something she hadn't been equipped to deal with in over five years, ever since large chunks of her short-term memory had started to fail.

She still remembered useless information, like the names of the kids' guinea pigs from thirty years ago, and the telephone number from their first marital home. But as for what she'd been doing five minutes before she was asked, like whether she'd lit a gas ring and left a pan of water to boil steadily away, you might as well have asked the wall. She'd start things with a conviction and focus that would fool anyone into thinking she was in complete control, but within seconds the circuits would short and she'd wander off, leaving the plugged sink to overfill; the iron to burn through the board.

Plus the gap between resets had shortened recently, to

the point where Ray could envisage her one day picking up a knife, forgetting it was in her hand, and scratching an itch on her face. That's why he was with her constantly these days, and where she couldn't come he didn't go. The golf range, the rugby, the pub, all his favourites abandoned because he had to be there for her.

Not that he minded. Wonderful flashes of his wife still emerged from time to time, coherent moments among all the haze, becoming ever more precious with rarity. He'd clung to them in recent times, afraid to miss even the briefest one, aware that each might be her last.

Until now a single thought had always comforted him. Whatever Maura was doing on *that* day, when she surfaced to say her final goodbye, he'd be there, by her side, to reciprocate and let her go.

But he'd never considered the possibility of them being separated. By force.

The worst part was that he had no idea why this was happening. What did the person holding him want, and why would they choose to kidnap Raymond Jewis? He wasn't rich or influential, he owed no money, nor had he upset the wrong people, as far as he knew. All of which pointed towards the whole thing being random.

But *why*?

If he could figure that out, perhaps it would give a clue as to who his abductor was, or even where this house was likely to be. For now, though, Ray just couldn't think.

He turned back to the window, staring at the dense foliage outside, which implied a secluded location. The view was limited, but the greenery appeared deep and unkempt, more like natural forest than somebody's garden. It didn't look like anywhere Ray had been inside Hainault Forest, either, and he'd explored most of it over the years.

He turned automatically towards the creak, too lost in thought to realise what it meant. Precious seconds passed before he registered that the door was slightly ajar, and that a plate of food was being carefully lowered to the floor inside.

'Hey,' he shouted, trying to launch himself forwards. But his bad ankle gave way and he fell. He scrambled up and kept going, desperately watching the hand retreat with the food.

Ray threw his arm in the gap, crying out as the heavy wood jammed against his flesh. But the door was still open.

And he had hold of his captor's wrist.

Rupert tried to jerk himself free, but Ray held on, reaching up with his free hand to grip the door's edge, wrenching at it.

They struggled, briefly cancelling each other out, stares locking through the fluctuating gap. Rupert's teeth were bared, but there was a cold determination in his eyes that chilled Ray. Already his strength was fading, but the adrenalin searing through his system allowed him to renew his efforts, keeping pressure up against the wood.

And without warning Rupert let go.

The door shot inwards, destabilising Ray, his hold on Rupert's wrist lost as he dropped to one knee, panting hard, closing his eyes against the pain gushing into his chest.

He heard the handle bang against the wall. The door was open, but Ray was in too much discomfort to look up, let alone continue the fight.

He forced his eyes open, raising a submissive arm, watching Rupert's feet step closer. 'Please . . .' he panted, ' . . . let me go.'

For a few seconds nothing happened, but then he felt hands being placed gently on his shoulders.

Did this mean it was over?

He was shoved.

Ray fell backwards, bouncing painfully off the bedstead, collapsing on to his back in the centre of the room. His first instinct was to get up, but he stopped himself.

The pain in his chest was subsiding, just the temporary effects of long-standing angina. But Rupert didn't know that.

He tensed and pretended to choke, maintaining the illusion of agony for a moment before letting his body relax, faking the heart attack he hoped Rupert would expect. If this man intended to kill him, perhaps he'd think the job was done, let his guard down long enough for Ray to escape. If not, maybe he'd call for an ambulance; or at least try to help. There was a brief moment of silence.

Then Ray felt something press against his right ankle, as his legs were shoved aside. Then the door was pulled shut.

And the lock turned.

25

Raymond lay on the floor till Rupert came back.

There had easily been half an hour of silence since their tussle, and the younger man must have approached with care, because Ray hadn't detected footsteps. But now he could hear Rupert breathing. Right outside the door.

He hadn't moved a muscle since landing next to the bed, despite the now spectacular ache in his back from being left in a twisted position. If his plan worked, Rupert would enter the room any moment, to check on his prisoner's physical condition.

At which point Ray would attack.

But the slow, heavy breathing continued. He felt Rupert's unwavering gaze. And the door stayed closed.

The problem was that soon Ray would have to move. His back was already murder, and the burning sensation in his hips made it harder and harder to disguise the fact he was breathing. Unless Rupert did something very soon, the standoff was over.

He went back to focusing on his damaged ankle, using the familiarity of its pain to distract from other screaming nerve ends. He was concentrating so hard that he hardly heard his captor's soft tone.

'I s . . . saw them.'

Ray froze, checking himself. Had he moved? He didn't think so.

But Rupert continued. 'Your p . . . pictures. I looked at them.'

Still Ray didn't understand, until he remembered his camera, which had been in his bag when he was taken. He wanted to swallow so badly it hurt.

Should he continue pretending to be dead?

After another twenty seconds he realised it didn't matter. His captor obviously wasn't coming in. Either Rupert knew he was conscious, or he didn't care.

Game over.

Ray inhaled hard and tried to look like he was coming round, slowly starting to shift his limbs. Doing his best to relieve the pins and needles.

'Your pictures,' Rupert repeated from outside. 'I l . . . like them.'

Ray swallowed, propping himself on an elbow, fighting the urge to get up and rush the door again. Somewhere under the pain and confusion, his brain was still functioning. Why this crazy bastard wanted to talk about photography was anyone's guess, but right now any communication was better than none. The guy was clearly a fruitcake, so he might be able to use that to his advantage.

He cleared his throat, trying to ignore the creepiness of normal conversation in such disturbing circumstances. 'Which ones do you like the most?'

'Trees. I like p . . . pictures of trees.'

'They're my favourites, too.' Ray fought his way to

the edge of the bed, and heaved himself into a sitting position.

'They remind me of w . . . walking in the woods when I was young. With my parents, and our d . . . dog.'

Ray reached back to rub his spine, tried to concentrate. 'What was the dog's name?'

'Tinker. She was a B . . . Border collie, but she died. Do you have any p . . . pets?'

'I have fish.'

For a moment neither man spoke, but Ray was glad not to hear footsteps moving away. He tried to revive the conversation on a subject that might benefit him. If he could just get out of the room, he might be able to negotiate his release. Or run.

'Do you take pictures?' he asked.

'No.' A small hesitation. 'I h . . . have no camera.'

'Why not?'

'. . . I'm not sure.'

'You can use mine.' Ray went for it, hoping it wasn't too soon. 'I'll teach you.'

'I'd l . . . like that.'

He stood up. 'Why don't you get the camera? We can start now.'

At first there was no response; just a quiet shuffling behind the door. Ray felt himself tense, imagining it being unlocked, the younger man stepping aside. Rupert had thirty years on him, at least, so he was unlikely to win a straight fight, but this might be his only chance. He'd have to time it perfectly; use the element of surprise to barge his way through as it opened, knock the guy for six if he could.

But the door stayed shut.

Ray pressed. 'We could go outside. I'll show you how to take pictures of the forest.'

'Perhaps we can d . . . do it tomorrow.'

He thought fast. 'But the light's good now. That's important. I think it's going to rain in the morning.' He held his breath.

'No.' Suddenly there was conviction in his kidnapper's voice, and a noise that sounded like him backing away. 'We don't kn . . . know each other well enough yet.'

Ray's optimism stalled, and suddenly tiredness swept in. He lay down on the bed, nausea forcing him on to his side.

'Please,' he said weakly, curling up in a ball. 'I need to get back to my wife.'

But Rupert didn't answer.

'Please,' he whispered again, resting his head on the pillow, feeling his eyelids starting to close. He tried to keep them open, listen for the distant voice. But Rupert was no longer talking, and slowly Raymond lost his fight with exhaustion.

As the blackness claimed him again.

26

'Jesus.' Aaron Sharpe rubbed his forehead, spinning slowly, dead leaves crunching under his boots. 'What if half of London is buried out here?' He motioned at the various gangs of SOCOs and search teams tramping back and forth around them in the mild autumn darkness, making the centre of White Post Wood look like an al fresco airport terminal. They stood near where the latest body had been uncovered, just over two hours ago. 'We could be finding bodies out here for weeks.'

Hawkins shook her head. 'It's unlikely. There are established tracks all over this place, which means people come here all the time. So the more bodies our killer dumps, the more chance that someone would have seen him, or stumbled across one of the graves.'

'Yeah,' Aaron wasn't finished, 'but he won't be doing it on his lunch break, will he, and I bet this place is deserted at night.'

'He'll need some light, though,' Yasir cut in just in time to stop Hawkins from saying something she might regret. 'The Chief's right, if he does it too much, eventually someone's going to notice.'

Sharpe raised his eyebrows. 'Let's see if you're still saying that after they find stiff number fifteen.'

Hawkins let it go, secretly hoping he wasn't right.

The three bodies they'd uncovered so far had been spaced out far enough that it had taken dedicated Met search teams three days to find them, and there was plenty of the area still to be searched. Plus, there were several other woods just like White Post within ten minutes' drive, so who was to say they *wouldn't* be digging human remains out of the East Havering soil for evermore? She pushed the nightmare scenario away and turned back to Sharpe, who was now arguing quietly with Amala, although it was good to see the female sergeant standing her metaphorical ground.

Hawkins shushed them politely, wary of putting either off side, even though Amala was always professional, and Aaron's work ethic had improved slightly since he'd started lodging with Frank Todd the previous year. Unfortunately, he'd acquired a dose of the more experienced officer's cynicism, too, and since Frank's departure to hate crime, Sharpe had taken it upon himself to fulfil the DI's self-appointed derisive role in the team. Todd had never done much to hide his disdain for Hawkins. He saw her as an extension of gratuitous management, all qualifications and no common sense, and made sure their every interaction was a chore. So she had no desire to fall out with his effective replacement: the newly vocal Aaron Sharpe.

Their small group included all four members of her current team plus Simon Hunter, the psychological profiler whose job was to offer insight and advice on the potential motivations and behaviours of London's worst serial killers. A profiler's involvement was mandatory now they had three clearly linked victims, but his assistance had been pivotal in their last two serial murder cases, and Hawkins was glad to have the scruffy but talented Hunter to hand.

She had gathered everyone together in response to the discovery of their third corpse, found earlier that afternoon in yet another shallow grave, within a hundred yards of the first two. She and Mike had come across to view the latest scene, while Sharpe and Yasir had been interviewing residents in the area anyway. Hunter had driven over to join them.

But getting everyone there had taken time, and daylight was now almost gone. Floodlights were clicking on around the latest burial site, and a fresh team of SOCOs were suiting up to dissect what remained of the scene. The body itself had been excavated swiftly, a virtue of having preliminary necessities like cordons and personnel already in place. It was now at the same mortuary as its predecessors, being prepped for autopsy as they spoke.

Briefly she recapped events for Hunter's benefit, starting with the discovery of Pete Barnes' body two nights ago, and the subsequent unearthing of the still nameless second victim the following day, their eventful arrest of Mitch Coleman, and her suspicions about his treatment of his wife's potential lovers – although that theory had fallen over with their discovery of a young female victim. Unless Lauren was experimenting sexually, it was unlikely her husband's jealousy was behind the deaths.

She was still sore about having to release Mr Coleman earlier that afternoon, albeit after charging him with double assault, against his wife and Mike. He even had an alibi for the date forensics said the young woman had died, supposedly having deposited a long-distance fare at Manchester airport that night. That claim was still to be verified, but they'd reached the maximum time they could hold him without indicting him for anything else. The annoying fact was that they had far less evidence in this fast-developing case than she would have liked; certainly not enough to charge anyone.

Given the choice, of course, Hawkins wouldn't have put Coleman back on the street. She just had to hope he wouldn't head straight home and take fists to his wife, or grab his passport and disappear to the furthest-flung backwater he knew. She tried to console herself with the fact that she'd watched Coleman sign out his belongings with his left hand, thereby contradicting the pathologist's assertion that the killer was right-handed.

And at least another body meant new leads.

She went back to addressing the team. 'We think this is Viola Clarkson.' She held up two photographs, one of a pretty teenager smiling through blonde ringlets, the other a battered facsimile of the same, 'seventeen-year-old student from Barking, reported missing by her parents twelve days ago, which tallies with Scene of Crime's estimate of her being strangled and deposited here twenty-four hours after that. It also follows our killer's established pattern. Last known sighting was at the house where she worked part-time, cleaning for a wealthy couple in Ilford. Obviously parents and employers will go on the list of potential suspects, but they're unlikely to have any connection with our other two victims, so for now it's purely routine. Viola disappeared at some point after leaving her employer's property at six thirty p.m. on the night she was last seen, to catch a bus towards home. It's a fair walk either end to each stop, so I've requested CCTV from the entire route.'

She glanced up at the darkening patches of sky visible through the trees. They'd been lucky with the weather so far. It hadn't rained since before the first victim had entered the ground approximately eleven days ago. That gave them at least a fighting chance of finding DNA from the killer, a possibility that only increased with the number of graves. But there was rain in the forecast, which would degrade evidence anywhere not covered by tarpaulins or tents.

She went on. 'Victims one and three, that's Viola here and Peter Barnes, went missing twenty-four hours before being manually choked to death and buried in these woods, which means mystery victim number two, who spent just over a week in the ground, was probably taken that far in advance, as well. Both men had Benzodiazepines in their systems, probably given forcibly by the killer, so I'm expecting similar results for our latest victim. What we don't understand is what happens to them between these times. So far we haven't been able to connect the two men, none of Barnes' family or friends claim to recognise the unidentified guy, and it's too early to say for this girl. However, we know that Pete Barnes was beaten heavily during his initial abduction, whereas the second victim wasn't assaulted until he was strangled. It'll be interesting to see where this girl falls into that pattern.'

Hunter stared briefly at the grave. 'Autopsies prove anything else?'

She thought for a moment. 'Well, neither of the men ate during the twenty-four hours we assume they were being held, and both have scratches to hands, faces and forearms, as if they were chased through woods like these, presumably just before they were killed. As far as we can tell, the girl has fewer scratches, so perhaps her chase, if there was one, didn't last as long.'

He nodded. 'What about logistics . . . do we know how the victims got here?'

'Probably by road.' Hawkins waved towards the car park, hidden behind the trees to their left. 'The only building within a quarter mile of here is the farmhouse, but if the owner's doing this, he'd be mad to bury them on his own land. So unless they're being held in the open, the killer must be shipping them in, dead or alive, from elsewhere.'

He hummed agreement. 'Motive?'

'Well, I think we can rule out blackmail or coercion now. I can't imagine a plasterer or a student having skills or influence that would interest the local mafia.'

'Sounds reasonable.' Hunter pulled thoughtfully at his chin. 'Were there ransom demands?'

'I considered that, too. No demands were made to either of the families we know about.'

He shrugged. 'It was a long shot. Twenty-four hours is a little fast to cash in the assets if that's their game, especially before contact is made. A nervous amateur might make that mistake once, but no one's stupid enough to do it three times. Unless . . .'

Everyone seemed to lean forwards.

Hawkins lasted at least five seconds before pushing him. 'Unless *what*?'

The profiler held up a hand. 'Let me get this thing straight. We know nothing about our killer, it could be one person or a gang, but the victims are taken and held for a day, possibly starved, and then chased through woodland before being killed.'

'That's the size of it,' Mike said.

'Well,' Hunter scruffed his own hair, 'as theories go it's a little unorthodox, but it could happen.'

He scanned their faces, as if waiting for someone to finish his sentence. When it became clear his thoughts were exclusive, he drew breath and posed the scariest question Hawkins had heard in a while.

'What if this is some kind of sport?'

27

It was almost dark when Ray opened his eyes.

For a moment his mind remained clear, encased in the warm blankness that followed sleep. But something about the stillness felt wrong. He scanned the space around him, seeing nothing but ethereal shapes. Everything was calm. *So what was bothering him . . . ?*

He began noting detail. The ghostly outline of the window was at the foot of the bed; not to his left as it should be. And there was no rush of tyres outside . . .

Then he was sitting bolt upright, his heart rate instantly rapid. Those differences meant only one thing.

The nightmare was real.

Ray scrambled off the bed and lurched to the opposite wall, his head already banging from the shock. His hands found the desk, then the lamp, and he managed to click it on, lighting the room with a dim yellow glow. He saw the unimposing farmhouse bedroom around him.

His prison cell.

He screwed his eyes shut, images of Maura coursing through his mind, as fear and desperation hit him again. He felt the heat of frustration.

'You can't keep me here,' he shouted.

He dropped on to the chair, hunched, panting;

helplessness sweeping through him. He pictured his kids being called to the scene, a few hundred yards from his house, where their elderly mum had been knocked down, having wandered into the road.

I'm sorry sir, madam, we couldn't save her. And I'm afraid we can't find your father.

Ray stood, fighting emotion. He no longer cared what they did to him; he just wanted this over with; to get home and make sure Maura was safe.

He looked across at the door, only then seeing the food.

The plate sat on the floor just inside the room. On it were a poorly made sandwich and an apple. Next to it a glass of clear liquid. He stared at them, confused.

Then he remembered his last encounter with Rupert, when his captor had tried to leave the plate and Ray had charged the door, causing him to retreat. Soon afterwards he had fallen asleep from exhaustion, and Rupert had obviously taken the opportunity to deposit the food. But it still didn't make any sense.

Previously he'd assumed he was being deliberately starved, denied sustenance to weaken his body or his resolve, in preparation for whatever his kidnapper had planned. *So what did it mean if he was now being fed?*

But all thoughts fled Ray's mind as a familiar voice reached him from the door.

'Aren't you g . . . going to eat?'

Ray looked at the hole in the wood, aware now that he was being watched. There was no light reaching the gap from the kitchen, which had allowed Rupert to stand there in the darkness, looking in without being seen.

'You can't keep me here.' The words just came out, shaky, but with conviction.

A short pause, then the same, quiet tone. 'Aren't you h . . . hungry?'

'Are you listening?' Ray moved forwards, his voice rising as he spoke. 'Let, me, go.'

' . . . You should eat something. K . . . keep up your strength.'

'This is fucking madness.' Ray reached the door, banging the heels of his hands against the wood. 'I told you my wife needs me. What the hell do you *want*?'

The shadows beyond the peephole shifted slightly: Rupert must have moved back. Ray rested his head against the door, pulse thumping in his ears, waiting for a response. But his energy faded and he sank to one knee, his head stopping level with the lock.

He fought the nausea, trying to concentrate on the handle; keep himself awake.

Slowly it came into focus, the spherical knob, and the keyhole just below it in the plate. His brain was pounding.

Then he saw it.

Ray blinked, not convinced at first he was right. He could see the latch from the regular handle, spanning the gap between door and frame. But the deadbolt underneath wasn't engaged, unlike when he'd inspected it earlier on. Which had to mean . . .

The door was unlocked.

Instinctively he reached for the handle, the urge to break free almost overwhelming, but then he stopped, forcing himself to think.

Did Rupert *know* the door wasn't locked? It was possible he'd forgotten to re-lock it after leaving the food, more focused on getting out quietly than securing the room. It seemed implausible, and yet the only other option was that he'd unlocked it on purpose. But *why*?

Was he being given a choice: stay here and eat, or run? Was Rupert waiting for him to wrench the door open and make a break for freedom, and what would happen if he did? Would he be attacked or punished somehow, maybe even killed? If Rupert wanted him dead, he'd already had plenty of chances, when Ray had been drugged or asleep, or both. Besides, if he didn't eat soon, he'd die anyway.

Ray's head was light with hunger, and the grogginess slowing his thoughts suggested there were still drugs in his system. If he tried to escape now, the younger man would easily catch him. The alternative was to wait; assume his captor had made a mistake, and hope for a better opportunity to leave, before Rupert realised the door was unlocked.

But neither option would work if he let himself starve. And regardless, it was best to wait until Rupert moved away from the door to make his move.

He looked down at the food.

Immediately instinct pulled at him, a rush of appetite telling him to grab the crooked sandwich and the glass of water; devour them both. He hadn't eaten since leaving his house, however long ago that was now. At least a day and a half.

What if this food was laced in some way, to put him back to sleep, or worse?

It was a risk he had to take.

Conscious of drawing attention to the unlocked door, Ray reached down, picked up the plate and the glass, and returned unsteadily to the chair, calculatedly placing himself back in his captor's line of sight, lit by the dull glow from the lamp. He sniffed the water, re-assured to find it odourless, and drained half of the contents. Relief burst as the liquid hit his throat. He placed the glass on the desk and picked up the sand-wich, hesitating for a second before impulse took over and he crammed the corner into his mouth, tore off a chunk and started to chew. The bread was stale, the cheese inside it dry and hard, but there was no foreign flavour that might have suggested the presence of drugs, and somehow it tasted incredible. He barely fin-ished the first mouthful before taking another.

Rupert spoke again, his voice muffled by the door. 'Bread is a g . . . good source of fibre.'

Ray stopped chewing, trying to process the odd statement.

In the absence of a reply, his captor went on. 'Fruit c . . . contains vitamin C.'

Ray swallowed hard, his heart beginning to sink. This man was clearly divorced from reality, having ignored Ray's statements about his ailing wife, any direct questions about why he'd been kidnapped, and all his pleas for release. Now he was talking about the nutritional values of food.

It was like talking to a child.

All his attempts to reason with Rupert had failed, so continuing his tactic of feigned compliance made sense for now, trying to build familiarity, find out things that might help later on.

Ray finished the sandwich and picked up the apple, projecting his voice towards the door, forcing out the words. 'Thanks for this, I was hungry.'

The usual pause. 'You're welcome.'

'I like the house,' Ray continued. 'Is it yours?'

'. . . It was my parents', but they d . . . died. Now it's mine.'

'Oh. How long have you lived here?'

'S . . . since I was born.'

'How much land do you have?'

'I don't know.'

There was a moment of silence as Ray tried to think of more questions. He bit into the apple, its tangy freshness suggesting it had been recently picked, but his kidnapper interrupted his thoughts.

'I t . . . tried using your camera.'

Ray stayed silent, unsure of how to respond.

'I took photographs. Would you l . . . like to see?'

Ray's mind froze. *What would happen if he said yes?* Would Rupert pass the camera into the room, realise that the door was unlocked and re-secure it, killing any chance of escape? But if he said no, he risked upsetting his captor, maybe unleashing whatever demon lurked under this childlike facade.

'Yes, I'd like to see.'

Ray heard footsteps moving away and almost bolted from his seat, but forced himself to stay put, aware that he had to play the percentage game. His decision proved correct as Rupert returned seconds later, and Ray saw the light from his camera's display being lined up with the hole in the door.

He stood, trying to block out the anxiety twisting his guts. He placed the remains of his apple back on the plate and crossed the room, testing his senses for any signs that the food had been drugged. But he felt OK as he reached the hole, leaning in to view the photo on screen.

'C . . . can you see?'

'Yes.' Ray studied the image, immediately looking for clues to where they might be. But the picture had been taken in the centre of dense woodland, before darkness fell, presumably not far from the house, considering that Rupert was unlikely to have left him unsupervised for long. Yet no signs, roads, or even the farmhouse itself, were visible anywhere in shot.

'I f . . . found the instructions in your case and followed them,' Rupert said. 'Is it OK?'

'It's good,' Ray told him. 'Did you take any more?'

The screen was removed for a moment before it reappeared; now showing a different picture. This time an off-kilter horizon was visible through the trees, and Ray's heart missed a beat when he saw tarmac snaking its way through the back of the frame. A road.

If he could only make it there.

He was trying to work out from the position of various shadows which direction the road would be in, when the camera vanished again. It was replaced a second later by Rupert's eye, staring at him through the darkened, jagged hole.

Ray took a step backwards. His first instinct was to grab anything sharp he could find and ram it into the psychopath's eyeball, but then his rational brain cut in. First he'd need a sharp object, which he didn't have, and second, if it didn't work, he'd only expedite whatever atrocities were in store for him. Yes, he might cause sufficient damage to slow the younger man down enough to escape, but he was just as likely to fail.

He had to stay calm.

He was ready to go. He'd slept in his clothes; even his walking boots were still on his feet, so there would be nothing untoward about his appearance that might tip Rupert off about his plan to escape. The only thing he needed was his jacket, still slung over the back of the chair, but that wouldn't take a second to grab, whenever the chance presented itself.

Ray drifted back to the desk, retrieving the apple. He took another bite and sat chewing, conscious of the need to replenish his energy, short of anything else to say.

Eventually Rupert spoke. 'Maybe tomorrow we could g . . . go into the woods. You can show me how to take better photos.'

Ray looked up, half expecting Rupert to open the door and step inside, wondering what he would do if

that happened. But the door stayed closed, and he realised he ought to reply.

'Yes, of course.'

'Good.' The tone of the disembodied voice altered
slightly, although Ray couldn't tell what that denoted.
More silence followed, this time a heavier lull that
seemed to signify a change of atmosphere. Then he
heard Rupert move away from the door.

Ray sat, waiting for him to come back, working out
ways to build further rapport. He was composing a
basic explanation of the rich mixture of colours and
textures offered by water and rocks when he heard what
sounded like a door closing elsewhere in the house.

'Hello?' he said.

No reply.

Louder. 'Hello?'

Nothing.

As calmly as he could, Ray flicked off the lamp and
made his way to the door. He peered out through the
hole; heart pounding suddenly, expecting to meet his
captor's eye. But as his face made contact with the
wood, Ray saw the kitchen was deserted, the remnants
of the fire and two candles in jars on the worktop
mutedly lighting the space. But Rupert had gone.

This was his chance.

He checked the deadlock again, relieved to find it
still apparently disengaged. Then he reached out,
gripped the handle and turned, praying there was no
additional security on the outside. The mechanism

scraped round, as he watched the upper latch edging slowly aside. And at last it jumped out of the stop.

Ray held the door in place, trying to regulate his breathing, aware that once he left this room there was no turning back. He glanced around at the window, and the darkening forest beyond, knowing this might be his only chance. So if he was going, it had to be now.

He stepped back and pulled gently at the door. It didn't move, and Ray felt a flutter of panic in his chest. He steadied himself and pulled harder. At first it resisted, but then a tiny chirp preceded movement.

As the door came free of the frame.

28

Daylight was gone by the time they had all trooped back to the car park on the edge of White Post Wood. Hawkins glanced up as they left the trees, now being whipped by strengthening winds. A partial moon added its glow to the light from several underpowered lamps spread along the perimeter, emphasising the fact there was still no cloud, although given the time of year, rain was unlikely to remain elsewhere for long. Tents were being erected over each burial site, but the forensic teams' greatest enemy was adverse weather, so the more they got done before it changed the better. Which meant finding any more graves.

Up ahead the team had regrouped near the cars, as Hawkins had asked. She joined them and began dishing out tasks in a positive tone, reminding everyone to stay open-minded, keep their heads up. Think of the overtime.

She told Sharpe to do background checks on the latest victim, and cross-reference her past with Barnes, looking for undiscovered links. Yasir agreed to visit Viola's family and friends, to see if any of them recognised either of the men who had shared her unsavoury fate. Mike was ready to chase the young woman's bank and mobile provider, to obtain details of calls and transactions she made in the days before disappearing. He would ask for locations of where she'd been at relevant times. Hawkins herself had the short straw that was explaining their negative progress to the DCS, in that they had more victims and fewer suspects now than just hours ago.

At least the body count remained at three, the constantly expanding on-site teams having found no further bodies since Viola's, although there was no way to know how many graves were still out there waiting to be found.

Hawkins dismissed her people, watching Sharpe and Yasir take the pool Astra they'd arrived in, and Hunter needing three attempts to start his battered old Vauxhall. Then she and Mike walked to his Range Rover and climbed aboard.

'All right, *Miss Positive*,' Mike said as soon as the doors closed, 'give it up. What's eating you?'

She gave him a sideways glance. 'Nothing. I just wish this case would settle down.'

His face scrunched as the 4x4's engine kicked in. 'What the hell does *that* mean?'

'Well, not finding any more dead people buried in the bloody woods might help.'

Mike snorted. 'Hey, if you don't like dead people, homicide detective was a shitty career choice. Come on, Toni, what's with the badly hidden crankiness?'

'You weren't up at three this morning,' she fired back, 'comforting two bawling sprogs because your sister downed half a bottle of vodka, and wouldn't have woken if the fucking sky had fallen in.'

'Maybe not, but you only drop the F-bomb when

you got something to hide, so don't give me bullshit excuses. Spill.'

'Ugh. Why do you have to *know* me?' Hawkins rubbed at her temples, feeling Mike's stare. 'I messed up royally with Sturridge today.'

'The shrink?'

She nodded.

'What happened?' Mike's seat creaked as he leaned closer.

'I might have . . . accused him and Vaughn of trying to oust me on grounds of mental instability.'

'*What?* Why?'

She flared again. 'Because they bloody well *are*. Ever since the attack, everyone's been watching, just waiting for me to collapse in a blubbering heap.'

'Hold on.' Mike touched her wrist, but she snatched it away, afraid that he'd feel it shaking. 'Psychoanalysis is tough, I get that, but it's meant to help.'

'It *doesn't*, though, does it? All he wants to talk about is the fucking attack, over and over like I'm just some pathetic victim.'

'So if you ignore the whole thing, it'll go away?'

'Far from it, obviously.' She snorted. 'I missed a couple of sessions and Vaughn was on the phone, ordering me to *get this sorted or else*.'

'Or else what?'

'I don't know. I went.'

'So what happened?'

Hawkins rolled her eyes. 'Well bugger me, we talked about the attack.'

'And . . . ?'

'I tried.' She rubbed at her forehead. 'Really. But I lost it . . . told him it was all a big conspiracy to fire me. Then I stormed out.'

'Geez, Toni, what were you *thinking*?'

'Stupid. I know.'

'But . . . you said the whole thing was tick-box.'

'Yes, I remember.'

Mike breathed for a moment. 'Why didn't you tell me you were flipping out?'

'Because . . .' Hawkins began, not realising until she'd started the sentence how hard it would be to finish. '. . . Specifically *not* thinking about the attack is the only way I can get through it.' She poked at the side of her head. 'It's in *here*. Permanently. Threatening to pull me under if I even acknowledge it's there.'

Maguire's hand arrived gently on her shoulder. 'Does Vaughn know?'

'About my insecurities, or about walking out on Sturridge?'

'Either.'

She shrugged.

'OK.' Mike was already in solution mode. 'This is salvageable, but you gotta come clean. Don't *call* Vaughn; go see him first thing. Tell him what happened; that you're struggling.' He reacted to her cringing response. 'I know that's the last thing you wanna do, Toni, but you said it, this thing ain't going away. You gotta face it down.'

Hawkins let her head drop back against the seat,

stared at the roof lining, huffed. 'Fine. I'll go in the morning.'

'Good girl. You realise that means you'll need to keep seeing Sturridge. Actually talk this stuff through.'

She nodded.

'You know I'm here. If you need me.'

Hawkins managed a smile. 'It's still a fucking conspiracy.'

'Sure it is.'

'Mike?' She waited for him to look over. 'Thanks.'

'Just doing my job, ma'am.' He engaged drive and pulled away.

Silence descended as Hawkins turned to look out of the window, watching the trees begin to skim past, wondering how to explain the latest developments to Vaughn. Fortunately, their chat had freed up her thought process. But then a horrific possibility occurred.

She turned to Maguire. 'What if Hunter's right?'

He paused, then smirked. 'A half-hour ago you said he was nuts, that hunting humans is a movie plot; not something that happens for real.'

'I know what I said. I was trying to stop everyone panicking. But the more I think about it, the more it makes sense. I may have misinterpreted what Hunter meant when he said it could be a sport. I was thinking cults or organised gangs, kidnapping people off the streets and advertising on secret websites; you know, experience days for your thrill-seeking psychopath, paintball for the insane.

'But,' she continued, 'if we're thinking it's just one

guy, doing this stuff on a smaller scale for his own twisted gratification, maybe it makes sense.'

He glanced at her. 'So why the long face?'

Hawkins crossed her arms. 'What worries me is how long it's been going on. Granted, the ones we've already found were killed recently, but this might not be the only burial site. How many bodies are out there? You know how many missing persons cases go unsolved every year.'

'I'm not saying you're wrong,' Mike swung the Range Rover into a bend, 'but a certain DCI once told me we trade *facts*. So let's deal with what we know, and quit sweating stuff that might never happen.'

'Fair enough, but we should consider the possibility. It might be crucial in decoding our killer's mind-set. If he's playing some sort of game, that tells us something about him.'

'All right, Holmes, deduct away.'

She thought for a moment. 'Predators like to have an advantage, whether it's a gun or a big set of claws. Every poacher stacks the odds in his favour, takes his prey by surprise if he can. We know the victims are held for a while before being killed, but we still have no idea *how* they were taken. We know he uses sedatives, but how's he administering them? It looks like Peter Barnes was drunk on the night he was abducted, so he might have made a soft target, but it still isn't easy to drug people without them noticing. So how's he doing it?'

'Whatever it is, it works. So what's our move?'

'We go back to the victims,' Hawkins said. 'Trace

their final movements; work out when they came under the killer's control. If they were all abducted by force, how and where did it happen? If some were from social situations, who's setting those up? The scenario probably involves a vehicle at some point, so identifying that's a priority if we can, but there must be another connection, someone or some*thing* that exposed these people as targets; that's where our focus should be.'

Maguire blew out his cheeks. 'Theory's solid, but where do we start?'

'Hendon. We've pretty much exhausted the search for CCTV footage of Barnes' kidnap without success, and we don't even know victim two's *name* yet, never mind where he lived or socialised, so our best chance of success is tracing Viola's movements on the night she disappeared. The CCTV I requested should be available soon. I'll call the night shift and get them started on trawling through it. We can take over in the morning.'

'OK, but isn't there another call you should make first?'

Hawkins turned to face him with a frown. 'Who to?'

'Hunter. To apologise for panning his big idea.'

'Oh. That.'

They rode on in silence as Hawkins found her mobile and toyed with different ways of apologising to the profiler without humiliating herself entirely. Hunter was right almost *too* often, and his puckish sense of humour meant he'd be teasing her about such a dramatic U-turn for months.

But it looked like he was on to something, which was good and bad in equal measure. Good because it gave them potential insight into a killer's psyche; bad because if he was correct about it being some kind of sport, his subsequent caveat was a worrying prospect.

If this was all just a game, only the killer knew how long that game had left to run.

29

Ray's heart pounded as he stepped clear of the bedroom, every sense buzzing for signs of his captor's return. The old building murmured around him, a symphony of timbers groaning in time with the wind, as if the place was calling its master; trying to report the breach. But its complaints went unanswered as Ray pulled the door closed behind himself, and began crossing the rough flagstone floor.

The kitchen was almost in darkness, lit only by the fire's creeping glow and the candles flickering at either end of the worktop, each casting its glimmer into the shadows, rendering movement on to the walls.

Ray took another stride towards the exit, too far from safety now to double back if he was interrupted. But the exit was just yards away.

And still there was no sign of Rupert.

He noticed his camera on one of the worktops, his rucksack on a chair just beyond, and almost reached out for his property, stopping when he realised their additional weight might slow him down.

Only then did he remember he'd left his jacket inside the room. But there was no time to go back, even if it was cold outside. He had to keep moving; get as far away from here as he could.

Ray reached the exit, preparing himself to search for a key, try a window, or retreat if the outer door was secure. But as he pulled at the handle and felt the mechanism shift, he was surprised to find the front door open as well.

Suddenly it all felt too easy, and for a moment he wondered if this might be some kind of trap. But he was free, for the first time in over twenty-four hours, so there would be no turning back now. Whatever the reason for it, he had a chance to escape, and he wasn't going to give that up.

Not while Maura needed him.

Ray held his breath and pulled the door open, to find woods similar to those on the far side of the house. A feeble glow bled from the open doorway and windows, reaching a short way out into the dark, but above the trees a clear half-moon shone in the autumn sky, shedding pastel white beams through the canopy, giving him just enough light to see.

And beyond the small clearing around the farmhouse, thick forest stretched away, an eerie mix of leaves and bare branches clawing the air, patches of mist carpeting the ground in between. The cold air was thick with moisture. Somewhere in the distance, a wild animal bayed.

The house was surrounded by an open gravel drive, leading into a narrow dirt track that snaked away to his left, disappearing among the trees. The rear of a car was just visible, parked in a recess next to the building, and for a second he considered going back inside, trying to find keys.

But that would mean risking his freedom.

He pulled the front door closed behind him, to prolong the illusion that all was as it had been, and strode away from the house, stepping as softly as possible to minimise the noise of his boots on the grumbling stone drive, trying to decide which way to go.

Keeping the moon dead ahead would stop him going round in circles. Eventually he'd hit civilisation.

He reached the edge of the clearing, glancing back to check he wasn't being followed, seeing no one.

Then he turned.

And ran.

Ray entered the forest at speed.

Branches snatched at his clothing, bracken crunching under his weight. Within seconds the light fell away, plunging him into blackness, pouring greater focus on to his other senses, emphasising the immediate discomfort in his ankle. He lost sight of the moon, forced instead to concentrate on the foliage rushing at him out of the dark, ducking the spurs that jabbed at his face.

He tried to check over his shoulder, to see if he was being pursued, but the foliage had swallowed him, blocking his view. And before he turned back he had stumbled, his foot dropping into a rut.

He fought the uneven ground for balance, kept on forging ahead, despite the burning pain in his lungs, and the hammering deep in his chest. He felt the heat rise up his back, a mixture of exhaustion and panic, but he hadn't gone far enough yet. His vision was starting to cloud, and he had to keep pushing his glasses up his nose, making it harder to see. The next time his ankle turned he sprawled sideways, crashing into a tree. His shoulder took most of the impact, the rough bark wrenching him round. He fell in an awkward heap, panting loudly, muscles singing, pulse thumping loud in his head.

Ray tried to stand and keep moving but his body resisted, clinging to its moment of rest. He slumped, trying to ignore the panic tugging at him. He couldn't afford to stop.

He pushed over on to his back, scratching at his cheek as something unseen brushed his skin, blowing air from the corner of his mouth and shaking his head. The blackened woods loomed, stars glinting through gaps as the forest chattered around him, a buzzing background overlaid with the calls of predators stalking their game. At night the wilderness came alive, but tonight its murmur felt hostile, as if it were casting him out, sentencing the intruder to his preordained fate.

Then a new sound cracked the air, at odds with the underlying tone.

Ray's head jerked towards the noise, ears straining, every sense primed; a breath catching deep in his throat. Something large had moved in the undergrowth not far away. Animal or human, it was impossible to tell.

But whatever it was had stopped moving.

Ray's senses raged, the combined odours of pine and damp earth flaring, threatening to make him cough. He managed to hold it down.

Another crunch, louder this time, but still cautious, as if its maker was trying to move without being heard. Petrified, Ray lifted his head, trying to glimpse whoever, *whatever*, was there.

His line of sight cleared the bracken, and he stared out across the forest floor, trying to locate the source. For a second he saw nothing, just charcoal shapes shimmering in the half-light. Then a glimpse, the slightest of movements, pulled his attention right, and he saw it. Twenty yards away a shadow ghosted through the trees, sliding past gently snapping vegetation, its angular profile marked out by two malevolent green eyes that scanned the horizon, turning slowly this way and that.

Searching.

Ray's heart missed a beat when he realised it was a night-vision mask, like the one Bernard had shown him a few weeks ago at camera club. It allowed the wearer to see in the dark, and it meant only one thing.

He was being hunted down.

All of this must have been planned: the deserted kitchen, the unlocked door; the opportunity to escape. It was the reason he'd been brought here and held in that room for a day. Then he'd been offered the chance to escape and he'd taken it, only to find himself out here in the woods, lost and unprepared.

He didn't want to imagine what would happen if Rupert caught him, but somehow he'd been lucky so far. His inadvertent fall had dropped him out of sight and kept him still, hidden from his kidnapper's view. But he couldn't just wait here, hoping not to be found. As soon as he got close Rupert would see him. And then . . .

He needed to move, as fast and as far as he could, and just pray he reached safety before Rupert reached *him*. He checked again and saw the mask facing briefly away, realising that his best shot was now.

The involuntary rest had at least allowed him to recover, and Ray felt stronger as he rolled up on to his haunches and threw himself forwards as hard as he could. His ankle felt OK for the first few strides, but as he began weaving in and out of the trees, crashing through dense vegetation, the pain returned. He ignored it and drove himself harder, trying to listen above the ragged sound of his breathing for signs that he was being pursued.

And they came; secondary noises of someone running behind him, closing him down. Panic rose inside like lava as he tried to guess how far back his assailant was. But the forest seemed to shrink around him, slashing at him with increasing force, a million branches cutting off his options for flight. He raised his arms to keep the clawing talons from his face.

Then the ground disappeared.

Ray pitched forwards, weightless for a second before his outstretched leg hit something and folded, throwing him into a spin. His right hip crashed into the ground and he rolled, skidding painfully to a halt on his side.

Still dazed, he looked around, trying to locate his

pursuer and regain his feet at the same time. His vision blurred, and the forest seemed even darker than it had seconds before. There was a strong stagnant odour, but no signs of movement in the trees and bushes nearby.

Ray tried to scan his surroundings, clutching his side where it hurt from the fall, trying to fathom the black night enveloping him. There were stones underfoot, set in soft mud beneath intermittent shallow puddles that sploshed quietly as he moved. From what little he could see, he'd run off the edge of a slope. Now he was in a vee-shaped channel, the base of which was scattered with debris, plastic sheeting and broken pieces of timber.

He stumbled across and picked up one of the wooden shards, cursing as a splinter forced its way under his skin. He dropped it and selected another, relieved to find this length smoother and sturdier in his palm. He limped away, afraid to stay in the open, even though the relative silence suggested the chase might be done.

He reached a clump of trees and sagged against one of the trunks, pausing to catch his breath and listen, trying to tune out the underlying babble of wildlife. This part of the woods was even denser, and the leaves around him hissed in the breeze. But still nothing interrupted the natural hum of the forest, and Ray allowed himself a moment's rest, leaning back against the tree and closing his eyes.

He heard movement behind him too late.

Ray spun, raising his weapon, but the wood was wrenched from his hands. He reached after it, drawing back when the green eyes folded out from nowhere, right in front of his face. He staggered backwards, tripping, falling again. The shadow dropped above him, the evil mask bearing down. Powerful hands clamped Ray's neck, hard and tightening.

'Help.' He screamed, but only a whimper came out.

He thrashed at the arms, head still light from running, his thoughts starting to liquefy.

He was choking.

White patches crept into his vision, a ringing sound built in his mind. And all the time those green eyes bored into him, glinting as Ray began to shake. His last thoughts, as the glare invaded his sight, were of Maura. Had someone found her, and if not, how much longer could she survive without him?

Somewhere in the back of his mind, Ray realised there would be no tomorrow for him to find out.

Consciousness melted away.

30

'Go on,' Ash insisted. 'Just a lug. I dare you.'

Rupert looked at the small white stick smouldering between his friend's fingers. 'Mum will s . . . smell it on me.'

'No, she won't.' Ash took another drag and held the cigarette back out, his hand curled over it from above, white smoke bleeding away in the wind. 'She wouldn't expect you to smoke in a gazillion years. Besides, it'll wear off before you get home.'

Rupert held his breath and stared out across the square, watching the small groups of other kids drifting down the hill from school towards the bus station, trying to think of a way out of this. Ash had offered him cigarettes in the past, but normally he gave up if Rupert refused enough. Today, though, he wasn't letting it go.

'They're yours,' he protested, but straight away he knew he'd made a mistake. Ash hadn't paid for the things; they were too young to buy them, anyway. His mum worked on aeroplanes and was always bringing home big packs for his dad, who was too drunk most of the time to notice if Ash stole a few here and there.

Ash pulled a face and grabbed his wrist, making him take the cigarette.

Rupert looked down at it, hating the smell; dreading the taste. He wanted to run, but Ash would be mad at him for days if he did that. So he stayed where he was, adjusting his grip so the filter was pinched between his thumb and forefinger, the way he'd seen his friend do it.

'Go on, then.' Ash was watching him.

Slowly Rupert raised his hand towards his mouth, but it was trembling so much that the embers fell into his lap. He jumped up and began desperately brushing them away, before they burned through his trouser legs.

Ash laughed.

Embarrassed, Rupert glanced around them, to check if anyone else had seen. Two kids from the year below were standing across the square, looking straight at him and laughing as well. They seemed to be the only ones who'd noticed, although another, larger group was just crossing the road to their left, talking amongst themselves. Rupert felt the kick of awe. They were the cool, popular kids; the ones who had nice clothes and parties, and who didn't hide themselves away behind the music block on breaks. And right in the middle, at the front, was Jenny.

Rupert's heart gave a little leap as he sank on to the bench, his guts already starting to churn. Jenny Masters was the prettiest girl in school, but he turned to jelly whenever she was around. He had trouble talking to anyone he didn't know, let alone the most beautiful girl he'd ever seen.

Ash twisted to see what he was looking at, turning back to him with a smirk. 'Hey Rupes, it's your girlfriend.'

Rupert shrank. 'She's n . . . not my girlfriend.'

'No, and she never will be if you won't even talk to her.'

He shook his head. 'I . . . I can't.'

'Course you can. And you know what I heard? She's into guys who smoke and ride motorbikes.'

'I don't have a m . . . motorbike.'

'I know that, stupid, but take a drag on that thing in your hand and you'll be halfway there, though, won't you?'

Rupert looked down, remembering the cigarette.

Ash shoved him. 'Quick, retard, while she can see.'

He shut his eyes. This felt just like all the other moments he'd bottled out in the past. Times he'd wanted to talk to Jenny, but hadn't had the guts. The electricity jolting through him now was worse than ever, but maybe that meant it was more important; a last chance, perhaps.

He looked up and raised the cigarette, suddenly determined to prove himself. He put the filter between his lips and drew on it hard, hearing a crackle as the orange sparks flared. He held the smoke in his mouth for a second, then inhaled.

'Jenny!' Ash shouted.

Smoke hit his lungs just as the whole group stopped and looked at them.

Then he choked.

Rupert lurched forwards; dropping the cigarette, coughing so hard that he thought his throat would burst. He could hear everyone laughing in the background, as he felt the heat of humiliation shooting up from his chest.

'Nice one, dickhead,' somebody called when he finally stopped choking and slumped on the seat next to Ash. The group drifted past, some jeering, others throwing screwed up bits of paper at him as they passed. His skin felt like it was on fire until Jenny turned the far corner and disappeared. He'd never get to speak to her now.

'Don't worry about it, mate.' Ash punched him on the arm and stood. 'She's a million miles out of your league anyway.' He started walking towards the newsagent's. 'Come on.'

Rupert sighed and lifted himself off the bench, slouching after his friend.

The shop was busy, the after-school rush filling its small aisles, a dozen people queuing in front of the till to pay for papers or drinks or sweets. He spotted Ash in the back corner by the magazines, and eased past a gang of first years to join him.

'About fucking time,' Ash whispered. 'What took you?'

'I . . .'

Ash rolled his eyes. 'Look, just get me the third one from the left, the one with the red cover, yeah?'

For a moment Rupert didn't understand. Then he followed Ash's gaze upwards and realised that he meant the third magazine *from the left.* On the top shelf.

'I don't have m . . . money,' he said. 'And I'm t . . . too young.'

Ash scowled at him. 'Who said anything about paying for it?'

Rupert glanced at the old woman behind the counter, then back at Ash, slowly shaking his head.

'You'd better fucking do this,' Ash hissed. 'Or you can find yourself a new mate. And who else is going to put up with your stupidity like I do, huh? You're fucked without me.'

Rupert looked at the floor, blinking back tears.

Ash shoved him. 'Don't start that shit. And hurry up, OK, while it's still busy in here.' He began walking away. 'I'll be outside.'

The whole shop started to spin as Rupert watched his friend leave. He felt hot and cold at the same time, and it was getting hard to breathe. Stealing was wrong, but Ash wanted the magazine. He had no choice. Their friendship depended on it.

He looked around as a few more kids walked out, opening bags of crisps as they went. The queue at the counter was half the size it had been, and there were as many grown-ups as children left in the shop.

He glanced up at the magazine rack, seeing the lady in underwear on the cover of the one Ash wanted.

Rupert swallowed hard and reached up. He was tall for his year, so on his toes it wasn't too much of a stretch, and the magazine slid out easily. He lifted it down and held it against his body so no one could see.

His head was pounding, and he felt the sweat on his neck as he crouched behind a display, pretending to look at something on a low shelf. Then he slipped the magazine into his belt before zipping his jacket up.

He straightened as a man in jeans and a light-coloured jumper stepped into the aisle to his right and looked straight at him. Rupert walked towards the man, trying to smile as he turned off between two other rows.

He passed the counter, where the lady was serving the last couple of kids, and turned towards the exit. He heard footsteps behind him, but there was no turning back now.

He stared straight ahead, kept heading for the door and the bench across the square, where he could see Ash, smoking again. But Ash was looking the other way, as if he didn't know Rupert was there.

He made it to the doorway and walked out into the light. But the footsteps behind him were the closest they'd been.

Then he felt the hand on his shoulder.

'Hold it there, son. You'd better come with me.'

31

He remained motionless in the shadows as Stony Wood swayed around him, leaves and branches stirring as breezes washed through, a bulbous moon drenching everything in its tepid hue. The temperature well above freezing, despite the time of year.

A good night for predators.

The killing zone stretched away in front of him, the dry bed once home to a small creek, now an open strip of stony ground snaking through the trees, providing a clear line of sight across the spot it had taken him weeks to identify.

He imagined the applause; the swell of pride as the announcer spoke. *Our Young Wildlife Film-maker of The Year is . . .*

Lionel Andrews.

He let the fantasy play for a moment before parking it. He needed to concentrate.

Then it happened.

The tiny leaves brushing the forest floor a short distance ahead shivered, out of sync with others nearby, betraying the position of something moving behind.

As prey came.

Two mice scampered out from under the bush, tiny

noses investigating every stone; each piece of debris, moving in bursts, searching for food. He tracked them for a while before looking up to scan the trees.

Within seconds his subject arrived, the wild barn owl he'd first seen two weeks ago, landing silently on a branch high in the canopy, its stare locked on the mice in the canyon below.

Lionel checked the camera, playing events forwards in his mind.

The owl sweeps soundlessly down from the trees, as the mice continue their search, oblivious. The nearest one raises its head at the last second, but before it runs the talons snap shut. The owl touches down before launching back into the air, the tiny rodent flailing in its grasp; its fortunate companion fleeing as the predator soars triumphantly out of frame.

It all sounded so simple in his head. He'd found the location, saved for months to buy the right kit, yet so far, visit after midnight visit, the crucial sequence had evaded him. But tonight would be different.

Lionel put his eye to the lens, switching focus quickly from owl to mice and back. The predator's staring black pupils were fixed on its prey.

But then its head turned.

Lionel glanced up, hearing it too: the low hum of an engine somewhere beyond the trees. He looked at the owl, saw it edge backwards.

No, not now. I'm so close.

He reassured himself that the owl hadn't fled. It was fine, the vehicle would pass, leave things as they were.

This would be an amusing anecdote he could tell in interviews.

But the vehicle didn't pass; it stopped. A short silence followed, then a door banged.

The owl flew away.

Lionel swore several times under his breath. For days he'd been the only person out here. Then, on the very night his patience was about to pay off, some fucker had ruined the whole thing. He wanted to march over and find the driver; tell him that wildlife photography was hard enough without idiots scaring the subjects away. Then he realised they had as much right to be here as he did.

Plus it was quiet again now, and the mice were still there. The owl might return.

He settled back down.

For a moment there was calm, but then the crunching sounds began, coming nearer; loud enough to startle the mice, who shot back under the bush.

Annoyed again, Lionel raised his head, to see a dark shape pushing through the foliage away to his left. Then he froze, for it wasn't a single figure but two; one carrying the other, slung over its shoulder in a fireman's lift.

What the fuck?

Nightmare scenes crowded Lionel's imagination: gang murders, mafia hits; newspaper stories about a young film-maker found dead in Stony Wood. His heart leapt when he realised his improvised camouflage, chosen to hide him from an airborne predator, might prove useless against this new threat. But he had to stay put; any movement or sound might draw attention his way.

He shrank, keeping the figure in view as it dumped its victim and unslung something from its shoulder, watched it lean forwards and begin swaying back and forth. He couldn't see past the bushes, but it was obvious the figure was digging.

He stayed perfectly still, watching the stranger. Soon his body ached from not being able to move. And then he needed to pee. He held on for what felt like hours, but the man was still there, only just heaving the body into the hole.

Lionel let go, feeling the urine spread, warm and comforting at first, soon turning to a cold itchiness that made the rest of his wait torture.

At last the man finished, stamping down the earth, turning to leave. Lionel stayed motionless for another few minutes after hearing the vehicle drive away, feeling a relief that outweighed any photographic high.

Then he rolled over, pulled out his mobile.

And dialled 999.

32

'Settle down in the back!' Hawkins shouted, bringing the Giulietta to a sharper than intended halt at the crossing, jolting everyone in their seats. 'Or we're going straight home.'

Her outburst yielded a moment of exquisite peace as a tide of pedestrians broke in front of the car, heading for the low facade of South Ealing underground station on the far pavement.

'Better.' She pulled away as the lights changed, nodding at Mike to emphasise how quickly she'd picked up parenting. 'Now let's see who can be the quietest until we get to Matthew and Jemima's.'

Emphasising the point, she turned up Heart FM and let CeeLo Green fill the cabin, suddenly willing to endure the music's jinking effect on her sleep-deprived brain. Once again they'd all seen three a.m., Hawkins loading wet sheets into the washing machine while Siobhan tried to coax her kids back to sleep, and Mike made hot chocolates.

She would have traded most things for a lie-in after that, but the case wasn't going to investigate itself.

Obviously this twenty-five-minute diversion was going to delay the start of their day's investigation, not to mention the meeting with the DCS she had organised through his assistant before leaving home. Fitting children's car seats to a vehicle designed by Italians had been a nail-mangling nightmare. Normally Hawkins wouldn't have entertained the idea, but Siobhan had surprised her the previous night with news that she had two interviews for part-time work lined up. If she got either, it *had* to increase the chances of her menagerie vacating the spare room this side of Christmas.

The best part was that both kids seemed agreeable to spending time with their similarly aged equivalents at Siobhan's best friend's place in Brentford.

They drove on, with Mike giving directions from the navigation software on his phone, and the children re-immersing themselves in whatever distractions their iPads provided. Hawkins' mind was just starting to process elements of the case again when a screech from the back seat demonstrated that control had been no more than a fleeting illusion.

She turned to see her nephew cowering under renewed attack from his sister. 'Oi.'

The hand was retracted. 'He started it.'

'I don't care.' She glared at her co-pilot. 'Are you on crowd control here or not?'

'Excuuuuse me.' Mike wrung out the words in a cartoon voice, glancing around. He finished with a raspberry, drawing mischievous laughter from the back seat.

She slapped him. 'You aren't helping.'

'Sorry.' Maguire winked at his audience. 'We'll be good now, right, kids?'

Mercifully the ceasefire lasted the remaining few minutes until they arrived at the decent-sized end-of-terrace property on one of Brentford's slightly less crowded roads.

Hawkins pulled on the handbrake. 'Everyone out.'

Mike waited for another car to pass before stepping into the road to let Kyle out of the back. Hawkins opened Rosie's door as Maguire was dragged past towards the house.

'Somebody's keen,' he observed, as Kyle pulled him to the porch and insisted on being lifted up so he could ring the bell.

Hawkins leaned in to undo Rosie's seat belt.

'Come on, madam,' she urged, physically lifting her niece out of the seat when she still didn't move, plonking her down on the pavement. 'Do we need the iPad?'

For a second Rosie looked wounded, but then she sighed and held out the tablet. 'I did this for you.'

'Oh.' Hawkins took it, turning the device over to look at the screen, finding herself oddly touched. On it was a brightly coloured drawing: five stick people and a stick cat, outside the crude approximation of a house, the words *Thank you, Arntee Antonia* written neatly at the top of the screen.

Rosie moved in beside her, pointing at each stick person in turn. 'That's me, Kyle, Mummy, you and Uncle Mike.'

'That's very professional.' Hawkins grimaced at her attempted compliment, looking closer. 'Why aren't Mummy and I holding hands like everyone else?'

'Because you don't like each other,' Rosie said brightly, as if the answer were obvious.

'Right.' She glanced towards the house, where the others were now being let in. 'I suppose we do argue a bit.'

'Don't worry. Mummy argues with most people.'

'Yeah,' Hawkins led her towards the house, 'I know the feeling.'

33

'Sorry, love, couldn't move your knees, there, could I?'

'If you must,' Hawkins mumbled, rising to fight her way over the knotted power cord.

'Cheers, darling.' The older woman bent and lifted the front edge of her chair, shoved the vacuum cleaner head underneath. 'Be out your way in no time.'

Hawkins shared withering looks with the Chief Superintendent's irritatingly attractive PA, wondering if the sanitation department's desire to clean under her chair had more to do with a need for interaction than work ethic, especially when the cleaner moved on, completely ignoring the carpet under the remaining, unoccupied furniture.

She stood quietly while the woman buzzed around the rest of the seating area, watching Vaughn's office door, across the hall from the glass-fronted waiting area. Thanks to obligatory, already-made cups of tea at the house where she and Mike had dropped the kids, Hawkins had arrived six minutes late for her reluctantly booked appointment. At which point Vaughn's assistant, Amy, had rung through to let the DCS know she was here. That was ten minutes ago.

But the door remained shut.

Which probably meant Vaughn knew about her

dramatic over-reaction and exit the previous day and was taking time to compose her dressing-down. Or he was letting her stew.

Hawkins was about to retake her seat when Amy's phone buzzed, and after a short conversation she was directed to enter. She nodded authoritatively and headed for Vaughn's office, feeling the familiar twang of apprehension as she crossed the corridor.

Rarely during her career had this room offered a welcoming experience. More often than not, her visits were to deliver or receive bad news, and normally she left feeling worse than when she arrived. Admittedly the phenomenon had been more emphatic under Vaughn's predecessor, but the current DCS was almost scarier for the fact she'd never heard him shout. At least once you'd experienced the full force of someone's rage, you knew its extent. Tristan Vaughn retained that air of mystery.

She neared the door, playing out the conversation in her head. Her plan was to start by updating him on the case. That would be his primary concern, anyway, and if she could relax them both by giving a good account of the current situation, hopefully it would lessen the perceived severity of the real reason for her appearance.

To explain what happened with Sturridge.

She paused as her fingers reached the door handle, glancing back to find Amy watching from behind the reception area desk. Hawkins gave her as pleasant a smile as she could muster, conscious that any concerns the young woman had about her employer's visitors might find their way back to him. She took a breath and went in.

'Sorry to book you at short notice, sir.' Hawkins bustled into the room, twisting to close the door before turning back to the desk. 'Especially on a Saturd—' She stopped.

Having locked eyes with Brian Sturridge.

The counsellor had been sitting in one of the two chairs in front of Vaughn's desk, facing away as she'd entered. Now he stood looking back at her with a calm expression, giving away the fact that she was the only party surprised by their collective presence.

'Sir?' She looked at Vaughn.

'Antonia.' The DCS waved at the chair next to Sturridge's. 'Take a seat.'

She did so, cautiously drawing out the process, engineering time to recalculate her approach given these new parameters. Clearly her hesitation in requesting an audience with Vaughn had allowed the competition to get in first. Now her boss knew the whole embarrassing episode, told without the mitigating veneer she'd planned to apply.

In the opposition's words.

'I realise Brian's attendance at this meeting is unexpected,' Vaughn said when all were seated. 'But frankly, if you knew, I was afraid you might not turn up.'

Hawkins shook her head slightly, unsure if he wanted a specific denial.

'Anyway,' he continued, 'further to concerns raised last time we spoke, I asked the counsellor to update me personally after each of your subsequent sessions, which he did. So when I saw you'd booked this meeting, I took the initiative and asked Brian to be here. Obviously I'm glad you went back yesterday.' He paused to glance at the other man. 'What worries me is the way you curtailed the meeting.'

'I . . .' Hawkins rummaged, 'I shouldn't have, it was unprofessional.' She turned to Sturridge. 'My apologies.'

'Well that's fair enough,' Vaughn said as Sturridge nodded. 'But it isn't my primary focus.'

Hawkins looked back at him.

The Chief Superintendent met her gaze. 'I told you my team, especially those of senior rank, must be beyond reproach. I cannot allow harm sustained in the line of duty to affect my officers' judgement or behaviour. Which means that when one of you goes through a traumatic event, as you absolutely did, it's my responsibility to see that any lasting damage, physical or psychosomatic, is addressed.' He leaned back, crossing his arms. 'I know you're an abrasive character; you put heart and soul into your work, and I applaud you for it, especially when you demonstrate such a low percentage of cases unsolved. However, I also can't ignore the possibility that I reinstated you prematurely to active duty. If there are underlying psychological complications that still need dealing with, then I have a decision to make, about whether to do this in post . . .'

Don't say it.

' . . . or whether to relieve you until such time as these problems can be resolved.'

'Sir,' Hawkins jumped in, 'let me assure you that I'm perfectly capable of leading this investigation. Granted, there are some private glitches I need to work through, and I'll absolutely do that. But don't take me off the case at such a critical stage.'

Vaughn regarded her. 'I admire your commitment, Detective, as always. But you'll also appreciate the decision isn't simply a matter of faith. Like I said, we have to cross every T.' He turned to Sturridge. 'What's your professional opinion, Counsellor?'

A barbed silence descended.

Heat ran up the back of Hawkins' neck as she stared at the man whose session she'd stormed out of less than twenty-four hours ago. Such discourtesy wasn't going to make his assessment more positive, but even without it he might condemn her. If Sturridge opined the slightest chance of personal demons impairing Hawkins' judgement, Vaughn would exercise caution. She'd be off the case.

Why did you have to mention the nightmares?

Then Sturridge was speaking.

'There are unsettled emotional disputes, yes, but are they sufficiently prominent to affect the Chief Inspector's ability to lead an operation?' His calm gaze drifted, as if the crucial decision was still being made. He drew breath, and Hawkins stopped picking at the underside of her chair as the noise became audible.

This was it.

'Actually, no.' Sturridge answered his own question at last. 'Perhaps counter-intuitively, the work environment provides important structure and stability for DCI Hawkins at a key stage in her rehabilitation. I also think we're close to a breakthrough, so relieving her of duty would create avoidable stress and disruption, thereby jeopardising our chances of a successful result. As long as you agree that her current conduct is sound . . .'

Hawkins fought the urge to kiss him as all eyes turned back to Vaughn.

'Fine.' The DCS nodded. 'I have no cause for concern there.' He looked at Hawkins. 'So, providing your counselling appointments are maintained, and continue to deliver progress, I recommend that you remain in post. Thanks for your time, Brian.'

'My pleasure.' The counsellor stood, and with courteous nods to both parties, left the room.

'OK,' Vaughn said as the door closed. 'That's sorted, so what did you want to see me about?'

Hawkins caught up with Sturridge in the car park, having offered Vaughn token updates on the case and extracted herself.

She called his name as he opened the driver's door of a large green Citröen. The counsellor turned as she arrived, slightly out of breath.

'Why cover for me?' she panted.

'What do you mean?'

'Come on,' Hawkins eyed him, 'I walked out of yesterday's meeting like a teenage prima donna, and we aren't on the verge of a breakthrough, not even *close*. If you were honest about that, by now I'd be handing the reins of this investigation to my second in command. How clear is your conscience that I won't have a debilitating relapse at some pivotal moment?'

His brow gathered. 'Have I misjudged the situation?'

Now it was her turn to frown. 'No, but I'd like your assurance that you meant what you said.'

'I did. So we have no problem.' He started lowering himself into the car. 'Just call my office and book your next appointment.'

Hawkins positioned herself so he couldn't shut the door. 'You still haven't answered my question. And I warn you now, if you're expecting a blow job, you'll just about live to regret it.'

Sturridge looked up at her, pulling himself upright, bringing them face to face. 'Look, Detective, I did what I did in there because successful counselling stands or falls on one thing: trust. I genuinely believe you're better off doing your day job for two reasons. One, because without it you'd be even *more* unbearable than you are now, and two, because people who are exceptional at what they do generally have a point to prove. Which clearly you do. So I hope that here begins trust between us. I've never forced anyone, patient or otherwise, to do anything, so the first thing we'll address at our next appointment is your atrocious diplomacy.' He lowered his voice. 'And I'll thank you not to make baseless allegations regarding improper thoughts about my clients. That happened once, twenty-five years ago. Now the lady in question is my wife, and she wouldn't like it. Good day.'

With that, Brian Sturridge dropped into the driver's seat and started the engine. Hawkins stepped clear, allowing him to shut the door, watching him back up and pull around her, out of the car park.

She stood for a moment in the empty space, Brian Sturridge's words ringing in her ears.

Unbearable.

Failing to convince herself he wasn't right.

34

The Range Rover's huge tyres ground to a halt on the gravel drive and Mike whistled. 'Geez. What the hell did taste ever do to these guys?'

'That's it,' Hawkins told him, 'vent the sarcasm out here, so it doesn't break loose in front of the nice civilians.'

'Oh sure, like you weren't thinking it.'

She frowned and looked up at the house.

Several decades ago, prior to big alterations, the property had been a mid-size detached with space either side. But, like the majority of others around it, the place had been heavily modified, and now threatened to overwhelm the plot, with a large, two-storey extension on the left, and a double garage tacked on to the right. Mock-neoclassical pillars and large stone lions flanked the porch.

As it happened Mike was correct: far more money than taste had been involved in the changes. The overall effect would have struggled for credibility in Cheshire, never mind North East London.

Hawkins undid her seat belt and opened the door, stepping on to the treacherous stones, spike-heeled boots threatening to turn her ankles. She steadied herself against Mike's car as her gaze fell on the large, charcoal-coloured

Audi parked alongside. The saloon was pure business-man's express, perhaps no surprise given its owner's position as director of his own accountancy firm, but firmly at odds with the vulgar property beyond.

Hawkins pictured a trophy wife sitting inside on a cream leather sofa, flicking through catalogues, oblivious to the concerns of people who had to work for a living.

But they weren't here to judge.

The reason for their excursion to Ilford was that this had been Viola Clarkson's part-time place of work. She had carried out domestic cleaning chores here, one evening a week, the last occurrence of which happened to be on the night she disappeared.

According to the missing person's report her mother had filed almost two weeks ago, Viola had come here by bus straight after finishing her day at Barking College, worked her usual ninety-minute stint, and sent a text to say she was leaving for home just after six thirty. Her homeward-bound journey comprised a ten-minute walk to the nearest stop, a short wait for the bus, a thirty-minute ride towards home, and a further few minutes on foot to her front door at the far end.

The set-up had been a wholesome attempt by Mum and Dad to teach their only daughter independence. Allegedly it had been working, too, right up until Viola disappeared.

By eight o'clock, forty-five minutes after Viola was due home, and with no answer to repeated calls and texts, both parents had been out, driving her route. By nine, the first desperate call to local police was made, and by the next afternoon, the official missing person's report filed.

Investigators established that Viola's mobile had been switched off immediately after sending the text home, as it hadn't triangulated its position after that, fuelling speculation that her disappearance was more likely a reckless adventure with some secret boyfriend than kidnap, although such contention lent meagre comfort to Mum and Dad.

For them began the pattern of growing panic, where progressively worse best-case scenarios came and went. Two weeks in, with television appeals for Viola or anyone with information to make contact unanswered, *second*-worst nightmares were starting to look pretty good. Pure abduction, even *injury*, bettered death.

Unfortunately, those meagre hopes had shattered the previous night, when liaison officers arrived at their door, asking them to formally identify the cold, lifeless form that had once been their child.

With a positive ID in place, and a clear connection to the other bodies found in close proximity, Hawkins had adopted responsibility for what was now a murder investigation. But she had decided not to approach the Clarksons personally at this stage, who would no doubt press for more information about their daughter's murder than she was allowed to provide. Withholding necessarily classified details regarding a killer's MO was neither easy nor pleasant; the most suitable alternative being to solve the case, and at least present the family with answers backed by the possibility of some justice. So she had chosen to focus first on Viola's last hours, a trail that began with the last available sighting of the victim herself.

On Hawkins' instruction, the night shift had already scrutinised every minute of CCTV from Viola's homeward-bound journey on the day she died, a task already completed by the missing persons team, but it was best to be sure. They had managed to pick up one camera site missed by the original investigators, at a small convenience store near the bus stop, but still the results of both checks tallied.

Viola had been caught on CCTV a few times before boarding the bus from outside Barking College towards Ilford, but due to its upmarket, out-of-town location, the roads around her employers' home were covered by precious few cameras, and none that showed the early parts of Viola's walk to, or boarding of, the relevant bus home. Neither did the news improve.

Despite the end of her journey being covered by a number of CCTV stations – one near her alighting bus stop, several on her walk along a wide avenue called Broadway, and another near home on Gascoigne Road – at no stage had Viola passed any of these lenses that night. Her regular bus paused at several stops, but there was no sign of her leaving the vehicle, and no way to tell if she had still been on board. Also complicating matters was the fact that her regular route, the 366 from Ilford to Barking, was generally busy, running every twelve minutes in the evenings, putting no pressure on Viola to catch a particular bus if she was early or late, and decreasing the odds of a specific driver remembering her.

But first they needed to establish at which point Viola had deviated from her normal route home, however voluntary that action might have been. It was something the missing persons team hadn't been able to establish, although Hawkins doubted that every possibility would have been followed up, given that until last night it had been lumped in with every other case of defiant teenagers deserting home, and neglecting to inform a predictably distressed mum and dad.

Maguire arrived beside her. 'Need a piggyback?'

'No.' Hawkins released her steadying grip on the 4x4's wing.

'Only you look a little unstable.'

'That's down to the job, not the boots.' She cast off and began negotiating the shingle towards the front door. Mike followed, throwing in the occasional '*Whoa there!*' whenever she listed. Hawkins ignored him, eventually reaching the safety of the ruthlessly garlanded porch.

There was a protracted pause between the bell being rung and the lady of the house finally opening the door, although Hawkins had experienced similar behaviour too many times to be surprised. Situations involving death in suspicious circumstances made those caught up in the subsequent investigation understandably nervous. The natural assumption was that, unless they had a cast-iron alibi, secondary acquaintances like colleagues and employers made easy targets, and that any inconsistencies in stories between husbands and wives who, for example, had previously employed the deceased, would provoke immediate distrust. The hiatus would have been used for last-ditch alignment of collective memory, which often made the events most clearly described worth challenging.

At last the door swung inwards, and an anxious-looking woman peered around it. She looked fiftyish, and might well have been the trophy wife Hawkins had envisaged, once. Recent stress might have accounted for the dark circles showing through her expensive make-up, but she wasn't ageing well.

'Helen Shawcross?' Hawkins asked when no verbal greeting was offered. Receiving a terse nod in reply, she continued, 'DCI Antonia Hawkins and DI Mike Maguire. We spoke on the phone.'

Their host nodded again and stepped back, allowing them to pass. They crossed a brightly decorated hallway that smelled of new paint and cigarettes, to emerge in a large kitchen with an island and great swathes of pristine white worktop. On the far side of the room, a suited man perhaps five or ten years Helen's elder turned to face them, his expression one of discontent as he drained a cup. Hawkins watched his head incline, half expecting the remarkably thick black hair on his crown to drop off.

'Mr Shawcross?' She moved towards him once the danger had passed, offering a hand, introducing herself and Maguire again.

He insisted on being called Keith and half-smiled as

they shook hands, but the eyes said he was unimpressed by the short-notice request for a chat.

Hawkins watched his wife slide quietly into view nearby. 'Apologies for disrupting your day. I'm told you're aware of the latest developments in our search for Viola Clarkson.'

Mister replied, in what Hawkins now picked out as a carefully veiled Yorkshire accent: 'That's right. The officer previously dealing with the case was good enough to call first thing this morning. Tragic, of course, but I still don't see what it has to do with my wife and me, or why we're now explaining ourselves again to different officers.'

She ignored his undertone. 'Well, Keith, as I'm sure you can appreciate, this is now a murder enquiry, hence the change of investigation team. It affects you and Helen because current information suggests that you may have been the last people to see Viola alive.'

'Oh.' Shawcross broke eye contact at last, looking at his wife. 'You'd better speak to her about it, then. I was at work that evening, where I should have been half an hour ago, in fact.'

She let his abruptness pass again. 'So you didn't see Miss Clarkson at all on the night she disappeared?'

He gave a curt nod. 'The girl came once a week to help my wife clean; I work late to pay for it, along with everything else, which I think you'll find concludes my involvement.'

He moved to leave, but Hawkins blocked his path. 'How well did you know Viola?'

The accountant frowned. 'We passed the time of day. She was only here because her father works for me. He asked if I'd give her work experience, and being the charitable type I agreed. Only she wasn't the brightest bulb in the chandelier, so she ended up here, polishing floors.'

Hawkins nodded. 'When did you last see her?'

'We talked briefly when she first came to my practice, and a couple of times the following week when she struggled with basic accounting, at which point I suggested she help Helen instead, for the same money, of course. That must have been two months ago. Since then I haven't been home in time for our paths to cross.' He raised a hand, requesting passage. 'I have meetings, so if there's nothing else . . .'

'Thanks for your time.' Hawkins moved aside, handing him a card. 'We'll be in touch, but please let us know if you remember anything that could be relevant.'

Shawcross agreed and lumbered into the hall, without acknowledging the existence of his wife. He collected a briefcase from the carpet and disappeared outside, closing the door gently behind him.

Hawkins watched his shadow retreat through the frosted glass and turned to Mrs Shawcross, who was lighting a cigarette from a gilt-edged pack unrecognisable enough to be expensive. 'So, Helen, you *did* see Viola on the night she disappeared.'

Their host blew smoke out of her nose, and replied in a chafing tone that implied a twenty-a-day habit: 'I let her in when she got here, if that's what you mean.'

Hawkins savoured the fusty aroma, now craving a drag. A manic work schedule was the only thing that kept her currently dormant habit at bay, but secondary smoke was still a guilty pleasure. 'Did you talk?'

'I told her the lounge needed cleaning, then I went upstairs.'

'No pleasantries?'

'No.'

'Your husband said Viola *helped* you. That sounds as if you were normally here when she came.'

'Normally, yes.'

'What were your impressions of her?'

Their host took a longer pull on the cigarette and stared at the high-gloss cupboards before answering. 'She never said much to me, and I don't like to pry. I suppose she was polite enough when we did talk.'

Hawkins wondered if she was being deliberately vague. 'Any particular subjects spring to mind?'

'No. But she was late more than once; usually said the bus hadn't turned up. Wasn't keen to make up the time, though; out the door on the stroke of six thirty, rain or shine.'

Hawkins suppressed a sigh, mentally condemning her interviewee. She scanned the spotless kitchen for signs of benevolence – kids' drawings stuck to the fridge; soft toys rammed into wine racks by marauding grandchildren; anything that denoted a stake in the lives of others. There were none. Then she realised that, until a few days ago, her own house had fitted the same profile.

She softened, and was preparing her next question when the doorbell rang.

'Sorry.' Shawcross left the room. But when she returned a moment later, instead of the package Hawkins expected her to be carrying, their host wasn't alone.

A young man followed her into the kitchen. He looked early twenties, his skin still bearing the remnants of juvenile acne, and he wore half-mast jeans with a black polo shirt, the letters *CSS* picked out in white above the pocket. He made a fleeting scan of Hawkins and Maguire before turning to Shawcross, the look on his face somewhere between hesitation and panic.

'Oh.' Shawcross realised that Hawkins' cocked head meant an explanation was required. 'This is Martin, Viola's . . . replacement. He works for the firm who clean Keith's offices. He's covering here, until we find someone else.'

'Hello, Martin.' Hawkins moved closer, introducing herself and Mike for the third time in half an hour. 'Did you know Viola Clarkson at all?'

There was an awkward pause as the young man's eyes darted from her, past Maguire, and came to rest on his employer.

At last Shawcross answered for him. 'No. He joined the company last week.'

Martin looked back, just about managing a nod of confirmation.

'Fine,' Hawkins said. 'Could we have some privacy, then?'

Trepidation flared again in the young man's expression. He twitched, but stayed rooted.

Shawcross cleared her throat. 'Start with the bedrooms today.'

Relief burst visibly as Martin backed out of the room and disappeared, poorly fitted jeans rasping as he drifted upstairs.

'Another of Keith's strays,' Helen explained when he'd gone. 'Scared of his own shadow, but he does a damn-sight better job than—' She stopped, clearly thinking better of slating the dead.

Hawkins gave a stoic nod. Cleaners weren't hard to find, of course, but considering that until the previous night Viola had only been *missing*, no time had been wasted in finding a replacement, reinforcing the suggestion that this woman had barely given a thought to her employee *after* death, let alone before. But the line of enquiry was still worth pursuing.

She regarded Shawcross. 'Did you ever discuss personal issues with Viola, mates or boyfriends, for instance?'

The woman frowned. 'How is that relevant?'

Hawkins felt her eyebrows rise.

Fortunately, Maguire knew her expressions well enough to step in. 'Well, ma'am, we need to establish how and when Viola went missing, trace anyone who might've seen her later that night. Say she was meant to hook up with friends after work that day. Maybe she left a little early, took a different route, caught another bus. Anything unusual helps.'

'Look,' Helen Shawcross reached for the crystal ash-tray on the side, dragged it closer, 'I didn't know the girl, she came once a week, made an average job of cleaning the toilets, and left. I wanted a professional. It was my husband's idea to take her on.'

Hawkins chose to summarise, because her patience was beginning to wane. 'So on the night she went missing, Viola arrived and left on time, seemed neither stressed nor preoccupied, cleaned your house in regular, sub-standard fashion and left, mentioning nothing about going anywhere other than straight home.'

Shawcross suppressed a cough. 'Right.'

'Did you see her leave?'

'I heard the door go from upstairs.'

'What time was that?'

'Six thirty on the dot, like I said.'

'And did you see which way she went along this road?'

Their host shook her head.

'Well then . . .' Hawkins produced another card, positioned it on the granite island, ' . . . we'll leave you in peace.' She turned without hesitation, and was waiting beside the Range Rover when Maguire caught up. She watched the front door close firmly as her DI approached the car.

'That was the best example of community policing I've seen all day.' He grinned and unlocked the doors. 'No contest.'

Hawkins didn't rise as they took their seats. 'So Viola left here at normal time, and frankly why wouldn't she?

Then she texted her mum to say she was heading home. That means either she had plans she wanted to keep secret, which then went awry, or that she was abducted somewhere along the way.'

'Right.' Mike started the engine. 'But unless we dredge up some new CCTV that shows where Viola deviated from her normal route, we're fresh outta luck.'

'Not quite.' Hawkins watched the windows as they backed off the drive, but Helen Shawcross obviously trusted them to fuck off without supervision. 'I want officers out here, knocking at every house along the sections of Viola's route she did on foot.' She waved at the houses now sliding past. 'There must be an army of dirty old men living around here who enjoy watching attractive young girls saunter by, especially if it's at a regular time every week. Get uniform down here, and tell them to keep looking until we find someone who saw her pass. If we can narrow the window in which she must have disappeared, at least it'll focus the rest of the investigation.'

'Sure, boss.' Mike flicked on the wipers as spots of rain began hitting the screen. 'Unpopularity hangs OK with you, huh?'

Hawkins frowned as her handbag started to ring. 'I've got three dead bodies, two IDs, and no idea how any of them ended up buried in the bloody woods, so until we get a handle on this case, yes, unpopularity is just fine with me.'

35

'Gin,' Ash said flatly, and began laying out his hand.

Rupert sighed and placed his cards on the creaky wooden table, spacing them out in groups of three and four, the way his friend liked. Some curled at the edges, making it hard to read their faces in the narrow beam from Ash's dad's old army lamp. The battered metal box sat wedged in a hole in the wall, patches of rust showing through its flaking green paint, light from its large silver eye dim because Rupert didn't have enough money this week for new batteries.

He put the last card in place and looked at his friend for approval.

'For fuck's sake.' Ash stood suddenly, screeching his chair backwards across the floorboards, making Rupert flinch. He pointed at the cards. 'You're not even sorting them right.'

He leaned over and began rearranging the piles, checking to make sure Rupert was watching. 'How many times? Runs of three or four from the same suit, or sets of the same value card.' He banged the last one into place and sat down, started making notes on his pad. 'How am I supposed to work out the fucking points if you can't even follow basic rules?'

Rupert stared at the floor, wanting to tell Ash that he hated cards. He rarely understood the rules, or why winning every game made Ash so cross. But he'd spoken up before, and only made things worse. Besides, he had just two pounds left, and the game would end when he ran out.

Ash dumped the notepad and pencil. 'You owe me a quid.'

Slowly Rupert picked up one of his coins and placed it in his friend's outstretched hand. Ash snatched the money and stuffed it in his pocket. Then he gathered all the cards and shuffled them, staring at Rupert the whole time.

He began dealing two new hands. 'Last game. And this time you'd better fucking concentrate.'

Rupert took his cards in silence, careful not to meet Ash's eyes, and started grouping the numbers and kinds. Outside he could hear the wind lashing the dirty old house. Now and again small puffs of debris fell through gaps in the ceiling, as if the place was trying to frighten them, tell them to leave. It was a horrible night, but it might get even worse.

Ash was in one of his moods, had been all afternoon. He only stayed here when things got really bad at home, and Rupert had spotted his sleeping bag laid out in the corner, so it must have been one of those days. Rupert's watch said it was almost eight thirty, the time he needed to leave in order to get home for curfew at nine. But tonight he was worried Ash might force him to stay, as he'd already threatened a couple of times. The place was horrid in darkness.

Since finishing their GCSEs, they'd spent a few weekends over the summer, boarding up the smashed windows and blocking off some of the doors, trying to make the rooms a bit warmer, stop the wind rushing through downstairs. Ash still said the place wasn't haunted, but Rupert had never known a house to make such terrible noises, screeching and banging through the night.

'It's your go, stupid.'

Rupert looked up to find Ash glaring at him again. Quickly he reached out and took a card from the pile, placing another back down. Ash watched him without blinking, slowly removing his *lucky cigarette from behind his ear and lighting up, flicking the embers on to the floor.*

Their game continued in silence, as Rupert watched the time slip past eight thirty; tried to concentrate like Ash said. Somehow his cards began to fall into groups, more easily than they usually did. Two kings were joined by a third, three clubs became four, and when he collected an eight to add to the others, it took him a moment to realise he'd finished.

He looked up as Ash reached for the pile, excited to have done as he was told. He'd kept his mind on the game and made two sets of three and a four. If winning made Ash miserable, surely this would cheer him up.

'Gin,' he announced, holding out his cards.

Ash's fingers stopped over the deck. He looked up. 'What did you say?'

'G . . . Gin,' Rupert repeated, placing his winning hand down.

Ash stared at the cards, his eyes flicking left and right over them. He put his cigarette down on the table, burning end over the edge, and linked his hands in front of his chin. Eventually he spoke, his voice so quiet that Rupert hardly heard it.

'Cheat.'

Rupert stared back at his friend. The room shrank around them, and shadows swirled as the army light flickered.

He shook his head. 'I d . . . didn't . . .'

'No?' Ash leaned over the table. He grabbed Rupert's sleeve and yanked it. 'Come on, idiot, where are they?'

None of it made any sense.

Ash let go and banged his fist on the table. 'Tell me, you little shit, or I'll make you wish you had.'

The tears were coming now, hot traces stinging Rupert's cheeks. But Ash's glare didn't ease. He sniffed.

'Put your arm on the table.'

Slowly, Rupert did as he said.

Ash took hold of his wrist, turned the palm up and pinned his hand down with a knee. He slid Rupert's sleeve up to the elbow. 'Keep still, or I'll fucking kill you.'

Then he picked up his cigarette and ground the glowing end into Rupert's bare forearm.

Lightning shot through Rupert's skin. He screamed. The table screeched and juddered as he jerked left and right, but Ash didn't let go.

'That's what you get for cheating,' he growled, screwing the butt down even harder.

Rupert felt himself shaking as the room turned red. Something exploded inside him, and then he was standing, wrenching his arm back. A roar burst from his throat as he slammed both hands into Ash's chest, launching him backwards with a frozen look of fear on his face. The cigarette spun away, leaving a trail of sparks in the air.

Everything moved in slow motion as Ash hit the rickety wall, breaking the surface and half crashing through it, chunks of dry plaster falling away. There was a bang as the army light dropped from its ledge on to the floor. Its beam flickered but stayed on, although it was now pointing upwards, casting its glare at the ceiling, leaving the rest of the room even darker.

But as quickly as it had come, the redness lifted and Rupert stumbled forwards, calling out to Ash.

His friend lay slumped in the gap he'd made, like a puppet hung up for the night. Rupert shouted to him again, as waterfalls of dust and debris rained down between them. A heavy crunch made Rupert jump. He looked up to find the ceiling sagging above them, tearing itself away from the wall.

'Ash!' he yelled, reaching out to grab his friend's clothing, trying to haul him upright. Ash didn't respond.

Another bang as a slab of ceiling landed inches away.

Petrified, Rupert gripped his friend's arm and wrenched. They crumpled together in the centre of the floor.

Rupert scrambled to his feet, pulling Ash up and dragging him towards the hall. They neared the door as a louder crash came from the hallway. The whole place seemed to shake as Rupert struggled into the passage.

He kept going until they were clear, and dry grass crunched under his feet. Then he stopped and lowered Ash to the ground, turning back to look at the house against its background of towering, shadowy trees. A pale glow from the army lamp crept out through gaps in the boarded-up windows. The noises from inside had finally stopped.

They were safe.

But the same moment kept repeating itself in his mind; the moment that would haunt him for years. The reason he'd never been back.

He'd done something terrible that night; allowed his anger to break free, a fury he couldn't hold back. He'd lost control, harmed his friend. If Ash forgave him, he'd never do it again.

Except his fear ran deeper than that.

His mother had been right: there *was* evil here. He'd felt it on his first visit, growing stronger every time he returned, slowly building into an unstoppable force.

But the thing that scared him most was *where* that evil had grown. Because it wasn't in the house, like his mother thought.

The evil was growing *in* him.

36

'For fuck's sake.' Hawkins looked down at their latest corpse. 'This makes four. In a sodding week.'

'Sure does.' Mike glanced around, as if her French might have upset the locals. He had just returned from the ground floor of Haringey mortuary to join her in the basement, where banks of stainless steel doors marked the place out as cold storage for London's recently deceased.

She regarded him impatiently as he tucked his mobile back into the breast pocket of his sharp charcoal suit. 'Did you get hold of the station who responded to the call?'

'Yeah.'

'So who is he?' Hawkins realised her tone conveyed irritation, still frustrated by the morning's events: mainly because they were viewing this corpse at eleven in the morning instead of eight, and at the mortuary instead of the scene where it had been buried in the early hours of that day. The reasons for these particular annoyances were that the local shift officers who attended the scene had bugger-all knowledge of their ongoing investigation. As with most other admittedly stretched forces these days, only senior officers took an interest in major homicide cases outside of their own jurisdiction. Which meant no connection to the umbrella investigation had been made until the resident inspector started his day shift at eight thirty, by reading reports of overnight events from his team.

At that point he'd called Hawkins, who was on the system as Senior Investigating Officer, just after she and Maguire had left the Shawcrosses' house in Ilford, to tell her the unhappy news. All he'd known at that stage was that someone had buried a body in nearby Stony Wood, fortunately an occurrence still unusual enough to remind him of the report he'd read earlier in the week about recent events in Havering.

The upsides were that, thanks to a teenage student named Lionel Andrews, who happened to be filming wildlife in the woods at the time, they'd known about the body straight away, plus it gave them a witness of sorts. Unbelievably, Andrews had watched the body being buried, and called it straight in. Thanks to a quiet night on other fronts, an incident van had been on site within the hour, to excavate the body and move it here before sunrise. The preliminary coroner's report said the corpse showed signs of recent widespread bruising to the body and legs, as well as the now familiar scratching to arms and face, along with traces of Benzodiazepines in the blood. There was no doubt he was the killer's number four, but they'd have to wait for the full post-mortem to reveal at what stage the various injuries had been sustained.

Hawkins would have preferred to see the corpse in situ, of course, as she had its predecessors, though at least swift refrigeration meant any evidence recoverable from the corpse would be field-fresh for the autopsy scheduled to begin at midday.

Here, however, the cons came flooding in behind. First, all the witness could tell them about the body's depositor was that it had been an adult male, wearing some sort of night-vision goggles and black clothes, although at least this evidence suggested they were after a single perpetrator, rather than two or more. Neither had their witness seen the vehicle used to transport this victim to the scene. *Sounded like a petrol car* was the best he could do.

And finally, the fact their killer used a new location to dispose of this body, and hadn't prepared the grave in advance, meant he could have been forced to change his plans at short notice, even though no pre-dug graves had yet been found elsewhere. This also indicated that he was not only aware of their investigation, but also capable of adapting to stay one step ahead.

'You receiving me over there, boss?' Mike's voice cut her silent deliberations, highlighting the fact she'd asked him a question, and then completely tuned out.

'Sorry,' she refocused, 'keeping my head on anything's a challenge at the moment.'

Since Operation Cavalier had broken three days ago, Hawkins had hardly looked at her other assignments. She had a lead on a robbery gone bad at an off-licence in Hackney, leaving three bystanders dead, plus a series of nasty rape-murders that smelled gang-related, and had been hanging around unsolved for almost a month.

Superintendent Vaughn was already twitchy about that one, but for the moment, with bodies popping up at such an alarming rate, this investigation demanded her full attention.

Not that she was being rewarded for it, of course. Since their unsatisfactory interview with Viola Clarkson's former employers earlier that morning, no positive progress had been made. Door-to-door checks along Viola's route from the Shawcrosses' house to the bus stop had yielded no witnesses at all, while ongoing enquiries regarding the identity of the unnamed victim still hadn't produced any leads.

Hopefully the update Maguire was about to give her would start turning things around.

'No sweat.' Mike shrugged, repeating himself. 'I spoke to the sergeant who went to check out the call. He thought it was gonna be a waste of time; expected to find Andrews whacked out on drugs, having hallucinated the whole thing. But he found freshly packed earth right where the kid said. He stressed that no one's ID'd this guy yet, but they think it's Raymond Jewis, retired sixty-six-year-old from Lambourne End. Fits the description given by the daughter, who rang the local cops an hour ago to report him missing. Nobody realised till then, because the wife has advanced Alzheimer's; didn't even notice he'd gone. Daughter rang the house last night but got no answer, so she called a local friend who went over this morning to find Mr Jewis already AWOL. Wife was upstairs in bed; hadn't got up, even to use the bathroom, in twenty-four hours.'

Hawkins grimaced. 'Is she OK?'

'As OK as she gets, I guess.'

She nodded, her mind flicking to her own father, and the increasing regularity with which he made excuses for forgetting names, shared memories, or where he'd left pretty much anything. She shook off her worry, tried to focus on the case. 'So how was Jewis taken?'

'Unknown, though apparently he was a keen amateur photographer. Daughter says he spent a lot of time in Hainault Forest, just up the road from his house. Area's real quiet, apparently, so if he was out there alone taking pictures, he'd have made easy meat.'

'What about timings?'

'Sketchy right now, but the medics who checked the wife say she can't have been home alone far over a day. Often as not, if no one fed her she didn't eat; so much longer and they'd have been dealing with malnutrition.'

Hawkins did some quick maths in her head. 'So Pete Barnes and Viola Clarkson were both taken twenty-four hours before being killed and dumped, and it looks like Jewis's timeline is broadly the same. That puts a three- or four-day gap between each person being taken, including the day each was held before being killed.'

'That figures, but what does it mean?'

She snorted. 'Buggered if I know. Are the gaps just because it's taking him that long to find each victim, or is there something else going on?'

'Right, and what's with the twenty-four-hour captivity thing? What's he doing with them?'

'We need to speak to Hunter again. I'll see if he's available later, but I want to get back to Hendon and update Vaughn in person.' She rolled her eyes. 'I'm sure he'll take our latest shitty news with typical good grace. Can you handle things till I get back?'

Mike assented, and they began walking back to find the mortuary attendant. 'If it's cool with you, boss, I'll pull the guys off Viola Clarkson for now, free up some assets to get a formal ID on Jewis, talk to the wife and daughter, and ask around to find out when he was last seen near the house. By the time you're done with the big man, we should have some results from the post-mortem.'

'Fine.' Hawkins pushed open the door to the stairs. 'Update me if the search crews come up with anything.'

A team had already been cobbled together and deployed in Stony Wood to look for more graves, though Hawkins was still clinging to the hope that this was the killer's first deposit there, in a move necessitated by the discovery of his earlier victims in White Post Wood. Hence his decision to dig the grave upon arrival.

Because if there were bodies scattered all over Stony Wood, too, the implications didn't bear thinking about.

37

Tristan Vaughn looked up from behind the monitor on his desk. 'Say that again.'

Hawkins considered rephrasing her statement – the true purpose behind her end-of-the-day visit to the DCS's office – but quickly concluded that there was no other way to say it. So she simply repeated herself. 'We should go public.'

Vaughn gave an incredulous chuckle. 'Just clarify something for me. By *public*, you mean releasing full details of this killer's MO. The kidnapping, the twenty-four-hour imprisonment, the drugging slash starvation, and the hunting down bit in the forest.'

Hawkins hesitated, not having phrased it quite so bluntly in her head. Now her commanding officer had said it, suddenly she could picture the front pages. But her last chance for a U-turn, or even a tempered proposal, had already passed.

'Yes, sir.'

His brow dropped a good inch. 'That's what I thought.'

He stood, reaching full statuesque height – at least six inches taller than Hawkins – and turned to look out of the window. The immediate view from the third floor of Becke House was hardly beautiful, starting on a low with the car park, improving slightly in the middle distance, where it encompassed the distant rooftops of Hendon's western fringe.

Silence fell.

Hawkins glanced around the room while she waited for a decision. The Chief Superintendent's office was a much brighter place since the advent of Vaughn's regime. Where his predecessor had preferred dark colours, eighteenth-century paintings and permanently lowered window blinds, the current DCS favoured daylight and crisp modern art. Compared to the previous incumbent, Vaughn's demeanour was also refreshingly weightless. Except today.

Hawkins' train of thought broke as he rotated back to face her, clearly prepared to continue their discussion.

'As I'm sure you appreciate, my concern is whether releasing these details will create public panic.' He moved back to the desk. 'I'm going to need a substantial upside.'

'Well, sir.' Hawkins tried to make her thoughts sound unrehearsed. 'We've reported three deaths in as many days now, and tomorrow news of the fourth will break. So far no witnesses have come forward, because the appeals were restricted to the area where each victim disappeared, as we tried not to spook the killer. But he's already changed where he's burying them, so he must know we're on to him. We should capitalise on the shock factor; use the press to our advantage before someone beats us to it and the opportunity's lost. Let's steal a march and release the facts voluntarily. That way the story's about these murders, and not about our choice to cover them up. It might be just sensational enough to reel in some new witnesses.' She took a breath. 'It might be the break we need.'

Vaughn let her finish. 'Or the moment we all regret.'

He sat down, put both elbows on the desk, and massaged his temples with his fingertips. A long time seemed to pass before he drew breath and spoke again.

'I'm going to trust your judgement on this. Go ahead and release the information. I just hope for both our sakes it has the desired effect.'

'Thank you, sir. I'll send you the press release for approval as soon as it's done.' She turned to leave.

'Antonia?' Vaughn said as she reached the door, waiting for her to look round. 'Sometimes I wish your male colleagues had balls as big as yours.'

38

Hawkins eased her chair away from her desk and stood, waiting for the laptop to shut down. She had spent the last half-hour reviewing the surfeit of information now rammed into the investigation file, hoping for fresh inspiration. Phone and text message records; social media and bank account histories of the deceased; information gleaned from door-to-door checks near the burial sites; interview sessions with family and friends.

All to no avail.

Her last hope had been that Lauren Coleman might volunteer something to the family liaison officer Hawkins had dispatched earlier that evening to check on her.

Her intentions were honest, of course, conscious that their investigation had stirred up a potentially hazardous situation for the young woman, only for new discoveries to then drag Met interest, and therefore its protection, away. But that didn't make it wrong to give her conscience another nudge.

Fortunately, Lauren had been fine, according to the phone call Hawkins received as the liaison officer left. But she'd also maintained her silence, however tactical it might be, on all the questions still hanging over the case.

And Hawkins was still waiting for a response from Vaughn regarding the final draft of the press release she'd mailed over, including the alterations he'd specified. Its real emphasis was a fresh appeal for witnesses to any of the abductions so far. A description of whoever was taking these people, or even the vehicle he used, would be a major breakthrough. So far they had only approximate locations for two of the four kidnappings, and footage of none.

Once satisfied, the DCS would forward it to the press office, who would distribute the information to the British media.

Then she just had to hope the rewards outweighed any backlash.

She yawned and stretched, looking up at the mucky tiles of her office ceiling, ambivalent about her decision to leave for the day. It was almost seven thirty, and self-preservation said it was time to stop flogging herself; time to go home, to eat and try to relax. Common sense, however, maintained that returning to an environment spilling over with stress of its own wouldn't help.

She had approached Siobhan again before leaving for work that morning, hoping her sister would at least have rung a few letting agencies over the past few days, making good on the promise that her stay would be strictly short-term. Typically, a child-related crisis had presented itself at the perfect moment, swiftly becoming the one time since their arrival that Siobhan had shown interest in her constantly skirmishing young.

And so, unbelievably, here was Hawkins twelve hours later, loitering in her office, contemplating something that, in contrast to most of her colleagues, had barely crossed her mind since joining the force. As she closed the lid on her laptop, she was on the verge of calling Mike . . .

And hitting the pub.

Right now, a gastro meal and a few glasses of wine in adult company, not having to break up juvenile fist-fights or being pestered to *watch my new dance* for the hundredth time, surrounded by Disney memorabilia and half-finished bowls of alphabet spaghetti, sounded pretty damn good. It might not clear her mind of the case altogether, but pinballing back and forth between two chaotic environments just wasn't healthy. Yet regardless of whether her audacious plan to fling open the proverbial doors on the case bore positive results or not, she needed a clear head to deal with the fallout.

Technically she was still on probation, full promotion to DCI level still two weeks from permanent ink, and requiring Vaughn's signature. Mercifully, he hadn't mentioned the fact in their first meeting of the day, but high-profile gaffes tended not to travel up the chain of command without being noticed.

Still, the press release was the right thing to do.

The fact was that four bodies had appeared in less than ninety-six hours, with no guarantee they'd yet found the earliest example, or that the perpetrator would stop there. Identifying three of the four victims had been hard enough, thanks to the killer's practice of stripping the bodies and burying them in various secluded woodlands, which meant there were no personal effects, and that DNA evidence was muddied at best. The families and friends of Peter Barnes and Viola Clarkson had produced almost no leads towards any kind of suspect, with no guarantee that the loved ones of body number four, recently confirmed as Raymond Jewis, would deliver anything more. One victim remained unidentified, and they still had no idea how or from where the unlucky four had disappeared, mainly because whoever was taking them had a knack for doing it away from electronic prying eyes.

Every time it felt like they might be nearing answers, someone dug another corpse out of the dirt, and the nightmare cycle started again. On top of that, the homes of the dead they *had* identified were spread across North London, and things were happening so fast that the team was already stretched to breaking point. But if she went to Vaughn for support four days into a new case, regardless of how challenging the situation might be, it wasn't going to look great.

Timing was critical. Get it right, by deploying exactly the right amount of force when required to bag a baddie, and you were a hero. Get it wrong, by missing the key opportunity to react, and your reputation could be damaged for good.

Yet in some respects the investigation was perfect: high-profile enough once cracked to reinforce her full installation as DCI; sufficiently low-key to avoid attention from the Commissioner's new multi-jurisdictional task forces.

But with an escalating body count, such exclusivity would be short-lived. While it had been a relief to conduct the investigation away from the public spotlight, the corresponding lack of pressure on her superiors meant the proverbial purse strings that funded extra personnel weren't being pulled.

With each new victim it became less likely that they were either linked or targeted, thereby fuelling Hunter's theory about this being some kind of sport for the killer, prey selected at random, purely for convenience. All the bodies showed signs of desperate flight prior to death, while some had been physically abused during the twenty-four-hour captivity all had endured. Hawkins shuddered when she thought about them: trapped, tortured, petrified. Then set loose, to be hunted down like game.

The latest complication came in the form of Raymond Jewis. Confirming their early suspicions, now that Mike had spoken to the deceased's family, the most likely scenario was that the sixty-something hiker and amateur photographer had been out walking in Hainault Forest when he was snatched. And approximately twenty-four hours later, his battered remains were dumped thirty miles away in Stony Wood. Two rural locations hardly brimming over with witnesses or CCTV.

Hence her bid for press coverage.

Hawkins collected her things and left her office, heading for the exit. She began crossing the floor as clattering doors marked the arrival of two young constables, both creasing up. One had an arm twisted behind his back, clearly impersonating a memorable arrest as he stumbled theatrically.

'*D'you know who the fuck I am?*' he squawked, trying not to laugh, freezing when he looked up, following his colleague's stare towards Hawkins.

He stood, straightening his shirt. 'Sorry, ma'am.'

She nodded, letting them scarper without reprimand, pausing to look around the Serious Incident Suite. The large open-plan area took up most of the second floor at Becke House, desks and investigation boards plastered with names, dates and high-definition photos of the repulsive things human beings did to each other.

For once the place was almost deserted, shift change having happened long enough ago that most of the teams were now out in the field; only a few jaded faces reflecting their monitors' glow in the darkened corners where sensor-operated lights had gone out.

Hawkins was about to resume her journey towards the frosted exit doors when she caught sight of familiar dark hair twisted into a bun, and found herself staring across the room at the back of one of her team.

She wandered over, clearing her throat. 'Amala? I thought you left an hour ago.'

'No, ma'am.' Yasir looked up from the impressive four-screen display she was using as Hawkins arrived beside her. 'I've been waiting ages for a go on here.'

'Aren't you youngsters usually in the Dog and Dragon by now?'

Yasir smiled. 'Not really my scene. Anyway, you have to come out of hours if you want to get your hands on this kit.' She waved at the pin-sharp images. 'Fantastic, isn't it?'

Hawkins studied the floating bank of flat-panel monitors, recently installed in a bespoke perspex cubicle between two windows along the north wall, recognising a couple of the CCTV camera angles being displayed. She pointed at a high-mounted shot with house-lined pavements stretching downhill into the distance. 'Isn't that Viola Clarkson's road?'

'Yep.' Amala leaned nearer, studying a lone figure approaching slowly from the rear of frame, tutting as it came close enough to be recognisable as someone other than the victim.

'We've already checked this footage.' Hawkins looked at the time signature in the bottom corner of each frame: just before seven p.m. – the early end of the window when Viola would have been arriving home. 'Nothing was found.'

Amala glanced up, obviously catching her confusion. 'This footage isn't from the day Viola disappeared; it's from the previous week.' She continued as Hawkins' frown deepened. 'Everyone presumed she came from this direction because it's the most direct, but we don't actually know. What if she popped into a friend's house or went via a local shop? I called Viola's parents earlier. Neither of them knew her exact route . . .'

'You're trying to find her arriving home the week before.'

Yasir smiled. 'You always say we should check our facts, ma'am.'

'Nice thinking. It'll speed things up if I help.'

Hawkins grabbed a chair and took the screens on

the left, covering the main aspect nearest the Clarkson residence, and the camera positioned above the bus stop. Amala had one camera further along Gascoigne Road, and a second covering the corner between the bus stop and Viola's street.

With only two screens for them each to assess, Yasir cranked up the speed, and they sat largely in silence, occasionally drawing each other's attention to figures entering their respective views, at which point they slowed the footage and zoomed in. But as time on the cameras rolled past seven p.m., despite regular buses and the resulting foot traffic as people returned home after work, there was still no sign of Viola.

Fatigue was soon nagging at Hawkins, and the images started to blur. She rubbed her eyes one at a time, still glancing back and forth between the displays, but she kicked herself when Amala pointed at one of her screens, obviously watching all four. 'There she is.'

Hawkins squinted, leaning closer, barely able to make out the figure in shadow towards the rear of shot. 'Wow, your eyesight's better than mine. Are you sure it's her?'

'Must be.' Yasir brought up the menu bar and scrolled forwards until Viola Clarkson was right under the lens, waiting for a break in the traffic on the pavement opposite home. The time signature said 19:15.

Hawkins recognised the seventeen-year-old, wearing the same denim jacket as in the Facebook profile picture they were due to use for a witness appeal in tomorrow's papers.

'I guess that's it, then.' Amala sat back and folded her arms. 'This is obviously Viola's regular route, so she would have passed these cameras on the day she died. If she'd made it back.'

Hawkins nodded, now massaging her neck.

Yasir went on. 'Which means that either she didn't make it on to the bus in the first place, or she got off at a different stop, voluntarily or otherwi—'

'Wait,' Hawkins interrupted, reaching for the controls. 'How do you rewind this thing?'

Amala showed her before sliding aside. Hawkins wound the film backwards at double speed, sending Viola back the way she had come. 'Where did you first see her?'

The sergeant stood and tapped the pavement behind the retreating figure. 'About here. Why?'

'Because we didn't see her get off the bus.'

Hawkins kept going; eyes locked on Viola as she passed the position Amala had indicated. Admittedly she was tired; maybe not watching the screens as closely as she could have been. But she hadn't seen *anyone* exit the last bus that had pulled over to collect passengers before Yasir had spotted Viola, even though the stop was right under a street light. *Surely she would have noticed that.*

On screen the teenage girl was still retreating, becoming harder to pick out as distant shadows enveloped her. Seconds later she disappeared into the darkness at the rear of shot. Simultaneously both detectives shifted focus to the bottom right screen, which showed the tributary view across Gascoigne Road from an adjacent street. Parked cars lined the far pavement, beyond which Hawkins expected to see Viola ghosting through the back of shot. Traffic jerked back and forth in the foreground.

But Viola didn't pass.

The seconds stretched, and Hawkins glanced back at the original screen, wondering if she had misinterpreted the camera's position. There appeared to be only one street on the corresponding side, and she followed a large van as it backed across the end of the adjoining road, watching its headlights slide past the parallel lens. She had the right street.

So where was Viola?

'Have you seen her yet?' she asked, her eyes not leaving the screen.

'No, ma'am. She should have reached the end of the road by now.' Yasir waved at the third monitor, where the two main roads met. 'No sign here, either, so we can't have missed her.'

'Hold on.' Hawkins stopped the film and ran it forwards again, this time at half normal speed. 'Watch for exactly when she appears.'

They both stared at the spot where Viola Clarkson had disappeared from view. Vehicles crept up and down the gloomy street, their headlights stabbing pools of brilliance between other cars. Hawkins watched the seconds crawl forwards. She blinked stinging eyes, losing focus. But when she looked again, she was just in time to witness the reason they'd missed Viola up to now.

'Did you see that?' She eased the footage back; played the sequence again.

They watched Viola slide into view, not out of the shadows further along Gascoigne Road, but from a side turning away to the left.

'That's why we didn't see her,' Hawkins said. 'Because she didn't *use* the bus.' She tapped the screen. 'Get me the name of that other street.'

Yasir picked up her mobile; began typing the Clarksons' address into an app.

But she looked up when Hawkins put a hand on her shoulder. 'Hold on, Amala.' She paused the footage. 'I don't think we need it.'

She pointed at a car waiting to join the roundabout at the end of Gascoigne Road. 'This vehicle left the side street a few seconds after she did, and turned the opposite way. It must have driven Viola home and dropped her in that side street, leaving her to walk the last part of the way, maybe so her parents would think she caught the bus.'

Amala shook her head. 'I don't understand. How do you know Viola was in it?'

'Because I've seen it before.' Hawkins grinned. 'And you know the best part about that car?' She glanced back at the vehicle in the centre of frame.

'I know whose it is.'

39

Rupert reached the top of the slope, worn out from the climb. He stopped the bike in shade at the side of the trail to get his breath back and looked ahead, along the corridor curving away through the trees.

Almost home.

Behind him, the pitted mud track dropped gently back towards the outskirts of Loughton. Next to it the biggest tree in Bury Wood, an ancient oak with gnarled, blackened limbs, groaned in the wind.

'Hi, George.' He nodded at the whorled section of trunk that looked like an ugly, screaming face. Every time he passed, the warty nose seemed a little larger, the pouting lips a bit more pronounced.

Rupert dragged a sleeve across his forehead, wiping away the sweat. The sun was still high overhead and he was glad when a breeze came at him out of the forest, rustling the leaves; cooling his skin.

It was a long ride to and from the garage on the main road, especially on a hot summer's day like this. He wanted a drink. There was milk in the bag, but without permission he knew better than to open it. He looked at his watch. If he wasn't back soon the milk would spoil, and then there'd be hell to pay.

He set off again, pushing down hard to launch himself as he found the left pedal with his other foot. The bike wobbled, its awkward handlebars making balance difficult. Rupert hated its creaky old frame and noisy brakes that hardly worked. It had been his father's years ago, and all that was ever said when he suggested replacing it was that it still worked fine. Recently he'd been even bolder and asked for a car, saying it would speed up his errands and allow him to carry more when he went for supplies. He was twenty-one now, plenty old enough to drive, and he'd already passed his test. But it didn't matter; the answer was always no.

He bumped onwards, weaving from side to side, keeping the bike's skinny tyres away from the sharp stones spilling out of potholes here and there. But the going was much easier now the track had levelled out, and Rupert was able to admire the greenery as he swept by.

All too soon he rounded the final bend in the track, dismounting as he hit the gravel drive, pushing the bike towards the house. His parents' home always looked so peaceful, hidden here among the ancient trees, vines climbing its soft grey walls, as if the forest were reclaiming borrowed slate and stone. Originally, when Bury Wood was still privately owned, it had been the groundsman's cottage, a job his father held for fifteen years before a local trust had taken over when the landowner died. Dad bought the house from the trust, at a bloody good price, he said, and it had been Rupert's home since birth.

He neared the front of the building, looking for movement behind the wooden window frames, beneath the triangular porch roof, where green leaves and small white flowers hung above the entrance. But no one was there.

Rupert propped his bike under the small lean-to cover against the near wall and shrugged off his rucksack, rotating his shoulders to peel the damp T-shirt away from his back, letting the air reach his skin. He crunched around to the entrance, front door creaking as it scraped across the flagstones and wedged itself against the floor. Rupert stepped inside and eased it closed, turning to face the room.

'Get everything?' Ash looked up from the chair in front of the fireplace, resting his book on his knees.

'Yes.' Rupert walked over to the kitchen. He unzipped his rucksack and took out the milk; put it in the fridge. Behind him, he heard Ash get up.

'Hope that didn't get warm.'

He shook his head, not looking round. 'It's still c . . . cold.'

He waited for Ash to say something else, but nothing came. He tried to swallow, but his throat was too dry. Instead he dug in his pocket for the change and began sorting the coins, arranging them in neat rows on the bench so they were easy to count. Then he placed the receipt beside them and carried on unloading his bag.

Ash appeared beside him and stood over the money.

Rupert put the bread in the cupboard, holding his breath. He turned to find his friend facing him.

'Cashier try anything today?' Ash asked.

'No. I watched her the whole t . . . time.'

The frown eased. 'OK. But what do we know about these people?'

Rupert struggled to remember the exact words. '. . . If they're b . . . being friendly, they're probably stealing.'

'Good.' Ash smiled, and Rupert relaxed.

'I m . . . met Mr Matthews outside the shop,' he blurted. Ash liked to know these things. You had to pick your moments, but now felt like the right time. Roger Matthews had been a close friend of his parents. He ran the Warren Wood, a pub next door to the garage where Rupert bought the groceries.

His friend's eyes narrowed again. 'Much to say for himself?'

'H . . . he said to say hello,' Rupert stuttered, remembering that Ash didn't really like Mr Matthews, now wishing he hadn't spoken up.

'And . . . ?'

'A . . . And, he offered me a j . . . job.'

'A job.'

'Yes. He promised my p . . . parents he'd look out for me. He said I could work in his pub, collecting g . . . glasses at first.'

'You don't need money. What the fuck would you want with a job?'

Rupert took a step backwards. Ash rarely swore these days; not unless it was something serious. 'Mr M . . . Matthews said I'd m . . . meet people.'

'You don't need a fucking job.' Ash moved nearer, glaring at Rupert. He was shaking, but his voice was low and his hands stayed by his sides. 'Your parents left you this house, and enough money that you never have to work again. But everyone knows you can't be trusted. That's why I'm here, to stop you giving it all away, to whichever arsehole asks you first.' He nodded at the room. 'And where would you be without me watching you, making sure you don't get screwed over?'

'I . . . I'd be h . . . homeless.'

'And what happens when you try to make friends?'

A tear escaped and ran down Rupert's cheek. 'They wait t . . . till I leave, and laugh at me.'

'Exactly. So how many friends do you have?'

'One.'

'And how many friends do you need?'

He sniffed. 'One.'

'Right.' Ash picked up the bottle of bleach from the counter and handed it to Rupert, himself again as he turned away. 'Dinner time soon. Best you get on with the cleaning.'

40

'Praise bloody be.' Hawkins pulled the Giulietta off the road into a bus stop, looking across the softly lit High Street at the place they'd both managed to miss the first three times they'd passed its door. 'At last.'

'No wonder we didn't see it.' Amala pointed at the bright facade of Luppolo, a modern restaurant bar next door to their destination. Several tables of fashionable thirty-somethings lined the pavement outside, enjoying the mild autumn night, while others with e-cigarettes stood further along, in front of the place Amala and Hawkins had wasted half an hour trying to find. 'It's minuscule.'

Hawkins nodded, noting the lack of light coming from inside the tiny frontage. The fascia was barely six feet across, comprising a single door and latticed window jammed between the trendy restaurant and a greasy spoon café, also closed. Although judging by the six windows above it and the bar, all bearing blinds with the same company logo, the entrance led to a substantial office area on the first floor. But that was in darkness too, as might be expected on a Saturday.

'Looks deserted, ma'am,' Amala said. 'Is there any point knocking?'

Hawkins twisted in her seat, looking back along the

surprisingly pretty main street running through the centre of Wanstead. Beyond the bar, a smart Tudor building marked the end of the row, opposite a leafy park. Between them, a junction led away to the left.

'Let's not call it a wasted journey yet.' She turned back. 'Jump out and wait over there by the office door.'

Yasir gave her a questioning look.

'Just a little hunch I want to check out.' She waited for the sergeant to step out on to the pavement, waving her mobile when Yasir turned back. 'Don't do anything till I call, but stay close to that entrance, OK?'

'No worries.' Amala closed the door and began crossing the road. Hawkins started the car and waited for a gap in the light traffic before swinging the Giulietta around and turning left by the park. As she'd hoped, twenty yards in she was able to turn again, into a parking area behind the buildings.

The restricted space was packed with various cars, most of which probably belonged to the restaurant's customers. But among them, right at the back, was the car they'd seen near Viola Clarkson's house.

Hawkins pulled forwards, blocking in a pricey-looking Jaguar, to get a clear view of the first-floor office windows. The blinds on this side were drawn, too, but as soon as her eyes adjusted to the darkness, Hawkins picked out a pale fluorescent glow behind the shades. Either someone had left a light on before going home, or her suspicions were right.

She got out and locked the Alfa as she wandered across to what looked like the rear entrance, noting the company name on a plaque beside a windowless PVC door. There was no point ringing the office number displayed; they'd already tried twice and got the answer machine. If there *was* someone inside, they clearly weren't there to take calls.

Hawkins rang the bell mounted on the wall, waited a good thirty seconds, then banged four times, hard. She looked up just in time to see the glow behind the shades disappear, confirming that the office was occupied, and moved closer to the door to listen for footsteps inside. There was no sound, and Hawkins had just retrieved her phone to call Amala when the door was unlocked from inside. It swung open to reveal three faces.

Behind a dishevelled Keith Shawcross stood a much younger woman and a bemused Amala Yasir.

'Your hunch was right, ma'am.' Yasir grinned. 'Look who I bumped into, trying to leave through the front.'

'Hello, Keith,' Hawkins addressed the accountant. 'Let's go back up to the office, shall we? You've got some explaining to do.'

The offices of Hart Shawcross were quaintly attractive. Hawkins admired the dark wood beams criss-crossing the white, vaulted ceiling as the four of them climbed the narrow staircase and turned left into a reception area, now brightly lit by flush-mounted bulbs their host had flicked on from the bottom of the stairs. To their right, four leather armchairs faced each other across a large coffee table, flanked by three oak desks and several healthy-looking houseplants. Along the opposite wall, two glass cubicles presumably offered private workspace for the eponymous directors. The only noise came from several PC base units, humming quietly as they backed up the day's business.

The young woman, still unintroduced, stomped across to slump in one of the leather chairs, arms defiantly crossed. Her matching pencil skirt and jacket were provocatively cut, and Hawkins wondered whether her day-worn make-up was always so liberally applied. She had attempted to excuse herself as soon as it became clear the unannounced visitors were here for Shawcross, at which point Hawkins had identified herself and Amala as Met police, and politely ordered her to stay.

Keith Shawcross ambled over to perch on the arm of an adjacent chair, not inviting the two detectives to sit. Hawkins remained between staircase and seating area, with Amala just behind. A few seconds of uncomfortable silence followed.

At last Shawcross cleared his throat with a wheeze, still out of breath from scaling the stairs. 'I would have appreciated some notice concerning your arrival, Detective, especially so far outside office hours. To what do we owe this interruption?'

'First things first, now we're all comfortable.' Hawkins turned to the girl. 'I don't believe we've been introduced.'

'This is my assistant,' Shawcross answered cautiously. 'Jasmin.'

'Lovely.' Hawkins turned back. 'Do the two of you often work late together, and on a Saturday too?'

'When our clients require us to do so, yes. Are you implying something specific, Chief Inspector?'

'Nothing relevant to the Viola Clarkson case at this point.' Hawkins held his stare. 'Is all your prep work done with the lights out?'

He blinked twice. 'We had just packed up for the night. Anyway, I have a dinner reservation, so get on with it.'

'There's been a development we need to discuss with you urgently.' Hawkins watched the accountant closely. 'We called and spoke to your wife. She said you were working late, but there was no answer on your business line or mobile, so we dropped by on the off-chance you were still here.'

'How diligent of you.'

'Thanks. Does that mean you're ready to tell us the *real* reason you offered Viola Clarkson work experience cleaning your house, rather than here at your practice?' Hawkins caught the scowl Jasmin fired at her boss at the mention of Viola's name.

Shawcross frowned. 'That's a rather cryptic question, Detective. But like I told you this morning, I barely made her acquaintance.'

'So there was no conversation on the half-hour car journeys when you gave her lifts home after work.'

The frown deepened. 'That's a ludicrous assertion. I never drove that woman anywhere.'

'Really? Even if we have CCTV footage of your

Audi dropping Viola in a side street, less than a hundred yards from her front door?'

A slight hesitation. 'Not on the day she died, you don't.'

'No, the week before, but it still means you lied. And I'm willing to bet that neither Viola's parents nor your wife knows anything about it.' She held up her phone. 'Shall we ask?'

Shawcross puffed himself up, still defiant. 'That doesn't prove I was driving.'

'Maybe not. But I'd advise you to take this whole thing a little more seriously, Keith. Viola was seventeen. She was abducted somewhere between your home and hers, before being murdered in cold blood. If you won't assist us, it makes me wonder what else you might be hiding. Then I'll have to take you in for questioning, which is how reputations get mangled.' She paused for effect. 'What do you say?'

The accountant stared into space for a moment, drew breath as if he was about to speak, then turned to stare at the wall.

'OK then.' Hawkins sighed. 'For the record, Mr Shawcross, you maintain that you did not, at any time, for any reason, give Viola Clarkson a lift in your car.'

He turned back, reddening, clearly aware that repeating the lie would land him in even deeper shit.

'Yes, he did.' Jasmin's voice broke the stand-off.

Hawkins looked at her. 'What?'

'He drove Viola home,' the girl repeated, turning a defiant stare on her boss, 'both days she worked here.'

'Be quiet, Jasmin.' Shawcross turned back to Hawkins. 'My legal representative will deal with this in the morning.'

But Jasmin wasn't done.

'I saw him touch her up, too,' she said, matter of fact, pointing at the far desk. 'Over there.'

'She's lying,' Shawcross asserted.

'Oh, am I?' Jasmin stood, now talking to Hawkins. 'He did the same thing to me when I started here.'

'Don't you dare,' Shawcross warned, but his assistant was in full defiant stride.

'He can't even get it up.' She jabbed a finger in the direction of his crotch. 'He gives me money to play with myself while he watches. He calls it "Pay Per View".'

They eyeballed each other across the coffee table for a moment before Shawcross found his voice, emitting a barely contained rasp: 'You're fired.'

'No, my darling; you are.'

Everyone spun to see Helen Shawcross at the top of the stairs, vindictive eyes burning into her husband, holding the keys she must have used to enter the building without being heard above the commotion.

'Helen. I can explain.' The accountant swallowed. '. . . This shameful child is trying to set me up, and the rest is simple misunderstanding. Go home and let me deal with it, please.'

'Misunderstanding?' His wife advanced, barging past Hawkins and Yasir. 'You swore this wouldn't happen again, but I knew as soon as the sergeant rang to ask

you about Viola something stank.' She reached her husband and began battering him. 'How dare you use this office for your perverted games? You're fired, you fucking piss-taker.'

'You can't fire me.' Shawcross tried to shield his head. 'I built this business from nothing.'

'Nothing but *my parents' money*,' Helen screamed, hitting harder. 'I'm majority shareholder; none of it's yours. The business, the house, that stupid car; say goodbye to everything, you wanker.'

'We'll see about that,' he wheezed, backing away. 'I'll sue you for it.'

'Oh will you?' she screamed, shoving him so hard that he bounced off the edge of a desk and fell. 'I'd like to see you pay for legal advice when all your accounts are frozen.' She dropped on top of him, grabbing a hefty metal stapler from one of the desks and raising it above her head.

'Help!' Shawcross implored, as Hawkins and Yasir waded in. 'I'll tell you what you want to know. Just get this madwoman off me!'

41

Hawkins flushed the loo and washed her hands, leaning towards the bathroom mirror, fighting her frustration at yet another night's broken sleep. She pulled at the bags under her eyes, reassuring herself they were temporary symptoms of exhaustion and stress.

Rather than the petrifying approach of her forties.

Unconvinced, she applied some moisturiser and used mouthwash before turning off the light and padding blindly out on to the landing, pausing outside the spare room, thankfully no longer able to hear the muted bawl that had woken her.

She moved on, hoping the disruptive effects of sleeping away from home would lessen with time. Perhaps her niece and nephew were beginning to settle, but she'd already seen plenty of the small hours since their arrival, and her sensitivity to midnight disturbances must have grown in response.

She had just found her bedroom door handle when creaking floorboards made her turn back, to see her sister standing in the soft night-light glow from the adjacent doorway.

'I heard you get up,' Siobhan whispered. 'Everything OK?'

'Just a bit frazzled. Are the kids all right?'

'Fine.' Siobhan stepped forwards, easing the door halfway closed. 'If I'm honest, I think they're missing Malcolm.'

Hawkins nodded. 'Why hasn't he seen them?'

'Probably because I forbade him.'

'Oh. And now you regret it.'

'I think . . . yes. I don't want to hurt these two.'

'All this must be confusing for them.'

Siobhan studied the carpet for a moment before looking up. 'Come and sit with me for a minute?'

Hawkins let go of the door handle, encouraged by the prospect of civilised conversation between them; just wishing the possibility hadn't presented itself in the middle of the night.

She trudged over to join her sister on the top step, shoulder to shoulder; bare feet together on the second stair down. They sat for a moment, both staring down at the orange glow creeping through the front door into the hallway.

Hawkins broke the silence. 'How did your interviews go?'

'John Lewis said I can start on fashion next Monday. Ten till three, four days a week.'

'That's good. Isn't it?'

'I suppose so.' Siobhan sighed. 'I'm just not sure it's what I want.'

'Retail?'

'Independence.'

'I know. I thought you were coping.'

'Hardly.' Siobhan picked at the hem of her pyjamas.

'My life's spinning out of control, but the more I try to stop it, the worse things seem to get.'

Hawkins frowned. 'You think leaving Malcolm was a mistake?'

'No, but now we've got nowhere to live.' Her sister's eyes flicked towards the bedroom. 'Coping with the children was hard enough at home with Malcolm helping. Now . . .' She trailed off. '. . . I do appreciate you letting us stay.'

Hawkins rubbed her back. 'Hey. As long as you need.'

'Thanks.' Siobhan pinched the bridge of her nose. 'I realise I've been a nightmare. My head's all over the place.'

'You realise you don't have a monopoly on psychological baggage around here, right?'

Siobhan smiled weakly. 'Remind me why we fight all the time.'

'Too similar for our own good, I suppose.'

'I don't think so.' Her head dropped. 'You know I was always jealous of your achievements, don't you? You're a senior police officer; I can just about work a till.'

'A career doesn't compare to what you have.' Hawkins nodded towards the spare room. 'I know they're a handful, but they're amazing. That's down to you.'

They sat in unusually comfortable silence until Hawkins asked, 'So is your marriage definitely over?'

'I don't know if I love him any more, if that's what you mean.' Siobhan half stood. 'Look, it isn't fair to dump all this on you.'

'Oh no, you don't,' Hawkins hissed, pulling her back

down. 'You're more than welcome to stay until everything's sorted out; you know that. But board is going to cost you some honesty for once, OK?'

Irritation flashed across Siobhan's features, but it dissolved into despair, and she burst into stifled tears, her shoulders jerking. 'What am I supposed to do, Antonia?'

Hawkins pulled her close. 'Supportive bullshit or hard truth?'

The reply from near her armpit was muffled. 'Truth.'

'Call Malcolm.' She waited for Siobhan to look up, met her questioning gaze. 'This is just as tough for him as it is for you.'

'But . . . you never liked him.'

Hawkins snorted. 'I'm not always crazy about *you*, but it's family. I'm not saying move back in, but he's part of their lives, and frankly, you need his help. So I suggest you try to salvage any bridges that aren't already burnt.'

Siobhan dabbed at her cheeks with a sleeve, still breathing in little bursts. 'When did you get so worldly-wise?'

'I spend my life investigating other people's mistakes.' Hawkins shrugged. 'After a while you realise there are only two personality types: the ones who put things right whatever it takes, and the ones who'll do anything to avoid paying for their mess.'

Siobhan thought for a moment before smirking. 'Did you just make that up?'

'Maybe,' Hawkins returned the grin, 'but the sentiment holds. Call your husband.'

42

'Sheila?' There was a pause before the soft voice continued, somewhere on the edge of her senses. *'Can you hear me?'*

'Yes,' she whispered through dry, cracking lips, trying to turn her head towards the sound. She became aware of a musty pillow; the warm bulk of a duvet. But her limbs felt heavy, as if she'd been . . .

Oh no.

Slowly she opened her eyes, to blurred colours and cartwheeling shapes. She almost threw up and shut them again, cursing herself. It was daytime, that much she could tell, and there was a chill in the air, yet everything was spinning around her, and she couldn't focus at all. But there was something else, something worse; something she'd convinced herself was under control.

She'd been drinking.

She lay still, trying to dredge up recent hours. All she remembered was driving. *So where the fuck did she get alcohol?*

'Sheila?' the voice interrupted, louder this time. 'Are you OK?'

'I don't know,' she answered. 'Did I crash?'

'No . . . you didn't crash.'

'What, then?' Her brain throbbed as her temper flared. 'What happened?'

'You f . . . fell asleep in the car.'

She tried to unravel the words, coming up short. 'I don't understand.'

Silence greeted her, as she strained to remember something, *anything* that made sense. At first there was blankness, a void of random daily events. Brushing her teeth, checking her bag for keys; getting into the car. Except those things happened every morning. How could she be sure they were from this year, let alone today? She recalled nothing specific, least of all where she was, or how she had come to be there.

'Where am I?'

'A . . . At my house.'

'What?' She forced her eyes open again, able this time to pick out a room she'd never seen, with dark wood beams and a low ceiling. 'Who are you?'

'I'm Rupert. I s . . . saved you.'

'Saved me? What the hell does that m—' Sheila stopped as it came back to her.

In the face of his harmless demeanour, she hadn't given safety a thought, dropping down off the verge, opening the passenger door.

Thanks so much for this.

She'd strapped in as he'd driven away; taken the flask without knowing what it contained. By the time he said it was whisky, her resolve had already frayed.

A single moment of weakness. *Justified by the stress of the day*; words that rang in her ears as she tipped her head back and drank.

43

Hawkins dropped her window and eyed the row of garages at the end of the cul-de-sac; a squat line of six identical flaking wood doors, all the same distressed shade of erstwhile red. Tall weeds stretched upwards in front of each one, suggesting that whatever was inside probably hadn't seen twenty-first-century daylight, while disparate piles of sun-bleached rubbish littered the grimy parking area in front. And yet, despite its proximity to the outskirts of the housing estate they had driven through to reach it, the dilapidated square of tarmac was quiet and secluded, hemmed in on either side by rampant greenery, overlooked by nothing but railings and trees.

She turned to her passenger. 'This is where you used to bring her?'

Keith Shawcross nodded, early signs of a dense grey beard riding the undulant mass of his second and third chins as he moved. He looked exhausted, wearing the same crumpled suit as he had been the previous night, having slept unexpectedly at Her Majesty's pleasure, in the cells below Forest Gate police station.

Yet had she been pushed, Hawkins still wouldn't have listed him as a suspect, despite his admission, once freed from under his rampaging wife, that he *had* seen Viola Clarkson on the day she disappeared.

She hadn't even arrested him, partly because he had no motive where the other victims were concerned, but mainly because Jasmin had reluctantly provided him with an alibi for the day Raymond Jewis disappeared. He'd also accepted the deal she'd offered him: to sleep voluntarily behind bars in exchange for not being formally detained, and then to provide a full explanation and daylight tour of his sordid exploits with the teenager.

The arrangement had allowed Hawkins time to have background checks carried out. The results were mailed to her phone at six a.m., and showed no historical arrests or convictions for *anything*, let alone violence or kidnap. The accountant's temporary detention had also guaranteed he wouldn't disappear in the small hours, kept his name out of the papers, and ensured that he wouldn't have to worry about returning home; an intimidating prospect in light of his wife's assertion as she was levered off him:

Set foot in the house, and I'll rip your bloody bollocks off.

It had also allowed them to start at first light.

Shawcross' only demand had been that Hawkins alone witness his exposé; terms she'd accepted. Here was an outwardly respectable man being forced to broadcast his Freudian depths; unaccustomed to the ignominy of using a regulation wash kit provided by the state's penal system. Divulging darker sides didn't come naturally to his demographic, and she couldn't afford for him to clam up now. Plus, of course, being sole escort allowed her to press harder for dirt.

'How long would you be here, typically?' she asked.

'No more than fifteen minutes; the time we saved over her taking the bus.'

'So you'd park up, recline the seats, and the show would begin.'

Shawcross squirmed. 'Must we go into such detail?'

'That was the agreement,' Hawkins reminded him. 'You got caught, so now it's my business.'

He crossed his arms. 'I don't recall signing anything.'

'It's disclosure time,' she warned, 'or I'll arrest you for formal interview, and I guess we'll get to see how certain members of your staff react after all.'

She watched the colour drain slowly from the accountant's face, as they both pictured Viola's father finding out that his boss had not only violated his daughter, but was also being questioned in connection with her death.

He sighed. 'It was just entertainment. I never . . . *touched* her.'

'Oddly, I believe you.' Hawkins heard Jasmin's words from last night: *He can't even get it up.* 'How many times did it happen?'

'Five, maybe six.'

'Always here?'

'Yes.'

'OK.' Her eyes drifted from the nearest houses, no more than thirty yards away, to the footpath running directly past the garages. 'This is all a bit public, though. Weren't you seen?'

He shrugged. 'The Audi's windows are tinted, and it was always after dark. Viola wasn't fully . . . naked, and

249

it would have been easy to drive away had anyone approached the car.'

'But they never did.'

He shook his head.

'Fair enough.' Having greased the wheels of conversation, Hawkins returned to blacker themes. 'Did cash change hands?'

Shawcross actually managed to look hurt. 'No. She was over sixteen. We were consenting adults.'

'Oh come on; a teenage girl and a man in his sixties? You'll have to do better than that.'

Shawcross frowned, but he soon caved. 'She had the use of a company credit card.'

Hawkins suppressed a smirk. Perhaps Viola hadn't been so innocent after all. 'When did it start?'

The accountant's gaze broke adrift, alighting somewhere in the middle distance. 'The second time I drove her home. The first night they were digging up the main road and we got caught in traffic, so I suggested we come this way instead.'

'Fully intending to proposition her, of course.'

'I didn't force her to do anything.'

'Maybe not, but she was up for some action, and you didn't refuse.' Hawkins thought for a few seconds. 'So did you suggest the credit card, or was she blackmailing you?'

'Neither at that stage.'

'Then why risk the cleaning job, which placed her in your house, with your wife, when you weren't even there?'

'Like I said, I couldn't keep her on at the practice; she wasn't sharp enough—'

'So you suggested the job as a way to maintain regular contact.'

Shawcross stewed for a moment, indirectly confirming the allegation.

'OK.' Hawkins let him off more lightly than she would have predicted. 'Let's go back to your movements on the day Viola disappeared. You left work just before six p.m., drove to Ilford and waited at the bus stop near your house, where Viola joined you at approximately twenty-five to seven. This was your normal arrangement, designed to avoid raising suspicion from your wife or her mum and dad.'

'Correct.'

'You drove here, another five minutes using the route we just took, and she . . . *performed* for quarter of an hour.' Hawkins waited for his affirmative grunt before going on. 'Then you drove to her parents' house in sufficient time to drop her in the side road, from where she'd finish the journey on foot, arriving home around twenty past seven, as if she'd taken the bus.'

Another nod.

'But that day things went awry, because you had a blazing row, during which you pulled over and threw her out. Only now you can't remember where.'

Shawcross swallowed hard. 'My mind was on other things.'

'Like the fact Viola had threatened to tell Helen about your arrangement.'

'Yes.'

'Well.' Hawkins started the Giulietta. 'Let's hope a tour of the route jogs your memory.' She pulled away, heading back along Woodbridge Road, approaching the side street they had come in on. 'Which way?'

'Straight ahead, left at the roundabout.'

Hawkins took his instructions, turning on to Westrow Drive, another conduit of seventies housing, set apart from the previous road only by cleaner cars and more accurately manicured hedges. She crashed over a speed bump, only then noting the twenty mile per hour signs and slowing to preserve the moral high ground.

'Keep going to the T-junction, then left again,' Shaw-cross said, as the well-tended terraces slid on and on, only the occasional front garden breaking an otherwise relentless stream of asphalt and block-paved drives.

'What did you argue about?'

He grimaced; made her wait for an answer. Eventually: 'She wanted commitments I wasn't prepared to give.'

'She wanted you to leave Helen?' Hawkins glanced over at him.

He snorted. 'Absolutely not. She wanted money.'

'Right. Hence the credit card.'

'Yes, although that novelty soon wore off, as soon as she realised there was a limit on the account.'

'She started making demands?'

'At first her requests were modest – items of clothing or jewellery – but soon she was asking for holidays with her friends.'

'That's what caused your big fight?'

'No, I talked her out of that one. This time she wanted me to rent her a flat. I told her it was madness; that her parents would know she couldn't afford a place of her own, but she wouldn't let it go.'

'You held your ground,' Hawkins speculated, 'so she threatened to tell Helen. But you called her bluff and threw her out of the car.'

He nodded. 'I didn't think she'd follow through. Viola knew that if Helen found out, her first act of vengeance would be to call her parents.'

'And then she disappeared before you had a chance to find out.'

'Yes.' The accountant's gaze dropped into the footwell.

They drove in silence to the T-junction at the end of the road, and Hawkins stopped opposite the manicured borders of a modern apartment complex, waiting for a gap in the early-morning traffic before turning left.

Upney Lane was wider than the previous street, its houses set back twenty yards from the road, behind wide pavements with tree-lined grass borders, and Hawkins' hopes rose at the decent number of pedestrians wandering by on either side. If Viola had left the car in this area, she would almost certainly have been seen.

As if on cue, Shawcross pointed ahead. 'It was somewhere around here.'

Hawkins dropped their speed, noting that the houses on their left had given way to a small row of shops, including a bookmaker's that would stay open long after office hours. But her guide stayed quiet as they left the shops behind, passing Upney Underground on a raised section of road, before descending the far side.

They were between a row of trees and a set of houses covered in orange plastic netting when Shawcross finally waved at a side street. 'There.'

Hawkins braked and changed down, swinging on to Merton Road, a shabby offshoot lined with fifties housing. She brought the Alfa to a halt, looking at her passenger. 'Are you sure?'

'Yes.' He turned in his seat, looking out through the car's rear screen. 'I remember that scaffolding.'

Hawkins glanced over her shoulder as a bus thundered past on the main road, twisting to watch it pull into a stop further along Upney Lane. The pavements weren't busy here, but they were surrounded by houses, so the chances of Viola being seen once on foot were reasonable. On the down side, with a bus stop one way, an underground station the other, and not too far to walk if she chose, the teenager would have had plenty of options for ways to get home. And the more possibilities there were, the longer it would take to identify the route she actually took.

She turned back to Shawcross. 'So you stopped here and told her to get out?'

He nodded.

'Was she upset?'

'Crying, perhaps.'

'Did you see which way she went?'

'No. I made a U-turn and drove away.' He twitched. 'Towards home.'

'And that was it? No further contact; apologetic texts or phone calls?'

Shawcross shook his head.

'OK.' Hawkins dipped the clutch, restarting the engine. 'I'll drop you back at your office, but don't go leaving town in case we need you again, and until I decide what we're doing about the withheld evidence charge. It won't be long until news of Viola's death breaks, though I'm sure I don't need to tell you not to discuss this with anyone.'

She was about to turn the car round, already working out how many officers she'd need to canvass the various routes between here and Viola's house, when she noticed the curtains twitch in the house at the end of the road.

'Stay put.' She undid her seat belt and got out. 'I'll be right back.'

44

Rupert jumped as the buzzer shrieked again. He shut his eyes, trying to block out the rapid squeaking sounds and yelling that followed. The noises passed quickly, and he peeked as they retreated, watching the gang of blue pyjamas disappearing along the corridor, shouting at people coming the other way to mind out.

He shuddered, wanting to be somewhere else; somewhere away from the chaos, and the stench that reminded him of being ill.

He stood. 'C . . . can I wait outside?'

'Sit, idiot.' Ash grabbed his coat. 'Relax, for fuck's sake.'

'Sorry.' Rupert sank into his seat. 'I don't l . . . like these places.'

Ash spread his hands. 'It's just a stupid hospital.'

'I don't like it.'

'Go home, then. I don't want you here, anyway.'

'But . . . you s . . . said I could come.'

'Only to shut you up. Make up your retarded mind for a change: stay or go. I don't give a shit.'

Rupert hugged himself and turned away, watching the old lady a few seats along digging in her handbag for something.

He turned back, keen to make up. 'Why are we h . . . here again?'

Ash rubbed at his forehead. 'I told you yesterday, I got a letter. They want to run some tests.'

'For your b . . . backache.'

'Yes.'

'What s . . . sort of tests?'

Ash rolled his eyes; shook his head.

'You'll be all right, though.'

'Jesus. How the fuck should I know?'

They both stood as someone called Ash's name.

'Uh, uh.' Ash stopped him. 'Just me.'

Rupert looked at the nurse waiting by reception, then back at his friend. 'But I w . . . want to—'

'It's private. I'll tell you what happens, yeah? Wait here.'

'Promise you'll t . . . tell me later.'

'Whatever.' Ash went with the nurse, leaving Rupert alone.

He swallowed hard and sat down. The noises around him seemed even louder somehow. He heard a couple arguing, a baby's cry, an announcement over the tannoy, telling Doctor Whetstone to call extension five hundred. Shoes squeaked endlessly against the shiny floor.

He tried to concentrate on the clock above the desk, counting each minute as it went by. Thirty, then forty-five.

But still Ash didn't come back.

45

Hawkins drummed at the desk with her nails, determinedly keeping her cool; drifting in and out of the idle conversation between Mike and Amala away to her right. She glanced at the clock on the far wall of the incident suite, then back at her office door, open in case her landline rang.

No one had seen or heard from Aaron Sharpe since the previous afternoon, and now he was late for the morning brief as well. What annoyed her was that he knew how much that annoyed her. *If you're ill, fair enough; delayed, don't let it happen again, but whatever you do, call in.* Those were her rules, and ever since his best mate's stag, six months ago, when he'd felt the full force of Hawkins' irritation, Aaron had managed to follow them. But not today.

To make matters worse, his mobile was going to answerphone, and his home number just rang.

She doused her frustration by thinking about the case.

A radio news update on the drive in had offered Hawkins the first interpretation of her press release. And, despite predictable focus on the meaty headline, the dates, locations and her underlying appeal for witnesses had survived pretty much intact. Any time now the press-office phones would start to ring. She just had to hope that somewhere among the time-wasters looking for attention, and the reporters after associated dirt, there would be genuine calls from witnesses previously unreached. Hopefully then they could put the case to bed before people started panicking about whether they might be next.

But their chances of delivering such a result relied on her team turning up for work. And at twenty to nine she gave up.

'Let's get started, shall we?' Hawkins stood. 'Hopefully Mr Sharpe will grace us at some point.'

She moved across to the map of Barking attached to the investigation board. 'The good news is that we now have more information about Viola Clarkson's movements on the day she disappeared.'

Mike and Amala were both aware of the voyeuristic arrangement Shawcross had brokered with his teenage employee, so she moved straight on to the dispute that ensued when the girl tried to turn events to her advantage. She traced the pair's regular route, from near his home to the garages, then on to Merton Road, where Shawcross had dumped a distressed Viola Clarkson and driven away.

'If Viola were the only victim,' she continued, 'her attempt at blackmail would be sufficient motive for us to be questioning Keith Shawcross right now. However, another of his female companions, a trainee accountant called Jasmin, has provided him with an alibi for the period covering Raymond Jewis's abduction and death. The pair stayed together in Taunton, *on business*, over those couple of days. So he isn't a suspect for now.'

She turned back to the map. 'We also have a witness, an elderly resident at this end of Merton Road. She saw Viola get out of Shawcross's Audi and head south on Upney Lane, which makes sense because that would be towards home. All of which suggests she was abducted somewhere in between. Our next job is to establish where Viola went after she parted company with her boss, what method of transport she used, and how far she got.'

'What time did she leave Merton Road, ma'am?' Amala asked.

Hawkins watched the sergeant flip her notepad over to start a second page. 'Just prior to seven p.m., so it would have been almost dark at that point, but the lighting's good because it's a main road.' She tapped the Clarksons' home address. 'There's a mile and a half between the two locations, so unless she fancied a thirty-minute walk, and explaining to her parents why she was late, Viola probably went looking for a faster way to get home. There are regular taxis and buses on Upney Lane, or she might have doubled back towards the tube. The nearest bus stop is further down on this corner, which according to our witness statement is the direction she went, but they only run once every thirty minutes at that time of day, at ten past and twenty to the hour.'

She was about to move on when the door behind her opened, and everyone turned to see Aaron Sharpe.

'Sorry I'm late, ma'am.' He moved towards Hawkins

with such uncharacteristic speed that she was forced to park her anger. 'But I have an ID for the unidentified body.'

He handed her the photocopy of a passport. Straight away she recognised their mystery victim.

'His name's Henri Delarue,' Sharpe said. 'French gap year student; came through Dover two months ago, which explains why he wasn't on anyone's radar. I submitted an ID request to immigration on the off-chance when he was found, but they're snowed under, so it only just came back. And our bloody printer's on the blink, so I ran down to . . . Anyway, Delarue said he was here to backpack round the UK; some nonsense about wanting to see every beach in Britain. But he got smart with an immigration officer, so border control strip-searched and fingerprinted him before letting him go.'

Immediately there were questions. Sharpe fielded them well, while Hawkins enjoyed the novelty of being impressed. Then Mike asked how Delarue had been getting around.

'He was thumbing it,' Sharpe told him. 'His Facebook page is full of posts about wanting to hitch-hike round the planet.'

Amala began to ask something else, but Hawkins interrupted. 'Hold on.' She moved back to the investigation board as her thoughts crystallised. 'Maybe that's the connection . . .' She turned back to confused faces, revealing her theory. 'What if he isn't *kidnapping* them at all?'

No one seemed to follow, so she continued thinking out loud. 'Look at the victims we know about. Viola Clarkson was dumped at the side of the road in tears, and now it looks like Delarue was hitch-hiking. If Peter Barnes and Raymond Jewis were in similar situations, they would all have been visibly in need of assistance.'

'You think the killer's looking for people who need help?' Amala asked.

Mike was nodding slowly. 'Which means they weren't targeted in advance, because their predicaments were unforeseen.'

'Exactly,' Hawkins agreed. 'The easiest way to abduct someone is if they don't realise they're being abducted. If he's helping people out he's a Samaritan, not a hijacker, so they have no reason to fear him. No force required.'

Sharpe interjected, 'But he still has to overpower them at some point.'

'Not if the tranquillisers come into play at this stage,' she argued. 'All the victims had traces in their blood. Administered in sufficient concentration, the drugs would render them unconscious in minutes.'

'That makes sense,' Amala said, 'but why would he bother looking for people who need help? Why not just pretend to be a minicab? He'd get a lot more takers.'

Mike answered first. 'Maybe he *wants* them to be injured or distressed? If Hunter's theory about killing for sport is correct, it gives him the upper hand when it comes to the chase.'

'Possibly.' Hawkins nodded. 'Or he sees them as

already being damaged in some way, and therefore expendable.'

Sharpe rubbed his neck. 'That's all fine in theory, but the victims came from such a wide area, it's still impossible to predict where he'll strike next, because even *he* doesn't know till it happens.'

'Don't write us off yet.' Hawkins grabbed her coat from the back of her chair, heading for the exit. 'Amala, use your new skills to assess any CCTV you can get hold of from Upney Lane on the day Viola disappeared. Start with the bus stop. If she caught a bus or a train, hopefully we can trace her onwards from there. Mike, organise a team to go door to door. We need witnesses, especially anyone who saw Viola getting into a vehicle after seven that night.'

Sharpe stood. 'What shall I do?'

'You're coming with me.' She paused beside the door, waited for him to catch up. 'You did well today, Aaron, and I want you to see how this develops.'

He smiled. 'Where are we going?'

'You've highlighted something I missed.' Hawkins was already moving again. 'So there's someone we need to find.'

46

'Can I help y—' Lauren Coleman looked up as Hawkins entered the battered Portakabin. 'Oh, it's you.'

'Hi, Lauren.' Hawkins waited for Sharpe to close the door behind them, wary of being overheard by the two cabbies chatting outside. 'Is your husband about?'

The young woman grimaced. 'I thought this was all sorted.'

'Not quite. We need a quiet word. Is he here?'

'No, and before you ask, I don't know where he is.'

Hawkins scanned the office for evidence that suggested a lie. But there was nothing; no second used coffee mug, no wallet, keys or coat to indicate Mitch Coleman had been around. All of which tallied with the absence of a black pickup in the car park outside.

'When did you last see him?'

Lauren snorted. 'He walked out the day you arrested him. Came home, threw some stuff in a bag and fucked off. Wouldn't talk to me. I haven't seen him since.'

Hawkins frowned. 'Has he done this kind of thing before?'

'Never.' She leaned back and massaged the bridge of her nose. 'I'm going out of my mind trying to keep this place running, and I don't even know if he's coming back. Why are you here, anyway? You let him go.'

'New evidence has come to light.'

Lauren's face fell and her gaze flicked back and forth between the visitors. 'Evidence that he murdered Pete?'

'Sorry, we really need to discuss it with him.'

Her head dropped. 'He'll only deny it.'

'What do you mean,' Hawkins said, 'deny *it*?'

Lauren fumbled, 'No, I . . . I didn't . . . it was a figure of speech.'

'Rubbish.' Hawkins placed her hands on the desk between them. 'You know something, and you're afraid to say because it makes Mitch look guilty, doesn't it?' She softened, adding, 'You almost told me before at the house. Come on, Lauren, you know it's the right thing to do.'

The phone on the desk rang as they stared at each other. On the fourth ring Lauren looked down at the display, clearly wanting to answer it. Hawkins leaned across, picked up the handset and placed it gently back on the hook. 'We're going nowhere till you tell me.'

Lauren shut her eyes and drew a long, dejected breath. When she looked up, tears had formed. 'Mitch didn't get home when he said, on the night Pete was attacked. I lay awake waiting for him. I heard the front door go at five a.m., but he still didn't come to bed. I didn't see him till I got up the next day.'

'You lied for him.'

She nodded.

'Where was he?'

'I don't know, really I don't. I came down the next morning to find him hanging out wet clothes. He never

265

does washing, but he must have come straight in and put it on. I think it was the stuff he'd been wearing the day before, a T-shirt, a sweater and an old pair of jeans. But he'd washed his jacket as well.'

'Go on.'

'He wouldn't talk to me, so I waited till he left and checked his clothes.'

'What did you find?'

Lauren dabbed at her cheeks with fingertips. 'Nothing.'

'That's it?'

'No.' She sniffed. 'He must have been in a hurry to get away from me.'

Hawkins frowned. 'Why, Lauren? You aren't making much sense.'

'Because he missed some of it.' Lauren burst into tears. 'When I went into the hallway ... there was blood on his shoes.'

47

Sheila sat on the bed, feet on the floor, hands clasped in her lap.

Staring into space.

Her sense of time was gone, persistent daylight the only thing telling her that less than twenty-four hours had passed since her unconscious arrival. Her breaths were shallow and quick, and she fought the anxiety swilling deep in her gut, her thoughts a seething mass of barely contained panic. Her brow tightened.

Don't let it beat you. Not this time.

She screwed her eyes closed; welcomed the twisting patterns that rose out of the blackness. But they were meagre distractions.

Had Barry remembered her saying she'd ring at lunchtime? Had he tried her mobile, left a message, and worried when she didn't return the call? Unlikely. He was probably enjoying his freedom, feet up in front of the golf. Which meant he wouldn't have reported her missing, while the Duke of Edinburgh party she was supposed to be supervising thought she was getting the car fixed.

So neither would they.

Desperation swelled as Sheila realised she might not even be *missed* for another two days. The situation meant each group would probably assume she was with the other, at least until she was due home after the trip.

No one was coming to help.

She felt the room shrink as her heart started to race. There was no point trying to force her way out; she'd already done that, and the sturdy wooden door had resisted easily. Her hands still hurt from the attempt. If she had any chance at all, it was going to come through discipline and strategy.

She needed a plan.

The other problem was hunger. She hadn't eaten since the previous afternoon, and her captor had provided no sustenance since her arrival, so there was a good chance he'd keep starving her. If she waited much longer, she wouldn't have the energy to escape, even if the opportunity came, let alone make freedom stick.

She looked at the door, at the spherical handle set in tired old wood, and the latch bridging the gap to the frame.

The noise reached her, petrifying her thoughts. A chill spread through her as she recognised the sound . . .

Of someone breathing outside.

'Let me out of here,' she demanded, repeating herself more firmly when no answer came. At last there was movement, a scraping sound as he shifted his weight. Then he spoke, with haunting innocence.

'Who is B . . . Barry?'

Sheila stared at the ragged hole in the wood, and the blackness beyond. It took a moment to find her voice: '*What* did you say?'

She waited as the silence stretched, trying to fathom how this insane stranger could possibly know her husband's name. She hadn't mentioned him, she was certain of that.

Her mind began listing the contents of her handbag, which wasn't here in the room; she'd already looked. He must have gone through it, but she recalled nothing inside that gave her partner's name. And just as she convinced herself a stray bank card or letter must be the culprit, his next statement stunned her again.

'Why are you u . . . upset with him?'

She stood, suddenly irate. 'How do you know *that*?'

Something creaked outside the door, and for a moment Sheila thought he was leaving, but then he answered, somehow managing to make things better and worse at the same time. 'You t . . . talked in your sleep.'

Sheila sank on to the bed, fresh exhaustion draining her. Had he been watching her the whole time? She put her hands over her face, trying to hold back desperation. 'Just let me out of here, *please.*'

'It isn't t . . . time for that.'

Emotion welled again. 'Why are you *doing* this?'

'I c . . . can't tell you.'

'Why not?' Her voice shook. And with that, emotion burst, spilling over into a sob.

'D . . . don't worry.' His voice was calm. 'There isn't l . . . long to wait now.'

Sheila tried to reply, ask what he meant, but her voice caught, and then he was talking again. 'You d . . . didn't tell me your name.'

Sheila frowned. 'What?'

'Your n . . . name. You didn't tell me. I'd like to kn . . . know what it is.'

She paused, chilled by his placidity. How could someone so outwardly docile take another person against their will, imprison them, and then ask for personal details as if they were sharing casual small talk at a party? And would it help if she told him? There was no way to know, but perhaps if she could build familiarity, it would improve her chances of walking away from this unharmed.

'Sheila,' she managed.

He didn't respond, for long enough that she began to wonder if maybe he'd gone, but then she heard him breathing again, and at last: 'What do you do . . . for a living?'

She thought about lying. 'I'm a teacher.'

More silence. 'My mum was a t . . . teaching assistant.'

Had there been a hint of sadness? She forced herself to engage. 'But not any more?'

'No, she p . . . passed away.'

'I'm sorry.' She gave the standard response without thinking, wondering if his stammer had been more pronounced than before. Had she tapped a vein of humanity, buried somewhere in her keeper's mind?

'You remind m . . . me of her.'

She couldn't think of anything to say.

Rupert went on. 'You're the s . . . same age she was when she died.'

Sheila paused. 'How do you know my age?'

'Your driving licence. I f . . . found it in your bag.' He spoke simply, as if he'd been invited to examine her personal things. But icy shockwaves ran through her when she realised the licence also showed her address.

She tried to stay calm, regroup and make another approach. But her emotions flared, and she blurted: 'Please don't do this. I have a family.'

Her mind flashed back to the roadside, stumbling along the verge, away from her car. She'd been grateful when he pulled in beside her, seeing a kind stranger offering help. She had no idea of his intentions, or what he was capable of.

How could she have been so fucking careless?

He started speaking again, but she cut him off as the creeping unease boiled over and she shouted: *'What do you want?'*

Then she was up, striding forwards. 'You can't do this.' She jerked at the handle; banged her fist on the door. 'Let me out. *Now!*'

He didn't answer, but daylight blazed through the hole as he stepped back. Adrenalin surged as Sheila pressed her face to the wood, pursuing him with her gaze.

Rupert stood a few feet away; the same timid man that had stopped his car the previous day. His head was bowed and he might have looked afraid, had it not been for the baleful stare he was firing back at her.

'I t . . . told you,' he said through gritted teeth. 'It isn't time.'

They glared at each other, breathing hard, neither one backing down. But Sheila sensed her resolve draining, as the natural high left her veins.

Rupert stared for a few seconds longer before he turned and left the room. Sheila slumped, her calves burning from standing on tiptoes. She dragged herself to the bed and dropped on to the mattress, mentally dissecting their exchange.

Force clearly wasn't going to work with her captor. In the face of her rage, Rupert might have backed away, but he hadn't backed down. He was gone for now, but she was still locked in the room, so whatever he had in store for her was probably still going to happen. And she didn't want to wait around to find out what it was.

Which meant she needed to act.

She heaved herself off the bed and stood, scanning the room.

Get yourself out of this.

Her gaze moved from one piece of furniture to the next, looking for something small but sturdy enough to smash a window pane, and then attack the bars outside. If the wood they were set in was old and fragile enough, she might be able to prise them apart far enough to get through. But everything in the room was too large or too rickety to be any use.

She crossed to the window, studying the metal bars outside the glass. But the more she tried to convince herself they were vulnerable, the sturdier they looked. They appeared to have been recently fitted, probably by her captor, which meant his actions were almost certainly planned. She hadn't been targeted, that much was obvious now she thought about it; he couldn't possibly have known she'd be stranded at the exact place and time he picked her up. So if it hadn't been her, would it have been somebody else? Her senses prickled as she looked over her shoulder at the room. What if there had already been others?

And if so, where were they now?

Heart pounding again, Sheila turned back to the window, even more desperate for the freedom so tantalisingly just out of *reach*. Come on, don't lose it.

Think.

Her mind darted frantically from one crazy idea to the next. If she smashed the window, would she be able to scream loud enough for someone to hear? *In this wilderness, probably not.* OK, why not wait till he came in and ambush him? *Because he didn't have to. He could simply wait till she starved or fell asleep, and do whatever he liked.* What if she pretended to collapse, and attacked him when he came to investigate? *No good, because he'd probably still be too strong.*

But as she rested there, staring at the window ledge, her vision came into focus, and a plan started to form. It was risky, maybe even stupid, but she wasn't exactly flush with options, and besides, it might just work.

Maybe there was a way out after all.

48

'Fuck me.' Mitch Coleman shot off his chair. 'How many more times? I didn't touch the cun—'

'Sit down, Mr Coleman.' Hawkins rose with him.

They locked stares across the table, accompanied by taut silence from the room's other occupants. Aaron Sharpe straightened in his seat, while Coleman's solicitor reached for his client's arm, which was jerked free.

Hawkins felt herself being assessed. Coleman looked ready to start using his fists but she held her ground, confident they were merely communicating on his level. If past experience had shown them anything, it was that Mitch Coleman understood threatening behaviour; worked almost exclusively on its terms.

Clearly they had riled the cab company owner, who must have assumed himself in the clear when their previous encounter was cut short by the discovery of a second body, especially one to which he had no obvious link. The shock on his face had been clear earlier that day, when Hawkins and Sharpe turned up at his best mate's gym, to find him knocking seven bells out of a bag.

After a short explanation from Hawkins regarding the reason for their call, it had been established that insults were all they'd get out of Mitch Coleman until legal representation arrived. The upshot had been a not entirely relaxed car ride to Tottenham station, followed by a tense three-hour wait for his solicitor, the pretentiously suited Morris Paul. Their detainee had spent the interim working himself into the scarcely contained rage that had just broken loose.

Hawkins watched the odds being calculated behind Coleman's furrowed stare, but at last he did the intelligent thing, sinking into his seat slowly enough to resume hostilities, should anyone flinch in the dying seconds of confrontation.

'That's better.' She followed him down; aware that seeing off such impulsively belligerent competition was a milestone in itself.

She checked the clock, amazed to find that the interview was barely five minutes old. Her first question had almost precipitated carnage, so she adjusted her approach, keen not to let things deteriorate further. 'Let's go back to what you were saying about Peter Barnes' disappearance.'

Coleman shook his head. 'Like I said; fuck all to do with me.'

'OK.' She nodded at Sharpe, who got up and left the room. Coleman watched him go, clearly suspicious, but Hawkins let him hang, waiting for the door to close before going on. 'So the story goes that you couldn't have attacked Peter Barnes because you were at your friend's gym all evening, and he'll stand up in court to swear that's the case, correct?'

'Hallelujah.'

She smiled as Aaron returned. He placed a large clear bag containing a battered pair of grey boots on the desk.

Hawkins nodded at them as Sharpe retook his seat. 'Are these yours?'

'Could be.' Coleman sat back. 'Standard workman's Daisies.'

'But you own a similar pair.'

'Yeah.' He glanced at his brief. 'So what?'

'Let me join the dots for you.' Hawkins eased the shoes nearer to him. 'These *are* yours, Mitch; we removed them from your hallway earlier today. You were wearing them the night Peter Barnes disappeared.'

Doubt crept into Coleman's expression as he looked at the boots. 'What are you on?'

'You didn't check them, did you?' Hawkins pressed her advantage. 'When you got home that night.'

'Why would I need to *check* them?'

'Because they're carrying traces of Mr Barnes' blood.'

Coleman's eyes narrowed and he sat forward, leaning from side to side as he examined the weathered footwear through the plastic. 'There's no claret on those.'

'Not that you can see with the naked eye,' she agreed, 'but only because your wife cleaned them the following day.'

'Tell you that, did she?' Coleman crossed his arms. 'Lying slut's trying to fuck me over.'

'Don't knock Lauren,' Hawkins warned, 'she tried to do you a favour, and now she's facing charges for destroying evidence. Anyway, if she wanted to screw you, why didn't she report it at the time?'

'I told you, she's a twisted cow. Who knows why you slags do any fucking thing?'

Hawkins ignored the insult. 'It's understandable you forgot to look. You had a lot on your mind, like trying to wash the blood out of your clothes. I have to say it's an interesting tactic, though; personally I'd have burned them.' She nodded at the designer label on his jacket. 'Though with an attitude like yours, I suppose it would cost you a fortune if you destroyed every piece of clothing you had a ruck in.'

He pulled a face. 'This is such bollocks.'

'Fortunately,' Hawkins continued, 'Lauren did the right thing in the end, and modern techniques can draw microscopic traces from the fibres themselves, so now we have a DNA sample from your clothing that matches Peter Barnes' blood.' She paused, hoping her bluff wouldn't be called, because in fact, only blood *type* could be ascertained so fast. They had taken samples from the shoes that afternoon, and sure enough the types matched, but Barnes was group O, the most common, and the limitations of the testing process meant they wouldn't know for certain that it was his until the morning at least. If her plan worked, however, they wouldn't need proof.

'So,' she said, watching their prisoner's unease grow, 'at some point on the night of Peter Barnes' death, your shoes picked up traces of his blood. Would you care to explain how it got there?'

Coleman turned to his brief. 'I'm being fitted up, here. Earn your fucking dough for a change.'

The solicitor shifted uncomfortably in his seat, adjusted his shiny pink tie and considered Hawkins as he drew breath. 'As you know, Detective, my client's wife was conducting an extra-marital affair with Mr Barnes at the time of his death. She may claim to have *found* blood on these boots, but I've heard no evidence to suggest exactly when or how it came to be there. Regardless of whether Mr Coleman was wearing them on the evening in question, it's perfectly possible that Mrs Coleman had her lover killed, and then purposely applied DNA evidence to my client's footwear in order to frame him for the murder. Until you have more convincing evidence, I see no reason for him to be detained. So if you don't mind . . .' He stood, motioning for Coleman to do the same.

Hawkins cut him off. 'Your client's going nowhere, Mr Paul.' She waited for him to sit before turning back to their suspect. 'Unless you can explain how the blood came to be on these boots, we have to assume you're in this up to your neck, which means we go looking for imprints that match them at every murder scene so far. As your brief mentioned, they're a popular brand, so even if we get a coincidental or partial match, it won't look good for you in court. Add that to the blood on the boots and your previous convictions, and how far do you think the benefit of the doubt is going to stretch?'

She let him stew for a moment, adding, 'I understand

why you want to distance yourself from this, Mitch, but come on, let's forego the macho nonsense and sort this out like adults. You knew Lauren was playing away with Barnes, but he was a big guy with twenty years on you, so it made sense to keep tabs on them and wait for a night when Pete was good and steaming before you tried taking him down. You saw them leave the club that night, and watched him put your wife in a cab. Right so far?'

Coleman said nothing, though his attention was complete enough to confirm that she wasn't far off.

She continued. 'I think you followed Barnes away from the club and, as soon as the opportunity presented itself, you beat the living daylights out of him.' The solicitor raised a defensive hand, but Hawkins talked over him, still watching Coleman. 'Except it might surprise you to hear that I don't believe you actually killed him.'

Coleman's frown deepened, and he studied her for a moment before answering. 'That what you think, is it?'

She nodded. 'Someone else took Barnes after you finished with him; the same someone who was responsible for his death. But I need to know where they picked him up, which is why I want you to fill in the blanks.' To her right, she was reassured to feel Sharpe fidget, which meant he'd correctly identified her strategy as high risk. Revealing your train of thought to a suspect, especially when it suggested his innocence, was rarely the best way to prompt disclosure, but with more victims likely, and few other leads, the gamble was worth a try. Plus she sensed that Coleman was ready to cave. All he needed was one final nudge.

'The faster we trace the real killer,' she teased, 'the sooner we can go back to charging you with plain old ABH. Come on, Mitch, tell us where you left him.'

This time Coleman didn't look at his solicitor. He paused long enough to illustrate that it was still his choice to talk, comfortable to leave the accusation hanging while he made up his mind. His next two words on the subject were somewhat confusing, but ones that Hawkins almost hugged him for.

'Clapton Common.'

49

Sheila clung to the last sliver of sunlight as it crept silently off the edge of another brick, on to the thin strip of mortar. But there it winked out, crushed between the window frame and the trees.

She was left in the dull hue of dusk, her pulse reacting when she realised the day was almost gone; that sundown would soon turn into night. It meant she'd been here almost twenty-four hours. More than that, it brought whatever this man had planned for her nearer.

Telling herself to stay calm, Sheila stood and crossed to the desk, fumbling in the half-light for a switch on the only lamp in the room. The low wattage bulb jolted to life. Its glow spread, casting rough crescents across the brickwork and picking out eerie shadows behind the furniture, ethereal spectres flushed out by the light.

But she spun, senses spiking, as the noise reached her ears.

She stared at the peephole in the door, holding her breath, trying to block out the renewed whump of blood in her veins. It had sounded like the creaking of a cupboard hinge, a harmless distraction under normal circumstances, but not here, not *now*. She realised he hadn't made a sound for almost fifteen minutes, and that in the lull, she had become distracted. But here was a reminder that her kidnapper remained just yards away.

Throughout the afternoon she had listened to him moving around outside her makeshift cell. Sometimes there had been clanking, as if he was tidying up, and occasionally he would mumble to himself, mostly indecipherable bursts under his breath. At one point he'd spoken a few sentences in succession, with short gaps in between. Sheila had sneaked to the door, thinking that he was addressing an accomplice, perhaps discussing what to do with her next. His speech had been clear; defined statements with emotion and lilt. She caught snatches about a hospital, something about doctors having done everything they could. But when she peered through to find him at the window, staring out into the trees, he hadn't been using a phone. Whoever Rupert thought he was talking to had been present only in his head. In that moment, Sheila's hopes of negotiating her way out of this, should her primary plan fail, fell apart.

Periodically he would return to the door.

Their resulting conversations had been awkward, stilted affairs, hardly surprising given the circumstances, although she still couldn't work out *why* he was trying to engage. She knew about things like Stockholm Syndrome: psychological bonding between captive and captor in hostage situations. It certainly felt like his aim was familiarisation, so maybe he was trying to incite some kind of dependence in her. On each occasion, his approach had been to ask if she was OK. She'd said yes every time, because that seemed to be what he wanted to hear. How the hell were you supposed to react when someone kidnapped you, locked you in a room, and then asked you *that*?

He'd move on to basic but personal questions about her hobbies, her job, the kinds of food that she liked; which was ironic when he still hadn't fed her. The headache beginning to work at the base of her skull meant she'd require sustenance if this went on much longer, but she refused to beg. And he must have drugged the alcohol he'd given her in the car, so who knew what he might put in her food?

Obviously he knew how long she'd been here, and that eventually she'd have to eat something, which meant that either starvation was part of his plan, or whatever he had in mind was going to happen pretty soon.

She turned her attention back to their previous inter-actions. Communicating through the door wasn't easy, and at times she'd struggled to hear his words. The rudimentary answers she'd given seemed to placate him, though, and each time he'd offered information about himself in return. But that was a worry in itself.

He talked freely about his past; the names of his former schools, the history of the house where she was being held. She'd memorised as much as possible, conscious that such facts would help the police track him down. If she got the chance to tell them.

That also assumed any of what he'd told her was true. But the most frightening thing was that he'd allowed her to see something about which he was unable to lie.

His face.

Rupert's features were imprinted on her memory, like the residual glare from looking at the sun, visible whenever she closed her eyes, whether she liked it or not. She could give a detailed description of him, to allow photofits to be made. Although maybe that was the point? The terrifying, uninvited question repeated itself in her head:

What if you aren't supposed to leave this place alive?

Another bang from the kitchen focused her thoughts.

As far as she could tell, Rupert hadn't left the adjoining room for more than a few minutes since she'd woken earlier in the day, and there was no indication that pattern would change. The gaps between him coming to the door tended to be about an hour each time, and his last visit must have been thirty minutes ago. But hunger was already making her sleepy, and the thought of what he might do next petrified her. Every slim chance of escape passed up might be her last.

So it had to be now.

Sheila drew breath and slid a hand under her pillow, feeling for the cold metal shape. Her fingers found the rough corner and she pulled it free, transferring it to her lap before hiding it between her knees.

She glanced back at the window, eyeing the splintered wood at the base of the frame. From where she'd prised the lever.

Earlier, while Rupert had talked to himself, Sheila

had initiated her newly formed plan. She had already established that the sturdy metal bars made it pointless trying to open the window, but only when she came to lean on the sill in despair had she noticed the wooden frame splitting in places, clearly having borne years of condensation and damp. She'd lifted the lever off its rest, turned it ninety degrees against the plate, fetched the plug from the lamp and wedged it underneath, then leaned on the far end as hard as she could. After a couple of goes, the screws had ripped clean out of the wood, leaving Sheila triumphantly holding the rusted metal length. Quickly she'd returned the lamp to the desk and concealed her prize, hoping that Rupert would be too focused on her to notice it missing the next time he came to the door.

Success. But it was only the first step.

Her original plan had been to wait for him to leave the kitchen area. Clinging to that hope, and having already obtained the lever, Sheila had made herself wait. A short while later Rupert had returned, this time curious about her children. She'd given him two made-up names, which he hadn't questioned. As usual he'd withdrawn after a short interaction, but had remained inside the house. Sheila had stayed hopeful that eventually he'd leave her alone, but as the afternoon stretched on, those hopes had faded. And he still hadn't left.

She took a breath and let it out slowly, gripping the lever tight as she stood, holding it down by her side.

Her guts felt as if they were being wrung out as she

moved to the door, risking another peek to make sure Rupert wasn't waiting on the other side.

The kitchen was almost in darkness. Rupert hadn't turned on any lights, but she picked him out in the gathering gloom near the back wall, moving slowly from cupboard to cupboard, as if looking for something he'd mislaid. He was still muttering, the same extraneous bursts of dialogue she'd heard before. But he didn't notice her.

She scanned the kitchen for her bag. She'd been carrying it when he picked her up, so it had to be here somewhere. It contained her mobile phone, and even though there was no guarantee she'd have a signal in the woods outside the house, if she managed to get out of here it was worth taking with her. She couldn't see the bag.

You're wasting time.

Her pulse raced as she stepped back and pushed the lever carefully between door handle and jamb, counting on the fact that all the wood in the room looked to be of a similar age, solid once; now fatigued. She kept pushing till the tapered end wedged itself in the slot. Then, as quietly as possible, she began working it left and right, widening the gap a little each time, wincing at every dull creak as the fissure began opening up.

She stopped every so often to check on her progress, and listen for clues that might suggest she'd been overheard. But the sounds from the kitchen continued, new noises of chiming crockery suggesting that food might soon be on its way. Her stomach protested but she ignored it, the tantalising prospect of freedom now too strong a draw. Instead she renewed her efforts, sawing back and forth, ignoring the pain of the sharp hinge digging into her palms.

At last she had opened the gap almost far enough to lift the frame clear of the bolt; most of the metal pin now visible between the rent pieces of wood.

She gave the lever one final shove. At first it resisted, but then there was a dull crack as the wood split and the lever jerked free, slicing her palm. Sheila yelped and snatched her hand away. She slunk back to the bed, posting the tool under her pillow.

Footsteps.

She raised her right knee, holding the ankle in fake distress, heart pounding as he arrived outside. She heard him breathing, felt the weight of suspicious eyes. All she could do was focus on her act, and pray she hadn't blown her only chance.

Then he spoke, his soft tone shot through with distrust. 'Are you OK?'

'Yes.' Sheila rubbed her leg, feigned insolence.

'I heard a n . . . noise.'

'I tripped,' she lied. 'I'm fine.'

Silence returned. Did he believe her? She heard him fidget.

Sheila dropped her gaze to avoid eye contact, still afraid that he might notice the window, see its frame damaged; lever gone. But the panic grew when she noticed the red smear on the duvet. She pressed her torn palm hard against her jeans, trying to stem the flow of blood.

At last his response came, but the words were so unexpected, they took a moment to decode. 'This p . . . place is always chilly. I hope you aren't c . . . cold.'

Sheila turned her head towards the door, trying to work out whether he could see the blood on the duvet from outside. She glanced down at the crimson wetness soaking into the fabric. But Rupert's tone remained detached, as if he had already assessed her honesty and moved on.

'There's n . . . no heating,' Rupert continued. 'But it was my parents'. I c . . . can't leave.'

'What happened to them?' Sheila asked. He seemed eager to talk, so maybe this was her chance to connect.

'They d . . . died in a car accident. Four years ago.'

'And you've been here alone ever since?'

'No. My f . . . friend Ash came to stay.'

A housemate? Sheila had seen no one else up to now, but that didn't mean they weren't working together. 'Is he here?'

'No . . . He died, as well.'

'It must have been a difficult time.'

There was a hint of melancholy when his response finally came, but it was the undertone of acceptance that sent dread shooting through her.

'Everyone dies.'

50

Rupert gripped the steering wheel and pulled himself forward in his seat, staring up at the curve-fronted structure dominating the far side of the road, the words St Margaret's written vertically on its white plaster facade. 'Everything's g . . . going to be OK, isn't it?'

Ash shoved him. 'Chill out, for fuck's sake.'

The knots in Rupert's stomach were as bad as they'd ever been. Today was the big day, after all, but somehow Ash seemed less angry than he'd been in a while.

He turned to his friend. 'What if the drugs f . . . fixed you?'

Ash shook his head. 'Doesn't work that way.' He opened the door.

'Wait!' Rupert grabbed his arm, recoiling when he realised what he was doing. Ash hated being touched.

But this time he smiled. 'You're such a pussy.'

'They're g . . . going to hurt you.'

'They'd better not. I'll fuck them up.'

Rupert brightened. 'You p . . . promise?'

'Yeah. Look, go home and come back in a few hours. I don't want you in there, winding everyone up.'

'But what if something b . . . bad happens?'

Ash thought for a second, then shrugged. 'Make a new mate.'

'N . . . no. No way.' Rupert looked down; picked at his jumper. 'People hate me. They th . . . think I'm weird.'

'You are weird, but most people are. Some are moody fuckers like me; others are knobheads, like you. If someone doesn't like you, just fuck them off and move on, got it?'

Rupert nodded at his feet.

'Good.' Ash got out: 'Now piss off. I'll see you later. And don't forget my cigarettes.'

He stood beside the car for a minute, bending down to look at Rupert with an odd expression. Then he limped off across the car park. Rupert watched him getting smaller and smaller, the knots in his stomach twisting harder.

It was a warm autumn afternoon; visitors walking in and out of the hospital were dressed in skirts, T-shirts, shorts. But he shivered as Ash got to the front doors.

He wanted to jump out of the car, run over and tell him not to go in.

He had a bad feeling.

At the last moment, Ash turned and looked back; gave him a quick thumbs-up.

He smiled and waved till his friend turned and disappeared through the hospital doors. Then he started the car and drove away, thinking about Ash.

And how it felt like friendship again.

51

Sheila sat motionless, her mind racing as she tried to think of something to say; anything that would steer the conversation off death.

Nothing came.

It had been at least a minute since either of them had spoken. The only sounds came from outside: the intermittent smattering of water droplets driven against the window; an aeroplane somewhere high overhead.

Her thoughts returned to her captor, the apparently benign, stuttering man who had offered help when she was in need, and then abused her resulting trust to kidnap and imprison her. The more she found out about him, the more enigmatic and frightening he became. She didn't scare easily, but at that moment, Rupert, and the things he might be capable of, terrified her.

She began to sweat as she pictured Rupert outside the room, unsheathing a burnished metal cleaver. Reaching for the lock.

Sheila glanced down, looking for dark patches between the floorboards; traces of blood in the cracks that even sustained cleaning couldn't erase. There were none.

But still there was silence.

Then she realised what was missing. Until now she'd

always known whenever Rupert was at the door, simply because of how heavily he breathed. She waited, straining to detect any sound from outside.

Nothing.

'Hello?' she said, loudly enough for him to hear.

No reply.

Carefully, Sheila lifted her hand away from her jeans, checking to see if the cut was still bleeding, but the crimson blot around the small gash had almost crusted over, and only a small amount of fresh blood leaked out when she flexed her palm.

Encouraged, she stood and walked to the commode, her strategy to assess whether explicably innocent movement would prompt a response from her captor. But no response came, and there was no change in the shadows around the hole in the door when she turned to check.

Reaching down, Sheila tore off a few sheets of toilet paper and wadded them in her cut palm. Then she moved over to the door and pressed her face against the wood.

He wasn't in the kitchen, still unlit in the fast gathering gloom.

So where was he?

The noise made her glance up, the unmistakeable sound of a creaky floorboard telling her exactly where Rupert was. He'd spent the entire day in the kitchen, bouncing around like a slow-motion pinball. And now, for some reason, he'd left mid-conversation and retreated upstairs, quietly enough that she hadn't heard him go.

But why?

It doesn't matter. This is your chance.

Sheila grabbed the doorknob with her good hand before she had time to back out, gripped, and twisted. She watched the latch retracting into the door, willing the metal bolt to clear the freshly damaged jamb. The corner emerged and she pulled excitedly, losing her grasp as the bolt snapped back into place.

Panic flared as she reached for the handle again. This time the latch moved further, but it still wouldn't release. She leaned closer, just able to see in the lamp's dismal glow that she hadn't opened the gap evenly; the lower left edge of the bolt was still trapped by the strike plate. She wanted to scream.

Another creak from upstairs, and for a second Sheila thought about going back for the lever, prising the gap open the rest of the way. But then a faster possibility occurred.

She twisted the handle one more time and held it there, bracing her right foot at the base of the door, heaving upwards as hard as she could. Tired hinges groaned as they moved, wide tolerances allowing sufficient play for the door to rise, millimetres, but maybe enough.

Already beginning to shake from the strain, Sheila edged backwards, keeping upward pressure on the handle, and pulled. There was the briefest resistance, followed by a high-pitched squeak.

Then it came loose.

Sheila wrenched the door open and ran for the exit

on the far side, through it before she had time to think about what would have happened had it been locked. She stumbled out into the darkness, finding herself in a small clearing surrounded by trees; freezing spots of rain burning her scalp, her eyes adjusting to the moonlight.

Get away from the house.

Gravel crunched under her feet as she went for the treeline. She slowed as the forest engulfed her, hands out to protect her face, and began trampling undergrowth, feet now slipping on damp mud and foliage. It hadn't crossed her mind up to now, but she couldn't have chosen better footwear than the sturdy walking boots she'd worn for the intended camping trip.

She risked a glance behind, half expecting to see Rupert bearing down. Through the trees she glimpsed the house: a squat, two-storey building of dark grey stone. One of the upstairs windows was lit, but she saw no one inside.

A few metres in she stopped, panting hard as her mind and heart raced. Unbelievably she was out, but that was only the start. Forty-eight-year-old legs had brought her this far on adrenalin, but she couldn't maintain that pace for long. And besides, as soon as Rupert realised she was gone and probably came after her, crashing arbitrarily through the trees would simply reveal her position.

She waited, picking up the scent of pine, the sound of a distant canine howl. White clouds of her breath curled away in the half-light, and she felt the forest's clammy wetness settle on her skin. Somewhere high above, the faint roar of an aeroplane was the only indication she was anywhere near civilisation. Except to reach it, she'd have to escape this rasping wilderness.

But how?

Using her brain had got her this far, so her best chance now was to stay one step ahead; do the unexpected, find something Rupert would miss.

Think.

She dropped into a crouch and edged to her left, until she could see the whole front of the house through the trees, reassuring herself that no one could cross the gravel drive without creating a fair amount of noise.

As the thought entered her head she heard it over the pattering bassline of rain; the soft crunch of someone placing their weight on loose stones. Her heart rate leapt as she studied the darkness, fighting to keep her breath under control. At first there was no change in the shadows, and she cursed the lack of light. Was he skirting the rear of the area, too deep in the blackness to be seen?

Then she caught movement.

A silhouette ghosted out from near the house, accompanied by a faint shush from the stones as it took each slow, deliberate step. Her kidnapper moved into a patch of moonlight, now dressed head to toe in black, wearing some kind of angular headgear. Sheila watched him turn, slowly scanning the trees, her heart leaping when she realised it must allow him to see in the dark. She shrank behind the bushes, losing sight of him, aware that the odds had just tipped even harder against her.

The thought barged its way into her head.

Had he *let* her escape?

He knew you damaged the door. That's why he went upstairs: to encourage you to run. He set the trap, and you fell right in.

He's hunting you.

Sheila closed her eyes and held her breath. Every instinct told her to run, but she forced herself to wait.

He knows you're here. He's trying to flush you out.

It was only a matter of time before he started scouring the trees.

Another shush. Nearer this time.

Sheila compacted herself even further, willing the mud to swallow her up. She had to do something, but *what*?

She leaned forwards and placed her hands on the cold, damp ground, trying to catch a glimpse of him through the trees. And as she shifted, the answer came.

Sheila steadied herself and began to dig at the soil, fingers working to free the large stone she'd found by touch a few seconds before. The wetness of the mud seemed to help, and quickly it came free. She sat back, hefting its weight, judging the clearest route through the trees. She chose a path heading diagonally away from the house and launched the stone on a low, flat trajectory into the gloom.

It skitted away into the darkness. She heard it land and roll, making a noise that could convincingly have been someone dislodging foliage in the dark.

Immediately stones shifted as her pursuer turned and entered the trees, small rushes of sound giving him away. Sheila held her position, letting him pass. At the same time, she unlaced her right boot and slipped it off, removing her long, thick sock and replacing the shoe. Then her fingers returned to the mud, prising the largest stone she could find from the soft ground, dropping it into the sock. She tested its mass before tying one knot above the fist-sized stone, and another into the opposite end to make a ring, which she slipped over her palm.

Her heart hammered in time with the rain as she went back to listening for Rupert, and within seconds she had another fix: a muted crunch ten or fifteen yards to her right.

The best chance she was going to get.

Tentatively Sheila rose and, staying low, picked her way through the undergrowth, back towards the house. She stopped short of the treeline, as soon as the moonlight penetrated far enough for her to see the ground, and turned to follow the edge of the clearing, pausing every few steps to listen again.

Repeating the pattern, she soon reached the road that led away from the clearing and followed it, keeping just inside the trees. Her plan was to stay close to the track until she hit an intersection, and flag down the next driver to pass. But it was impossible to guess how far she was from a public road, while her pace was hampered by trying not to make any noise. She was still less than twenty yards from the house, covering just a few feet every minute, so if Rupert realised he'd been duped and doubled back, he'd easily find her.

You need to move faster.

Sheila closed her eyes and tried to concentrate on the forest, clenching her jaw to keep her teeth from chattering. She tried to tune out the clicking raindrops, and the rustle of wind in the leaves, listening for noises at odds with the natural rhythms around her. There were none.

She sped up, no longer slowing to negotiate branches or scrub, treacherous vegetation hissing as she passed. She paused less frequently as the distance stretched, confidence growing that she might make it out of this alive.

But then it came. A dull crunch, behind her and to the right.

Sheila dropped back into a crouch, heartbeat leaping into her ears as she tuned into the sound, telling herself it was an animal; a fox or something like that. But just as she started to think it was nothing, it happened again.

For a second Sheila froze, too scared to move. But then survival instinct kicked in.

She half stood, turning to scan the trees. At first there was no sign of her kidnapper among the deep shadows. But then she caught two pinpricks of emerald green, glinting in the middle distance.

He had found her.

She ran, veering on to the road outside the trees. Behind her, a crash indicated that Rupert had given chase, and panic rose when she pictured the younger, faster predator closing her down. She tried to focus on the road ahead. No junction was visible yet, just a sloping track stretching off round a bend.

But more noises from behind boosted her resolve, reminding her that he had twenty yards of thick forest to get through before he reached the road and could get up to full speed in pursuit.

Her boots gripped the glistening surface as she entered the bend, staying near the trees on the inside to shorten her route. Everything was burning now, her muscles starved of oxygen as she tried desperately to maintain speed. But she drove herself onwards, clutching the stone in her makeshift flail, not daring to look back.

She heard the final swish of undergrowth, followed by a second pair of feet crunching on to the road in her wake. The footfalls were still distant, but they repeated faster than hers. He was closing.

For a second she thought about stopping, turning to reason with him while she still could. But instinct said keep going.

Had this chase been his intention all along? And what would he do to her when he caught up? Would she die here, tonight, on this road?

Her thoughts flipped again as she came out of the turn to find another gentle slope stretching down and away, except this time she saw a T-junction at the far end; and hope flared when she saw lights flickering through the trees away to their right.

A car.

'*Help!*' she screamed, raising her arms, knowing it was too far away. '*Help me. Please!*'

The lights swept past, turning red as the car accelerated away.

No.

Tears welled, though she couldn't be sure if they were due to exhaustion or fear, or the wind rushing into her eyes.

She was less than fifteen yards from the junction, and the slope of the track had increased, pulling her on. The trees thinned near the intersection, letting the moonlight in. If another car passed now the driver might see her, but there were no more headlights, and she could hear Rupert breathing behind her, closer than ever.

He was right with her.

Pain flared in her ankles as she fought to stay upright on the treacherous stones, her pace dropping again on exhausted legs. She wasn't going to make it to the road.

Then she was shoved.

Two hands punched the centre of her back, pitching her forwards. Her legs crumpled and she fell, just managing to get the heels of her hands out as she landed, wet gravel ripping her palms before she twisted and rolled, skidding to a halt on her side.

Immediately he was there, grabbing at her, trying to pin her down, his mouth twisting below the angular black mask. Sheila kicked out, her boot making solid contact. Her attacker grunted and dropped aside, briefly releasing her. She tried to roll away, but he grabbed her arm with frightening strength, wrenching her back.

She raised her leg to kick again, but he dropped his weight on to her shin, bracing the leg against her chest. Sheila yelled as it cramped, but she couldn't move to ease the pain. Her body bucked as they clawed at each other, a flurry of movement focused on gaining or breaking the decisive hold.

She lost.

The strength in her arms was fading fast as trembling weakness took hold. He wrenched her wrists together across her stomach and pinned them there with a knee, driving the breath from her. Then his hands were on her throat, gripping hard, cutting off the air. Her neck tensed as she tried to inhale, but her chest heaved helplessly. She drove her chin downwards, trying to crush his hands. It made no difference.

She heard the stones grind beneath them, the noise fading as fight abandoned her. Her throat clicked, pulsing as reflex tried to drag oxygen into her lungs, but his grip was absolute. All she could do was stare up at the jagged black mask, pleading with its callous green eyes.

Let me go. Please.

Her vision started to blur, and her gaze drifted upwards, past his shoulder to the moon, round and bright, part obscured by patchy cloud. An odd calmness descended, and everything softened. She no longer felt his hands or his weight on her stomach. Her mind tuned in to minute sensations: the cold drizzle hitting her face, the scratchy fabric of the makeshift flail against her palm, the rough road surface against the back of her hand . . .

The flail.

Then she realised; Rupert had adjusted his position. So her arms were free.

Slowly her fist clenched as she looked at her attacker, lining up the shot. She was light-headed, like being drunk, and her throat still pulsed, trying to draw breath, even though there was no pain. She summoned what resilience she had left, and swung the flail.

She watched it hit the side of his head, heard the muffled crack of connection. He grunted and collapsed, releasing her. Instinctively she dragged at the air, lungs burning as she drew the oxygen down. She blinked the streaming tears from her eyes, glancing at Rupert, aware that she didn't have long. He lay beside her, apparently stunned. His hands were righting the mask, which had twisted on his head, one of its lenses smashed. But the remaining green eye turned slowly towards her, fixing her with its merciless stare.

Run.

Pain exploded in Sheila's head as she twisted away. She rolled up on to hands and knees, still gasping for breath, managing to get a foot down and launch herself upwards, staggering aside when Rupert lunged at her ankles. She stumbled away, the road ahead coming in and out of focus as she headed for the junction.

There was a growl from behind as her attacker regained his feet, followed by the slurred swash of gravel when he came at her again. This time Sheila didn't look back; just kept driving forwards, fighting to stay on course. At last she reached the road and staggered to its centre, aware that he was just inches behind.

But there were no cars.

In the split second she had left, Sheila realised that reaching the road meant nothing. It had been her whole focus, but it was pointless if there was no one there to help. She started to turn.

As he crashed into her.

They fell together, Sheila crying out as her head hit the tarmac, setting off a shockwave that rang in her ears. The disfigured mask leered down at her, its remaining lens just inches from her face as she caught his rancid breath, ragged from the chase, hot on her cheeks. He rammed his forearm across her throat, while his free hand tore at the sock wrapped around her palm, ripping away her only defence and launching it into the trees.

Sheila began to choke, desperate coughs jerking through her as the air supply was severed once more. Her vision started to flash, interference arcing in from the sides, and her teeth ground as she clawed at him with her free hand. But her resistance was fading, and she felt consciousness slipping away.

The lids began to close over Sheila's eyes, and everything started to fade. Vivid light grew to her left, and she jerked her head towards it. *Was this what it felt like to die?*

It took a few more cycles of languid thought for her to realise they were headlights.

For a second the crushing weight on her neck lifted as her attacker's watery silhouette turned towards the glow. Sheila saw her chance, ramming her chin downwards, biting as hard as she could into his exposed wrist. He yelled and wrenched it free, jerking her forwards. She felt his flesh tear.

Whiteness flared as something slammed into the side of her face, sending a jolt of agony through her skull, forcing her jaw to release. She slumped, feeling his weight increase as he launched himself off her, hearing his feet crunch in retreat as the brightness peaked. Her eyes closed, stung by its intensity, leaving the maelstrom of agony to fight for attention in the black void of her brain.

For what seemed like forever, she listened to the sound of an engine at idle, but then it stopped.

The last things she heard.

'Can you hear me, love?

'Jesus Christ.'

52

Hawkins leaned back in her chair, trying to savour the creak of leather as she reclined, still unable to shake her growing sense of unease. The gap between the hands on her wall clock and nine thirty p.m. was growing desperately small, and even the short break she'd forced herself to take from the activity going on outside her office wasn't helping her to relax.

They were in that tantalising window she often craved and resisted in almost equal measure; the tapering knife edge you danced before falling either into the cosseting embrace of a breakthrough, or the ignominious pigsty of another dead end.

She had extracted herself from the ongoing investigation ten minutes ago, hoping that her absence would have the desired effect on the proverbial watched kettle. Unfortunately, the only outcome so far was the realisation that she hadn't eaten since breakfast, and that calorie-laden junk was fast becoming her only option if she preferred not to starve.

More disconcerting still was the unfamiliar urge she'd been fighting all afternoon. For the first time she could remember, Hawkins was frustrated that if things went as planned, work would occupy her till the early hours. Dropping exhausted into bed after midnight, a few hours of feverish sleep, and half-comatose returns to work the next day were a familiar routine to most detectives. Yet for once she found herself resenting the prospect, and, oddly, not because of the ludicrous imposition of it all.

But because she wanted to see the kids.

'Crazy,' she said aloud, shaking her head.

She'd been exhausted for almost a week now, but Hawkins had started looking forward to getting home more than she remembered in years. The resultant sniping between her and Mike had also reduced in recent days, despite their growing fatigue and the pressure of an escalating body count.

She had even begun to empathise with Siobhan, never previously having understood the demands of parenthood. The two of them had managed another civilised conversation earlier that evening, their second in as many days, when Hawkins had rung to say that she and Mike would be forced to work late.

She checked the time, calculating that both youngsters should now be asleep, it being Sunday night. Rosie had infants in the morning, and Kyle pre-school, so Siobhan would have picked the necessary fight early, giving herself the best chance of both children being settled by half-eight. Had the idea of managing bedtime been proposed to Hawkins just a week ago, she might have run for the hills. Tonight she was genuinely annoyed to have missed it.

Sarcastic Storytime had been invented by mistake, but

both kids thought it hilarious whenever Hawkins read their favourite books in her less-than-apposite tone.

The biting click of knuckles rapping glass lifted her from thought.

'Yes?' She looked up as the door opened and Amala leaned in, one hand on the jamb. 'Think you'll want to see this, ma'am.'

'Coming.' Hawkins rose as her colleague withdrew. She followed the retreating sergeant through the investigation room and out into the main incident suite, turning left to see Amala retaking her seat in front of the department's new favourite toy. Hawkins approached, noting four bright images frozen on the large display screens in the rear section of the open-plan area.

She passed other officers dotted here and there among the tessellated desks, heads down, in the productive first flush of their night shifts. Handover had occurred two and a half hours ago, so the flurry of baton passing and task allocation had passed, dispensing incomers to their duties; outgoers towards home or pub, leaving calm in their collective wake.

Hawkins joined Yasir at the desk, already aware of what she was likely to see, expectations pre-tempered by the flatness of the sergeant's tone, and the fact she hadn't waited to accompany her boss to the video suite. On a daily basis Amala's optimism was almost impervious, except on the rare occasion she failed to deliver. Granted, the potential lack of a result here would reduce that afternoon's revelation to less of a breakthrough, although there must be something to see, or she wouldn't have been summoned at all. Hawkins' instincts were on alert – after all, they hadn't let her down earlier in the day.

She'd been right about Mitch Coleman.

That afternoon, after what felt like the hundredth time of asking, the cab company owner had finally cracked. Hawkins' admission, that she no longer suspected him of murdering his wife's most recent lover, had prompted long overdue honesty from their detainee.

Clearly encouraged by the prospect of eliminating himself once and for all from the suspect pool, Coleman had at last owned up to having attacked his other half's recently deceased boyfriend, Peter Barnes. Apparently Coleman had known of his spouse's various affairs for a long time, but until now he'd vented his frustration on Lauren. He maintained that none of the previous men had received personal attention from him, or from others on his behalf, and that Barnes had simply happened to be in the frame when his patience had finally frayed.

Hawkins suspected the truth was that Lauren's previous partners had been less intimidating to her husband's turbulent sensibilities. But her affair with Pete had outlasted its predecessors by a long way, perhaps due to the connection between them, not to mention his tuned physique and relative youth, all of which made Barnes the first credible threat to their marriage.

Whatever his motivation, Coleman now admitted tailing his wife on various nights out, waiting for an opportunity to provide corporal incentive for his rival to back off. The fact he chose to do so on a night Barnes had been drinking heavily was purely coincidental, of course, and while Coleman agreed that his attempts had been zealous, he maintained that his rival had definitely survived. But the critical part of the story was location.

On the night in question, after watching Barnes exit the club on Ferry Lane with Lauren and put her in a cab bound for home, Coleman had planned to follow his inebriated foe on the usual five-minute walk to his nearby flat, intending to ambush him once they reached sufficient distance from the busy main road. Except on this occasion, Barnes hadn't followed his regular route. Instead of staggering home, the plasterer had rejoined the growing queue for taxis outside the venue, allowing Mitch time to retrieve his pickup from a side road and follow the car that eventually carried Barnes towards Tottenham Hale.

Fifteen minutes later, Coleman watched Barnes exit the cab near Clapton Common, a multi-egressed hotspot growing in popularity with the area's recreational drug dealers, and begin weaving his way slowly towards the park's west entrance.

Mitch parked up and followed on foot, observing from a distance as his younger rival conversed briefly with another man who then departed, leaving Barnes alone.

Coleman had seen his chance, ambushing his target as he retraced his steps through the common's deepest shadows. He beat his victim half senseless, stopping while Barnes was still conscious enough to understand his instruction to stay away from Lauren; a warning Pete hadn't lived to heed.

With Coleman's confession tucked away on the station's server, Hawkins had curtailed the session, although she had held on to him, at least until they could verify his story. Then she'd called Yasir and instructed her to chase CCTV records from every lens pointing at Clapton Common. Amala had quickly obtained footage from three cameras on the park's periphery and begun her analysis. Meanwhile, Mike and Aaron had driven to the scene, tasked with identifying any private cameras overlooking the site – shops or businesses with an eye on security, for example, potentially plugging holes in the coverage they already had.

And it seemed Hawkins might be about to get an idea of where those gaps were, as she pulled up a chair. 'What have we got?'

'Well, the good news is that I found them.' Yasir waited for her boss to settle and started the footage on three of the displays.

Cars began traversing the two lower screens, headlights blazing through the darkness, washing out detail from the park's interior. The third image showed a quieter road without cars, overlooking a large pond.

'These images are from the three council-run cameras near the common.' Amala pointed at the aerial map on the remaining screen, Clapton Common a diagonal oblong surrounded and split by pathways and roads. 'The first two are on the park's west perimeter, while the other one's on the far side.'

Hawkins checked the time signatures. All showed 11:28 p.m. on the night Peter Barnes disappeared, around thirty minutes after he left the club with Lauren, and approximately twenty-four hours before he was buried in White Post Wood.

For a few seconds the pavements remained empty, as cars continued sweeping back and forth. But her attention was drawn to the lower left screen when a lone figure ambled into shot.

'Is that Barnes?' Hawkins leaned closer, trying to decipher the pixelated image, noting the patterned red shirt and dark grey trousers that Lauren Coleman had described.

'I think so, ma'am. I've sent a screen dump for enhancement, just to be sure, but it has to be him.' Yasir rewound the footage a short distance and replayed it, pointing out a car with Rapide written large on the passenger door, passing through the frame a moment before their target arrived. 'I rang the Boilerhouse, and they use a local cab company called Rapide. Barnes must have got out further along this road.'

'Makes sense.' Hawkins watched Barnes enter the scene again, noting his heel-heavy gait. He trudged to centre screen and turned off into the park, soon disappearing amongst the gloom. Cars continued to pass, but there was no immediate sign of his attacker.

Amala used the controls to skip forwards three

minutes, returning to normal speed just before Mitch Coleman appeared from the lower left corner, clearly having used the interlude to deposit his pickup in Castlewood Road, a side turning further along the A107, and walk back, just as he claimed.

In contrast to Barnes' lurid shirt, every piece of Coleman's clothing was black, down to the beanie hat and gloves. He'd come prepared.

They watched him follow Barnes on to the common.

'There's nothing else for another twelve minutes,' Yasir said, rolling forwards to 11:43, when the black-clothed figure walked briskly out of the park and crossed the road before passing out of shot.

'Do we see Barnes exit?' Hawkins asked.

Amala nodded, fast-forwarding again. 'He doesn't reappear till 11:57. I suppose it took him a while to recover.'

She hit play, and Barnes staggered out of the darkness, moving even more slowly now. One arm cradled his ribcage, the other braced intermittently against a knee to keep him upright. He headed back the way he had come, eventually disappearing from shot.

Hawkins looked at her colleague. 'Can we track him?'

'Sorry, ma'am, the other two cameras are in the opposite direction. There may be non-council systems further out, but it'll take time to get footage from those, and given how badly Barnes is moving, chances are that he was picked up nearby, so unless there's another camera pretty close, we're unlikely to see the car stop.'

Hawkins swore, drumming her nails on the desktop as she thought. The good news was that this new evidence supported her theory. Whatever Barnes' reason for visiting Clapton Common, be it to buy drugs that his best friend was convinced he didn't use, or even steroids to maintain his striking physique, the list of fatalities now included an assault victim, a stranded teenager and a hitchhiker, all three convincingly *in need*. It remained unclear what misfortune had befallen Ray Jewis, but three out of four was enough. Now the critical element became the killer's mode of transport.

'OK.' She pointed at the traffic skimming back and forth on the screens. 'You can read the number plates on a lot of these cars, and if we assume Barnes was picked up nearby, the vehicle would have passed at least one of the cameras.' She waited for Amala's nod of agreement. 'So I need registered keepers for everything that passes within thirty minutes of Barnes leaving the common, then I want that information cross-referenced with the equivalent material from Upney Lane, in the hour after Keith Shawcross dumped Viola Clarkson there on the day she disappeared. I'll call Mike and Aaron, tell them to focus their search in the direction we've just seen Barnes go. It's probably stolen or on dodgy plates, but if we can identify any car present at both locations, we'll be a lot closer to apprehending our murderer.' She shrugged. 'It's a long shot, but you never know.'

Hawkins was retrieving her mobile to call Mike when it rang. She answered, and listened with a slowly deepening frown.

'What is it?' Yasir asked when she ended the brief conversation.

'Keep working on those plates,' Hawkins instructed, already heading for the exit. 'I'll update you as soon as I get to Harlow hospital.'

But Amala's confused silence prompted her to offer clarification as she neared the stairs.

'We may have a survivor.'

53

'Come *on*.' Hawkins pressed the call button again and jabbed impatiently at the Sani-Foam dispenser as she waited, her charge through the Princess Alexandra Hospital halted by Winter Ward's security door. Twenty seconds of being ignored later, she turned at the sound of a depositing lift, hoping for a nurse, or at least a regular visitor who knew the access code.

Instead she found her DI.

'Ten sixty-six.' Maguire saw her and strode over, leaning past a bemused Hawkins to punch in his prediction, frowning when the light stayed red. He shrugged. 'Read somewhere it's the most common pin code used by you Brits. Any news?'

'No.' Hawkins thumbed the bell for the fourth time, hoping that someone had enforced her demand for the nurse who called 101 just over an hour ago to be available when she and Mike arrived. Maguire had come from Upper Clapton and she had raced there from Hendon, to find the hospital's labyrinthine parking area buried under Portakabins and temporary railings. She had finally abandoned the Giulietta on a verge, hoping that whoever patrolled the area wouldn't still be around ninety minutes before a cold autumn midnight.

She was about to send Maguire for assistance when the door clicked open and a drawn, slightly overweight nurse with red highlights and a name badge that said *Natalia* stuck her head out. 'You are police?'

They followed Natalia on to the ward, a long, dimly lit corridor punctuated by various abandoned trolleys. Windowed rooms ran along the left side, four curtained beds in each. Natalia ambled ahead of them, apparently in no rush.

Hawkins drew alongside as they walked. 'Was it you who called, about the injured woman?'

'Yes, I call.'

'Good. What happened?'

The nurse stopped to peer inside one of the rooms before turning to face Hawkins. 'Older lady is brought in two hours ago. She has bad cut to back of head. I prep her for theatre, ask questions about injury. She is . . . drowsy, not making lot of sense, but I understand. She was . . . kidnap, held prisoner inside house.'

'What sort of house – where?'

'I don't know.'

'OK, what else?'

'She escape, but man chase after, try to . . .' she motioned with her hands, '. . . strangle her.'

Hawkins nodded. 'And then?'

'A car stop. Evil man run away.'

'Then the driver brought her here.'

'Yes.'

'So how did you know to call us?'

'This morning I read paper, story about people

whose daughter was taken same way and killed. I think it must be connected, so I call.'

Hawkins felt Mike pat her gently on the back, but she didn't turn, already aware what his action meant.

You were right to go public.

She asked, 'Where's the driver now?'

The nurse shrugged. 'He leave.'

'*Leave?* Did anyone take contact details?'

'I ask. He say no. What can I do?'

'Why would he leave?' Mike said.

Hawkins sighed. 'He saved her life, didn't he? But who wants to hang around and get dragged into the mess of a court case, risk backlash from whichever crazy bastard attacked her in the first place?' She turned back to the nurse. 'He must have said where he found her.'

Natalia shook her head. 'Only that he find her in road, see other man run away. We treat patient, but when I go back to find him, he is gone.'

'Brilliant.' Hawkins took a deep breath, let it back out. 'Can we speak with the victim, at least?'

Natalia glanced along the corridor, turned back with a frown. 'No. We sedate her, after operation. She is unconscious till morning.'

Hawkins bit her lip to contain the swearing, took a moment to compose herself, and fixed the nurse with a stare. 'I want to see her. Now.'

Her irritation only increased when they were shown into a dimly lit cubicle, to find the victim – Natalia's idea of an *older lady* – in her late forties, a demographic that, in little over a decade, Hawkins would join.

The woman lay prostrate, inclined; her head turned aside. Clear tubes networked her pallid face, and her skull was heavily bandaged, verifying how close to death she had come. Blue and white covers barely moved in time with monitoring equipment that beeped and hummed in the background. Hawkins shuddered, picturing herself the same way, still less than a year ago.

She swallowed the moment, addressing the nurse. 'We need to talk to her.'

'This is not possible.' Natalia moved round the bed and peered at one of the monitors. 'She lose lot of blood; lucky that driver find her while wound is fresh, otherwise she die. She has concussion, needs rest. You talk with her in morning.'

'Morning's not *good* enough.' Hawkins stepped closer. 'You told us the killer ran when the car turned up, so as far as he knows, the driver could be leading us to him right now. That means he'll try to escape, so we need a description of the attacker, or at least an idea of where she was found, except you've mislaid the only other person who can tell us either of those things. That's why we have to speak to her. Do you understand?'

Natalia frowned. 'I understand. But I cannot help.'

'Then get me someone who can.' Hawkins managed not to shout.

'Ward manager will tell you same thing.'

'Hey.' Mike stepped between them, keeping his voice

down. 'Look, Toni, if the wound was still fresh when she came in, this whole thing can't have happened that far away. The driver probably lives around here, and wherever he found her, he's gonna take her to the nearest hospital, right?'

'Go on.' Hawkins forced herself to listen, picking up wheezing snores from at least two of the other beds.

'This complex has to have cameras,' Mike continued, 'so we check the film, get the guy's plates and look him up. Then we go ask him.'

'Fine.' Hawkins looked at the nurse. 'How do we get hold of your security footage?'

Natalia shook her head. 'System upgrade. Cameras not working at moment.'

'Of course they aren't.' Hawkins rubbed her forehead. Mike started to say something else but she shushed him, turning back to the nurse. 'I suppose it's too much to hope that she had a bag with her. Some kind of identification.'

Natalia shook her head.

'You must have a name, at least.'

'Sheila.'

'Surname?'

'No.'

'Good.' She rolled her eyes at Mike. 'We're going backwards here.'

There was a moment's silence as they all stared at the patient.

'Effects,' Hawkins said at last. 'Can we see what she had with her when she came in?'

'No problem.' The nurse ushered them both aside, apparently relieved to finally deliver *something* she'd been asked for, stepped round the bed and started digging various items of clothing out of a cabinet.

Natalia hefted the pile on to the bed and began spreading the items out below Sheila's feet. Aside from a small plastic bag containing a bra, there were walking boots, jeans, a T-shirt and sturdy jumper, and a plain black bomber jacket. Most were streaked with dirt, while the cream woollen jumper and grey T-shirt had significant bloodstaining around the collars. The prevailing smell underlined the fact that everything was damp.

Was that significant?

Hawkins picked up the jacket and checked the pockets, turning up nothing but a cheap lighter and some chewing gum wrappers. She turned to Mike, who was holding one of the boots, peering at the mud stuck in its tread.

'Beats me,' he said. 'This stuff could be from Hackney Marshes or the Himalayas for all I know. We could have it tested for composition and clay content, I guess, maybe get a rough location from that, but your perp'll be in Mexico with a mortgage by then.'

Hawkins dumped the jacket and picked up the T-shirt. 'Same story with the blood. The patch around the neckline will be Sheila's, but if she put up enough of a fight to survive, these spatters on the front might be his. Testing will take time, though, and there's no guarantee we'll have his DNA on file, even if he's been picked up by the authorities before.'

'More blood here.' Mike was holding the jacket up to the light, revealing a large rusty blot inside the neckline. 'Geez, she was lucky to make it *this* far.' He stopped in response to Hawkins' tilted stare. 'What?'

'That jacket.' She reached for it. 'It isn't hers.'

Mike frowned and handed it over.

'See?' Hawkins pulled it taut in front of him. 'This thing's too big for *you*.'

They both looked at the woman in the hospital bed, probably no more than two thirds of Mike's width, then back at the coat. Hawkins checked the collar before holding it up. 'Triple XL.'

Maguire clicked. 'It's the driver's.'

'Exactly. He was trying to keep her warm, and forgot or just decided to leave it when he scarpered.' She turned to the nurse. 'The man who brought Sheila in, did he have any unusual features, maybe scars or tattoos?'

Natalia's expression hardened. 'No. He is tall with dark hair. Just normal guy.'

'OK.' Hawkins thought for a second before digging the lighter back out of the jacket, assuring herself there were no markings on it. Exasperated, she checked the whole garment again for hidden pockets, scrunching the padded sections in her hands; looking for anything that might provide a clue to its owner's identity.

She was about to give up when she felt a tiny rough section on the upper left arm, at odds with the smooth surrounding material. She held the patch up to study it, but the ward's after-hours darkness made it impossible to pick out any detail. She grabbed the lighter and was about to strike it when Mike stopped her.

'Whoa there, missy.' He pointed up at the sprinkler head in the ceiling above them. 'That ain't the kind of bed bath I ordered.' He retrieved his mobile and activated its LED light.

'Thanks.' Hawkins moved the patch into the beam, realising straight away why she hadn't noticed it upon first inspection. Two words and a number had been intricately stitched into the jacket's upper left arm, black thread on black material: *one9five*.

Mike peered over her shoulder. 'One nine five, what's that, some kinda fashion label?'

'Let's find out.' Hawkins took his phone and opened the browser, typing in the logo exactly as it was written, waiting for the mobile signal to drag the page down from the server.

'Bingo,' she said at last, tapping the first search result.

Mike raised an eyebrow. 'It's a bingo hall?'

'Nope.' Hawkins ignored his joke, holding the phone up for him to see the page popping into life on its display. 'One nine five is a nightclub in Epping.'

54

They heard the club before they saw it.

Maguire followed the satnav's instruction to turn right, off Epping High Street into Cottis Lane, a narrow side road between Starbucks and a clothing store called So Glam, both now shut for the night.

The buildings closed in around them, appearing to loom inwards as the Range Rover's lights cut a channel through the darkness, and the thumping bassline from their destination grew as they slid towards the far end.

'There.' Hawkins pointed ahead, at the silver lettering mounted high on the left wall: *One9Five.*

Below the sign, a few dressed-up teenagers huddled against the wall, smoking as the cold drizzle fell around them, dripping off an A-board that shouted: *Monday is student night!*

'Slow down,' Hawkins instructed as they passed the entrance, craning her neck to peer in through the open double doors. She glimpsed two brawny white men standing just inside, obviously bouncers staying out of the rain. The first was in a bomber jacket just like the one at the hospital, but the other wore the classic doorman's overcoat, long and black, entirely too heavy for mid-autumn. Both men looked up as the Range Rover rumbled past, their eyes tracking it in the split second before they disappeared behind the wall again.

'He's here,' Hawkins reported as Maguire turned into the club's almost empty car park. Either Student Night wasn't a crowd-puller, or the weather was putting the punters off. Mike steered into a space and they both got out, Hawkins glancing around at the other cars, trying to guess which one was the coy Samaritan's. She chose a black 5 Series BMW and cleared the water off its passenger window with her sleeve to check inside for blood, but the seats were black leather and it was too dark to see.

She backed away as a shrill bleep warned that the vehicle had proximity sensors, and joined Maguire at the corner. They turned back towards the club and moved along the whitewashed wall, inside barriers rendered obsolete by the lack of a queue. Everything around them vibrated in time with the intermittent bassline leaking from the building, its gaps punctuated by the muffled clatter of the unseen DJ's voice. Hawkins raised a hand to shield her face from the worsening drizzle.

They neared the double doors as three girls tottered down the step on to the road, each in hot pants and six-inch heels, apparently oblivious to the rain. Once stabilised, they linked arms and headed for the High Street, drawing gazes from the smokers now finishing their cigarettes.

Hawkins reached the entrance first, rounding the open door into a small but flamboyantly adorned entrance area, now containing only one oversized doorman.

'Evening,' the bomber-jacketed bouncer mumbled without expression, although Hawkins had already caught the flicker as forced indifference settled on his face. He was also doing his best to ignore the fact that she and Maguire, who had moved in behind her, clearly weren't dressed for a night's clubbing. He motioned towards the open door in the back wall, through which Hawkins saw another woman behind a velvet-fronted desk, waiting to take coats and entry fees.

Hawkins didn't move. 'Where's the other guy?'

He stared at her for a second, forced indifference being superseded by forced confusion. 'Sorry, love, not with you.'

'We don't have time to muck about here.' She pictured the killer racing towards the nearest airport. 'We drove past a minute ago and there were two of you.'

The bouncer drew himself up. 'What's the difference?'

'We're Met Police.' Hawkins produced her warrant card. 'But you already knew that, didn't you?'

He bent to study the ID before taking a long, attitude-adjusting breath. 'You mean Dominic. He's just gone for a quick break.'

Hawkins peered past him into the blackened depths of the club. 'When's he due back?'

'Fifteen minutes, twenty maybe.'

She sighed and looked at Mike. 'Go and wait on the corner. If he comes out the back or tries to reach one of those cars, stop him, would you?'

Mike nodded and left, as Hawkins turned back to the bouncer. 'What's your name?'

'Tony.'

'Mine too. Look, Tony, whatever trouble Dominic's in, we aren't here because of it. But we do need his help with a serious incident that took place earlier tonight.' She watched another affirmative tic cross her subject's features, confirming that the story about taking an injured woman to hospital had already been shared. 'Where did he go?'

The doorman's eyes narrowed as they stared at each other, but finally he caved, nodding over his shoulder towards the flickering strobe lights. 'He's in there. You can wait till he comes back if you want, or go in and find him yourself if you're in a hurry.'

'I'll go after him, thanks,' she said, wondering how hard it could be to find a six-foot-five bouncer in a club without a queue. 'What's his surname?'

She waited while the doorman procrastinated, judging after a few seconds that he needed some encouragement. 'The game's up now, anyway. We know he works here, so it's only a matter of time till we find out who he is. But we have an urgent situation, and talking to him now might just prevent a murder or two.'

Tony looked up at the ceiling, obviously weighing the merits of giving up the pal he'd been tasked to protect. At last he looked back at her. 'Dominic Locke.'

'Thanks.' Hawkins stepped around him as he gestured at the woman behind the desk to let her pass.

Club 195 was much busier than the lack of a queue suggested it would be, and Hawkins' pace slowed to a crawl as she hit the first crowd of students just inside the door. She stood on tiptoes and looked out across a sea of heads. What appeared to be the main dance floor occupied the centre of the large room, with an island bar off to the left, and various seating areas round the perimeter. The mirrored ceiling was lined with rows of glowing polka dots that flashed pink in time with a bass-saturated version of what had once been a Michael Jackson song, almost drowning out the rhythmic babble coming from a DJ she couldn't locate.

Satisfied that her oversize quarry wasn't among the crowd, Hawkins edged towards another bar area through an archway in the rear left corner. A quick scout round the low tables turned up no sign of him there, either, so she pushed and excused her way into the final room, which held more seated booths. She checked each in turn.

No sign.

She looked back towards the entrance, now wondering if Dominic had gone out of the front while she and Maguire had been parking the car, leaving his colleague to delay them further when they got to the door.

It was more than plausible. He'd avoided leaving details at the hospital after saving a woman's life and then, whether or not he realised his abandoned jacket had led them here, he'd scarpered at the merest sniff of someone having tracked him down. All of which reinforced her suspicion that Sheila's knight in shining armour had something to hide.

Hawkins retrieved her mobile and checked the display. Nothing from Mike, which meant either that he was otherwise engaged, or that he'd seen nothing of their missing bouncer.

She started composing a text, telling Maguire to look up Dominic Locke's address. If he wasn't here at the club, they might as well send a unit there straight away, in case he was naive enough to have gone home. Even if the killer was likely to be long gone by now, the faster they pinpointed exactly where Sheila was picked up after the attack, the sooner they'd find out wherever she'd been held, a location that would undoubtedly provide clues to the perpetrator's identity.

Hawkins was halfway through the text when someone patted her bum.

She looked up as a man in his early twenties, with scything blond hair, skin-tight shirt and pupils the size of saucers, slid into view.

'Boom!' He took a dramatic step away before closing back up to yell in Hawkins' ear, a week's worth of aftershave threatening to choke them both. 'I've seen some banging MILFs in here over the years, but you are *maxing* that look, girl. I'm Ewan, by the way.' He draped an arm round her shoulders. 'So, shall we fuck in the toilets now, or do you want to dance first?'

Hawkins smiled, about to shrug herself free and deck her unwanted admirer, but as she was adjusting her stance, she caught sight of Locke appearing out of the gents' toilet. Instead of turning towards the entrance, however, the bouncer began crossing the room towards them. Hawkins glanced the other way, seeing the fire exit doors on the far side of the room that had to be his destination.

A strategy occurred just in time.

'I'd love to,' she shouted, 'but you'll need to ask my boyfriend if he minds.' She nodded at the approaching Locke, watching as Ewan turned, saw the bouncer and sprang off her like a scalded gazelle.

She tried not to laugh as Ewan held up his hands, drawing Locke's attention beautifully.

'Sorry, mate,' Ewan yelled as the bouncer leaned down to hear what he was saying, 'I didn't realise, OK?' He waved emphatically at Hawkins. 'Never touched her, I swear.'

Locke glanced at Hawkins. If he recognised her from when she slid past him in Mike's car, there was no indication of it on his face as he straightened, the doorman's bravado asserting itself instantly. 'Is he bothering you?'

'I don't think so.' She performed a slow, one-too-many blink, letting herself sway. 'But I could do with some . . . fresh air.'

She sagged theatrically at Locke, forcing him to stabilise her, watching Ewan slip gratefully into the crowd as she was whisked expertly through the hordes to the fire exit. Locke pressed a concealed switch, probably to prevent the alarm going off, and opened the right-hand door, guiding Hawkins out into a side alley and closing the fire exit behind them, supporting her throughout with one hand.

'Thanks, Dominic, I feel better already.' She stood as soon as the doors were secure, and held up her warrant card as Locke turned in response to her unexpected use of his name. 'Can we have a quick word?'

'Fuck.' He slumped against the exit. 'I thought we were done with this shit.'

Hawkins frowned. 'What shit would that be, exactly?'

Locke's face dropped into his palms. 'The court ruled in my favour, but she won't leave it alone. What am I supposed to have done *now*?'

'I think we've got our wires crossed here.'

He looked up. 'This isn't about my ex's bullshit rape charge?'

'No, although it explains why you didn't hang around at the hospital earlier tonight after saving a woman's life.' Hawkins watched realisation dawn on his face.

He nodded slowly. 'She was in a bad way when I found her. I couldn't just leave her there, but if she didn't make it, they'd only have my word for it that I wasn't the one who attacked her. There was blood everywhere, on me, in the car.' He shrugged. 'Shit sticks when you've got a reputation.'

'I understand why you ran,' Hawkins said, 'but running only made things look worse, and leaving your jacket behind wasn't exactly the work of a criminal mastermind.'

He grimaced. 'I realised after I left the hospital, but it was too late to go back. The woman, she OK?'

'Stable,' Hawkins told him. 'It looks like she's going to pull through.'

Locke gave a relieved sigh. 'So what now?'

She motioned back towards the club. 'Let's find your boss and tell him you're taking the rest of the night off. I need you to show me *exactly* where you found her.'

55

Rupert stood alone, outside the battered wooden door.

Darkness had come while he waited, but he hadn't let himself leave. Yet every time he reached for the handle, tears welled in his eyes. If he opened the door, saw the room again, somehow it would make the nightmare more real. If he left, it was like abandoning the memory of his friend.

He almost turned away, unable to face the sadness. But then it came: a tiny sound, less than a whisper, but he understood the words, recognised the voice.

What do you want?

He stared at the door, listening hard.

'Ash?' His words were thin and high-pitched. 'Is that you?'

No reply.

'Hello?' he said again.

Still nothing, as his fingers found the handle and turned it, letting the door swing open against the wall.

'I'm here.' He stepped inside, looking around. The room was exactly as it had been when they'd first turned it into a bedroom for Ash, shortly after his parents died four years earlier. There were no pictures or mess, or clothes on the floor like in Rupert's room. Ash hated all of that stuff.

A bedroom is just somewhere to sleep.

But there were still traces of him. The air was smoky and stale, because the door had been closed since it happened, but *otherwise it was just the way Ash left it every morning. The bed, to Rupert's left, was unmade, and across the room, the chair had been pulled away from the desk, where Ash sat to read by the table-top lamp. An old book lay on the surface,* James Herbert *picked out in gold letters on its spine, next to the dirty old cup he used to flick cigarettes in.*

Everything was so normal, so familiar. *It felt like Ash could walk in at any moment, Marlboro in hand, slump in the chair and throw an insult Rupert's way.*

He called Ash's name and waited again, but all he heard was the distant moan of the wind driving itself up under the eaves.

He'd imagined the voice.

Ash wasn't here.

He shuddered, suddenly feeling a chill in the air. The room had never been warm, even with a fire in the hearth next door, or a hot summer's day outside. This corner of the house stayed permanently cold, as if it was haunted, or wanted to drive people away. Condensation formed on the windows right up until late spring, and sometimes it felt like the icy winds blew in straight through the walls. His parents had never used it, not even for storage.

But it had never felt as empty as it did now.

Ash had been his companion, his best and only friend. Ash was smart; he understood life, and the way people behaved. Since childhood they'd hardly been apart. Ash had always been there to offer advice, to help Rupert through the difficult times. Without him Rupert would never have coped with his parents' death. But most of all, Ash accepted *him when no one else would. They'd fought, of course — everyone did — yet they always made up, and with none of their parents around any more, the two boys had become like family.*

Then illness had come, and Rupert had watched in horror as it slowly took his friend. Now Ash was gone.

And he was alone.

Rupert glanced out of the window, at the wind disturbing the trees, and felt panic rise inside. He hadn't thought about it till now, but it was almost autumn again.

His mind flashed back to that night, playing cards in the ramshackle house, the pain of the cigarette on his skin; the fury that seized him. Ever since, he had told himself the haunted house had been to blame; that something there had taken over, forced him to attack his only friend.

Never since had he felt that rage. But then, as he stood in his dead friend's room, Rupert felt something beyond the fear of being alone. He had never returned to the haunted house, and yet here in his parents' home, he recognised the emotion like it had never been away.

The rage had risen again.

56

They waited in silence.

Hawkins dropped the Range Rover's window a few millimetres, watching a neat line of droplets beginning to bead on the doorsill. The muted patter of rain hitting the forest canopy grew, broken occasionally by sharp winds that stirred leaves in the post-midnight blackness around them. For a moment nothing broke the background hum, but then Hawkins picked up the sound she'd been waiting for.

It started softly, a gentle hum that quickly grew into the unmistakeable rush of tyres against tarmac. Coming their way.

Seconds later, twin lights swept into view, edging closer and closer through the trees. The vehicle slowed near the junction, in response to Mike's double flash of full beam, casting shadows through the 4x4's cabin as it turned off the main road.

'Here we go.' Hawkins reached for the door pull.

The other car pulled up as the two senior detectives convened in front of the Range Rover. Aaron Sharpe dropped the passenger window, and Hawkins bent down to see Amala in the driver's seat.

'Kill the headlights and park up,' she said. 'Jump out and I'll explain.'

She and Maguire waited while Amala edged the unmarked Kia on to the thin verge ahead of the Range Rover, simultaneously buttoning their collars as the stormy night renewed its turbulent assault.

The four officers assembled, shoes crunching against stones on the dirt track that curved away into the trees.

'Any action since we spoke, Chief?' Amala asked.

Hawkins shook her head. 'Nobody in or out on this road.'

During their brief phone conversation half an hour ago, as she and Maguire had driven the short distance from Club 195 to Epping Forest, Hawkins had instructed Amala and Aaron to meet them on the road running through the north quarter of the national park. She'd kept her explanation brief, keen to help their passenger, Dominic Locke, identify the location where, three hours earlier on his way to work, he had almost run over the woman called Sheila and her attacker.

Quickly Hawkins explained that, following their conversation at Club 195, and Locke's agreement to help, she and Maguire had followed the bouncer's BMW along part of his regular commute, south-west on Epping High Road, into the forest. There, Locke had joined them in Mike's car, highlighting a quarter-mile stretch of the B-road as the approximate place he'd come across the struggling pair.

Yet, despite a few passes along the unlit, featureless highway, it had proved almost impossible to distinguish one section from the next. Mostly the route was bordered by scrubland or trees of varying density, all of which meant the chase could have come from almost any direction.

Their joker had been the victim's mumbled account of events to the hospital nurse. Before losing consciousness, Sheila had mentioned being held in a house, which therefore had to be within running distance of the road. And for a woman in her late forties, even one driven by desperation, that distance wouldn't be far. So if the house *was* accessible by road, that meant they were looking for a turning, only one of which they found on the entire run.

Closer inspection of the adjacent tarmac yielded residual traces of blood, partly washed away by the rain, while careful exploration of the side turning revealed a rustic farmhouse set in dense woodland, four hundred yards from the main road. The strange thing was that from a distance the place looked lived in, even well maintained, with a neatly raked gravel drive and a dull glow from the downstairs windows, as if a normal family might be inside watching TV. It certainly wasn't the run-down shell Hawkins had expected. And yet, according to a quick check of Google Earth on Mike's iPhone, it was the only building within running distance of where the latest victim had been rescued; inconclusive perhaps, but enough to convince Hawkins they'd found the place where Sheila had been held.

They had returned Locke to his car and parked up to

wait for the rest of the team, additional manpower crucial if they were to safely apprehend anyone still inside the property.

'How do we know it's just one person?' Amala asked.

'The latest victim mentioned a single captor,' Hawkins told her. 'And the driver who picked her up only saw one assailant.'

Sharpe frowned. 'Shouldn't we get SCO19 involved?'

'We tried already,' Mike said. 'But armed response are maxed out, covering some major drug bust south of the river, and a raid on a terrorist sleeper cell in Watford. They all have guns and high body counts, whereas our guy doesn't use weapons, so we got third on the priority list.' He put on a posh British accent. 'Your serial killer is important to us. If you still require an armed response unit, please stay on the line.'

'Anyway,' Hawkins cut him off. 'Our murderer isn't classified high-risk, but we don't have time to wait for back-up, so for now it's down to us.'

Sharpe sounded nervous. 'Do you really think he'll be here?'

Hawkins looked at him. 'Given that he's aware there are witnesses, one that knows this location, and another who might be able to identify him, plus the fact it's been three hours since the attack? No, I think he's on his way to Heathrow.' She glanced along the lane. 'But if this is where he's been keeping them, it'll hold clues. Either way, our job is to get inside before he disappears completely.'

She led off towards the house, explaining her approach strategy as the team fell in behind.

The woods rustled and buzzed on every side, seeming to close over them as they rounded the bend. Mist hung in patches, its icy dampness stinging Hawkins' cheeks. She eyed the forest, having warned the others about how well this terrain lent itself to an ambush. Hence her preference to wait until they could approach in numbers, rather than just herself and Mike.

They slowed as the house came into view, sunk in the darkness at the edge of a clearing, shadows grasping at its squat facade. Mike was carrying a torch, but Hawkins told him not to use it, keen to preserve any residual element of surprise. She studied the house for glimpses of movement in the blackened pools of the upstairs windows, or changes in the glow escaping the curtains on the ground floor. Seeing none, she switched to the exterior, noting a dark saloon car in a recess beside the cottage, although its presence didn't guarantee anyone was there.

She turned as they entered a patch of moonlight, nodding at Sharpe and Yasir. As instructed they broke off, heading for the rear of the house while she and Maguire resumed their advance towards the front.

Hawkins glanced back as they neared the entrance, taking a final sweep of the trees. She saw foliage dancing in the breeze, heard the rustle of spent leaves scratching their way across the drive. But still no sign of a trap.

They reached the front entrance, a low, centrally set

wooden door with a small triangular porch directly above. Some kind of plant climbed the brickwork, and again Hawkins was struck by the apparent normality as she gently knocked, wary of multiple occupants, hoping to alert only those near the door.

No response.

She checked the mechanism: a basic lifting catch, probably secured from inside by a manual bolt. There was no way to tell if it was locked, so she tried the latch.

It clicked open.

She pushed, feeling the door scrape on a flagstone floor. Adrenalin surged as the door swung inwards, allowing them to slip inside before Mike eased it shut.

Hawkins scanned the dark, deserted room. Heavy beams lined the low ceiling and walls, and to their left was a small seating area with a live fire, its clicking embers dying now, but its presence demonstrating that someone had been here in the recent past. Its fading flames cast the only light inside the house; the glow they had seen from outside. At the opposite end of the room, a kitchen area surrounded a solid wooden table and chairs. And in the back wall, two further doors.

Hawkins nodded towards them, maintaining silence, and moved across the room, alert for noises that might suggest they weren't alone. They reached the first door, her hand almost on the lever when she heard it.

A creak from the other side.

She froze, arm up to warn Mike as the worn handle dipped.

They stepped aside in unison, staying out of sight for

as long as possible, as the door creaked inwards. She felt Maguire bristle beside her.

'*Chief?*'

The tension broke as Amala stepped out from behind the door, and Hawkins breathed again as Aaron followed.

'Geez, guys,' Mike whispered, 'thanks for the heart attack.'

Yasir pulled a face. 'Sorry. We were being quiet.' She glanced behind her. 'The back door was unlocked, so we were coming to let you in through the front.'

'No need,' Hawkins said quietly. 'If anyone's here, they aren't big on security.' She pointed at the hallway and stairs now visible through the open door, nodding to Mike and Aaron. 'You two look upstairs. We'll make sure there's no one next door.'

The group split, and Hawkins watched Sharpe check the understairs cupboard before following Maguire towards the first floor. Then she joined Yasir at the second door off the kitchen.

Amala eased the handle down and pushed it open. The escaping air was notably colder than that of the main room, but the space inside remained a blackened void, beyond the reach of the fire's lazy glare. Hawkins felt the sergeant shiver as she reached past her shoulder and felt for the light switch.

A weary bulb stuttered to life near the ceiling, its languid glow fighting its way through layers of grime, revealing what had once been a dining room. Damp shadows scaled every wall, above a medium-sized table against the far wall, now almost lost beneath piled cardboard boxes that haemorrhaged junk. But still no occupants.

Downstairs was deserted.

Hawkins moved to the table and peered into the nearest box, finding mobile phones, two handbags and a black leather wallet, as well as various keys and change. She pulled her sleeve over her hand and picked up the wallet, flipping it open to remove a driver's licence. She showed it to Amala. 'I think we're in the right place.'

Yasir leaned in, read the name. 'Peter Barnes.'

'Exactly.' Hawkins nodded towards the door, indicating that her colleague should investigate the kitchen.

'Thanks, Chief.' Amala stepped away holding her nose, and Hawkins listened to the slow creaks shifting above her head. Then she returned to the table, breathing through her mouth to avoid the stale fug of neglect, and checked the next box. Mostly paperwork.

She moved a chipped ornament before lifting the flap on the uppermost folder, a beige cardboard wallet stuffed with ragged papers in the early stages of decay. The header on the top sheet addressed a Mr and Mrs Perkin.

She was about to dig further when Amala reappeared in the doorway. 'Chief? I think you should see this.'

Hawkins turned and followed her, hooking the dining room door closed as she went. The younger officer stood at the far end of the bench near the window, holding aside a tatty blanket moonlighting as a cupboard door. Hawkins joined her, crouching to look inside at the objects Amala was lighting with the LED flash on her phone.

Four items stood out, all recently handled, in stark contrast to the rusting tins and cloudy plastic bottles surrounding them. A bottle of cheap whisky and three white plastic bottles labelled Temazepam.

Sleeping pills.

Hawkins leaned closer, until she was able to read the printed label on the side of the tub: *Mr R. Perkin*. She ran a cursory finger across the stone floor by her boot, showing the powdered white result to Amala. 'That's how he got them here.'

They both looked up when footsteps descended the stairs, as Maguire and Sharpe re-entered the kitchen. Mike caught her eye; shook his head.

'OK,' Hawkins stood, returning to normal volume. 'Nobody's home, but that's no major surprise. Anything of interest up there?'

Maguire shrugged. 'Two bedrooms, though only one's been recently used. As for clues, hard to say till we take a better look.'

'Same here.' She gestured towards the dining room. 'The victims' effects are in there, along with most of the killer's domestic history, but for the moment we have to keep one eye on the long game. If we can't pick this guy up in the next few hours, any evidence we gather here will help us later. So let's bring the cars up and get some romper suits on before we search any f—'

She stopped mid-sentence, staring past Mike's shoulder

at the far corner of the lounge. Beside her, Sharpe and Yasir shared blank expressions, but Maguire's told Hawkins he'd also heard the quiet click.

She raised a hand, telling the others to stay silent as she moved towards the rear of the ground floor, and a darkened alcove almost impenetrable to the fading firelight.

Her eyes adjusted as she went, picking out detail in a recess she had previously disregarded as the building's extremity. The main downstairs area was L-shaped, deeper in the rear corner to accommodate the seating area, before thinning at the kitchen end, where the hall and dining room cut into the floor space. But what she'd assumed to be the back wall was actually a partition. And, set in the furthest corner, a door.

None of them had noticed it, probably because its sturdy wooden slats were painted the same murky shade of avocado as the room, while the lack of a frame allowed it to blend almost seamlessly into the wall. It looked like a cupboard, except now she could see soft light bleeding through a small, ragged gap in its surface. At eye level. And lower down, a spherical doorknob above a plain keyhole.

Gently she gripped the handle and turned.

It was secure; the mechanism almost certainly responsible for the click they had heard a moment before.

An occupant locking themselves in.

Hawkins looked round to find Mike right with her; Aaron and Amala still waiting by the kitchen.

Heart thumping, she positioned herself a few inches

from the hole, wary of the potential for harmful liquids or sharp points to be thrust at her, and peered inside.

It was a bedroom. Against the left-hand wall was a small bed, opposite a dark wooden chair and desk, from where an old-fashioned table lamp cast its feeble glow. A small window was set among the beams in the far wall, only the blackness of night beyond the glass. There was no other exit aside from the door itself, so whoever had locked themselves in a moment before must still be inside.

But she saw no one.

She glanced at Maguire, indicating that their mystery occupant had to be pressed against the other side of the dividing wall, purposely staying out of view. But there was only room for one. She held up a finger, estimating the number of potential assailants they faced. Mike nodded, silently questioning whether she wanted to force their way in.

Hawkins shook her head.

'Metropolitan Police,' she stated calmly through the hole. 'How about a civilised chat?'

No response.

'There are four of us out here,' she pressed, 'with more on the way. So as you don't have any better options, let's talk.'

More silence.

Hawkins was about to try the handle again when the quiet words came, uttered from just inside the door. A man's voice.

'What's your n . . . name?'

For a second she faltered. The voice was so hesitant that she wondered if it wasn't the killer, but a hostage. 'DCI Hawkins.'

'N . . . no. Your first name.'

'Antonia.' She kept her voice low. 'What's yours?'

A longer pause, one in which she was able to pick out the sound of his breathing, short, pointed gasps that suggested a verbal run-up to his reply.

'R . . . Rupert.'

With that Hawkins realised: his hesitation wasn't due purely to fear.

At first she had mistaken the stall in his speech for emotion, as if their unseen host were afraid of something. But instinct overruled that assumption. Numerous prolific killers suffered the physical manifestations of childhood trauma. Many referenced difficulties in their formative years as motivation to hurt others later in life, perennial torment over physical flaws or social ineptitude having scarred them so deeply that an eventual glut of revenge became inevitable at some point.

It was a stammer, perhaps the final trace of that bullied juvenile; the weak child grown strong. *The worm that had turned.*

He stepped into view.

Hawkins flinched, instinctively jerking away from the door. Mike started, too, but she raised a hand, telling him to wait. Through the hole she could see Rupert's torso, in a baggy green jumper. He'd stopped a few feet inside the room, breathing heavily, apparently without aggression.

Hawkins repositioned herself so she could see his face. He was standing between the lamp and the door, so his features were poorly lit, but she made out a slightly crooked, oversized nose and thin eyebrows above circular, unintelligent eyes. He was around thirty, of average height and build. His shoulders slouched.

He looked harmless.

She reminded herself not to be taken in by what could still be a diversionary ploy. 'Why are you here?'

Rupert blinked slowly, his head tilting, a frown slowly knitting his brow. 'This is my h . . . home.'

He was no hostage.

'OK.' Hawkins kept her tone soft. 'Why don't you come out so we can talk face to face?'

He didn't move. 'Why are you here?'

She glanced at Mike, then back at him. 'We're here because of Sheila.'

'Sh . . . Sheila,' he breathed, the word thick with recognition. Except this time there was a nervous undercurrent, lending detail to Hawkins' mental image: the damaged youngster grown up – still mostly placid, but sometimes, when provoked, a feral, merciless beast. 'She was h . . . here.'

'What happened to her?' Hawkins asked.

'She r . . . ran away.'

'And that made you angry.'

'No.' His head dipped. 'It made me s . . . sad.'

'What about the others?'

She watched his cheeks twitch; heard his breathing change, becoming deeper and more rapid.

'They r . . . ran away, too—' He broke off, anguish cracking his voice.

Hawkins saw him sag, recognising her opportunity. 'We aren't here to harm you, Rupert. Why don't you let us in so we can talk properly?'

He looked up, blinking slowly. Then, as if sleepwalking, he drifted forwards and unlocked the door.

Hawkins waited for him to step away before turning the handle, feeling the mechanism release. Gently she pushed the door open and stepped inside, aware of Mike moving in behind her, hearing the muted clicks as he prepped some plasticuffs.

Rupert barely reacted as Maguire stood next to him, pulling his arms into position and fitting the restraints.

With their quarry bound, Hawkins took a second to scan the room in more detail, noting metal bars outside the window; a small box commode beside the desk.

This is where they were held.

'OK, Rupert.' She turned back to their captive. 'Now you'll be coming with us.'

57

Loughton police station reeked of the sixties.

From its hopelessly dated attempt at a futuristic facade to its disintegrating lino floors, the place nut-shelled nascent Met underfunding. Closed to the public the previous year, the building's upkeep had since been completely overlooked, according to the duty sergeant who let them in – one of the resident officers silenced in their longstanding calls for a refit by growing threats of full closure.

Neglect extended to their poky interview room.

Three of the four bulbs in the ceiling weren't work-ing, and the other was in its final flickering throes. That left bizarre strip lighting set in the walls to provide most of the room's illumination, embellishing those at the table with reverse shadows above cheekbones and eyebrows, and ensuring that the duty officer in the rear corner stood head and shoulders in darkness, like a faceless mafia boss.

Hawkins would rather not have had time to contem-plate their surroundings in such detail, but she also understood the importance of keeping her cool when faced with such a deadpan interviewee.

So distraction it was.

Rupert Perkin sat hunched in the hard plastic chair

opposite her and Maguire, head down. Their suspect had neither resisted nor claimed his innocence since being arrested, hustled into Mike's car and driven the short distance to Loughton station, behaviour that had led Hawkins to contemplate the tantalising possibility of swift resolution. Perkin held himself like one of the rare breed who knew when the game was up; who did everything possible to avoid getting caught but were content, once ensnared, to hold up their hands. That pragmatism often led such individuals to wait quietly for the appropriate forum in which to unburden themselves, and as she had started the classic recording equipment a few minutes before, Hawkins had half expected a confession to spill forth.

It hadn't.

Perkin's benign expression hadn't lifted when she asked him to confirm his name, revealing what could have been calculated patience as genuine confusion. At which point he'd compounded the issue: *'I d . . . don't like it here. Can I go home?'*

Hawkins had sighed internally. After ten years on the force, she felt generally justified in assuming that the average murderer at least understood *why* they were being arrested. But either Rupert Perkin genuinely was limited enough not to know why they had brought him here, or he was a convincing actor determined to waste her time.

The trouble was it didn't look like an act.

And so far he had refused repeated offers of free legal representation, reinforcing her suspicion that he didn't appreciate just how much trouble he was in.

She drew in her frustration; focused on his sole concession of guilt so far: 'Let's go back to the kidnappings.'

Increasingly familiar panic contaminated his expression.

'You took those people against their will.'

'N . . . no. They g . . . got into my car. I didn't force them.'

'They got in because they needed help.'

'Yes.' He brightened, as if that justified the whole thing. 'Raymond f . . . fell in the woods, hurt his ankle. Sheila's car had b . . . broken down.'

Hawkins hesitated, picturing Henri Delarue thumbing a lift; a battered Peter Barnes stumbling along beside the road; Perkin pulling alongside in his car, offering help.

She eyed him. 'You put plasters on Peter Barnes' wounds.'

'Yes.' Perkin searched her face, as if he didn't understand the point of the question. 'He was b . . . bleeding.'

Hawkins swallowed her sympathy, remembering the tablets. Perkin had laced the alcohol in advance, and offered it to his unsuspecting passengers. Did he think that because he had *saved* these people, he somehow *owned* them?

'But they didn't volunteer to be drugged and kidnapped, did they?' she snapped. 'We found the whisky and sleeping pills in your kitchen.'

Perkin's cheek twitched. 'I d . . . didn't like doing that.'

'What if they refused the drink?' Mike asked.

'S . . . some of them did.' His gaze remained on Hawkins. 'I just t . . . took them where they wanted to go.'

She frowned. 'How many?'

'I c . . . can't remember. L . . . lots.'

Jesus. 'How long have you been doing this?'

'T . . . two weeks and one day.'

She gave an incredulous snort. '*You were out there every night?*'

Perkin nodded. 'When I had n . . . no guest.'

Hawkins felt Mike nudge her under the desk, telling her to rein it in. She took a breath; resumed her slow build towards a confession. 'But the people who accepted and drank enough to succumb, you took them home and imprisoned them.'

'Yes.'

'How many did you take home?'

His eyes flickered as he thought about it. 'F . . . five.'

'Are you sure?' She relaxed slightly. If that were true, at least they'd found all the bodies. 'Viola, Henri, Peter, Ray and Sheila. That's all? It won't look good in court if you've lied to us.'

'Y . . . Yes. Five.' His head dropped again, but he snapped back to attention as Hawkins raised her voice.

'Why?'

His eyes searched hers. 'I d . . . don't underst—'

'Why did you take them?' she snapped.

She waited, expecting his justification for taking random revenge on the weak, meting out the same punishments he'd once endured at others' hands. She pictured a young boy, demeaned, beaten, starved; growing to believe that torture was something to savour. Perhaps it was what happened when you systematically bled someone dry of compassion.

Perkin blinked several times in succession, now fighting to get his words out. 'I d . . . didn't want . . . to be alone.'

Hawkins sat forward, unsure that she'd heard him right. 'What?'

He shrank in his seat, cuffed wrists crossing in front of his chest as if he were cold. His answer, when it came, was barely a whisper.

'I w . . . wanted a friend.'

58

I wanted a friend.

There was silence as they stared at each other across the interview room. At last Hawkins opened the file on the table and withdrew a sample bag. It contained the only thing Rupert had been carrying at the time of his arrest, tucked into his jeans pocket as if he took it everywhere. A creased magazine page.

She positioned the bag between them on the table top. 'You're talking about this.'

Perkin looked down at it, then back at her. Nodded.

Hawkins glanced at Maguire. Under normal circumstances she would have dismissed any reference to the page as some kind of diversionary tactic, a pre-emptive move towards an insanity plea. But now, as she studied their suspect, Hawkins couldn't convince herself he wasn't telling the truth.

The article printed on the page was an opinion piece about friendship. It described how many of life's strongest relationships begin during traumatic experiences, often when one party assists another, and that most people know within twenty-four hours if they've found a lifelong friend.

Twenty-four hours.

The length of time he'd been holding them.

Was this confused individual living his life on the strength of a single piece of commentary from a disposable weekend rag?

And with that thought it became clear. This deluded young man wasn't playing games. It wasn't some kind of twisted sport; he really believed that what he'd been doing was justified, perhaps even *normal*. He was trying to achieve an ordinary goal, just in a tragically misguided way.

She held down her emotion, refocused on drawing out the relevant words. 'And what did you do during those twenty-four hours?'

'We t . . . talked.'

'About what?'

'About ourselves. The way f . . . friends do.'

Crazy, but consistent.

'So how did they get away?'

'I u . . . unlocked the door and went upstairs.'

'And?'

He sagged. 'They ran away.'

Of course they did. 'And that made you angry.'

'No, it m . . . made me sad.'

'But that didn't stop you going after them, did it?'

He breathed harder. 'What?'

'You chased them into the trees.'

'N . . . no.'

She managed not to shout. 'They didn't want to be your friends because you *kidnapped* them. *Obviously* they ran as soon as you released them, but that annoyed you, so you hunted them down.'

Perkin blinked rapidly and his head began jerking from side to side as if an important piece of behavioural code had suddenly malfunctioned. 'I d . . . don't understand.'

'Really?' Hawkins reopened the file on the desk, slid a picture of one partly exhumed body across the table towards him. 'How about now?'

He looked down at the image, stillness settling over him once again. Except for his eyes, which jumped erratically from detail to detail. Blanched skin smeared with mud; dirt-matted hair; black staining around the neck moving to purple as the permanent bruises set in. At last he looked up, deep creases around his eyes implying confusion. 'Wh . . . who—?'

'You don't remember Peter Barnes?' Hawkins raised her eyebrows, chewed her lower lip. After a dramatic pause, she shrugged. 'Why would you? I suppose you don't recognise *these* people, either.' She produced similar shots of Viola Clarkson, Henri Delarue and Raymond Jewis, spread them out in front of him, too. 'You drugged these people and held them prisoner. Then, when they weren't keen to hang around, you chased them down, strangled them to death and buried them. I imagine they all blurred into one after a while, right?'

Perkin's gaze flicked from her to Maguire, down to the photographs and back. 'They're d . . . *dead*?'

'Our coroner's quite experienced.' Hawkins was losing patience, but nightmare scenarios were already flashing through her mind. Hopefully it was only a matter of time before DNA from the house, the bodies and the swabs taken from Perkin's cheek upon arrival at the station would tally, giving them proof that he was responsible for the murders. Plus they had Sheila, of course, the survivor who would pluck him from a line-up as soon as she opened her eyes.

If she opened her eyes.

But that was only half the battle. Having the killer in custody meant conviction only if he was *fit* to stand trial.

Currently, Perkin was doing a good job of looking as if all this was news to him. And once you entered the realms of split personalities or full-blown psychosis, with a few well-chosen 'experts' muddying judicial waters, it was anyone's game. Unless she proved that Rupert Perkin wasn't the complete fruit-loop he was beginning to look like, four new families would soon join the fraternity of the grieving dissatisfied, their anger turning from perpetrator to police, while the inevitable media scramble would provide the perfect soapbox from which to level blame at the Met.

Her heart sank further as Perkin looked up from the photographs with tears in his eyes. 'You th . . . think that I—'

'Murdered four people?' Hawkins interrupted. 'Yes, I do.'

'Oh no.' He shook his head, the diminutive wail repeating itself as more of a cry. 'Oh no.'

'Let me guess,' Hawkins said as her mobile started vibrating in her pocket, 'you don't remember.'

Perkin looked up at her. 'I didn't k . . . kill anyone.'

'Of course you didn't.' She stood as Maguire paused the session, and they both moved out into the corridor, where Hawkins answered the call.

'Ma'am?' Amala waited as a tannoy announcement drowned out the background murmur on the line. 'I'm at the hospital. Sheila is awake.'

'Have you spoken to her?'

'Briefly. She's groggy, but she's already given me a description that matches Perkin exactly. He even told her his name.'

'Great. Get a formal statement as soon as she's up to it. Anything else?'

'Actually, yes. Sheila says that during the attack she bit him hard on the wrist, though she doesn't know which side.'

'Did she break the skin?'

'Looks like it. The nurse says there was blood on Sheila's teeth when she came in, although they've cleaned her up since.'

'Shit.' Hawkins thought for a second. 'OK, get her clothes to forensics straight away. If they can lift blood samples off any of it, we'll try matching them to Perkin. At the very least she'll have left teeth marks we should be able to use.'

'Right you are.'

Hawkins ended the call and turned to Mike. 'We need a doctor here, pronto. Sheila bit Perkin when he attacked her, which is great if it gives us more evidence, but not so good if this goes to court and we get pulled for neglecting our duty of care.'

She paced while Maguire made a swift call.

He hung up looking less than impressed. 'Sorry, boss, we'll be lucky to see anyone this side of three hours.'

'Fucking fantastic.' Hawkins heaved a sigh; stared at the scruffy poster on the opposite wall. *Officer of the Month, Loughton. July 2009.*

'Right.' She looked back at Mike. 'Let's check the wound. If it's bad, we'll have to take him to A&E. I don't want him picking up a tetanus infection while he's our responsibility.'

They re-entered the interview room to find Perkin still in his seat, hunched, rocking gently back and forth. Murmuring. But he straightened as the two detectives approached and stood over him.

'Hold out your hands,' Hawkins instructed, demonstrating.

Perkin hesitated, but then he complied, raising cuffed forearms in front of him.

'Keep still.' She leaned closer.

She gripped the left sleeve of his green woollen sweater and began easing it back towards his elbow, alert for twitches or steps in his breathing that might suggest discomfort. He didn't flinch, although he might already have dressed the wound himself. As the whole forearm was exposed, Hawkins found a group of small, circular burn marks peppering the delicate skin. But there was no evidence of a bite.

She repeated her actions with the right arm, constantly aware of Perkin's gaze, which remained locked on her, and his slow, unsteady breaths.

She finished and stood back, letting Maguire step in. He lifted Perkin's arms the same way she had, bending the elbows to inspect above and below. Then he turned to look at her, his face displaying similar confusion.

She shook her head, unable to explain.

There were no marks.

59

'Who are you protecting?' Hawkins demanded, plastic chair creaking as she leaned in to repeat herself.

Perkin's mouth opened a little further, and his eyes darted between her and Maguire, as if he were the butt of an incomprehensible joke. 'I d . . . don't und—'

'Fine,' she cut him off. 'Let me spell it out. Just over twenty-four hours ago, you drugged and kidnapped a woman called Sheila. You held her prisoner at your house until last night, when you *allowed* her to escape into the forest. All of this you've acknowledged. Sheila ran towards the nearest main road, at which point someone tried to murder her, though fortunately a passing driver stopped, scaring the attacker away, and took her to hospital, where she's now being treated.' She paused, emphasising the fact that his final victim had survived, carefully omitting the doctors' caveat that she wasn't in the clear by any stretch.

'Until a few minutes ago I was ready to have you up on four counts of murder and one attempted,' she went on, watching Perkin's brow knit further as she talked. 'Then we found out that Sheila bit her attacker during the fight, hard enough to leave a mark.' She studied Perkin's expression for signs of understanding. There were none.

'Except you don't have any bite marks, which means that either you're a medical anomaly, and that you'll spend several life sentences being studied by science, or that you aren't working alone. So which is it?'

'Th . . . there's nobody else. O . . . only me. But . . .'

Hawkins checked the tape was still running, expecting the truth at last.

'. . . I didn't k . . . kill anyone.'

Calm, Antonia. 'Then who's murdering these people?'

'I d . . . don't know.'

Hawkins dropped her elbows on to the table, massaged her temples with her fingertips.

Try a different angle.

'OK.' She looked back at Perkin. 'There are two bedrooms upstairs in your house. Whose is the second room?'

'It was my parents'.'

'And where are they?'

'They d . . . died. In a car accident. F . . . four years ago.'

'So why keep the room made up?'

'To r . . . remember them.'

'And you've been there alone ever since?'

'No. My friend Ash c . . . came to stay. The room d . . . downstairs. It was his.'

Bingo. 'And where is Ash now?'

His head dropped. 'He's d . . . dead, too.'

She frowned. 'Is it me, or is there a theme emerging here? What happened to *him*?'

'Ash was s . . . sick. He had c . . . cancer.'

Hawkins stood, chair legs screeching. 'So these people are murdering themselves, then, are they?' She stopped the session again and retreated to the corridor with Maguire in tow.

'For crying out loud.' She began pacing once more, talking half to herself. 'I genuinely can't tell if this guy is yanking our chain. You?'

Maguire shook his head; pulled a face.

'Then we call his bluff.' Hawkins shrugged. 'I want full searches; everything we've got on the three people he's mentioned. Birthdays, residential addresses, criminal records, the lot.'

Twenty minutes later they strode back into the interview room, to find Perkin nervously occupying the rear corner.

'We've checked our records, Rupert.' Hawkins dumped a stack of printed sheets on the table. 'Would you like to revise any elements of your story before we start?'

Perkin shuffled slowly back to the table and sat, looking up at her. 'I t . . . told you the truth.'

'Did you?' She retrieved the sheets and began flicking through them. 'You aren't protecting someone who'd prefer their name to be kept out of this discussion?'

Somehow, he managed to look even more confused. 'I d . . . don't un—'

'We pretty much take that as read these days.' She didn't let him finish. 'So I'll explain. We only found death certificates for two of the three people you lived with.'

He blinked heavily. 'Wh . . . what?'

'I've got a complete medical history here.' She flicked through the top set of pages on her pile.

'And it turns out your friend Ash isn't dead.'

60

Headlights.

He watched them approach through the forest, sliding behind the tree as a large white van entered the clearing. Two bright beams probed the undergrowth around him, splitting the misty shadows before moving away as the van turned, accompanied by the rush of gravel beneath its heavy wheels.

He gave it a few seconds before leaning out to take another look, squinting as pain flared in his head.

The van had parked up in front of the house. Its doors were open, and people were getting out. They wore civvies, but clearly they were police, called in by the others who had taken Rupert less than an hour ago.

The new arrivals gathered beside their van, opening the doors, starting to unload their kit. After a short conversation, one of them turned to scan the trees, her gaze sliding right past him. But this time he didn't bother hiding. He knew these woods, how to negotiate them and how to stay out of sight. Without the van's headlamps, the moonlight didn't penetrate the dense foliage far enough for him to be seen. And besides, the police weren't looking for anyone else.

They had their suspect.

He'd expected this development, anyway. OK, so

the woman wasn't supposed to get rescued, but something was bound to go wrong at some stage, so contingencies had been built in right from the start.

As soon as tonight's victim escaped, it had become just a matter of time until the police turned up. The woman ought to be dead by now – he'd felt the crack as he rammed her skull into the road – but obviously the driver had brought the cops here. He had to hand it to her, though; she'd been a lot smarter than the others, following the track rather than flapping off into the trees, then evading him long enough to make it all the way to the road. And his head was still ringing from whatever she'd hit him with.

After watching the car take her away, he'd stumbled back into the cover of the woods. Both the bite mark on his wrist and the cut on his head were surprisingly painful, but he hadn't fled, returning instead to watch the house, propped against a tree.

For a few hours he had drifted in and out of consciousness, and the time had passed without incident. But just after midnight he'd woken with a start, to the soft crunch of boots on gravel as two men and two women, obviously plain-clothes police, had crept towards the house.

They had entered the building and found Rupert.

Shortly after that, they'd brought two cars up and loaded their suspect, cuffed, into the large 4x4, which left with Rupert and two of the officers inside. The remaining two talked for a moment before the woman drove off in the second vehicle, leaving the male officer alone, presumably to wait for their colleagues. Now this new team were going to examine the house.

Soon they'd find all the evidence they needed to convict Rupert of multiple abductions and murders. At which point it wouldn't matter what excuses he came out with, because they'd be dismissed as desperate bullshit.

Leaving him in the clear.

He refitted his night-vision headset. Only one of the lenses was working now, after the feisty bitch had clouted him during the chase, but it still allowed him to navigate in the darkness. He turned and moved away, thinking about what happened next.

He dabbed at his temple, fingers exploring the rough, encrusted landscape of dry blood. The strike had been heavy, temporarily blinding him in one eye, and although his sight had since returned, he'd become increasingly light-headed.

So his priority had to be rest.

Now the police had someone in custody, they wouldn't be looking for anyone else. And even if Rupert worked out what was going on, he wouldn't be able to convince them of his innocence. So he had some time to recover. Although once his strength had returned, it was still probably wise to put some distance between himself and the police.

Just in case.

61

The Range Rover surged away from the junction, and Hawkins watched the black forest scenery outside the windows blur again.

Alone up front, Mike stretched the V8 to pass inter-mittent slower traffic, touching eighty on the straights as they retraced their route from earlier that night.

Beside Hawkins in the rear seat, Rupert Perkin sat hunched, staring through his cuffed wrists at the floor. The car's interior lighting bathed the three of them in a soft glow and she watched their captive closely, in case her instincts about him were wrong.

There had been little sign of fight from him in the three hours following his arrest, but since Hawkins' revelation thirty minutes ago that his former friend Ashley Jones hadn't died earlier in the year, as he clearly believed, Perkin had retreated still further into himself. At first she had upped the intensity, trying to snap him out of it, but despite Mike playing Good Cop with characteristic aplomb, her attempts to force answers from their suspect had failed. In the end, moderate coaxing had provided the most effective results, and Perkin had hesitantly filled in some of the blanks.

It seemed that his former house guest had been lying to him for months in advance of his supposed death.

The closest thing in Jones' medical history to the spinal cancer he'd described to Rupert were some vertebral cysts, which had required a few consultations and surgery, but certainly hadn't been life-threatening.

And yet, the day after what Jones' medical records described as *successful surgical intervention*, Perkin had received a call, telling him that his friend had passed away on the operating table and that he'd be contacted once the body could be released for burial. Whether Jones had made the call himself was unclear, but Perkin had been too caught up in misery, and his subsequent search for a replacement, to question its validity, or the length of time that had now passed since it came.

Loneliness had consumed him.

Thanks to the insurance fund released following his parents' deaths, and the unmortgaged property he occupied, a desperate and misguided Rupert Perkin had never been forced to seek employment, or interact with the outside world; circumstances that had given rise to his unilateral attempts to obtain new friendship by any means.

Within days of Jones' supposed death, Perkin had started making his excursions, inspired by the magazine article to look for those in need of help, then abusing their trust in order to drug any that accepted his offer of a drink, and imprison them for twenty-four hours.

During this time, he would converse with his reluctant guests through the hole in the door, hoping to build a relationship strong enough that, when tested, would inspire them to stay. Unfortunately, as soon as his visitors were presented with the possibility of escape, every one had taken that chance.

At which point, all but one of them died.

The natural assumption had been that Perkin, having seen his erroneous attempts to spark friendship rejected, pursued his hostages into the forest and capitally punished them, before hiding the evidence two feet below ground in various nearby woodlands.

Case closed.

Except that, while Perkin admitted everything up to that stage, he flatly denied having killed any of his victims; a claim backed up by the lack of teeth marks on his arm, following Sheila's assertion that she had inflicted such a wound on her attacker. The only explanation being that a second party was involved.

Swift background searches on Perkin's immediates had revealed a single anomaly: no record of the supposed terminal illness or subsequent death of his best friend Ashley Jones. Which meant they needed to act fast.

Because potentially, the killer was still at large.

If Jones *had* been murdering Perkin's hostages without his knowledge as they fled their kidnapper's house, he'd be aware not only that Sheila could have survived, but also that she, or the driver who interrupted her murder, might lead the police back to him. So he was probably heading for the hills.

Their best option was to pick him up now and ask questions later. Every moment they hesitated was more time for a potential murderer to put distance between them and himself. And he must have been near.

For events to unfold as it now appeared they had, Jones would have needed to be close; close enough to watch the house during hours of darkness, without knowing exactly when Perkin's captives would be released, in order to pick them off straight away.

Challenged on this point, Perkin had come up with one possibility: a condemned house deeper in the forest, within walking distance of his parents' home – where Jones had stayed on regular occasions over the years.

Except neither that house nor its apparently overgrown access road were visible on aerial photographs, and without any kind of address, their chances of finding it quickly were depressingly small. Hawkins' resulting question as to whether Perkin could lead them there had received a muted grunt she'd chosen to take as agreement. Assuming their guide followed through, it had to be their best chance of detaining Jones before he disappeared altogether. Hence Rupert's presence in the back of Mike's car as they sped along the tree-lined highway, back towards his home.

Admittedly, the plan was tricky to justify. Removing a potential murder suspect from the security of Loughton police station, in order to use him as a guide, broke several sizeable rules in itself. OK, so the lack of bite marks on his wrists suggested he wasn't the killer, and without him, finding the house might conceivably take much longer, but if his testimony turned out to be true, she was putting a material witness in harm's way.

For directions.

Hawkins wiped the discourse from her mind as the Range Rover's suspension jerked under hard braking. She looked ahead, deciding it was too late to question her instincts as Mike swung the car right, on to the lane she recognised from their previous visit, just a few hours ago.

She checked on Perkin as they bounced along the unsurfaced track, the 4x4's large wheels picking out imperfections in the rutted trail and transmitting them straight to the cabin. Rupert's head lolled in time with the jolts. He seemed even more withdrawn than he had at the station, where Hawkins had watched the shutters beginning to fall when the extent of his supposed friend's betrayal became clear. For several weeks, Perkin had been coming to terms with news of his companion's untimely death and trying, in his own way, to compensate. Now he was having to reconcile the fact that he'd been dumped.

It had been almost painful to watch the realisation invade his expression; the slow marches of denial, confusion, anger and sadness like successive curtains being drawn. She had got her questions in fast.

Why did he believe his friend to be dead?

All his information had come directly from Ash, who said he was dying. Blinkered trust had negated the need for proof, while repeated hospital appointments and an eventual operation, presumably for the cysts to be removed, had been enough to convince Rupert his friend was telling the truth.

Was Ash violent?

At first Perkin said no, but when Hawkins pushed for examples of what he referred to as *a temper*, it became clear that Ash had bullied and belittled him for years, so frequently that Perkin had come to accept it as normal.

Plus Ash had form.

His police record was strewn with misdemeanours; nothing of great concern in isolation, but sufficiently ominous in this context for alarm bells to ring. He had been cautioned several times as a teenager for shoplifting; instances that stopped as abruptly as similar charges then started to appear on Perkin's file. He'd also been questioned in connection with the disappearance of various pets near two separate addresses; nothing proven either time, but one or two of the animals' bodies had been recovered bearing evidence of torture. Add the cigarette burns on Perkin's forearms, which he wasn't keen to talk about, and a fuller picture of Ash started to build.

Hawkins still couldn't say for certain that she knew the full story, but either way someone else was involved, and right now, Ashley Jones was her guess.

They rounded the final bend and entered the clearing, wide tyres parting the gravel with a noise like unbroken waves on a beach. As instructed, Aaron Sharpe was waiting near the entrance, and Mike stopped to let him into the passenger seat before moving on.

Hawkins glanced at the house, every window lit from inside, as the white-suited forensic officers interrogated the place. And ahead of them, the SOCO truck was parked beside a silver Land Rover Defender with a wading snorkel and jacked-up suspension.

Mike parked up next to the Defender, aligning Hawkins with the driver's side, both windows opening so they could talk.

'Thanks for coming.' Hawkins smiled at the bald man in the driving seat of the other car.

'Any time.' He smiled back. 'What do you need?'

DS Dave Thurgood was an old friend from Hendon training college; one of Hawkins' most outstanding students from her last year of lecturing there. Not only did he drive an appropriate car for their needs, but he was now an authorised firearms officer with the local branch of Specialist Crime and Operations. He introduced the man in the Defender's passenger seat as Gary Dennison, an AFO colleague. Luckily, both men routinely carried Tasers, and had been in the area when she'd called Thurgood from Loughton. And, true to altruistic form, he had agreed to provide armed support for their prospective arrest.

Quickly Hawkins explained the situation: that they would be following Perkin's directions across off-road terrain, hopefully to locate the derelict house where she hoped to find potential killer Ashley Jones. Thurgood agreed to follow their lead.

Hawkins raised the window and looked at Perkin. 'So, which way is it?'

For a moment there was no reaction, as their captive continued to stare out of the opposite window, at the intermittent stream of SOCOs trudging back and forth, removing various plastic-wrapped possessions from his home.

Slowly he turned to face her, his quiet tone faltering. 'They d . . . died . . . because of me.'

Hawkins heard the soft creak of leather as the two men in the front turned to look at each other.

You shouldn't have let him see the house.

'We can talk about this later,' she tried, alert for signs of understanding. 'But right now we have to find Ash. Do you understand?'

Briefly Rupert looked at her, and she caught the glassy shimmer in his eyes before his head dropped. 'I d . . . did this.'

Hawkins thought fast. She had to keep him engaged, get the information they needed, before the window closed.

'Please, Rupert.' She leaned closer. 'Which way is the other house?'

At last he whispered. 'B . . . behind the cottage.'

Hawkins tapped Mike on the shoulder, relaying the instruction as her DI put the car in drive and set off, skirting the small structure. He dimmed the interior lights as they went, the off-roaders' headlights darting among the trees at the edge of the glade, firing slender shadows into the mist as Thurgood fell in behind.

They rounded the building, allowing Hawkins to scan its rear facade. No exits this side, but she noted the window with crude metal bars bolted on the outside; the tiny room where Rupert had held his supposed guests.

She looked at Perkin. 'Where now?'

'Turn h . . . here.' He raised his arms between the front seats to point.

Mike followed his command, easing the Range Rover in among the trees. Straight away the ground became uneven, pitching the 4x4 on its axis, forcing all three passengers to reach for grab handles or seat-backs.

They crawled for a while, wheels spinning here and there on the wet ground, but finding traction each time. At last the forest's density fell and their pace improved, joining a path that wound away into the trees.

'Left or right?' she asked.

Perkin's head rose, but his eventual reply wasn't the one she wanted. 'Ash l . . . lied to me, didn't he?'

Hawkins hesitated, but he looked at her, one side of his face lit by the second vehicle's headlamps. 'A . . . about his illness.'

She nodded. 'It looks that way.'

'I thought he was my f . . . friend.'

'We all want answers,' she said. 'But finding him is the only way to get them.'

Rupert thought for a few seconds. 'What will happen to Ash if you f . . . find him?'

'We need to ask him some questions.'

'About whether he k . . . killed the people I took.'

'Yes.'

'What if he d . . . did?'

Don't sugar-coat it. 'He'll go to prison.'

Rupert's eyes drifted off her, and he turned to stare out of the window, fingers working nervously away at his chin.

She followed his gaze along the moonlit track, imagining Ash Jones speeding through the darkness; towards somewhere he could go to ground until the investigation floundered. And in time, kill again.

She fought the urge to rush Perkin, reminding herself they were still effectively strangers, asking a confused young man to offer up his lifelong companion. She began calculating search perimeters, based on the worst-case scenario that their suspect had a seven-hour head start, had he departed immediately after his failed attack on Sheila Priest.

His ideal exit strategy would likely be Europe via rail, air or sea. But the ports had been her first thought, too, so his details had been circulated to each one straight away. If he had any sense, Jones would avoid the obvious routes and seek refuge this side of passport control.

Her thoughts arrested as Rupert turned back, the amplified rise and fall of his shoulders suggesting that a decision had been reached. For a moment they just stared at each other, but at last he answered,

'Left.'

She nodded at Mike, who moved them away as directed, the Range Rover's high-mounted headlamps picking out every detail of their narrow, overgrown route. At last they emerged from the treeline into open wasteland.

It was approaching three thirty a.m. when they rounded the final cluster of trees on to rising terrain dotted with coarse scrub in various stages of decay, as if disease had recently cut its way through. Above them, a bright quarter-moon drifted through a gap in gun-metal clouds, but Hawkins' attention slid straight to the top of the slope, and the shape looming there among the blackened, skeletal trees.

They had found the derelict house.

62

Something woke him.

There was a flash of blackness as cold air filled his lungs and jagged pain arced behind his eyes. He froze, picking up the familiar creaks and groans of the ruined house, felt the pulse of a migraine settle in.

Was he going to be sick?

He rolled off the mattress and tried to stand, chasing the floor with his feet when it shifted under him. He swayed, watching the ethereal glow from the window dance across the far wall, dropping into a crouch as dizziness took hold.

Reeling, he screwed his eyes shut, reaching up to check the wound on his head. The rough patch under his hair felt dry, although he couldn't be sure it had fully sealed.

Water.

This time he managed to stand, but the lightness in his head said his body needed fuel, too.

He edged forwards in the pitch darkness, choosing not to reach for the torch on the floor by the bed in case he fell. He didn't need it anyway. This place hadn't deteriorated much in the years he'd been away, and in the last couple of months his internal map of the house had come back. Instead he moved towards the grey smudge of the window; halfway point in the safest route across the room, free of broken floorboards or full-blown holes. It was only a few feet, but his breaths were coming hard and fast by the time his palms found the sill. He rested for a moment, going over recent events.

Tonight had not gone to plan.

Obviously he had allowed for that possibility, so when it happened his plan had been to return here, leaving Rupert perfectly positioned to take the blame for it all. He would gather his things, erase all traces of the time he'd spent living at the house, and disappear to let things resolve themselves. The news would tell him once Rupert was convicted. Only then could he relax.

Except now his contingency plan was fucked, as well.

For a start, Rupert's latest hostage wasn't supposed to evade him for so long. And when he finally caught her, the feisty bitch certainly wasn't supposed to fight back. His head was still ringing. It felt like he'd been hit with a brick.

Then, just as he'd been about to make her pay, some arsehole passer-by had stopped, forcing him to back off. He'd watched from just inside the trees, considering whether to go back and take them both out, but the guy had been fucking huge, leaving him no choice but to watch the BMW disappear with his unfinished business aboard.

After that he should have left straight away, but instead he'd gone back to watch Rupert's house, eager to see what happened next. Sure enough, the police turned up within hours, arrested Rupert and took him away. Only then had he stumbled back through the forest to his childhood bolt-hole.

And he'd only just made it, dragging himself the last quarter-mile, shaking due to loss of blood. Inside, he'd stuck the cleanest towel he could find over his head wound and slept, needing to recharge before clearing the place.

But he'd woken feeling even worse, and as he checked his watch in the dim light seeping in through the window, he realised it had been almost eight hours since the bitch had escaped. And there was always the risk that Rupert might mention this place to the police, leading some overzealous cop to come and check it out.

He needed to leave.

Except now it looked like he required medical help, but even *that* was complicated. At this time of night, it meant walking into a hospital and answering questions about what had happened to him; too much of a risk to take anywhere around here, even if he lied. He needed to be at least two hours away before he contemplated that. His car was a five-minute walk from the house, because the immediate terrain was too rough to bring a road car any nearer than that. And besides, right now he was in no physical state to drive.

He gripped the windowsill tighter and stared at the horizon, wondering how it had all come to this.

The whole thing had started by chance, soon after

his fabricated demise. He'd begun watching Rupert's house, curious about how the runt would cope on his own, after a lifetime leeching off his supposed best friend. Without him Perkin was fucked, and he'd been looking forward to watching the idiot disintegrate when he realised there was nobody left to carry him any more.

Except that evening, for the first time he could remember, Rupert Perkin had surprised him.

It happened on the third night he'd gone to watch. At first everything seemed normal, shadows dancing on the walls from a fire in the hearth; curtains open because normally there was no one around to hide anything from. His gaze had flicked from room to room, confusion growing as the minutes passed. *Where the fuck was Rupert?* He'd been about to check the rear when he'd noticed . . .

The car wasn't there.

Perkin's green Laguna had been missing; an event not unusual during the day, when he used it mostly to collect supplies. But the little coward hated going out after dark; avoided it whenever he could. So for him to take the car out at night, something big must have been going on.

An hour had passed, then two, and still Rupert hadn't returned. He'd grown more and more curious, and at last the answer had come.

At first he'd seen headlights cutting through the trees, coming towards him from the main road. He'd crouched in the bushes a few metres from the track as the old Renault passed, slowly bumping its way between potholes towards the house.

It had pulled up on the shingle, tail lights going off as Rupert climbed out and lurched round behind the car, possibly heading for the boot. But he hadn't stopped there. Instead he kept going, right around to the passenger side, opening the door and leaning in.

He'd watched in silent awe as Rupert lifted a young woman out of the car. She hung limp in his arms as he'd carried her to the house. *Maybe asleep; maybe drugged. Maybe dead.*

He'd stayed to find out what happened, of course.

For a few hours Rupert drifted back and forth inside the house, but there had been no sign of the girl. Just after midnight the last light went off, and nothing more happened before it started getting light just after eight a.m.

Camouflage gone, he'd been forced to leave, also desperately in need of rest by that point. Even so he hadn't slept much, his mind scratching away at the question. *What the fuck was Rupert up to?*

He returned to the house as soon as night fell again, although the first four hours of darkness produced nothing of interest. But then, almost exactly twenty-four hours after being carried inside, the young woman had come flying out the front door and run straight into the trees, narrowly missing him.

But the weirdest thing was that Rupert hadn't followed.

Clearly she'd been taken and held against her will.

And regardless of whether he'd intended to set her free, either Rupert wasn't aware she had gone, or he wasn't interested in stopping her.

He'd watched the girl disappear into the woods, turning things over in his head. He could let her go and wait to see if there were repercussions, or he could get rid of her and watch what happened next. Either way, Rupert took the blame.

So he'd switched on his night-vision glasses and gone after her.

The irony wasn't lost on him, of course. Yet again he'd ended up dealing with Rupert Perkin's mess.

But he hadn't expected to enjoy doing it quite so much.

Over the years he'd flirted with the idea of killing Rupert but had never followed through, because their *friendship* meant there was never any rent to pay; never any need to buy food. Obviously he'd since skimmed enough money from Rupert's bank account to survive on his own, but putting up with Perkin made life *easy*.

Except, ever since Rupert's parents had died, all of the kid's needy shit had landed on him, and one day it had stopped feeling like a stress-free ride. The thought had struck him as he read a letter from his doctor, saying he needed a follow-up appointment for the persistent backache he'd suffered in recent years. Shortly after that, several consultations and a minor operation had become his chance to break away, without then having to worry about an abject Rupert Perkin following him around like a rejected pet, wanting to know *why*.

Obviously he'd known Rupert would hate being alone, but he hadn't expected such a dramatic reaction as *this*, whatever it was. And as the young woman had stumbled away through the trees, he'd had another choice to make. If he let her escape, she'd go straight to the law, and Rupert would be arrested and charged.

Or he could stop her.

For good.

At first he had faltered. He'd killed plenty of animals before as a child, mostly local dogs that had strayed on to the fields. Nobody cared about them. But the rush he felt that first time with the knife had faded quickly, and soon he was knocking them out with bricks; finishing the job with his bare hands. Watching the sense drain from their bovine eyes.

Even that thrill had gone stale.

Now here was an opportunity to indulge his long-held curiosity about human death, an insignificant lamb with no risk attached. If he kept his gloves on and his wits about him, he could dispose of her without implicating anyone but Perkin, should things go sour. And, not only was Rupert the obvious suspect if her body was found, but he was also convinced the real killer was dead. Whatever means Rupert had used to obtain the girl, eventually they would lead the police to his door.

So where was the downside?

He went after her, his pulse racing, night-vision goggles allowing him to catch up easily. He'd kicked her feet out as she ran, followed her down into the sharp undergrowth. She'd been so weak, so helpless as he rammed one hand over her mouth and the other round her neck, and kept them there until she stopped thrashing. Then he'd transferred both hands to her throat, really clamping down as the ecstasy pounded through him, peaking only when her eyelids flickered one last time and went still.

He had knelt over her lifeless body far longer than he should have, just savouring the dying glow of his first human kill. The high had been incredible; unlike anything before or since.

But it never faded like those dogs.

At last he'd picked up her body and carried it to a secluded spot accessible by road. Then he'd gone home, collected the car and moved her across London to another small wood, buzzing the whole way.

The main rush had lasted longer than it took him to dig the shallow grave, his hands tingling like pins and needles as he worked. And the last of the adrenalin hadn't subsided for days.

In truth he'd expected that to be it. But he was still curious the following day, returning under cover of darkness to watch the house again. After thinking about it all afternoon, his best guess had been that Perkin had made some kind of abortive attempt at getting laid. The girl had been a hooker, off her face on drugs; a skank that no one would miss. She'd woken up with a tiny cock dangling in front of her face and fucked off at a sprint. An experience that Rupert wouldn't be keen to repeat.

But his best guess had been wrong.

The car was missing again when he'd arrived,

although this time it hadn't reappeared until much nearer midnight.

Rupert's second hostage had been a lanky bloke with a rucksack, also unconscious, who was dragged into the house across the ground. *So much for equality.*

Again he'd stayed until dawn, and waited for darkness before coming back. But just like number one, number two had stumbled out the front door almost exactly twenty-four hours after going in.

He'd buried that guy not far from the girl.

And so the pattern continued. He had no idea where Rupert was finding these people, or how they ended up comatose in his passenger seat, but the lambs kept on coming, and he kept on taking them down.

Number three might have presented more of a challenge. He was clearly a much fitter man, whose bulk almost led Rupert to burst a blood vessel as he was hauled slowly into the house. But as they crossed the light of the window, he'd noticed the wounds. There was no way Rupert could have taken this guy out, but he'd definitely taken a beating in the not too distant past. Another easy target in the end.

At which point one of the bodies was found.

Again he'd expected things to come to a head, picturing police cars slewing on to the drive, officers manhandling Rupert into the back. And yet, there was Rupert days later, calmly dragging another victim into his lair, an older man this time, clearly some kind of rambler. Those walking boots had been fuckers to get off the corpse.

Then came the feisty bitch.

He'd been circling the house at a distance, trying to keep the blood flow going in his legs, when she came out. Plus she was early, which had caught him off-guard. All the others had emerged within an hour of the full twenty-four, but she'd appeared at least two hours before that. Then she'd got clever, managing to stay hidden while he chased noises deeper into the woods.

By the time he caught sight of her, she'd been half-way down the track to the main road; somewhere he couldn't afford for her to be. He'd caught her near the junction, kicking at her heels. But as they struggled, she'd hit him with some kind of weapon. Luckily she'd connected with the plastic casing of his goggles.

Otherwise it might have been game over.

As it was, he'd managed to drag himself back to safety. But there was no more time for rest; he had to get moving, clear this place out in case the police turned up after he'd gone. He drew breath, trying to ignore the pain drilling into his head, about to push off the sill when he saw them.

He froze, attention fully back on the present as he stared out over the night landscape, following the four pinpricks of brightness as they left the trees and entered the far end of the field leading up to the house. Headlights. And there was only one thing their presence could mean.

Somebody knew he was here.

63

'Lights.' Hawkins nudged the back of Mike's seat, watching the ground in front of the car all but disappear as he pressed a switch on the dash.

She glanced out of the rear screen in time to see Thurgood's headlamps flick off, too, before turning back to stare up at the derelict house. Now in the misty pre-dawn darkness, it was easy to see there was no light coming from around any of the boarded-up windows. And no vehicle parked outside.

But that didn't mean Ash wasn't here.

It was the middle of the night, after all, so if there was anyone inside this rickety old house, they were likely to be asleep. Which, of course, suited her fine. With any luck they'd find Ashley Jones snoring in one of the bedrooms and have him cuffed before he knew what was going on.

She turned to Maguire. 'Get us a bit nearer, but keep the noise down.'

He nodded, engaging first, the off-roader's V8 torque allowing them to crawl up the incline without too many revs. The engine hummed quietly as they crept forwards, weaving between the larger foliage, bumping in and out of the ruts.

Mike brought them to a halt ten yards from the

house, then he and Aaron climbed out. Hawkins waited while Sharpe came to open her door, unable to do so herself because the security locks were engaged, then stepped out on to the damp ground.

The sergeant's ambivalence was palpable when she told him to wait with Perkin in the car. He glanced at their captive, sitting forlorn in the rear seat, staring out through the windscreen at the dark outlines of distant trees flailing in the late October wind. Perhaps Sharpe was less convinced than Hawkins by the younger man's innocuous demeanour, but clearly, venturing into a condemned building after a multiple murderer held even less appeal.

He got in.

Hawkins eased the door closed and leaned on it, muffling the noise of the mechanism as it engaged, keen not to alert anyone inside the house. Then she walked out from between the vehicles, looking up at the building. It seemed so out of place here, an ugly twenties structure with broken gutters and smashed windows, the whole place exposed to the elements, groaning in the wind that whipped already wet hair into her face.

She joined the huddle of her colleagues in front of the cars, taking the torch that Mike handed her, noting that both AFOs had drawn Tasers. Quickly they devised a plan. Then she and Thurgood waited for Maguire and Dennison to disappear behind the house before approaching the front door, which hung off broken hinges and had been propped against the inner wall, inviting the low mist in to swirl at their feet.

The darkness swallowed them.

Their boots clicked on to bare floorboards. As agreed, neither of them used their torches, and quickly Hawkins' eyes adjusted, allowing her to determine the layout. A staircase led upwards away from them, with an open door to the right of the medium-sized hallway and another, closed, at the far end. Above them, the discoloured ceiling was a mass of spiderwebs.

Thurgood paused with a hand up, telling Hawkins to stop. They stood close, listening for noises above the quiet wail of the wind breaching the exposed property's seams. Within seconds, soft footsteps reached them from deeper inside the house.

Hawkins tensed, watching Thurgood edge silently forwards, bringing his Taser up as the door at the end of the hall creaked open. But they both breathed again as their colleagues appeared in the gap.

Dennison came first, making a sign she took as confirmation that what looked like the kitchen was clear. Then he pointed upwards, indicating that he and Mike would check the upper floor. Maguire touched her shoulder as they passed and began climbing the stairs, while she joined Thurgood at the closed door leading off the hall.

The AFO nodded before gripping the handle and nudging the door to release it from the frame. It opened on to blackness, the moonlight coming through the open front door unable to penetrate the room's deeper recess, but the stale tang of body odour and damp that hit them suggested very recent use.

Thurgood flicked on his torch, leading Hawkins to do

the same thing, then he leaned inside to find the light switch. She heard the click, but nothing happened.

They stayed in the doorway, torch beams skimming the surfaces like fingertips across Braille. Both windows were boarded from the inside, and rubble lay in piles on the intermittently ruptured floorboards. Men's clothing was scattered across the surfaces. At the back of the room, Hawkins' beam skimmed over a camping mattress and sleeping bag, in front of a small settee. A torch stood upright on the floor.

Jones had been here.

They moved inside, Hawkins lighting the floor; Thurgood the walls. She turned to look behind the door as the AFO checked around the few pieces of furniture. But the room was clear.

Automatically she relaxed, becoming aware of the floor creaking above her as the others continued their search, but there were no warning shouts. It looked like their target had gone.

She and Thurgood returned to the hallway as Maguire and Dennison came down the stairs, now also using their torches. Mike shook his head, and Hawkins was about to suggest they return to the cars.

'Shit.' Thurgood raised his Taser.

She spun, following his stare past her shoulder to see Aaron Sharpe's face spotlit by the AFO's torch beam. He stood just outside the front door, head back, eyes wide, a trickle of blood running down his neck from the serrated point of a kitchen knife pressed hard against his throat.

Which meant the shorter man standing behind him, holding the blade, was Ashley Jones.

Hawkins suppressed the icy dread that chilled her vertebrae at the sight of a sharpened blade, mentally kicking herself. Clearly Ash had seen them coming up the hill and left before they arrived, skirting the house to target Aaron while they explored the building. Now he had a hostage, but this stand-off raised two questions. First, he'd been free, so why hadn't Ash simply run, and second, what had he done with Rupert?

'Back off,' he growled. 'Or this fucker dies.'

They all complied as the two men edged into the hallway; both blinking as three more torch beams joined the first, Sharpe choking quietly as the knife jerked against his skin.

In the overspill from the torchlight, Hawkins made out that Jones was in his late twenties. His features were twisted into a sneer, but his eyes were glazed, and the hair on the left side of his head appeared to be matted with dried blood. His knife arm, held up and over Aaron's shoulder, was half supporting him.

He was hurt.

Then the second of her questions was answered. As Ash and Aaron moved forwards, a third figure slid out of the darkness behind them.

'Get in here, freak,' Jones ordered.

Rupert obeyed, shuffling inside with his wrists still cuffed, hunched like a scolded child, as Hawkins weighed the odds.

Under normal circumstances Jones wouldn't have

been able to control two people with just a knife, but his hold over Perkin was obviously more established. He was facing four adversaries, including two trained AFOs with Tasers. The stun guns fired twin projectiles that debilitated the receiver with a highly concentrated electrical charge. But the system only worked if both darts made contact, and currently Jones wasn't providing them with enough of a target. Together, the four of them could easily overpower Ash, but not without putting Aaron's life at unjustifiable risk.

'Take it easy,' she said, watching the blade's edge press harder against her sergeant's windpipe. 'Let's be rational about this. There's no way out of here, so put the knife down.'

'Fuck off.'

'OK, keep the knife.' She adjusted her approach, wary of pushing too hard. 'What do you want?'

'Well now,' the suggestion of a grin formed on Jones' lips, although there was also a mild slur in his speech. He nodded at the two 4x4s parked outside. 'Give me the keys to both those cars, or this wanker's dead before he hits the floor.'

'And what then, Ash?' Hawkins asked, watching tears form in Sharpe's eyes. 'We know your name and your face, so how far do you think you'll get? Give it up now, and I'll do what I can for you when this goes to trial.'

He snorted. 'And what fucking difference is *that* going to make when you've killed four people? As soon as you muppets arrest me I'm screwed either way, so give me your fucking keys.'

Hawkins looked at the knife, and the crimson fissure starting to open up on Aaron's neck where the blade was rubbing. She turned and nodded at Thurgood and Maguire, both of whom retrieved their keys and held them up.

'Throw them to Rupert,' Jones instructed.

They did. First Thurgood, then Maguire, tossed their keys across the hallway to Perkin. He caught the first set but fumbled the second, stooping to recover them as Jones reeled off a string of insults under his breath.

Ash waited for him to stand. 'Now, the three of us are leaving, and unless you want your pal's throat slit, you'll stay right where you are, got it?'

There were nods.

'Good.' Ash tugged at Sharpe, and both took a step towards the door, but they were forced to stop there. Because Rupert hadn't moved.

Ash glanced at him. 'Fuck's wrong with you, retard? Go.'

Everyone looked at Rupert.

Perkin whispered something at the floor, but his head came up when it became clear no one had understood. He looked at Ash, this time raising his voice. 'I let them go, but you k . . . killed them.'

'Too fucking right I did,' Jones spat. 'And you should be thanking me for the biggest fucking favour anyone's ever done for you. You know what would have happened if any of them had got away? They'd have locked you up.'

Rupert began to rock from one foot to the other, breathing hard. 'Why did you l . . . let me think you were dead?'

Ash rolled his eyes. 'I didn't *let* you think it, idiot; I *made* you think it, because I wanted out, away from your stupid questions, on and on, day after fucking day. And I knew if I just pissed off you'd have followed me, like the pathetic worm you are.'

Rupert's shoulders sank as Ash talked, and his quiet reply was thick with emotion. 'We were f . . . friends.'

'You were a bloody meal ticket, mate.'

There was another pause as Rupert appeared to absorb the statement. But his response, when it came, was more definite. 'We aren't f . . . friends any more.'

'At last we agree on something,' Ash sneered. 'Now get your backwards arse outside and unlock the cars, or this copper's death will be your fault as well.'

For a moment, Rupert looked as if he might burst into tears, but then he gathered himself and looked up at Hawkins, who held his gaze as he backed slowly out of the door.

'Keep it calm,' Ash reminded them, renewing pressure on the knife at Aaron's throat as he followed, yanking his distraught hostage backwards down the step.

Hawkins felt her heart rate build as the three men retreated across the wet ground, slowly closing the ten-yard gap to the cars, indicators on both 4x4s flashing brightly in the gloom when Rupert followed Ash's instruction to unlock them.

She waited until Jones was out of earshot, and hissed

at the others, 'As soon as that knife comes away from Aaron's throat, we go for him, OK?'

'You sure, boss?' Mike whispered. 'That's a big distance to cover.'

'Then do it fast.' She looked back at Rupert, reassured by the fact that he was still staring straight at her. The men were almost at the cars when it happened.

Something caused Ash to slip on the soggy ground, and the knife came away from Aaron's neck for a second as he righted himself. Rupert must have been waiting for an opportunity, because he reacted surprisingly fast, reaching out with both hands, grabbing Ash's wrist, pulling it back.

'Now!' Hawkins shouted, sprinting down the step with the three men behind, feet slipping as soon as they hit the soggy grass, blunting their progress.

Ahead of them, Ash released Sharpe and head-butted Rupert hard in the face as the sergeant stumbled free. Perkin dropped, releasing his grip on Ash's arm, just as Aaron rounded and attacked, trying to disarm Jones.

But he was clearly off-balance.

'Aaron, no,' Hawkins yelled, slipping again as she tried to speed up.

Sharpe lunged for the knife, but Ash jerked it away before driving the blade up into Aaron's gut. Hawkins flinched as she heard the rip of flesh.

The sergeant doubled over, his head crashing into the mud as Jones stepped away in one fluid motion, grabbing the keys from where Rupert had dropped them, and darting towards the cars.

Hawkins heard a hiss from behind as one of the AFOs fired their Taser. The darts shot past her, narrowly missing Jones as he disappeared behind the car.

They skidded around the Range Rover in time to see Ash slam the Defender's door.

Hawkins threw herself at the outer latch, wrenching it back, feeling fingernails break. The door popped as the Land Rover's engine fired, and then Mike was beside her, both of them trying to pull it open. But the off-roader's tyres spun and it hauled itself clear, dumping them both on the ground as it slewed away across the wet grass, chucking up dirt, tyres fighting for traction.

Hawkins dragged herself upright, looking across to where Dennison was marshalling Perkin to his feet. Beyond them, Thurgood had turned Sharpe on his back and was adjusting clothes to assess the sergeant's wound.

She fought the urge to retch and turned away, pulling out her phone, but when the screen lit it was smashed. She swore and stuffed it back in her pocket.

'Mike.' She strode to the back of the car, where her DI was crouching with one arm under the 4x4. 'I need your phone to call an ambulance and air supp—. What are you doing?'

'Always have a back-up.' He stood, opening a small black box to produce a spare key. 'Now we go after Jones.'

'Great.' Hawkins grabbed the key, calling to Thurgood, cutting Mike off before he had a chance to point out whose car it was. 'Dave and I will go after Ash. Gary can hold on to Rupert; you stay here and fix Aaron.' She ignored his open-mouthed protest and opened the tailgate, pulling out the medical kit he kept there. She passed it to him. 'You're the most qualified here in first aid, aren't you?'

He paused, then rolled his eyes. 'Be careful, OK?'

'Of course.' She grabbed the key and skidded towards the driver's door, glancing down the hill, catching a flash of red as the retreating Defender braked.

She and Thurgood clambered aboard the Range Rover and she started it up, gunned the throttle, engaged first and floored it. She switched on the lights and wipers, simultaneously dropping the front windows to clear the rain.

'I'll call air surveillance,' Mike shouted as they slid sideways, all four wheels spinning on the wet grass. 'Don't engage; just keep him in sight. And don't scratch my ride.'

'Got it,' she yelled back, straightening up.

They hit the slope, quickly building speed. Beside her, Thurgood was trying to plug in his seat belt, jolting from side to side as they crashed through ruts and bushes. Hawkins fitted hers, too, fumbling with the buttons to move the seat. She found height and lumbar adjustment before the seat finally slid forwards, allowing her to reach the pedals without having to stretch.

She squinted through the mud being smeared across the glass by the wipers, pulling the screenwash lever. 'Can you see him?'

'There.' Thurgood pointed ahead and to the left, as Hawkins caught a glint of silver near the treeline.

She swore. 'He's miles ahead.'

'Don't worry,' the AFO shouted over the racket of vegetation smashing against the underside of the car. 'The Defender's built for strength, not speed. And he's driving without lights, trying to stay hidden, which'll slow him down, too. We'll catch him.'

'Good.' She pushed harder, veering around a large tree that appeared out of the darkness. The wheel bucked in her hands, but she managed to control it, wrestling the 4x4 back into line as they banged through another ditch. The steering went light for a second, jolting both of them in their seats as the bulky vehicle reconnected with the ground, splattering the wind-screen with lumps of wet mud.

'I can't see him,' Hawkins urged, speeding up the wipers.

'He went into the woods.' Thurgood sat forward, pointing through the muck-smeared glass. 'Where the treeline juts out.'

'Hold on,' Hawkins yelled as they reached the bottom of the hill, trying to pick the smoothest route through a rocky creek that ran in the seam between inclines, and began climbing the opposite side. Another spray of the washers cleared a patch of screen, allowing her to identify the point where Jones had supposedly entered the forest.

'Turn here.' Thurgood's voice rose as they shot towards it. 'Here!'

Hawkins braked as late as she dared, hauling the off-roader left on to the small path that disappeared into the trees, spurred on by a burst of red light fifty yards ahead.

But she was forced to slow as the forest contracted around them, foliage crunching sporadically against the screen as she fought to stay on the bucking pathway, although the next time the Defender's brake lights flickered, they were closer again.

'We're catching,' she said.

'Speed up,' Thurgood replied. 'He can't move as fast as we can.'

Hawkins flattened the accelerator, shocks entering the cabin less frequently now, because the track had evened out, just as she lost sight of the Defender behind thick foliage. But seconds later its headlights came on, and the silver 4x4 sped away to the right.

Hawkins swore. 'How's he doing *that*?'

'Must be a road,' Dave said. 'Keep your foot down. I think the trees are thinning.'

He was right. Almost immediately the overhanging branches began to retreat from their path. Hawkins reacted, pushing harder; gathering speed as they approached the point where Ash had turned. At last their headlights hit tarmac, and she bumped up the verge on to a medium sized road that stretched away through the forest.

'We'll definitely catch him now,' Thurgood told her. 'Old girl tops out at fifty-five.'

'About fucking time.' Hawkins floored the throttle,

feeling the surge as the Range Rover's V8 entered its stride. They built momentum rapidly, passing seventy as Hawkins corrected for an insistent tug on the wheel, obviously having bent something in their charge through the woods. Mike wasn't going to like it.

But they had to keep going.

'Have you got a phone?' she asked, glancing over to see the sergeant's mobile already pressed to his ear.

'On it.' He started talking as the call connected with control, giving the operator details of the chase and their approximate location, north-west of Loughton, heading south.

He covered the mic and raised his voice above the engine's roar. 'Chopper's on its way.'

'No rush.' Hawkins wrestled the wheel.

Up ahead the Defender, now easier to track thanks to its tail lights, had slowed for a sharp left, and they began to close at frightening speed. From the corner of her eye, Hawkins saw Thurgood grip the seat as she finally braked, tyres screeching on the wet asphalt, understeer threatening to carry them straight on. She eased off, controlling the slide, firing them along the next straight.

Hawkins saw Thurgood give a quick nod of appreciation, but her real satisfaction came from seeing the gap fall below forty yards and continue disappearing fast. Better still, the trees on either side were dense enough to prevent Ash from veering off into the forest.

There was nowhere for him to go.

By the time they reached the next series of corners,

the Defender's lead was gone, and Hawkins followed closely through the turns, lowering the passenger window as their speed dropped. Wind invaded the cabin.

'Can you hear air support?' she shouted.

'Not yet,' Thurgood yelled back.

Hawkins closed the window. 'We can't wait much longer. Find out where they are.'

Dave raised his mobile as she swung into a sweeping left, watching the other 4x4 almost lose control as Jones cut the oncoming lane. It skimmed the opposite bank before being yanked back into line.

'They're over Dartford,' Thurgood reported. 'Ten minutes.'

She banged the wheel. 'We need them *now*!'

'Why? We aren't going to lose him.'

'Maybe not.' She pointed at the Defender as it narrowly missed an oncoming car. 'But this guy's confused and dangerous. We have to stop him before he gets near a built-up area.'

She sensed Thurgood's stare as he asked, 'Are you even *trained* in vehicular intervention?'

'Of course.'

'Bollocks.' He shook his head as she glanced over. 'Your views on protocol haven't changed, then?'

'Not really. You in?'

'Absolutely.' Thurgood hefted the Taser. 'Let's get him.'

Hawkins nodded, punching the throttle to make the gearbox kick down as they entered an unbroken straight. The Ranger Rover complied, charging forwards so fast that she almost mistimed the manoeuvre, having to jerk the wheel to avoid the Defender's rear bumper.

Jones tucked into a right-hander as she tried to over-take on the inside, hoping to get ahead and brake both cars to a smooth halt. But he cut her off, veering right, forcing her back. She switched sides and tried again, but she was blocked the same way.

'Road's too narrow.' Hawkins fought the wheel, re-strategizing as a solitary car flashed past in the opposite lane, horn blaring. 'I'll have to give him a tap.'

Thurgood turned to look at her. 'Do you know what you're doing?'

Hawkins didn't answer as she drifted right, watching their target follow. Then she swung the other way, unleashing a burst of acceleration to bring them along-side. Ash took the bait, swerving back as her front wheel came level with his rear wing.

'Sorry about your car,' she said to Thurgood and Maguire at the same time.

And turned in hard.

There was a crunch as the two vehicles connected. Hawkins felt her passenger grimace, but she held fast, forcing the Defender sideways, watching its front wheels turn into the slide. She kept the pressure on, cancelling out Jones' correction, sending his car into a spin.

Then he braked.

Hawkins sensed the momentum shifting, and the Range Rover shunted forwards, tortured metal scream-ing as it ground along the side of the other 4x4. She felt their speed collapsing, aware that if it dropped too far, the Defender might flip. She eased off, allowing a gap to open up.

But Jones must have floored the throttle as they broke contact, because at that instant his tyres found traction, and the silver car catapulted sideways across the road, smashing into the kerb and launching itself towards the treeline.

Hawkins heard the bang as she tried to emergency brake, but control had already gone. Released from the stabilising influence of the other car, her front wheels bit, firing the Range Rover the opposite way. She managed to scrub off some speed, but it was too late.

The big 4x4 skidded across the oncoming lane, the rear slewing around so they were travelling backwards when tyre screech disappeared as they left tarmac. There was a split second of rumbling as they crossed the verge and crashed sideways into the trees.

A shockwave flashed through the cabin, wrenching them both in their seats. Something exploded, punching her backwards. Then there was nothing but ringing silence.

Hawkins blinked hard, trying to clear her vision as she looked over at Thurgood through the white haze from the now limp airbags, her heart jumping when she saw the sergeant slumped awkwardly beside her. The tree that had stopped them was right outside his shattered window, the door thrust inwards around its heavy trunk.

'Dave!' She tried to lean over, but was forced to retreat and undo her seat belt before she could reach him. She lifted his head, noting the welt on his brow where he must have hit the window in the crash.

She checked him for injuries, pressing hard enough against the major bones to prompt a reaction if any were broken. Thurgood groaned quietly, but he seemed largely intact.

'Lie still,' Hawkins commanded, squinting out through the badly cracked windscreen at the Defender's rear half, sticking out of thick undergrowth thirty yards away in the darkness, steam venting slowly into the night air. 'Help's on the way.'

She pulled the door release, unsure as she stepped out on to the muddy verge whether the pain in her collarbone and ribs was just bruising, or more serious damage muted by shock. Light rain dusted her face as she glanced upwards at the uniform grey slot of sky between the two avenues of trees, straining her still buzzing senses for any signs of imminent air support. There were none.

She looked back at the other 4x4, scanning the forest for any clues to Ash's location. There was nothing to suggest he wasn't still in the stricken car, although there was no way to tell for sure without going over and opening the door. Yet, without knowing how far away the cavalry were, the only logical choice was for her to go after the killer alone, a prospect she wasn't relishing.

But Jones had been injured before starting the chase, while the game of chicken he'd lost to Epping Forest wouldn't have done him any favours, either. So hopefully he'd be in worse shape than her.

She paused, concocting her strategy before climbing back into the Range Rover. After a moment's fevered digging she found Thurgood's Taser in the footwell, and checked it with a layman's eye under the interior light. The dart cartridge seemed undamaged, and if the red button on the barrel was a safety lock, it seemed to be off, although this type of Taser was a one-shot deal, so the only way to find out for sure was to pull the trigger and hope.

Having reassured herself one more time that Dave was breathing normally, Hawkins returned to the roadside. Her breath curled up and away into the mist-infused night air as she moved around to the boot, fighting her way into one of the stab vests Mike carried for special occasions.

She remote-locked the car to keep the sergeant safe and limped off down the road, alert for any distant signs of approaching traffic. But the backwater highway remained clear.

Her ears had recovered slightly by the time she neared the stricken Defender. The underlying murmur of unseen nocturnal creatures and the wind-agitated rustle of leaves enveloped her, broken only by the damaged car's engine, clicking itself cool.

She slowed, picking the clearest line along the gravel-strewn pavement, crouching to check under the car as she edged near. Above the muddy bank to her right, an eerie barrage of trunks and foliage offered a plethora of shadowy coves, but she needed to see if Ash was still at the wheel. Ominously, the 4x4's high suspension, and the fact it was pitched upwards against the bank, meant she couldn't see into the cab.

She raised the stun gun, hoping the creased wing wouldn't prevent the driver's door from opening. Her fingertips reached the old-fashioned latch. It moved with resistance, a cold metal scrape destroying any element of surprise she might have had. But it gave, and she wrenched the door back, bringing the Taser to bear.

On an empty cabin.

Hawkins backed away, heart thumping now. She rotated slowly through a full turn, keeping the Taser raised. But there was no sign of Ash.

She swung back to the forest, trying to regulate her breathing, reminding herself that she had the upper hand. Yes, Jones probably still had the knife, but her Taser offered superior range. Her body was starting to ache from the crash, but he must be in worse shape after a much heavier head-on impact.

Yet somehow he had made it out of the car and into the forest while she'd been preoccupied with Thurgood, which meant he couldn't be *so* badly injured, and that already he could be escaping through the undergrowth, or dug in somewhere just inside the trees. Watching her.

She shivered, feeling cold for the first time since leaving Mike's car, still edging along the treeline. There was no point waiting here at the roadside, hoping that air surveillance would turn up in time. Ash had gone into the woods.

So she had to follow.

As she accepted the inevitable, the forest seemed to yield, presenting her with a naturally worn aperture, just big enough for her to duck through. She took a final glance at the Range Rover, catching sight of Thurgood, head tipped aside in the passenger seat, reassuring herself that he was locked in.

Briefly she considered going back for a torch, discounting the strategy because it would give her position away and destroy her peripheral vision. She had to count on whatever natural light there was, which put them on equal terms, at least. She turned back, took a deep breath of icy air.

And entered the darkness.

64

Ash held position behind the thickest trunk he'd been able to find, watching the silhouette enter the trees. It was hard to tell from twenty yards away in the darkness, but the merging shadows suggested a single figure, which was good because he had definitely seen two faces in the other car as he'd scrambled free of the wrecked 4x4. So either they'd split up and were trying to corner him, or the other one had been hurt in the crash. The latter was more likely, and best of all the silhouette's shape and size suggested it was the woman. Slower.

Easier to overcome.

He'd have to be careful, of course. She might be armed, and he was still dazed from the crash. The blinding pain in his head meant he must have hit the steering wheel, and his lower legs were still burning. Plus he was still carrying the injury inflicted by the other bitch, and he didn't have his night-vision goggles. But after weeks of practice, he was adept at moving through the forest with minimal noise. And he still had the knife.

He just had to get close enough to use it.

Obviously he could still run, but he was injured and on foot, so his chances of escape weren't great anyway.

If he went down it would be for the rest of his life, so he might as well go out on a high. The start of several life sentences would be so much easier to bear if he went in with fresh memories of killing a female pig. And now they knew who he was, there was no point being careful about leaving traces.

So he could gut her as well.

Already buzzing at the thought, he leaned out again, scouring the patches of light where the moon's glow broke through the canopy. For a moment there was no movement, no sound beyond the forest's rhythmic swash; the underlying chatter of insects.

At last a quiet snap wrenched his senses right, towards the deeper shadows. Then came the quiet rustle of his enemy easing through the spiny undergrowth. Giving herself away.

Ash felt his heart rate climb as he crouched low, and with hands out in front to detect unseen foliage, he crept away to his left.

To get round behind her.

Hawkins kept moving away from the road, still cursing herself for stumbling into the noisy scrub that had grabbed at her ankles. Aware that she might be under surveillance.

Initially she had paused just inside the treeline, every sense straining, half expecting Ash to attack as soon as she left the pavement's relative safety. She had steadied herself, finger poised on the stun gun's trigger. But no attack came. Meanwhile she'd listened hard, hoping to detect her target's swiftly retreating footfalls. Then it would have been a case of staying in touch until air support arrived, making their relative positions known to the helicopter crew.

Game over.

Except there were no obvious signs of retreat, no sound beyond the natural clicks and whirs of the forest; nothing to say there was anyone else here at all. Given his probable state of health, Ash was unlikely to have covered enough ground since the crash to escape altogether. Which meant either he had gone to ground or collapsed from his injuries, and was still somewhere nearby.

Or he was hunting her, too.

She slowed, rendered almost blind by an even darker section of forest, scouring the mottled blackness, trying to filter the soft cracks of her own footsteps from the maelstrom of sound encasing her. Leaves rattled in the wind, backed by creaking boughs and the muted drone of crickets. Yet still no hum of rotor blades, or clues to the whereabouts of her foe.

Hawkins stopped altogether, willing the blackness around her to yield detail, feeling far more exposed than she'd expected to upon entering this natural maze. But there was no turning back. Ash could be anywhere.

Then she heard it.

A light crack, off to her right.

Panic flared, urging her to run. But she held fast, forcing her senses to do her bidding. The woods seemed to contract around her as she stopped breathing, limiting internal distraction to the machine-gun pulse assaulting her brain.

For a moment there was nothing except the vague hoot of an owl, more swirls of leaves disturbed by the breeze.

Another crack.

This one was heavier, although as she spun towards it, there was still nothing to see among the intersecting greys and blacks of the forest.

Hawkins edged away from the noise, adopting a crouched stance, Taser held at arm's-length. Ready to fire.

She swept the weapon from side to side, trying to remember the all-too-brief training session she'd attended when the weapons were introduced to the force. But the specialist's barked instructions, as she'd fired at a brown sack torso, were now just a distant blur.

Four quick footsteps. Much nearer.

Hawkins ran.

She crashed through a wiry bush that ripped at her face, instinctive counter steer sending her the opposite way, into a tree that snatched painfully at her shoulder, threatening to turn flight into fall. She kept going, boots scuffing the soft ground, hearing Ash behind her, running too, as she cursed herself for relinquishing what should have been the upper hand.

But she wasn't just running away.

Through the trees she caught glimpses of the place she wanted to reach, a small clearing between the trees, where moonlight punctured the canopy. A place she could see to fire the Taser, without fear of its projectiles snagging unseen foliage.

Hawkins' injured ribs burned, and her ragged breath grew louder as she ducked and wove through the undergrowth, resisting every urge to look back; knowing it would only slow her down. Both of them had abandoned any attempt at stealth now, crashing through bushes and bracken, fully consumed by the chase.

He could only have been yards behind when Hawkins reached the clearing. She didn't slow till she got to the far side, raising the Taser as she started to turn, planning to use her remaining lead to set herself and fire across the lit, open space; put him down before he reached her.

But she had overestimated the gap.

He slammed into her, knocking them both off balance, and she felt the knife slam into her ribs as they fell together, the stab vest doing its job. Brambles tore at Hawkins' scalp as they landed in the bushes on the far side of the clearing, the impact forcing the Taser from her grip. She tried to curl and roll as they hit the ground, but his weight came down on top of her, trapping her legs.

She twisted and lashed out, her fist connecting hard with the side of his head. He grunted and slid off her sideways. This time Hawkins managed to free herself, but she was only halfway upright when he slashed the back of her calf. Instinct snatched the leg aside as she turned, feeling the incision gape; pain searing her skin like a hot poker.

Weakness tugged at her, the underlying dread of helplessness that she fought daily flaring at the thought of cold, sharpened steel puncturing her flesh.

Beside her, Ash was scrambling to his feet, thin shards of weak light glinting off the blade in his hand; fury etched on to his face. But his movements were unsteady and laboured, underlining Hawkins' renewed advantage.

He was clearly in pain.

He came at her, leading with the knife, raised high because he must have felt the stab vest repel his previous attack. Hawkins let her combat training take over, holding position until the last moment before twisting aside, letting the blade slip past, flicking around to drive her elbow into the back of his head. Bones connected through the fabric of her jacket, and she felt the satisfying crack of heavy contact as Ash went down again.

She followed, dropping a knee in his back, forcing him to the ground. She felt his lungs empty as she went for the knife, banging his wrist against the ground to prise it from his grasp, launching it into the darkness.

She kept the pressure on, digging in her pocket for cuffs. But her weight wasn't enough as Ash bucked, unseating her, using that motion to drag himself free. Hawkins scrambled away, evading his grasp, scouring the shadows for the Taser. She saw it, half-hidden by low foliage, and began to move, but he barged her again.

Bushes broke their fall this time, but Hawkins fell

badly, her left arm folding under her, making her cry out as she felt the shoulder twist. She flailed at Jones as he straddled her, grabbing her wrist and pinning her down. His other hand closed around her throat with surprising strength, his fingers digging into her flesh.

She struggled as whiteness invaded her vision, flashing in time with the pulse thudding hard in her ears. Jolts of panic arced through Hawkins' body as jagged memories of the night she almost died reared in the darkness, but she fought them down. Breaths jerked in and out of her as she drove her chin against his thumb, dragging in air when the grip softened. Yet lack of oxygen had already blanched her senses.

And then he transferred both hands to her throat.

Hawkins' breath arrested again, chest heaving as the increased compression began choking her. Ash's contorted features blurred above her, greys and blacks dissolving into each other as she lost focus, and his face seemed to split in two, briefly becoming the man who almost ended her life ten months ago, and the man trying to kill her now. Her heels scraped weakly in the dirt, but then everything started to lift. The pain of his grasp and the rushing sound in her ears began to fade. Her thoughts softened and her body went light. She no longer felt his hands on her skin.

Was this the end?

For a moment she considered letting go; just allowing the flood of calm to wash her into white oblivion. Gently float away.

But something dragged her back.

Hawkins felt the muscles around her eyes tighten, once more registering the pain of his hands on her neck. She wouldn't give in, but she had just seconds to fracture his grip.

She clawed at concentration, her mind reluctant to lace one thought to the next. All she could think of was oxygen; and the crushing grasp denying her it.

Then: clarity.

If both of his hands were on her throat; *her* right hand must be free.

She focused everything through her shoulder, feeling the arm materialise at her side. It obeyed her instruction to turn and start trailing back and forth in the dirt, leaden fingertips too numb to identify texture, simply trawling form and resistance as her head went lighter still. But then it was there.

She gripped as hard as she could, letting the shape seat in her palm, and raised her hand, index finger slipping into position. She took aim at Jones' torso.

And pulled the trigger.

There was no sound, but Ash snapped rigid above her. Then she was dragging in air. She kept the button down for as long as possible before letting go, watching his blurred form slump aside, continuing to haul in oxygen between rasping coughs.

They lay side by side as Hawkins' senses began to stabilise, and she felt the pain rising up her neck, starting to bang inside her brain. Beside her Jones stirred, but all she had to do was pull the trigger again, hearing his limbs scuff the ground as he tightened once more.

This time she released him after a shorter burst, rolling up on to an elbow before pushing herself back into a crouch. She searched her coat for plasticuffs, and had just finished binding Ash's wrists behind him when she heard the faint sound of rotor blades.

A moment later the trees around them started to thrash as the aerial response team swept in overhead. The helicopter slowed to hover above the two crashed vehicles out on the road, and then moved back towards Hawkins, the crew clearly having detected the figure waving up at their infra-red camera through the trees.

'*We have you. Hold your position*,' a tannoy blasted, as the aircraft lifted and whirled away. And somewhere in the distance, beyond the retreating noise of engine and rotor blades, Hawkins picked up the sound of sirens.

65

Hawkins sat on the ambulance tailgate, wrapped in a big sheet of tin foil, letting the young female paramedic finish applying the bandage to her damaged calf. Electric-blue LEDs flickered around them in the pre-dawn gloom, intermittently lighting patches of the tree-lined channel scything its way through Epping Forest.

Twenty yards away, a still disorientated Ashley Jones was being half carried towards a waiting ambulance. Fortunately for Hawkins, a suspected lightly fractured skull from his encounter with Sheila Priest, plus the subsequent car crash, had concussed her assailant sufficiently for his well-rehearsed stranglehold to be weaker than usual.

Jones was guided into the back, before the ambulance's engine fired, and it pulled away as the paramedic stood. 'How does that feel?'

'Fine,' Hawkins reported in the steadiest voice she could muster.

The paramedic made a non-committal noise and started prodding at her neck. 'Any nausea, light-headedness, difficulty breathing or swallowing?'

'No.'

'Hmmm.' The younger woman pressed harder, while

Hawkins stared past her shoulder and tried not to react, aware that she was being assessed. 'Does this hurt?'

Hawkins shook her head.

'OK.' The medic let go. 'I'm going to release you, but if this redness doesn't disappear in a few days, or if you experience any of the symptoms I mentioned before, go straight to A&E, OK?'

Hawkins agreed and thanked her, looking further up the road to where Dave Thurgood's Land Rover was being callously extracted from the undergrowth by a low loader, its mangled front end tearing at the branches as it was dragged free. At least the sergeant wasn't here to watch, having already been taken to hospital for assessment. She cringed as the front bumper fell off.

'Forget that pile of junk. Look what did you did to my ride!'

Hawkins leaned around the open ambulance door to see Maguire, who had been brought down from the house by one of their response teams. First he'd come to check she was OK, but now he was standing beside his traumatised Range Rover. Recently levered off the tree, the 4x4's worryingly banana-shaped passenger side looked a lot worse than she had expected.

She smiled. 'Most of that will buff out.'

'Yeah, right.' Maguire moved back towards her. 'What is it with you and these big showdowns? I told you not to engage.'

'You also said not to scratch your car.'

'Oh, it's like *that*?'

'You're just jealous you missed out on this one.' Hawkins pulled her tin foil tighter.

'Maybe. But next time we're using *your* damn car.'

She ignored him. 'How's Aaron?'

'Should be hitting surgery anytime now, but he'll pull through. Somehow Ash managed to miss anything important.'

'That's a relief. And Rupert?'

'I sent him back to Loughton with two of the guys, but he was good as gold; helped us carry Sharpe to the chopper.'

Hawkins nodded. 'It's almost a shame we have to charge the poor misguided sod.'

Mike shrugged. 'It ain't so bad. The abductions were short-term, no weapons were used, and his motive was hardly sinister.'

'Maybe, but it was multiple pre-meditated counts, and he used drugs.'

'Think he'll go down?'

'I hope not. He doesn't need putting away; just a decent role model. At least it looks like Ash will own up to *his* part.' She tried to stand. 'Anyway, where's our lift?'

'Easy.' Mike took her arm as she faltered, helped her back down. 'I'll call for a ride.'

'Thanks. I am sorry about your car, by the way.'

'No sweat. Been thinking about upgrading for a while, actually.' He produced his mobile. 'We're going home, right?'

'Don't be ridiculous.' She pulled a face. 'We're going to Loughton to interview our protagonists. And hopefully they won't fuck about.' She checked her watch. 'I'd like to get home in time to do the school run.'

66

'Careful.' Hawkins rolled the biggest suitcase towards Mike. 'Last one's heavy.'

He took it from her, heaving it up into the Qashqai's boot and pulling the tailgate closed. Then they walked back to where Siobhan and the kids were waiting on the pavement.

'Is that everything?' Hawkins asked.

Siobhan nodded. 'Think so. I just did a final sweep.'

'It better be,' Mike cut in. 'Nothin' else will fit in that trunk.'

'Well then . . .' Siobhan stood behind Rosie and Kyle; a hand on each of their shoulders. 'I suppose it's time to go. Say thanks to Antonia and Mike, you two.'

Both children went straight to Maguire, as he bent down for a three-way hug, and Hawkins made a patient face at her sister. At last Rosie stepped away, and stood staring up at Hawkins.

They considered each other for a moment before Rosie stretched her arms wide. 'Thank you for reading us stories.'

'You're very welcome.' Hawkins stooped, surprised by the gesture, not expecting Rosie's launch into her arms.

'Wow.' She heaved herself upright, ignoring the complaints of a body still recovering from recent hostilities, supporting her niece's weight. 'What brought this on?'

Rosie whispered in her ear, 'Mummy says you're still a grumpy old cow. But I think you're funny.'

'Oh thanks.' Hawkins shot eyes at her sibling. 'I think I prefer your assessment.'

Rosie smiled, twisting one of her pigtails around a finger. 'Will we see you again soon?'

'Definitely,' she said, startled to find she actually meant it. 'I'll visit next weekend, if Mummy says it's OK.'

This seemed to satisfy Rosie, and Hawkins was about to move towards the car when something wrapped itself tightly around her right thigh. She looked down to see Kyle administering a limpet-like hug.

'Well take a look at that,' Mike said as she reached down to stroke her nephew's hair. 'Somebody's warming up to his Auntie Antonia after all.'

Their multi-storey embrace lasted a few more minutes before Siobhan called time, and the kids were loaded into the Qashqai. Mike said goodbye and disappeared into the house, leaving Hawkins and her sister together by the car.

'Are you really coming next weekend?' Siobhan asked.

'Work permitting.' Hawkins smiled. 'But you know this means you'll have to stop calling me a grumpy cow.'

Her grin was returned. 'I'll see what I can do. Work should calm down a bit now, though, shouldn't it?'

'I hope.' She glanced at the two tiny faces behind tinted glass, already submerged in their electronic toys. 'Though after spending a week in the same house as these two, I'm not sure I have much right to complain.'

Work had been uncharacteristically quiet in the three days since Ashley Jones' arrest, and somehow Hawkins had managed not to pick up any major new investigations in the meantime. Aside from attending follow-up interview sessions with Rupert Perkin and Jones himself, she had spent the downtime catching up on paperwork, and visiting Aaron in hospital.

It was still unclear if Jones had expected Sharpe to be wearing a stab vest. Either way he'd gone in well below the sergeant's ribs, where a generous love handle had taken most of the impact. Painful of course, but mercifully it meant Aaron's intestine, left kidney and lung had escaped unscathed. The ward sister said his greatest challenge would be overcoming the mental trauma of his stint as a human shield, but physically he was on the mend, and would be discharged in a few days.

The same couldn't be said for his attacker.

As she'd expected, Jones hadn't even attempted to talk himself off the charges; apparently unwilling to share what he saw as *credit* for his callous manipulation of circumstance. In interview he seemed almost proud of his actions, as if like-minded individuals might one day admire and try to follow his lead. Fortunately he also didn't seem to appreciate how quickly he would become yesterday's news.

It was hard to say whether the picture of childhood abuse they were slowly building was entirely responsible for his emergent fascination with psychological torture, but a decent judge and a following wind ought to ensure he'd never be free to exercise his twisted disposition on the unsuspecting again.

As for Jones' long-suffering companion, Rupert Perkin's condition was somewhat trickier to quantify. Hawkins still couldn't decide where the line between tragically misguided loner and poker-faced abductor lay.

For years, it seemed Perkin had played the monster's muse, until such time as Jones chose to extract himself from the situation by way of fabricated death. Except the manipulation hadn't ended there, moving instead to a higher level, where Perkin had become the unwitting accomplice in four and a half brutal murders.

When asked about his actions, Perkin seemed to be aware that drugging and imprisoning random strangers was likely to land him in trouble. But he stood almost heroically by the notion that ends would eventually have justified means. His theory was that, if he 'saved' enough people, sooner or later one of them would overlook his rather didactic approach and become a genuine friend. Hence his fatalistic decision to give each victim the thinly veiled opportunity to escape following the arbitrarily prescribed period of 'familiarisation'. His disappointment that every one had exercised that option was palpable but, as none had ever sent the police back to arrest him, he'd simply become more and more convinced it was just a numbers game. The irony, of course, was that the very 'friend' he'd been trying to replace was the sole reason his involuntary guests never reported his crimes.

Perkin was also in custody, awaiting routine psychological assessment to decide how much responsibility he should take, still patently distressed by the thought that he'd played any part in the deaths. In his mind, Perkin had lost not one friend, but five.

He was still asking to visit Sheila Priest.

'You're already back at work, aren't you?' Siobhan's voice dragged Hawkins from her thoughts.

'Yes, sorry.' She looked back at her sister, realising that she'd zoned out again; one of Siobhan's biggest irritations. 'So you'll be OK?'

'I'll be fine. I start at John Lewis on Monday, so if I end up needing somewhere for myself and the kids, I can probably afford to rent something nearby.'

'How likely is that?'

'I'm not sure yet. Malcolm's going to his brother's in Wanstead. He says we can have the house until we get things sorted out.'

'That's decent of him. Are you sure about this whole break-up thing?'

'We've got a lot to talk about.' Siobhan heaved a sigh. 'There'll need to be changes.'

'Sounds promising.'

They said final goodbyes, and Siobhan was halfway round the car when she turned with a frown. 'Is it weird that I don't want to leave?'

Hawkins shrugged. 'No weirder than the fact I don't want you to go.'

They met in the middle, embracing for the first time in years, as Hawkins tried to determine whether the tears she was holding back were due more to happiness or relief.

In the end, she decided it didn't matter.

Acknowledgements

This book had a difficult inception. I spent a two-week summer holiday in 2014 trying not to put pressure on myself to come up with an idea, so it was with frustration that I boarded the plane home still lacking a plot. As a result, my first acknowledgement must go to the man I found myself sitting next to on that flight, who will have had no idea that our various conversations inspired this novel.

Similar eternal gratitude to Rowland White and the team at Michael Joseph, as well as my agent and associates at Hardman & Swainson, plus friends and family for your continued support. Thanks also to Jim Coulton, my special consultant on (among other things) the intricacies of metal detection.

But as always, particular mention must go to Anna, because our many talks enabled me to retrieve the idea from the 'on-hold/abandoned' file on more than one occasion.

Without all of you, this book would not have made it to print.